Dropping the Keystone

Ashes of the Past Saga, Volume 2

Christina Dickinson

Published by Christina Dickinson, 2021.

To my cousin, Michelle. Happy Birthday from...What was it, five years ago?

1

~Irrellian~

THUMBING HIS RING ABSENTLY, Irrellian Thornne considered his current situation. He'd been removed from Arra's current events for twenty years. A drop in the bucket that made a lifetime of difference. The players had changed. His game board had altered.

Telgan Korsborn, a name out of history. A mortal name. And yet, also the name of the demon bound within him. How had a mere slip of an elf come across this ring? Did she understand the significance behind an immortal creature carrying such a name? If she did, she could be the key to everything he'd wished for.

It couldn't be a coincidence this girl, his savior, was Fortiva's daughter. Irrellian knew Genovar better than anyone–the way only a true enemy could. It was almost like friendship, this thing between them. Almost.

More likely the winds of fate were at play.

Snow whipped through his loose silk robes, coating the top of his jagged perch. Beyond him lay a vast mountain range of the demon world, stretched from below Seirane to the eastern border of Gyth, neighboring country of Eerilor. If the range had a name, the demon within him was unwilling to provide it. That suited Irrellian. He didn't wish to alter the Demon Realms. They held no interest for him. It was a place without sun. These unholy denizens were doomed never to know the taste of light. Flayer contracts were the only hope of escape, and they were often regarded with the same disdain below as they were met with above. To become bound to a mortal... To serve a lesser creature... Barbaric.

A faint smile tugged at the Flayer Mage's lips. Barbaric, indeed. Yet, these same creatures regarded him as some sort of legend. A mortal had tamed death. It made him powerful enough to be feared, even here.

There were times the demon pressed him. Why bother with this nonsense of taking the world a continent, a country, or even a person at a time? Irrellian Thornne had the power to tear everything down. The world could burn. Nothing would be left but ash. Things would be changed, forever. At these times, Irrellian would be tempted, but *Telgan* did not fully understand his mortal counterpart. He wanted to change the world for the better, which meant converting, sometimes conquering those who could not see his vision.

Which was part of his current dilemma. His followers had been left to their own devices for two decades. It didn't matter how devoted his subordinates were to his cause. They were still mortals–prone to their own desires, mistaken interpretations of his will, and corruption. While some of his people would be overjoyed to see the return of the Flayer Mage, there would be others greeting him with much less pleasure.

Irrellian was still weak from his prolonged slumber, though he'd been gaining ground against the gods. If he hadn't been woken by the Fortiva girl, his prison would've released him in another forty years or so. How unfortunate Irrellian had shed his trappings early enough for the high gods to retain a few believers. His legend was growing, while belief in the divine was on the decline. Gods of Arra only held power as long as the mortals retained a sense of devotion.

Arra was an old world. It had seen the rise and fall of many, many pantheons. Where did a god go once they lost their position? There was a reason most of the demon world disdained the mortals of the surface. Envy created monsters.

He should know.

2

~Khiri~

"GET UP, GIRL. DUST it off and move forward."

Khiriellen Fortiva: once an elf of the Life Trees, now a blooded killer and responsible for the reawakening of Arra's greatest threat, who also happened to be her Destined mate. The man she had killed still lay in the growing puddle of melting hoarfrost and magic ice crystal while the clammy air of the cavern coated her skin like a layer of shame that would never wash away. What little glow had been present before was fading with the enchantments that had coated the icy walls. She felt small. Smaller than she'd felt the first time she'd entered Jarelton and been surrounded by humans, smaller than when she'd first climbed out of the monstrous Life Trees as a child, smaller than a single ant in a forest.

"It will pass."

Khiri pushed against the voice that spoke inside her mind. There was enough to deal with without a tag-along.

"I am no mere tag-along," the voice reprimanded. *"The elves are not in my charge, so while I forgive your non-devotion, I'll not tolerate rudeness. I am **Imyn**. Heed me, Khiriellen, daughter of Genovar."*

One of the seven High Gods of the human lands, Khiri recalled from her lessons with Estan, Imyn was the Goddess of Power and Change. Imyn and her father had made a bargain more than twenty

years ago that had altered the fate of the world. Power and Change...
"Can you change my destiny?" Khiri asked.

"I cannot alter what you wish of me. Telgan Korsborn is within your mind in a way that affects the Elven people. Only the will of the Mother would be able to alter such a bond... Your people no longer have the ability to hear her, and only your elders can speak with your ancestors. If you agree to aid me without further argument, I do have something I could grant you."

"What do you offer?" Khiri sighed. Her hope had flared for a moment. The fragile shell of emotion plummeted and she felt it crash against the jagged edges forming in her soul. Too many things had happened too close together: gaining Micah as a brother, losing him to the Venom Guild, learning her mother was really human and her father had been a war hero who'd fought against the same Flayer Mage she was bound to, having Fennick–someone she had believed to be a friend–force her to kill him in order to undo her father's work. It was all too much.

Estan rushed to her side, his deep-set brown eyes filled with concern. Khiri noticed almost distractedly that his coal black hair, normally kept short to fit under his helmet, was missing entirely. His eyebrows were uneven and looked as though they'd been recently scorched. His full lips were pulled tight in his distress. She'd never really noticed before, but his face was the same shape as the leaf of an apple tree, with his wide cheekbones and sharp chin. It was getting harder to see him with the eerie glow of the Flayer Mage's prison fading. Khiri was sure his saddle brown nostrils were flaring the same way they had when she'd run off during the Flayer attack in Illesdale. He was tall and strong, this friend of hers. A knight. Estan didn't like it when he couldn't rescue people...when he couldn't put those muscles to use.

Kal, the most recent and mysterious addition to their small band, entered right behind the knight, an enigmatic smirk tugging at his thin lips. He carried a staff with sigils of light trailing down its shaft. A glowing crystal worked into the staff's top radiated with strong enough magic to make her ear tips hurt. Kal's golden, round, owl-like eyes glinted as they caught the light from his staff and his pale skin shimmered with ripples like water. His iron gray brows seemed to slide into his sharp nose like they were all one line on his face. There was no roundness to his cheeks and no visible stubble. Lanky and tall, even taller than Estan, Kal had Odlesk heritage, though he didn't talk about his people much. His gray hair had a wild, windswept quality to it, belying his casual nature.

Both were handsome in very different ways, and both were forbidden to her.

"Khiri, thank Taymahr you're alright! What happened?" Estan's words tumbled over her. Nothing was making much sense to her shock-addled mind.

"Leave me alone," Khiri said. She didn't deserve the knight's concern. It was too much. He was too much. All Khiri wanted right now was space. A little room to breath and piece herself back together.

Estan drew back like she'd slapped him. There was already so much guilt flooding her system, one extra pang barely registered. She didn't bother to call him back when he walked out of the cavern.

The Flayer Mage was her Destined. Somehow, Irrellian Thornne was also Telgan Korsborn. Khiri couldn't wrap her head around it. How could she possibly explain something like this to her friends? They'd never understand. Those that were born unbonded had a hard enough time digesting the idea that Khiri didn't have a say in her romantic destiny. Kal and Estan couldn't be told they were being turned down because she was bound to the Flayer Mage. Ullen had a history of fighting against Irrellian. Any one of her friends might label her a traitor.

For the time being, Khiri decided to keep her Destined secret.

Imyn didn't object audibly, but Khiri could feel the goddess disproved.

Dewin, her wavy, black bangs framing her large, brown eyes, entered the cavern with exaggerated steps. A former thief with wicked hatchet fighting skills, she was obviously trying not to sneak up on anyone. Dewin's nose was pinched and her face was as round as the moon. She had fine eyebrows and delicate lips. She was taller than Khiri, but still shorter than Kal by almost a full head and a half. Next to Kal, it was hard not to think of Dewin's complexion as the warm, orange fall leaves flanking his lake.

Right behind Dewin came Resmine. It was hardly surprising the one followed the other. The two were practically joined at the hip lately. They were similar enough in height, Resmine was practically Dewin's shadow despite her lighter countenance and thinner frame. Resmine's skin didn't have the shimmering quality that Kal's did, but it was nearly as fair. She had a heart-shaped face with pronounced cheekbones and a strong nose. When she smiled, dimples showed on either side of her mouth. They weren't showing at the moment, though. Her chestnut curls were bound in their normal tail, and her intelligent, hazel eyes were pinched with apprehension. It was hard to believe she'd managed to hide herself away as a slow-witted stablehand for years.

Ullen... Ullen who'd helped bind the Flayer Mage. Khiri felt a sharp pang of something other than dull guilt when he entered the cave at a trot. Anger, maybe. Why hadn't he ever told them he'd been one of the generals during the War of the Burning Valley?

Being the only dwarf in Khiri's acquaintance, she wasn't sure if he was tall, average, or short. He was certainly shorter than her, though Khiri was tall for an elf. But what Ullen lacked in height, he made up in stockiness. Ullen had almost as much muscle as Estan despite being half as tall. He cut a dashing figure with his hooked nose and sharp brows. Ullen's chiseled cheekbones were nearly hidden behind an intricately woven, inky mustache, adorned with red ribbons. Lacking much of a neck, his strong, stubbled chin nearly rested on his chest. His dark hair was pulled back into a single braid. Having just seen the version of Ullen from twenty years before, Khiri couldn't tell that he'd aged a day.

"Here." Dewin handed Khiri the bow that had once been Khiri's brother, Micah. Khiri recalled she'd left it leaning against the bunk she would've slept in back in Harish before things went cloudy and she was led away by Fennick. "I figured you'd not want to leave him with these oafs, love. A brother's right precious, no matter his condition."

Khiri took the bow and hugged it to her the way she'd clung to her mother's skirts as a child, as though Micah could reach out and embrace her through the bow's seasoned curve. They had grown up together. He'd been the only one in this strange land outside the Life Trees that understood... Understood everything. What Fennick's death meant to an elf.

"You keep it up and I may have to cry," Micah's voice echoed in her head.

Khiri jerked the bow away from her chest. It had to be shock. How else could she hear the voice of her departed kinsman? She looked around the cavern at her companions: Dewin, the former thief; Kal, the abandoned assassin; Resmine, the former stablehand; Ullen, the prince-turned-bard. The only two missing were Estan and his blue roan warhorse, Catapult. "Did... did anyone else hear that?"

Most of them seemed puzzled, but she caught a slight incline of Kal's head. The enigmatic smirk tugged at the corner of his mouth again. "Shydan, God of Death and Dreams currently shares existence with me. Your brother and I have been introduced."

Ullen's confusion melted away. He gave a nod of understanding before turning to Dewin and Resmine. "Life Tree wood holds the spirits o' the elven people. Seems those two can talk to our lad, again."

Dewin let out a gasp and a tear or two rolled down her cheeks. Resmine's eyebrows scrunched together as skepticism warred with grief across her delicate features. Khiri even detected a bit of jealousy in the mix, but the elven hunter was too distracted by the miraculous return of her brother's voice to pay it much thought.

"This Kal guy's not half bad for being part of the team that murdered me," Micah's voice held the warmth of a teasing smile. That warmth softened some of the edges that had formed in her stomach.

"I didn't kill anyone," Kal said.

"Didn't stop them though, did you? Khiri, nock an arrow so I can punch this guy."

"I was unconscious."

Imyn pushed against Khiri's thoughts, making it impossible to think of anything else. Her presence swelled against the constraints of Khiri's mind, darkening Khiri's vision, shortening her breath. **"You wanted your brother. I have delivered you the power to hear him... Do we have an agreement?"**

It was a struggle to stay coherent enough to answer the goddess. *"I will work with you to hunt down the Flayer Mage. I will undo the harm that I have done."* Almost immediately, the pressure inside her head eased. Khiri continued, *"But like you, I will not tolerate rudeness. If you pull something like that again, I swear by the Mother, I will find a way to expel you."*

"That's the Khiri I grew up with!" Micah's smile was audible.

"Come, lass, let's get you out of this dismal place and leave this valley of the dead. Can't imagine how many mashers have made it into me boots." Ullen offered Khiri a hand. "We left Harish burnin', but someone may be along to see the deed was done."

Taking her dwarven friend's hand, Khiri heaved herself off of the cave floor. "Sounds good. I've had enough of this place for a dozen lifetimes."

Relief loosened Ullen's shoulders as Khiri began to come back to life. She wasn't sure if he was relieved that she was responding now, or if he was happier to leave this place of sordid memories.

In a quieter tone, one the others couldn't hear, Khiri said, "Once we're well away, I think you and I should have a talk about the last time you were here."

Ullen's eyebrows rose slightly, but he nodded assent. As she continued to examine each of her friends, Khiri realized there was something different, something familiar... The same reason she wanted to talk to Ullen, a flashback involving his participation in the War of the Burning Valley, where her father's team had frozen Irrellian Thornne. Seven deities were released...

"Are we all–" Khiri paused, trying to find a delicate way to phrase the question "–hosting companions? Imyn is with me."

"Taymahr," Estan said, edging his way back into the group now that they were exiting the cavern. It seemed even when he was hurt, he couldn't stay away for long. Catapult trailed in his knight's wake, his head lowered as though even the horse couldn't take the gloom in this place.

Being a Knight of the Protective Hand, Estan was already sworn to Taymahr's service. It made sense that his goddess would seek him out.

"Locke," Resmine answered. Khiri seemed to recall that she had a similar history to Estan, though a lot more tragic. Resmine was also as deadly as she was lovely, which made her perfect for the God of Beauty and Battle.

Ullen paused for a moment before muttering Tharothet's name, the same deity he had housed before; God of Seeking and Knowledge. Suddenly, his predilection for traveling jobs and learning new trades made much more sense.

With a cocky grin, Dewin said, "Adari, patron deity of thieves. Corianne would be so proud, could I tell her."

Kal just shrugged, having already told her about Shydan. He wasn't one to waste words, and the God of Death and Dreams was probably just as enigmatic.

"So... Where is Numyri?" Khiri asked.

One by one, everyone shrugged and looked around the dimly lit cavern, where the only glow left was that of Kal's staff.

"It took all seven of them to subdue the Flayer Mage last time, and they were at full strength. What are we going to do without Numyri?" Khiri rubbed her temples in frustration.

"Numyri likely would've gone to Ardi Vorden had she come with us into the valley," Resmine said. "I wonder if we need to track her down?"

Estan looked around as though he only just noticed someone was missing. Khiri wasn't sure who Ardi Vorden was but, if she was their missing avatar, they needed to find her in a hurry.

"She's likely long gone from Harish, lass. We ain't likely to find her lessen' she be wantin' to be found. Said she were out to return to service now as she knows Genovar be gatherin' forces again," Ullen patted Resmine's knee the way taller people would pat someone's shoulder.

At that moment, Estan yelped in surprise, whipping around to face his horse. Holding a scrap of Estan's trousers in his teeth, Catapult let out a whinny that sounded disturbingly like a chuckle.

"I don't think we need to find Lieutenant Vorden. The Goddess of Mirth and Mayhem...is in my warhorse." Estan sighed. He begrudgingly caressed the blue roan's velvety nose as he reclaimed the fabric scrap. "Because you weren't mischievous enough, my friend?"

A playfully wicked neigh echoed into the shadowy valley of soot.

THE JOURNEY OUT OF the valley was made in silence. There was exceedingly high potential for an ambush in the ashes of the long dead ravine. Khiri and her friends had no way of knowing where Irrellian Thornne had gone when he stepped into the darkness and traveled through the paths that Flayers used. Whatever or whoever was left of Harish's populace was also likely to come looking for them before the night was out.

Despite the fact that Harish was a fair distance from the mouth of the Burning Valley, acrid smoke crawled through Khiri's nose and up her tongue. In hushed whispers, Khiri and Ullen discussed how best to avoid passing too close to the burned city. Until their holy passengers were stronger, they couldn't risk returning to Seirane; once the Gods' City, now swarmed with the Gray Army, it seemed Irrellian Thornne's most likely destination. Without a better plan, Ullen had suggested that they move on to Grimson's Pass where his family's scouts were to meet them in a few weeks' time.

Something rested uneasy on Khiri's shoulders. Staying in one place for more than a day or so seemed wrong. Maybe it was just that they'd been traveling for so long that she wasn't used to sitting still, but they had the Gray Army, the Flayer Mage, and the Venom Guild to contend with. Any of the three could easily catch up with them out in the open. The Venom Guild, assassins who liked to move in teams of three—always one Flayer—had declared war against Khiri. They'd managed to hunt her down several times already.

"It will be okay, Khiri," Micah soothed. *"You're not alone in this. Everyone beside you is exceptional. Your father is out there, gathering his old generals."*

"I know." Khiri tried to convey a grateful smile. *"But the last time we ran into the Venom Guild, you... well... you..."*

"I lost my charming limbs and face along with most of the bits that attached. At least I've retained my dignity." Although Micah was trying to make light, Khiri felt his frustration.

A wave of renewed guilt hit her in the chest. When Micah had died, she'd prayed for his spirit to find a way home but, also, wished that he wouldn't leave her side. Micah's last words had been a promise not to leave her alone and he'd found a way to make good on his promise. It may have been Micah's choice to stay with her, but Khiri's guilt insisted it was her fault. He should be at peace in the Mother's embrace instead of still being a part of her fight.

"None of that. It was my choice to follow you, and it was my choice to die for you. I'll not have you second-guessing my motives. They're mine. You, go on and do whatever it is you do with your two legs and I'll be at your shoulder if you need me," Micah said.

With a slight smile, Khiri gave the bow a squeeze, then rested her hand on the hilt of her knife. A bare stretch of ground lay between her group and the cover of the forest. With the valley behind them and the forest within sprinting distance, this would be their most vulnerable moment.

Estan walked up beside her. Without words, they had a brief discussion in eye movement where he agreed to take point while Khiri would fall back to guard the rear. Allowing the others to pass her, Khiri watched as Resmine and Dewin took their positions behind the knight. The two of them were so well paired, it was hard to believe that they were having issues. But Resmine felt Dewin wanted a deeper relationship than Resmine could deliver due to having lost Syara, Resmine's first love. Behind them, Ullen rode on top of Catapult. With the shortest legs, it made the most sense to let Ullen ride, even though the dwarf and the horse didn't always get along. Next, Kal stepped up behind the warhorse. His pale, reflective skin and gray hair made him look like living moonlight, especially now, in the dark before predawn.

Kal paused to brush a strand of Khiri's hair away from her cheek. A strand had escaped from its knot. His fingers left a trail of tingles in the wake of his touch. "I didn't get a chance to say this before: thank you."

"For what?" Khiri swallowed. Her nerves were already tense from a very eventful night. Surely, that was the reason that her stomach was turning like she'd swallowed a live fish.

He leaned in and whispered into her ear, "For living when I couldn't make it to you."

Khiri stepped back, feeling exposed.

She caught Estan glaring at the mage with a near-poisonous dislike. The spot inside of her that strummed the dull iron name *Telgan Korsborn* swelled in protest. She couldn't forget that she was bound to him, especially now that he was awake.

It was all so overwhelming.

3

~Ullen~

THAROTHET. GOD OF SEEKING and Knowledge. It was like putting on an old, comfortable shirt after it had gone missing for several summers in the bottom of a chest. Only, in this scenario, Ullen felt like he was the shirt.

"It's been a long time, my friend," Tharothet said.

Too long. Not long enough. Much like returning to Eerilor, this was a reunion Ullen could've put off for another hundred summers.

More of Ullen's secrets were about to come out. He could see it in Khiri's expression. It was only a matter of time before she asked questions about things Ullen didn't want to tell her, but really, they'd been secret too long.

After all, the return of the gods could only mean one thing. War had returned to the face of Arra. There was no way Irrellian Thornne would let himself be caught the same way twice. Ullen could feel the difference in Tharothet's power, too. Even if they were able to lure Irrellian into the same sort of trap, the seven high gods might not be able to hold him.

"There's no might *about it."* Tharothet seemed to sigh within Ullen's chest. *"Even at the peak of the Great War, we were already starting to decline. None of us were ready for the fade. Many of us still are unwilling to admit our pantheon is nearing the end of its cycle."*

Being the sort of dwarf to house a god like Tharothet, Ullen didn't have to ask what that meant, but it wasn't widely known by most that the current gods weren't the original gods. Very few books still existed from the previous pantheon, and fewer still from the one before that. Some of the lesser gods made the transitions from one pantheon to the next. Petora was one of the oldest goddesses known to Arra's scholars. Somehow she'd managed to remain seated in the heavens through three regimes. Likely because she'd never been one of the high gods.

"Petora is clever, more so than many of us realized when we formed the current council," Tharothet agreed. *"You and I knew it was likely we'd meet again. I'm as sorry for it as you are. But as bad as this seems, we must move forward and make new schemes."*

"Aye," Ullen grunted.

Catapult's ear swivelled back at the sound. The horse couldn't fool Ullen, though. Numyri had likely been listening in all the nearby exchanges between the newly christened avatars and the gods they carried. It was her way.

A chill wind cut through the valley, stirring the ashes of innumerable corpses. The Burning Valley, the last stand of the Great War, had been disturbed. With the coming winter winds, the footprints Ullen's party left behind would be swept clean. Unfortunately, the consequences of this visit would be much harder to scrub out.

"It is time to turn our eyes toward Eerilor. Every country we can get will be pivotal in the days to come, and Eerilor historically has far more allies than Mytana. Maybe even with your return, that silly water rights dispute can be put to bed."

Ullen didn't ask how it was that Tharothet knew about current events despite having been shut up in a cave for twenty years. There was a bond between the dwarf and the god, after all. A bond unlike the one shared by the others. Tharothet had never acted above his host, despite being a divine entity. When they spoke, it was like a meeting of like-minded individuals that shared a passion for learning.

They discussed, they argued, they discussed again.

It was good to have Tharothet back. Ullen was going to need the support when it came time to see his family.

And he'd need a stout drink when Khiri decided to break the silence.

4

~Estan~

LEADING THE CHARGE into the forest was something Estan could focus on. He needed a distraction from thinking about what Kal might or might not be planning for Khiri, or with Khiri, or against Khiri. Maybe he just needed a distraction from Khiri, period. After he'd flubbed his chance to be her savior, he'd frozen as she'd struggled to come to grips with whatever had happened in the cavern. Expecting a tearful embrace, he'd been stung when she told him to leave her alone.

She hadn't told Kal to leave her alone. Far from it. Khiri had even let the assassin touch her when she thought no one was watching.

Estan's eyes darted over the quiet field. He sought distraction from his thoughts about Khiri and her delicate grace. Her sultry mouth perched above her stubborn chin. Her long, rose-gold hair, and the way it caught the sun. Her gorgeous blue eyes, and how they drank in the world. Her tan hunting muscles, and the enticing way they flexed when she fought. Her skill with a knife. Her natural curiosity. Despite her diminutive stature, she had one of the biggest hearts he'd ever encountered. Estan wanted to be her teacher, her pillar, her lover. He'd even thought he was making headway before Kal arrived.

Tightening his grip on his sword, he shifted his balance forward on his toes and pelted his way across the turf. Both dew and smoke scented the air, clawing at his lungs as he drew in each fierce breath. He almost wished something would attack, just so he could burn some of his jealous energy.

"By Taymahr," he hissed, spotting several shadows against the tree line. "I wasn't serious!"

He felt Resmine tense behind him, readying her whip. Dewin was behind his other shoulder, ready to launch a hand axe once they were in range. One, two... a third one to the far right. The question was: were these shapes humans or Flayers? They were too tall to be dwarves or elves. If they were Flayers, there was no question whether they should die. If they were human, odds were good they were enemies, but it wasn't a surety.

Once they were close enough to make out the arms of individual shadows, Estan was almost relieved to see each shadow swaying, as though caught in a breeze that only they could feel. Chilling, thready whispers of *"Blood... Sizzling... Cracking... Bones... Rending... Tearing..."* crept into the damp, smokey air. Flayers, probably those that had escaped from the burning village of Harish, wandering the forest's edge.

A war cry sprang from Estan's lips, as though he could use his voice to cut through the creatures before he even reached them. The foremost Flayer roared a counterpoint. He had been a large man in life, and the grotesque mottling of his skin was horribly apparent on the round dome of his bald head. Estan's sword was met with a long buckler, fastened to the inside of the Flayer's wrist.

Estan ducked below a claw aimed at his face. A twin to the buckler blocking his sword glinted as it passed over his head.

Flayers rarely wore anything other than the clothing they formed in, but these bucklers were fitted. Buildings in Harish had been raised above the reach of their Flayer companions, as though the townspeople feared their allies. Probably not refugee demon-bound, then.

Sparks flew as Estan brought his sword around and the Flayer blocked again. He heard frustrated curses as Ullen hit the ground nearby, having made his own unsuccessful attempt on one of the three unusually armed Flayers. Estan blocked one of the Flayer's claws and slid the blade up along the creature's arm, managing to gain first blood on the interior of its armpit. He barely had a chance to register that he'd made contact before the Flayer pulled the sword deeper into its own wound. It gnashed its teeth, chomping at Estan's neck.

Though the creature missed its mark, Estan felt the rush of air as the Flayer's canines snapped together. He yanked his sword out of its temporary sheath and tumbled out of the thing's reach.

Khiri leapt over him, kicking both feet into the center of the big creature's chest with enough force to cause it to stumble backward. The elven woman sprung off the Flayer and out of reach. Without losing momentum, she darted toward the one Resmine was fighting, notching an arrow to her bow. Khiri had taken up the role of distraction for this battle, which was fine by Estan. Enough danger had befallen his flame for a lifetime, let alone one day. None of them had slept since the last sunrise.

Before the Flayer could recover fully from the surprise attack, Estan pressed into the thing's open guard and plunged his sword into its belly. He shoved the blade up and out, cutting through the creature's heart. As demon blood began steaming its way out of the big man's body, Estan spared a thought to wonder what the man's story might have been.

Another of the Flayers fell with one of Dewin's axes in its throat. It was wearing a fitted breastplate, one that was being eaten away by the acidic blood rushing out of the creature's skin. Who in all of Arra would outfit Flayers this way? Not even the Venom Guild took the time to give their Flayers gear. At least, not that he'd seen so far.

The last Flayer burst into flame, screaming as bits of its body fell to ash before it even died. Kal shifted back, leaning on the staff he'd borrowed. He looked spent, something that made Estan fight the urge to smirk. Even though the Odlesk mage had slept more than the rest of them over the last few days, he didn't have as much stamina.

"Your thoughts are unworthy of a Knight of the Protective Hand," Taymahr chastised.

Grimly, Estan acknowledged the truth of his goddess's admonishment. Kal had been showing his worth throughout the night, even saving Estan's life when he stupidly jumped into a magical fire. He'd done so begrudgingly, but Estan was still alive.

Pulling a rag from one of Catapult's saddlebags, the knight wiped his sword clean of Flayer residue and tossed the cloth to Dewin. She swiped it from the air with practiced ease and tended to her own weaponry.

"Right shiny bit o' polish on them toughs," she mentioned with exaggerated casualty as she rubbed at a nick one of her axes had acquired during the fight.

"Shame that dying Flayers leave so little behind," Resmine said. "Mine was wearing some nice bracers. They were made with that dye that deepens the browns in leather so they're almost burgundy. Complete waste of good equipment."

"Who would equip Flayers and then just leave them to wander the countryside?" Khiri asked. She was wiping her brow with one of his rags. She must've fished it out on her own, because he certainly didn't recall giving it to her. Estan wondered briefly if Dewin had been teaching Khiri some of her trade. Maybe he was just so tired that he hadn't noticed when she took it out of his gear.

"A team of three makes my immediate thought turn to the Venom Guild," Estan said with a sharp look in Kal's direction.

The former assassin shook his head. Still leaning against his staff as though it were the only thing holding him up, he seemed to have difficulty speaking. "Venom Guild would never send Flayers out on their own. They only ever send one per team... Easier to keep in check... Easier to keep... Focused," Kal managed.

"Are you alright, lad?" Ullen offered the mage a hand. The dwarven prince didn't seem to have any more qualms about trusting Kal. Either Ullen knew something about Kal that Estan didn't, or he was more willing to overlook the former assassin's previous allegiances. How would Micah take the news that his bond-sister was being courted by one of the assassins responsible for his death?

Granted, Kal was unconscious on the other side of the fighting, well away from where Khiri and Micah had been facing off against the oddly cognitive Flayer. Micah had given Estan a bit of a swollen jaw once, though, just for looking at Khiri too often. Kal was undeniably guilty of similar transgressions.

"I'll be fine," Kal waved away Ullen's assistance. "If Estan and Catapult would be good enough to allow me to ride for a time, I would be better for it."

"I still have the rope somewhere," Estan muttered. Resmine, overhearing him, punched him in the arm. It wasn't hard enough to hurt, but it wasn't really soft enough to be playful. "Go ahead. If Catapult will let you up, the rest of us can walk."

Dewin sheathed her weapons and took a few steps into the treeline. "I'll scout ahead. Give the elders a bit of time to catch their wind." With a grin, she melted into the shadows of the graying light.

Kal mounted Catapult without much trouble. Disappointment rumbled through Estan's shoulders and melded with his exhaustion. He refused to let his fatigue show. If Khiri could keep going at this point, so could he. She'd been through more than anyone else in the party, between Fennick the traitor and the waking of the Flayer Mage.

"So it's not likely to be the Venom Guild. Who else would equip a bunch of Flayers and let them run loose?" Khiri asked, waiting for

Dewin's signal to move forward. When it sounded, they began to move forward through the trees, two people at a time. Estan took Catapult's harness and fell in beside Ullen, while Khiri and Resmine were in front.

"Not sure we've enough to go on at this point, lass. They've a deep pocket, whoever they be," Ullen said. "Once we meet up with me boys, mayhap they'll have summat to say on it."

As the sun started to peak over the mountains, Estan began to regret his bravado. Khiri still plodded on, as though she were trying to outdistance her memories of the last few days.

"I don't know about anyone else," Resmine sighed, "but when we get to that pass, I'm going to sleep for the next two weeks."

GRIMSON'S PASS, LONG used by hardy merchants and smugglers to bypass the more easily accessed but more easily guarded and taxed portions of the Mytana-Eerilor border, was roughly five days of wooded and rocky terrain. During their first day out, it had taken all of them to convince Khiri to stop and make camp around noon. It was far enough that anyone fleeing the ruins of Harish would've been hard pressed to find them. Seirane was the most likely destination for survivors. Grimson's Pass was far more dangerous to an average citizen and didn't offer much in the way of shelter. Bandits camped in the nearby mountains. There were also roaming packs of gnorels—wild dog-like creatures with hooves like a goat—that didn't mind preying on unwary travelers.

"Vicious things, but mighty tasty iffen you catch 'em," Ullen grinned. "I know a cave we can hunker down in. S'probably where me boys'll be lookin' to find us."

"Seems sound," Khiri said. She was scanning the pass with a dark scowl. The grass around the mountain was already beginning to turn brown and leaves in neighboring trees were changing, as though summer was afraid to linger in the area.

Estan picked up a rock and hefted it in his hand before pitching it at a suspicious shadow. It bounced off with the clack of stone meeting stone, which made him feel slightly more at ease. As though Flayers, assassins and the Gray Army weren't enough to contend with, Grimson's Pass felt the need to add more to the list of things that would like to kill them.

"*You must return to Jarelton,*" Taymahr told him.

Confused, Estan hesitated to say anything. Was he the only one of his companions to receive such a change of instructions? *How soon?* he inquired silently.

"*If we are to make it in time, you must leave no later than tomorrow morning. You will have tonight to make your farewells, but we must depart with the rising of the sun,*" the goddess insisted.

"*Am I to go alone?*" Estan asked.

He listened with half an ear as Khiri, Resmine and Dewin discussed how best to divide the tasks of making camp for the night. With the number of threats in the area, there was a debate about whether anyone should be allowed to leave camp on their own. Ullen and Kal were chatting about Eerilorian structures that Kal had read about while studying magic. Catapult nipped at Estan's fire-shorn head, something he had only started doing recently. It occurred to Estan as he ducked away: with their holy counterparts riding along, his warhorse wouldn't even be a guaranteed travel companion.

"*Your friend Ullen must enter Eerilor. The rest are free to choose as they will,*" Taymahr answered after a few moments of silence. Perhaps the deities had been talking amongst themselves, or perhaps Taymahr had been consulting some sort of cosmic portents. There was no way Estan could fully understand the workings of his Goddess.

With a sigh, Estan followed the others in contemplative silence. He would leave in the morning.

Duty to Taymahr came first.

Tonight, he would broach the subject with the rest of their party about who would go with him, and who would stay with Ullen. Things could seem normal for just a bit longer. This small band, Kal notwithstanding, had gone through a lot together.

Estan didn't want to be the one to split them up.

5

~Khiri~

ULLEN'S SECRET CAVE had a small, easily overlooked entrance hidden behind a large patch of dogwood bushes. Khiri slipped past the spindly red branches behind Ullen and Kal, who had volunteered to scout the place. As magic gathered in the mage's hand, Khiri's ears tingled. Kal released a brilliant silver globe of light high into the dome of the main chamber. The light revealed milky pillars of stone, reddish brown stalactites draping down from the ceiling, purple-ish stalagmites bulging from the floor like frozen geysers, but nothing menacing. Nevertheless, fear tightened its grip on Khiri's chest as she slipped into the rocky cavern. Her latest, and only, experience with a cavern had been all too recent and none too pleasant.

Sensing her hesitation, Estan placed a hand on her shoulder from where he walked behind her. He had the largest of the saddle bags tossed over his other shoulder, the cavern entry being too small to leave their supplies strapped to Catapult. "Take it easy, Khiri. We're all here this time. The only evil in this cavern is Kal."

Kal turned back and fixed Estan with a deeply sardonic raised eyebrow. Somehow, the two of them feuding calmed her down more than she could have anticipated. It was becoming familiar... Homey. She hadn't thought any place would really feel like home since the day she had been banished from the Life Trees.

"You find the oddest things comforting," Micah interjected.

"*Including you,*" Khiri thought back.

Micah sighed at her, though she could tell he was enjoying their banter. Until Khiri and Kal were given the ability to hear him, Micah'd been restricted to the role of watcher. In the Life Trees, he would've had the companionship of all those that had returned to Mother Arra. Yet another thing their bond had stolen from him. She would put it right somehow.

The hideout Ullen had chosen was far larger on the inside than the entrance had led Khiri to believe. The central chamber had a natural chimney, so it would be easy to light a fire in the evenings. Despite the rock formations, the area around the firepit was nice and flat. Perfect for laying down bedrolls. Two chambers led out of the main room, and there was no sign of frost or ice crystals of any kind. Compared to the outside air, it was almost warm.

"How did you learn about this place?" Khiri asked.

"During my time as a smuggler, spent a lotta time on me own runnin' onions over the border," Ullen said. "An entire summer, Eerilor's onion supply dried up due to summat or t'other. Floods or pests... may have been a rash of feastin'. Anyhow, made a fair profit that year 'for I decided to move on."

"One of these days, you'll learn not to be askin', love." Dewin pushed Estan forward so she could squeeze into the cavern too. She was carrying one of the saddle bags and looked eager to drop it. "Stop pluggin' the barrel, Estan, we've still got Resmine and your horse waitin' on the all clear. Catapult's a tough, but he don't need to be facin' down a ring of gnorels on his own."

Instead of protesting his treatment, Estan moved slowly into the middle of the main chamber. He'd been rather subdued for most of the day, Khiri realized. The most animated thing he'd done was helping her through the cavern door.

"Is Estan alright?" Khiri asked Resmine the moment the former stablehand ducked into the cave. Short of asking the knight himself,

Resmine was the elven woman's best chance at insight into Estan's odd behavior. The two had been friends almost as long as Khiri had known Micah.

Resmine, carrying the warhorse's saddle in one hand, pulled on Catapult's reins twice.

Catapult stuck his head into the cavern's opening and nickered in frustration. He squeezed through the cavern's mouth, but it was a tight fit. Once the blue roan was inside, he trotted into the left-hand chamber and uttered a whinny that seemed to warn the rest of his companions not to follow him.

Shaking her head, Resmine let out a heavy breath. "That horse was odd enough before Numyri got a hold of him. Something's bothering Estan?"

"I think so," Khiri said. "He seems quieter than normal."

"You'd probably get more out of him than I would," Resmine gave Khiri a suggestive grin. "Not ready to push him that far yet, eh?"

Heat rushed into Khiri's cheeks. She shook her head and glanced from Estan to Kal before turning her eyes to the floor, feeling like a fool. *Telgan Korsborn* sounded in her mind like an iron-scented warning.

Resmine turned to watch her friend as he picked a clear bit of floor, swung his load off of his shoulder, sat down and pulled out a whet stone. As Estan began running the stone along his sword, she turned back to Khiri. "Now isn't the time. This is one of his I'll-talk-on-my-own-eventually funks, not the kind where he wants people to notice he's out of sorts."

Dewin called Resmine over to help her unpack the saddlebags so that bedding and dinner could be arranged. Khiri hesitated, still debating whether to try speaking with Estan or not. She finally decided not to pursue it. If she couldn't trust Resmine's judgment, it had been silly to ask. Instead, Khiri sought out Ullen's company.

"I had questions for you," she said without preamble.

"I imagined ya had, lass." Ullen eased onto a stalagmite shaped like a stump that had probably seen use as a stool many times in its existence. "I'm not certain what ya saw in that dark place, but it seems that ya know a bit more'n ya did."

Khiri sat on the ground nearby the stump-like stool of rock, watching the others go about their camp-setting tasks. Both Kal and Ullen had scouted the cave, so they were off duty until it was time to take their watches during the night. Having hunted the night before, Estan and Khiri were allowed lighter duties, such as mending and weapon maintenance. Setting Micah's bow where he could see Khiri's work and offer suggestions, the elven woman pulled out an arrow and began repairing its fletching. In life, Micah had been a journeyman fletcher and now that he was a bow, his insight was even more helpful.

Watching her hands move, Ullen waited for Khiri to speak. "Why didn't you tell us that you were one of my father's generals? Also, I thought none of you were supposed to be nobility, but we're about to head into Eerilor where you're a prince... What's going on, Ullen?"

There was a pause as Ullen smoothed the red ribbons that were woven into his long, braided mustache and scratched at his neatly trimmed beard. Shifting his weight from one side to the other, the dwarf huffed through his nose as he began to speak. "I knew yer father right well. We met 'fore any signs o' trouble started. What's more, I knew yer mum when she'd been no taller'n me. Thas' not to say either o' 'em knew me very well. There's few o' 'em that do... I ne'er told Genovar about me past. Most just assume that I were raised on the streets. May be that I encouraged 'em to think it. Is hard work, hidin' who ya are from the world. Easier when ya don't let people in. People assumed I weren't a prince 'cause I never let on that I was.

"As for the first bit, that's a might more complicated. As I said, I knew yer parents 'fore he was called to duty and 'fore the two o'

'em got involved. Yer mum, she t'wasn't born wit' the name Leyani...
The real Leyani, she was a right different creature. Yer father, he was
stuck because of yer people's ways with a right bad woman. Pure evil,
she were. He became friendly with the girl that would become the
Leyani that mothered ya, and the two o' 'em came to me, as I was always blessed with a multitude o' connections. Always knew who to
go to, ya see.

"That vision, the one that placed yer father at the heart o' everything... It weren't random. People were convinced it had to be, him
bein' an elf and all, but truth were that he owed the High Gods for
intervening. Unable to change the soul name he was born with, they
switched the girls' names. Swore they'd ne'er do so again, 'cause of
some sort of consequences. Now, I may be a lot o' things, but I ain't
a fool. Things were set in motion back then, and I had the stains all
over me gloves. When the seven o' us made a pact ne'er to speak o'
what happened back then, I started watchin' for signs o' the trouble
to start o'er.

"When I ran into that lad and he was lookin' for ya on Genovar's
orders, I knew I had t' follow. I wanted to talk to ya so many times on
the way, lookin' for Maleck ya said, but I didn't dare trust me secrets
to ya while I still didn't know ya too well, and t'wasn't about to let
that Fennick creature know any more'n I had to. For what it's worth,
I'm right sorry fer all you went through back there. If Maleck hadn't
lived so near Harish, t'would've been able to tell earlier summat more
than felt wrong."

Khiri's hands had stopped working somewhere in the middle of
Ullen's story.

"The name of my Destined was able to change because my father
changed his Destined," she whispered.

A kind of numbness flowed outward from around her heart. She
loved her mother, and her father, but anger at their actions all those
summers ago was welling up. Not only had they altered the course of

her future, but they'd never bothered to tell her. It had been a shock to learn her mother was human. But learning her parents had known there was a price stung like betrayal. She wondered if they'd known their daughter would be the one to pay for their decisions.

"Why couldn't he just leave the other Leyani?"

"As I understand things, that's easier said than done, lass," Ullen sighed and patted Khiri's knee. "I think yer aware just how difficult such a task'll be."

Thoughts tumbled through Khiri's mind like unwanted hailstones. Returning to her work on the arrow, she made a request. "Ullen, would you tell me about your time as a smuggler?"

A grim smile parted the dwarf's lips as he recognized the desired distraction for what it was. It seemed he knew Khiri would have more questions at a later date, once her anger had a chance to settle.

"Aye, lass. I'll tell ya about the time when I fended off a whole league of bandits. T'was toward the end of my smugglin' days... What I didn't know t'was an entire bushel of me onions, well, they were turnin' a might sour...."

WARM STEW, HARD CHEESE and stale bread composed their first meal in the semi-permanent encampment. Sitting down next to Dewin, Khiri exchanged smiles and complemented the former thief on the improvement of her cooking. None of them had the same level of skill Micah had possessed with herbs and spices, but it was becoming more tolerable for all of them.

Now that Khiri and Kal could both speak with him again, the others would sometimes talk to him through an intermediary. It wasn't the same as when he had occupied a seat by the fire, refusing to let anyone else near his cooking until it was done. But the fire did burn a little brighter.

Before Resmine could break out the card deck, Estan called for everyone's attention.

"I'm afraid I have some bad news," he said.

Khiri winced. A start like that rarely meant good news was going to follow. It was all she could do not to cover her ears like a child. There'd been too many unwelcome surprises lately.

"Taymahr has instructed me to leave for Jarelton, no later than tomorrow morning. Tonight will be the last night that all of us will be together in one place for... Well, I don't know, really. Until fate or the gods intervene."

"You knew of this?" Khiri asked Imyn silently.

"Whether I knew or not would have changed nothing. He must go, as his Goddess commands, Imyn replied. *I leave it to you whether or not you follow."*

"I don't know how much your own *friends* have told you. All Taymahr told me was that Ullen was required in Eerilor, and I must return to the farthest borders of Mytana. I will welcome anyone that chooses to travel with me; the rest of you, I wish you safe roads and swift feet until we meet again," Estan said, his voice soft with restrained emotion. It sounded as though he'd rehearsed his words carefully, maybe a thousand times, over the course of the afternoon.

Silence followed Estan's speech. No one wanted to be the first to speak. Khiri hardly dared to move, the quiet was so tense. Her mind changed three times, four, and a fifth time for good measure. She opened her mouth to say something, hardly certain what was about to come out when Dewin's voice cut through the stillness.

"I'll go with you."

Estan started to smile, and then hesitantly looked at Resmine. Looking around the circle, Khiri realized he wasn't the only one. Everyone's attention was on the other member of the camp's only couple. Resmine didn't seem happy.

"I'm going with Ullen," Resmine said, her voice choking a bit. She got up, leaving her unfinished stew behind, and walked into the left-hand chamber where they could hear her whispering softly to Catapult.

Dewin frowned at her lover's disappearing form before returning her gaze to the fire, her expression pensive. "I'll give her a bit to think things over. She's not a love what likes to be rushed."

It was unlikely Kal would choose to travel with Estan unless he was forced, and Ullen didn't have a choice. Catapult, being Estan's horse, would likely be going to Jarelton with Estan and Dewin. Not that the warhorse was in the room to voice his opinion.

Khiri considered the tenuous attraction she occasionally felt for the knight. It left a bitter aftertaste after what she'd learned about her parents. She thought about how much Ullen had hidden from her. There was still so much she didn't understand about the shadows gathering on the horizon. Besides, she had a duty to the people of Arra. No matter what else was going on, she had to take responsibility for what had happened in the Burning Valley. Glancing from one companion to the other, weighing all possible outcomes, she gritted her teeth against the pain of such a decision. "I'm going to Eerilor with Ullen."

Disappointment, anger, guilt, understanding–they all warred against each other on Estan's face as he digested her decision. He scooped stew into his mouth a few times, though he didn't seem to taste it. After a few more mouthfuls, he turned and wandered toward the cave's mouth.

"I think I'm going to get some air," he mumbled.

"Are ya sure, lass?" Ullen asked, concern filling his gaze as he watched Khiri pick at her remaining bread. "Ya may never be seein' 'im again. These things, these people we be facin', they don't play games and these divine bein's we carry, they aren't a guarantee we all be walkin' out clean."

Khiri nodded, depressed but resolute, "I understand, but I need answers about things he doesn't know. And I have to go where I could do the most good. Standing at your side as the only person that witnessed the reawakening of the Flayer Mage as you make our case to Eerilor–that's where I belong. I don't know what calls Estan to Jarelton, but I know he'll have allies. Dewin's going with him, which means Corianne and Evic will stand by them."

Ullen stirred his stew with a hunk of bread and bit into the soggy crust, chewed quietly, then continued, "And what of the Venom Guild? They've still got feelers out for him."

"All the more reason for me to go elsewhere," Khiri answered. "They've declared war on me. If I were to travel with him, the Venom Guild wouldn't even let us rest. I don't like that we, any of us, will be divided, but I am making the best decision I can."

"And that's...why ye'll be an even better leader than yer father," Ullen said, a touch of pride seeping into the dwarf's expression.

A small, surprised bloom of warmth sprouted in Khiri's chest. She offered a trembly-lipped smile of gratitude as she set her mostly untouched stew down.

"I think I should go say goodbye," Khiri pushed herself off the ground and began her way around the fire.

"Khiri," Kal caught her by the wrist as she passed him, his intensely large owl-like eyes glinting with reflected flame and magical light, "I will follow you, whichever path you choose."

Swallowing the lump that rose in her throat, Khiri slowly retrieved her wrist from Kal's tingle-inducing grip. After a brief struggle to find the words she wanted to say, she gave up and hoped the mage could read all of the emotions she wished to convey in her brief nod.

The small curve of Kal's lips hinted at a smile that would make her knees weak. Khiri hurried toward the cavern's portal, clamping down the confusion the mage caused within her.

Estan was leaning against the outer stone wall, still hidden behind the cover of the dogwood bushes. Night was approaching. A few stars were already shining through the edge of darkness opposing the setting sun. Keening howls echoed over the mountain range, but none close enough for concern.

"It's really pretty out here," Khiri observed. "I never thought I'd say that about rock."

"Khiri..." Estan pulled her away from the cavern mouth. His tone, an unintended echo of Kal's only moments before, made her shiver. She didn't resist when he wrapped his arms around her, despite the protesting pulse of her Destined's name. "There's so much that I wish..."

Gently, Khiri pushed away from Estan's well-muscled chest. His earthy brown skin smelled of leather and forest, familiar and comforting.

"I'm sorry," Khiri said. "It's not..."

Before she could finish whatever she was trying to say, Estan's hand was on the back of her head, pulling her face toward his. His lips embraced hers; urgent, firm, devastating. There was nothing gentle about his desire, and Khiri almost lost herself to it. Except... She pushed him away.

"Estan, stop. I can't do this."

He moved his hand to her neck, stroking her cheek with his thumb. "Khiri, come with me."

She wasn't immune to his pleas, but with the sting of his kiss still on her lips, Khiri understood that he was asking for more than her company. And she couldn't be what he wanted. Not now. Maybe ever. She was pulled in too many directions.

"I can't." Tears threatened at the corners of her eyes. "Estan, you're needed in Jarelton. My place in this is next to Ullen."

"That's it, then? All you have is...duty," Estan's jaw tightened; a flicker of anger danced through his gaze.

Resentment blazed back in Khiri's heart, "What more do you want of me? I've never asked you for anything, never offered you anything... This, this was not what I came out here for. I came to wish you well, tell you to be safe. I hope, as a friend, you would wish the same for me."

"Don't pretend you never felt anything," Estan let his hand slide off of her face, but his gaze still held her. "I know I'm pushing right now. But if there was ever a time for me to push, it's tonight. I'm leaving tomorrow and if I don't say it now, I might never get a second chance."

Estan took a deep breath. Khiri braced herself. She knew what was coming and she was powerless to stop it.

"Khiriellen Fortiva... I love you."

6

~Resmine~

SHAKING WITH FRUSTRATION, Resmine sought comfort with the only friend she'd been able to consistently count on since the death of Syara. Resmine had been on the path to a knighthood, same as Estan, but things changed drastically for her after Syara discovered the corruption of the Grey Army which had wormed its way into Temple Hill. Syara, Resmine's first love, died and Resmine kept herself safe by playing the simpleton. She failed her squire trials and got shifted into stable duties. Horses were still easier to deal with than people. Catapult had been a favorite of hers even before he'd been assigned to Estan.

"Catapult, I need a horsey nuzzle right now," Resmine said. She produced an old withered apple she'd pocketed from the saddle bags while unloading.

Seeing the bribe, Catapult hurried over and butted his head into Resmine's torso. Wrapping the big head in a hug, the former squire held on as long as she dared before the war horse started to pull away. He'd earned his treat.

"Dewin just volunteered to go with Estan. Didn't even ask if I had a preference," Resmine told the horse in a low voice, not meant to carry. "I told them I was going with Ullen, but I'm not sure—"

"Resmine?" Dewin's tone was tentative. "You're not coming with me? For true?"

Light coming through the door from both the fire and what little dimming sunlight broke through the chimney cast pink and yellow shadows on the thief woman's features, causing Resmine's heart to constrict. Dewin was so beautiful it made Resmine ache. She wished... She wasn't sure what it was she wished for.

In spite of what Resmine had been whispering to Catapult only moments before, she felt her resolve stiffen. She'd barely let her guard down with Dewin. The former thief was wedging her way into Resmine's heart bit by bit. This was the first major decision where they'd both been given a choice, but Dewin hadn't paused. She hadn't bothered to ask what Resmine's preference would be. Resmine's feelings on the matter were merely an afterthought.

Syara would've asked. Before the words could fall out of her mouth, Resmine bit her tongue. Bringing her late lover into this wouldn't help anyone, though truly, Syara's shadow was always hovering over Resmine. She couldn't seem to escape it these days. More so now than when she'd been working in the stables.

"Does it matter? You didn't seem to care when you volunteered to follow Estan. You didn't even hesitate!"

"I didna think you'd hesitate either! Is it right daft of me to want to see my family! Or for me to assume you'd want to protect yours?"

"It is daft for you to risk your life to return to a place where the Queen of Thieves has signed your death warrant!"

"And you're so stubborn that choosing not to go with us will somehow protect me?"

The words stung. Mostly because they were true. There really wasn't any reason to believe that Resmine would've refused to follow her lover and her best friend into the fire. She'd already followed Estan across Mytana twice. Maybe Resmine had been looking for a reason to fight. Things would be so much easier if Dewin and Estan were allowed to go their own way and Resmine could follow a new path for a while. She could start fresh. Not worry about Estan's lack of common sense or Dewin's expectations.

Lips tightening as she faced her lover, Resmine dug in her argumentative heels. "I refuse to be a party to another decision where there's been no discussion!"

Dewin's tourmaline brown eyes widened. She looked utterly gut-punched. The former thief spread her delicate, tapered fingers in a gesture of surrender. "Okay, there, love. I came in here for your discussion, and that's not what you're after. I don't right know why you're lookin' for a word-brawl, but I'm not gonna do this on what's apparently our last night in close quarters."

"Syara would've fought for me," Resmine said. It was only after she heard the words in her own voice that she realized they'd slipped through her guard.

"Sweet Adari! I can't do this!" Dewin shouted. "I can't keep competing with a dead woman! Resmine, I know what she was to you, and gods know that I've tried to be accommodating for your grief. But I'm not Syara! I've never tried to be, and I don't want to drop her out of her place in your heart! It'd be nice if you'd recognize we can both be in there, love. Someday, you're gonna push so hard that you'll have no room left for yourself there either. Then who'll it be? Somebody'll be tasked with pickin' up the pieces, and no one'll have the claim to you."

The two women stood in excruciating silence while Catapult swished his tail. It was obvious the horse didn't appreciate them bringing their issues into his chosen stable for the night. Slowly, Dewin turned back toward the central cavern. She was waiting for Resmine to stop her, apologize, something, but Resmine couldn't make the words come out. Her throat felt welded to her tongue.

When the thief left the room, Resmine collapsed against Catapult's flank with a rush of tears. How had she let things go that badly? She didn't really want Dewin to leave. Her pride was preventing her from rushing to seek forgiveness, but Resmine could practically feel Dewin's embrace. Was pride worth losing that forever? Was guilt?

"Sometimes pride is all we have," Locke said from within her. *"But this was a battle poorly chosen."*

"Whose side are you on?"

Locke was right. Dewin had been right, too. Hell, Resmine couldn't hear Catapult, but he was probably chastising her as well. It just made Resmine dig in further, though. This was for the best. If Dewin left, she had a shot at finding someone that truly deserved her, instead of tying herself to the bitter leftovers of Resmine's heart.

Dewin would find some way to get out of the trouble she was in, or her siblings would handle it. Or her goddess. It wasn't like Syara. There was no way Resmine could survive another Syara. Dewin would be fine, and she would move on.

Resmine would get over it. They both would.

7

~Estan~

ESTAN COULD HARDLY believe that the words had finally been spoken. Searching Khiri's azure eyes, he waited for a response. When he had kissed her, he felt as though lightning had coursed through his body. Surely, surely, she must have been struck as he was.

"I'm sorry, Estan," her tears shimmered in the dimming light. "I can't."

"You can't," he felt his heart hit the ground. He wondered how Khiri couldn't hear it shatter on the stones near her feet. "What do you mean—you can't?"

"I mean I can't. I'm bound to someone else," Khiri said. "The name of my Destined is as in my head now as it ever was. I'm sorry."

Estan reeled back. Between his rivalry with Kal and the excitement of their mad dash through Harish, to the return of the Flayer Mage and becoming the bearer of his goddess, somehow Estan had managed to forget the quest that had driven Khiri out of the Life Trees to begin with.

"So if Kal were to confess his feelings to you, you'd say the same thing?" Estan asked, failing to keep the acid out of his voice.

Displaying more wisdom than Estan had, Khiri held her silence. She threw her arms around his neck and clung to him, interrupting the impotent fury before it had a chance to swell into a storm. He could feel her crying. Something inside of him, something he hadn't realized was frozen, thawed. Despite his desperate attempt to keep her with him, nothing inside of him had wanted to cause her pain.

"I'm sorry, too," he said, finally. "Perhaps, if things were different..."

Khiri didn't respond to that verbal nudge either.

She held on until the sun had vanished and thousands of stars had come to bear witness to their parting. Holding her close, Estan allowed himself to imagine a better world, one that would permit him to make a home with the woman he loved without having to worry about assassins, armies, or Flayers. It would help if the woman he loved was also in love with him. Not that any of it mattered.

For one night, all that mattered was Estan's ability to hold Khiri in his arms.

AS HE FINISHED TENDING to Catapult's saddle, Estan took one last look around Grimson's Pass. In the early morning haze, not much was visible beyond the lip of the trail. Dewin was having a quiet word with Khiri. Resmine was avoiding eye contact with her lover. Releasing Catapult's reins, Estan approached his childhood friend.

"You do know that this may be the last time you see each other," he cautioned her.

Resmine glared at him, her lips pursed in irritation, "I realized that the moment she volunteered to leave me. I'm not the one who didn't pause to consider things."

"You could still come with us," Estan said. "Dewin's not the only one that made a decision yesterday."

"Fine, she chose to go and I chose to let her. I'm just as guilty. Maybe I was even a little relieved... Because this way... She can move on. She can move on and we can stop wasting time while she loves, and I..." Tears started falling down Resmine's cheeks. "I'm just broken."

Estan pulled her into his arms, making soothing sounds. In less than two days, he'd managed to make two of his friends cry. If he were to stay, he was pretty sure Ullen would be his next victim.

"Resmine, this is your chance to say goodbye. You shouldn't miss it," he urged her.

"Be well, Estan. May the Goddess be with you," Resmine sniffed. "Watch out for my thief."

Before he could say anything else, she darted away from him and back into the cavern. Dewin's sad gaze followed Resmine out of the open pass, possibly out of her life. The thief woman turned and gave Khiri a hug, then Ullen, and even Kal. Gathering Catapult's loose reins, Dewin smiled sadly and walked over to Estan as he watched. "Well, love, no use lingerin'. What say we dig our hooves into the soil?"

"I'll be right behind you," Estan said, taking a deep breath of damp mountain air. He raised an arm in farewell, which was answered in kind by Ullen and Khiri. Kal made a motion as though he were trying to shoo a fly, only to turn it into a wave when Khiri looked at him.

The day before, Estan would've seethed at leaving Khiri alone with the mage. Now, Estan felt a grin twitch at the corners of his mouth. It was only a matter of time before Kal got himself snubbed for a name in Khiri's head. Too bad the knight wouldn't be there to see it.

"Let's hope it's a fine day for travelers."

TWO DAYS OUT FROM GRIMSON'S Pass, the fair skies were filled with clouds tall enough to rival the mountains they were drifting over. As Estan and Dewin were entering a valley, the thief woman approached Estan with a determined grimace. "If Khiri were here, she'd already have knocked you flat."

"Have I done something wrong?" Estan asked. He tried to think of what he may have done to set Dewin's dark amber-toned jaw so rigid. They'd barely spoken more than five words the whole journey.

"Training, you great lunk. We've not had a match since we left, and I can tell you plain as Catapult likes grass that we both need it."

Dewin lengthened her stride to keep up with Estan's longer pace. "We're only two toughs—" An irritated nickering from Catapult corrected her. "—three toughs against whatever should want us dropped, where we used to be ten. Used to be a proper little army, the lot of us."

Estan managed a small grin, "Doubting my prowess?"

"Doubting your sense, more like." Dewin punched him in the arm. "Though you'll probably be more effective now that your head's not bein' turned by someone else's...prowess."

"Was I that obvious?" Estan sighed. "And here I thought I was being subtle."

"About as subtle as Ullen's mustache," Dewin said. She bent down and picked up a stone off the path and threw it into the trees. A flock of small birds took flight, startled by the sound. "Seems we're safe enough from Flayers, should you be inclined."

Taking a look around, Estan thought it over, "What about our lookout?"

"Catapult's good enough for the gods. Surely he can cry a warning well enough for us," Dewin said. "What say you, Catapult?"

The roan whinnied, bobbing his head in obvious ascent. Blinking in surprise, Estan looked from his horse to the former thief and back again. "Did you teach him that?"

"Hardly had to," Dewin said, looking around for a good sparring area. "He's got a goddess inside him, hasn't he? We're all bein' improved upon, or ain't you noticed?"

"Have I been 'improved upon'?" Estan asked Taymahr internally.

"You've received what gifts I was able to give. Your healing has been permanently and significantly increased. And as I told you before, should you ever ask for aid, you will always find it," his Goddess responded.

"Come, then," Dewin said. "Found us a proper spot, if you're feelin' man enough." She grabbed him by the arm and dragged him to a small open area surrounded by oak and birch trees.

Drawing his sword, Estan hefted the weight, testing his grip. He wasn't sure that he felt improved, but he did feel a bit stiff. Dewin was correct. They were two days overdue for this.

She positioned herself in front of him and signaled she was ready. Estan assumed the extra formality was because the two of them were on their own. The only person they had to intervene was the warhorse that was also their guard.

Before Estan saw any sign of movement, Dewin was on his right. Her hatchet was arcing down toward his collarbone. Rolling away, Estan thought he still saw a glimmer of Dewin's figure where she'd been standing only seconds before.

Confusion made him falter, nearly missing the block on her follow-up swing.

Axes flashed in the dappled light. Dewin charged again, pinning Estan between her and one of the tree trunks. Borrowing a move he'd seen Khiri use, the knight waited for the former thief's approach on the balls of his feet. Once Dewin was truly committed to the charge, he leapt, grabbed onto one of the tree's hefty limbs and swung himself back into the center of the make-shift practice ring.

The move should've put Dewin behind him, but she came at him from his left. Again, Estan found himself struggling to meet her attack. He managed to bring his sword about. Metal clanged against metal. It was enough to prevent her from earning first blood, but it wasn't fast enough to hook either of her axes. Estan felt himself losing ground against the constant barrage. She was pressing too far into his reach for his sword to be effective. Estan needed to open some distance.

Dodging as Dewin fully extended, Estan tumbled to the side. He lunged back onto his feet and began pumping his legs in full sprint, almost tripping over Dewin as she...sat...in his...path?

"Dewin!" Estan shouted.

Peering down Dewin on the ground in front of him as she convulsed into giggles, he glanced back to the Dewin he'd been fighting. His sparring partner was no longer there. Estan began to feel dizzy.

"What in the name of Taymahr is going on?"

"I believe this is actually in the name of Adari," Taymahr corrected.

"I told you, they been improving upon the lot of us," Dewin chuckled, wiping a tear from her cheek. "I just been wishin' to see it in action. So I looked over to your glum self, an' I thought it may cheer you to have a bit o' rough. Worked fair well, my compliments to the Goddess Adari. She be a right one for thieves, no doubt!"

"But what was that?" Estan demanded. "Were you really all over the place, or were you just watching me run around like a moron?"

Picking herself up and dusting off her breeches, Dewin pointed at the first tree she'd backed him up against. "That one was really me. While you watched the non-real one get ready for battle, I snuck up beside you. Then I shifted the false to your other side so you'd not be seein' me get out of the way for a turn. To be right fair, love, you needed the stretch a bit more."

Estan shook his head. He gripped his pommel and did a practice thrust, parry, reverse. It seemed to feel lighter in his grip than before. Maybe there was something to Dewin's assertions. His chest felt a bit looser, too. With a grin he beckoned to the thief with his blade, "Alright, no games this time. Let's go again."

"I make no promises," Dewin replied. She flipped one of her axes into a better position, and launched at him.

They traded blows back and forth for a few rounds. Estan's sweat was pouring into his eyes more than usual, thanks to his partially burned brows. Just as Estan was starting to get into the rhythm of fighting against Dewin's new ability, Catapult whinnied a cautionary whinny.

Dewin hurried to recover the hatchet Estan had hooked from her grip. Estan was sporting a shallow gash across his chest plate. He leveled his sword to guard the gap in his armor as his gaze swept the trees for the newest threat.

"Don't mind me."

A stranger stood next to Catapult, his hands folded into his deep brown hair, well away from any weapons. "I was just passing through when I heard a scuffle. Thought I'd poke my head in and see what it was about but, since it's all friendly, I'll just amble along."

Estan ran a trained eye over the man. Stance of an experienced fighter, though his preferred weapon was not immediately visible. Shorter than Estan by only a hair's breadth and just as broad. If this man wanted a fight, he could be trouble.

Having made a similar assessment, Dewin tilted her head at the newcomer. Catapult trotted in behind, cutting off the strangers escape.

"I think we'd prefer introductions, love." She lowered her axe so it was no longer threatening, but her stance stayed ready. The former thief never loosened her hold on her weapons.

"My name is Tharkern Anverin, though most just call me Tak," he said, grinning as though he weren't trapped between two armed fighters and a trained warhorse. For all the concern he showed, they may have been meeting in the taproom of the local tavern. His eyes, a very light brown–catching light from stray sunbeams like chips of amber–carried the same sort of carefree expression. He very nearly appeared young and foolish.

Estan had his doubts that Tak was either of those things.

"Who are you, Tak?" he asked. "What are you doing out here?"

"You know, that's a very odd set of questions. I'm pretty sure I just told you my name, which most people would take that as an answer for the first. I gather that you're wanting a bit more than that, handsome." the stranger grinned and offered Estan a wink.

Tak began moving forward, as though he was planning on either walking between Estan and Dewin or impaling himself on Estan's still-raised sword. Before Estan had to make the choice between moving or attacking, Catapult reached forward and clamped his teeth down on the back of Tak's shirt and pulled him backward.

Hardly seeming to notice that he'd been detained, Tak said, "You see, what I'm doing out here is very closely tied to what you seem to be asking with who I am. Though I believe the proper phrasing would be more a question of what I am, because people aren't always what they do. Sometimes we are more than our stations make us, and sometimes we are less than we should be. What I am, is a very humble trader, seeking to make his way in life. I pass through this area often, seeking to trade what little I carry in order to make a profit."

Estan risked looking behind the blue roan and around the clearing. Tak was wearing light leather hunting armor–little more than bracers and shin guards. His clothing consisted of a cheaply made tunic that had started life as some indeterminable shade of blue, clashing against the olive undertones in the man's complexion, and patched trousers that had certainly seen better days. A coarse brown sack hung over one of Tak's shoulders, but it probably held little more than a change of clothes or some food. Maybe a few loose trinkets.

"A trader?" Estan's skepticism dripped through his teeth, coloring those two words a dangerous shade of disbelief.

"Ease up, love," Dewin said, dropping her hatchets into their loops on either side of her belt. "This one be no harm to us. He's a trader right sure. None too regular, mind, but he's got the mark sure enough."

"What mark?" Estan asked, only lowering the tip of his sword from the stranger's chest to his navel.

Dewin sighed, then gestured to Tak. "If you don't mind being a love, show this lunk-minded tough your neck."

Tak reached up slowly, making no sudden moves, and adjusted his shirt collar so that Estan could see the outlines of a small red tattoo against Tak's bronze skin. Three rings were woven together; one had a tally mark, while the other two had been slashed with knife wounds. Dewin walked up to the stranger and pointed at the rings. "It's smuggler code, telling what he's to be trusted with. Most of them I've seen, they've the tallies in all three rings and nary a slash were merited."

"So what does it mean?" Estan asked, still not understanding the significance.

"Look here, the rings represent trades; farm goods, weapons, secrets. Tally means you carry it, slash means you're above suspicion–you're backed by local toughs what can be spared by the Thieves Guild, should you carry it. He's got slashes on farm goods and weapons, and he carries secrets.

"Tak's bound dutiful to any what's carry the seal of Thieves." Dewin pulled a chain out of her own shirt. "Which I have."

8

~Khiri~

FOUR DAYS AFTER ESTAN, Dewin and Catapult had split off from the rest of the party to return to Jarelton, Khiri was on hunting duty. She took cover behind a large elm while the-bow-that-was-Micah had an arrow nocked and ready for the first sign of game. Or trouble. It was the first time since her banishment that Khiri recalled things being so quiet. No Flayers, no assassins, nor a trace of treacherous Gray Army sympathizers. A lone man had traversed the pass a few days ago, but Ullen had advised them to leave him be and stay in the cave.

Only a few feet away, Kal ducked behind an oak, his borrowed staff surrounded by swirling shadows. *A camouflage spell,* Micah informed her.

Being the only two that could speak through Micah, Khiri found herself being paired with Kal more and more often for scouting through the mountains and scavenging for food. Dewin and Estan had been allowed to keep most of the rations in the saddlebags based on the idea that being in one place would allow Khiri's team more hunting time. Ullen's men would likely bring their own rations. If not, there would be at least that many more hands to hunt and forage until they reached the inner regions of Eerilor.

During these ventures, Kal hadn't made any more advances. Khiri was uncertain whether he was waiting for some sign from her or if he'd taken Estan's rejection as a warning. There were times when she caught him looking at her. His gaze was heated and a mysterious smirk played over his lips. Estan, for all that she liked him and missed him, had never made her feel quite so off-balance.

A scuffing sound alerted her to the presence of a creature nearby. She made a quick glance around her elm and spotted something on two legs rather than four. The creature could've been a person, but it also could've been a Flayer. It was impossible to tell from where she was hiding.

"I'm going to take a closer look," Khiri relayed through Micah.

Giving her brother a moment to pass along the message, Khiri began to edge around her tree. Cautious of each foot placement, she swept through the undergrowth with all the stealth her father had taught her. As she neared the passing figure, she knelt beneath elven eye-level. Most humans would never see her but, this close to the more diverse country of Eerilor, she still risked being seen by a dwarf. Or she would've, if Kal wasn't with her.

It was a dwarf that Khiri found herself nearly face-to-face with. He was peering into the underbrush, not three feet from where she stood. Alarm faded as she recognized his fading blonde hair and Eerilorian issued armor.

"Kal can drop my camouflage," she informed Micah.

"Ho, there," she said. Khiri hoped she was announcing her presence in a way that wouldn't startle the dwarven commander into attacking.

He leapt back into a battle stance, only to relax when recognition glittered in his eyes. "Fortiva, you're a bit far from Grimson's Pass. I trust you're not alone," he greeted her.

"We've been awaiting your arrival," Khiri said. "We can guide your team in, assuming you brought provisions... Otherwise, you may want to give me another hour or so."

The dwarven commander contemplated her answer, searching her eyes for hidden agendas. Khiri waited, aware his suspicious nature was likely part of the reason he'd been chosen for a mission across the Eerilorian border. Finally, he loosened his grip on the pommel of his sword.

With a nod of respect, he said, "We have enough food. No prince of Eerilor will be allowed to go hungry."

Khiri signaled Kal with an all-clear, visibly for the commander's sake, and followed the dwarf back toward his troop.

"FORGIVE MY EARLIER behavior, Fortiva. I wasn't certain that I was dealing with the real you until I spotted your ears," the dwarven commander said.

"Who would impersonate me?" Khiri asked. She was genuinely flummoxed at the notion. How many people even knew of her existence? If they looked enough like an elf to disguise themselves in the first place, would they have forgotten her ears?

"This commander thinks himself quite clever," Imyn commented. *"Don't worry too much about his posturing."*

"Those who seek to take my prince's place would've done their research," the commander said, unaware of the goddess's derision.

Khiri and the commander were inside his tent, a grand pavilion with carpets and a field desk, in the Eerilorian troop's base camp. Originally, the dwarves had planned on making their way up into Grimson's Pass the next day, as they had believed they were still early for the prince's arrival. A handful of humans and dwarves, both men and women, scurried about the base camp, pulling down tents and stashing things into packs. Khiri hadn't seen any horses, but five or six donkeys had been led from one side of camp to the other, their burdens growing as the camp was packed away.

Kal stationed himself outside, though the commander's pavilion had the walls pulled back and roped in a way that made the pavilion more of a sunshade than a shelter. If walls were needed, they could be drawn back out and lashed to the poles. The tent illustrated the commander's rank though, and Kal was visibly marking himself as Khiri's subordinate.

"It was my advice," Micah told her. *"Judging from our last encounter with these people, I figured they'd respect us more if we seemed to operate more officially than the rag-tag bunch we are. Kal agrees. Says it's more in line with the way his guild used to function. Armies prefer dealing with those that understand order."*

"It's been a hard road. I'm sure my people will be glad to see home for a few weeks. Unfortunately, Fortiva, I fear we've yet to complete our primary mission," he sighed. "My pardon, I just realized I've yet to introduce myself. I am Captain Horis Aldash of the Eerilorian scout division, currently first officer."

"What exactly is your mission, Captain Aldash?" Khiri inquired. She didn't realize until the words were out of her mouth that the captain might see her as overstepping her boundaries. Hurriedly, she added, "If it's not too much to ask."

Captain Aldash studied her quietly for a moment. "It would be daft for me to doubt your loyalties, given your heritage and the esteemed company you travel in. But that daftness has saved my hide all too often out in the field. I'll get into what we're doing out here once you've taken me to my prince. Not before."

"Don't let him dictate without a say in the proceedings. Acknowledge his position, but make it sound like you're granting a request," Imyn advised her.

"I will consent to that."

Khiri wished that Ullen had been the one out scouting when the Eerilorians ran across their group, but realized it may have reflected poorly on their team. Granted, Captain Aldash had been out in the woods on his own, but that wasn't the same as having a prince out scouting for a scouting party.

Unease settled in her chest as she realized the easy rhythms of their group's campfire would all change in a big way once Captain Aldash and his people were added to the mix. Ullen's lively stories and casual nature wouldn't suit the image of royalty.

At least there was a trade-off. Since Estan and Dewin had left, Khiri had feared that somehow the Venom Guild would catch wind of their division and move to strike. With a full Eerilorian scouting party in tow, the Venom Guild wouldn't pose such a large threat. She wasn't quite certain the two issues balanced out, but it was something.

The captain moved to her side and had opened his mouth to say something when he was interrupted by shouts from a different quarter.

"If you'll excuse me, Fortiva, I see that there is some confusion with the cook's equipment." Captain Aldash gave Khiri a brief salute and trotted out of the command tent yelling at his people to move one donkey out of the way and bring in another.

Khiri strolled slowly to the edge of the pavilion. Her hands itched to be useful, but she had a feeling she'd give her lack of experience away. Kal's head didn't turn toward her at all, but she could feel his awareness as she approached. There was a jolt between them, not eased at all by the impossibilities standing in the way of her affection.

"So, this seems fun," Kal said lightly, as though nothing had happened.

"Doesn't it just," she replied. Sarcasm didn't come naturally to Khiri, but she'd picked up a lot of things since leaving the Life Trees.

Like a penchant for attracting the unbound.

KHIRI SENT KAL AHEAD to warn Ullen that Captain Aldash and his crew had arrived. The Odlesk-hybrid mage could easily move up the mountain without drawing attention with his camouflage spell. If Kal did run into trouble, he would be able to call for help through their connection with Micah.

"Someday, we'll have to test your range," she told her bond-brother.

"I'm a long bow. It's pretty decent," he said.

Fighting the urge to swat the weapon in front of the Eerilorian team, Khiri groaned under her breath. It wasn't like she could let Micah get away with that kind of thing, though. Instead of visibly hitting him, she envisioned several things she could do without the strangers questioning her sanity: letting Ullen borrow him when he had to answer nature's call, leaving Micah unwrapped during the night, or leaving the bow near one of the donkeys while they were being groomed.

Khiri wasn't entirely sure what it was about the donkeys Micah found so unnerving, but her last threat left him stammering apologies until she promised never to leave him within their reach. She couldn't see why the steady creatures struck Micah as a fate worse than Flayers. With their big, furry ears and soft noses, they were pretty cute. Maybe it was because they were herbivores and he was made of plant matter.

As the scouting troop crested the hill, Ullen stood in the center of the pass with Kal on his left and Resmine on his right. He'd stepped fully into his role as Prince Ut'evullen Dormidiir, second son of Eerilor. Even though Ullen stood shorter than Khiri, when he decided to be regal he seemed like the tallest being in Grimson's Pass.

"Thank you, Khiriellen, for escorting my guests."

Khiri dipped her head in return, not entirely sure how far was appropriate. She wasn't familiar with the rules concerning royalty. Her people knew stories about kings and queens but, until she left the

Life Trees, she'd never dealt with nobility personally. The day she'd learned Ullen was a prince, Khiri'd told him he would always just be Ullen to her. Her bard friend seemed uncomfortable with his heritage. She doubted he would have identified himself if their situation hadn't robbed him of options.

"He must return to Eerilor," Imyn reminded her host. *"There are portents in motion."*

Swallowing a sigh, Khiri kept her expression as neutral as she could. She'd had more than her fill of fate lately.

"Well met, Captain Horis Aldash." Ullen gripped the man's forearm with one hand, patting his shoulder with the other. "I believe we have much to speak of before we return to my ancestral home. Why don't you and your second join my team for a light lunch while your people set up outside?"

Captain Aldash made a series of hand signals and grunted a series of commands, before beckoning his second, a Lieutenant Pecryn Frosthill, to join them as they entered the cavern.

Even though Estan, Dewin and Catapult had left half a week before, there was still a horse-like mustiness clinging to the walls. Khiri spared a thought for her absent friends, hoping all was well with them. Estan would've been very handy with his knowledge of military history and procedure. Whatever his task was in Jarelton, Khiri hoped that knowledge would serve him well.

A bit of camp bread, the last of their cheese and a stew of wild carrots, onions, and the remnants of Khiri's prior hunting trip were waiting in the center of the main chamber. Khiri noticed the bed rolls, which had been spread in a ring around the fire, were all packed away. It looked like they were hiding the fact they'd all been sharing the same sleep space. Studying his surroundings, Captain Aldash seemed to have come to a similar conclusion.

"If I may speak informally, your highness," the captain asked, inclining his head.

Ullen dipped his head to indicate the captain could continue.

"Your highness," Captain Aldash said again, seeming hesitant to speak the words currently safe inside his head. "I am under no illusions that, prior to our encounter, you lived in a manner customary to Eerilorian nobility. If you and your companions continue to be this uneasy in my presence, I will constantly be questioning your motives. I'm well familiar with the need for lines to be drawn within the ranks, so I don't think I ask this lightly: when we are within private quarters, such as this, would you do me the honor of dropping rank and speaking with me as you would your associates?"

Silence followed Captain Aldash's speech. Khiri's heartbeat sounded much too loud and she hardly dared breathe. Ullen had cautioned them to not drop character unless the four of them were alone behind Kal's shields only two days ago. He'd been gone too long to know who to trust. Most nobles would've assumed an absent prince would be holed up somewhere befitting his status, regardless of necessities like coin. Eerilor was a prosperous, industrious nation where nobility and status were synonymous with riches, unlike Mytana's farm-based economy. Some of Mytana's nobility wore patched linens and last year's silks, saving their finery for the most special of occasions. Temples in Mytana were far more powerful than the average nobleman, especially in Seirane. Jarelton was the only true exception, being a city built on trade rather than faith.

All of those things must have been weighing themselves in Ullen's head as well, for he seemed every bit as still. Only two people dared move; Lt. Frosthill was practically squirming in discomfort, and Kal, standing behind the two visitors, seemed to be on the verge of laughter.

"He's laughing on the inside," Micah said.

"Tell him he's very peculiar." Khiri fought the urge to roll her eyes. There were many times that she did not understand Kal's sense of humor; this was one of them.

Kal met her eyes, his mirrored pupils twinkling with merriment. *"He finds that even funnier,"* Micah reported.

Returning her attention to Ullen, Khiri tried to ignore the feeling that her brother and the mage were ganging up on her somehow.

"Tell you what, Horis," Ullen said. "I'll stop acting all pompous if you will."

A deep chuckle sounded in the light haired captain's throat, "Fair enough. Pecryn, I'd like you to meet an old friend, whom I've known since we were children. Ullen, this is my protege, Pecryn Frosthill. Be kind."

"You know each other?" Resmine asked. "Then why did you attack us that night?"

"The last time I saw the lunker, neither of us had facial hair," Captain Aldash, Horis, responded. "I couldn't tell him from any other blighter, and he was traveling in the company of one that I thought I recognized from the front of the current war effort."

"You more'n likely had," Ullen admitted. "Our friend, Estan, was stationed there as a Knight of the Protective Hand. He got into a dash o' trouble and then some, before stumblin' on Khiri here."

Horis looked around the chamber, seeming to notice for the first time how few were around him. "This was a much larger team the last time we met. What happened?"

"It's a long story, one that we'd best not go into without shields," Ullen nodded to Kal. "While we're about it, let's hear what you've been doin', traipsing about the hills of Mytana ."

Kal gripped his staff, pouring a glowing bronze puddle of glitter along the cavern floor. It flowed up the walls slowly, as though the entire cave was flooding with a layer of goldstone. Leaning down, Khiri touched the layer of magic and quivered as the feel of it flowed up into her eartips. It was the first time she could remember a spell feeling pleasant as it brushed against her sensitivity to human magics.

She picked up her hand and watched as flecks of magical dust faded against her skin.

"I can teach you," Kal's voice sounded in her head. Without using Micah as an intermediary.

9

~Estan~

SHARPENING HIS SWORD while Dewin and Tak faced off, Estan tried to shrug off his growing feelings of anxiety. In the bright morning sun, their surroundings should have seemed idyllic; at the edge of a wooded thicket, overlooking the golden rolling ocean of a grain crop as it ripened for harvest, there was little chance that anyone should notice the oofs, thuds and clangs as thief and trader exchanged blows. Tak dropped low and swept Dewin's legs out from under her, landing the thief solidly on her backside. Almost immediately, Dewin jumped up and asked him to do it again, but slower and with explanations on how she could copy it.

Tak was an expert in unarmed combat, claiming that weapons just tripped him up. From what Estan had seen, the latter portion was a lie Tak had created for the sake of modesty. Granted, the man was better with his bare hands than many of the knights Estan had trained with, but Tak could hold his own with just about anything thrown at him. He proved to be very useful as a traveling companion; every morning they were near a stream or river, Tak would pull fish out like a bear "to stay in practice." He was also as good at cooking as Micah had been.

Estan's sense of unease was not tied to Tak's presence, although neither Estan nor Dewin had mentioned anything about their divine travelers since the trader had joined them. No. Tak was not the issue.

It was the lack of Flayer attacks.

Before Irrellian Torne had been released, there had been roving bands of decaying Flayers and the odd fresh Flayer, not to mention the ones tied to the Venom Guild. The last time Estan had seen a Flayer at all, it had been that band of outfitted demon-bound near the Eerilorian border.

Catapult, grazing on the dropped fruit of a crab apple tree, stopped eating to neigh at Dewin as she over-extended an attack, leaving her entire side open. Giving the roan an odd look, Tak almost let Dewin sweep him with the move he had just taught her.

"...drip...crunch...rend...scream..."

On his feet in an instant, Estan dropped the whetstone and honing cloth off his sword, not caring where the items fell. He didn't spare a glance at Dewin and Tak, just barked out the warning "Flayers!" before they were on him.

Two of the creatures launched out of the shadows, their arms extended to plunge rancid claws into the knight's flesh. Five more Flayers came gliding out of the trees, hissing for blood, meat and bone. All of the cursed beings were outfitted with various bits of leather armor; a pair of bracers, a belt, breastplates, studded boots, none of it matched but it was all quality craftsmanship.

Catching one Flayer's arm on his shoulder guard, Estan rolled his way through the first wave of the demon-bound before stabbing one of his adversaries through its back. Screeching a death cry, it began to sizzle on the end of his sword. The knight spared a brief prayer of thanks to his goddess that these attacking creatures were older Flayers, which were markedly weaker and more feeble-minded than their younger kin.

Another Flayer started to wade in to replace its brother before Estan could yank his weapon free. Dodging its attack, Estan swung the corpse on the end of his sword into the wave of oncoming opponents.

A third Flayer found Catapult's teeth wrapped around its shoulder only seconds before it flew backward. The war horse reared and pounced on yet another Flayer, landing squarely on the creature's head. Squealing a war cry, Catapult cantered to the next node of fighting centered around Tak.

Making sure the Flayer thrown by Catapult was truly dead, Estan followed his horse into the thick of the fighting. As he approached, Dewin's hatchets severed the jugular of an unusually tall and skinny Flayer that had been wearing an ornate helmet. Tak jumped into the air and slammed his knee into one creature's jaw. The jawbone cracked loud enough to be heard over the sound of Dewin's Flayer sublimating as its blood boiled away. The last two Flayers were dropped with ease, finding themselves caught in a ring of steel and muscle.

Wiping her axes on the grass, Dewin sighed, "Was hopin' we'd lucked out and would've made it back to Jarelton without seein' any more of their type."

"How often have you two fought Flayers?" Tak asked. Estan noticed the trader's olive-toned skin was a shade more green than normal. "You seem a bit young to have been in the Great War."

"More often than we'd like," Estan admitted. He made his way back over to his polishing kit and picked up his cleaning rag, running it over his blade while he searched for any sign of his whetstone. "You're right about our being too young for the war, though. I assumed you were close to the same age. How many summers have you seen?"

"Roughly thirty-two, give or take a few in the middle there," Tak attempted a smile. "I could've participated, had my mother been alright with sending her boy of twelve out into battle against those things. Well, I suppose I also could've run away and joined the army had I been that determined, but I was alright with staying home until I was older. These days when I see Flayers, I'm usually alone and it's best to find a way around them. It's like fighting a gnorel, you know? Only if there's no choice and preferably with someone friendly at your back."

Estan nodded in agreement. Gnorels and Flayers were equally vicious, though gnorels were natural creatures and Flayers were anything but. "You make your trade in information, right? Do you know anything about Flayers being equipped and sent to wander the countryside?"

Dewin picked up Estan's whetstone, brushed the Flayer ash off of it and tossed it to him. "He's in the trade," she reminded him. "Anything he knows, it ain't going to be free, love. First, ask payment then ask the tough for what he's got."

Waving away Dewin's objection, Tak said, "No charge this time. The two of you," Catapult neighed an objection, "three of you carried me through my first real battle with Flayers and I have no broken limbs. It seems fair to say you earned a bit of credit."

"Assuming you know something," Estan returned the whetstone to his polish kit and then thought to examine his blade. With a sigh, he pulled it back out and began sharpening his sword all over again. He'd forgotten he hadn't gotten the notch he'd been working on buffed out when the Flayers arrived. "It'd be a shame for me to agree to this, just so you could turn around and say, 'Great, we're settled. As for your question, I know nothing about it.'"

"Nothing like that," Tak assured him. "This is what I've got: they're equipping Flayers somewhere along the border of Eerilor. The crown's concerned, of course, because if it gets out that they're doing this, trade's going to dry up. Who's going to openly trade with the bleedin' Gray Army, you know? They've got teams out hunting the things on the quiet all over Mytana, Gyth, Verem... All the way to Chultha."

"Any idea how long that's been in the works, love?" Dewin asked. She pulled a brush out of one of the saddlebags and began working on Catapult's left flank. Too late, Estan realized that they were being a bit too casual around someone that made a living by ferreting out secrets. He was surprised that Tak's nose hadn't literally started twitching.

"It's been a few months since they set out the first team. No one I've talked to seems sure of when the first of these blighters were released, though," Tak said, less easily than before. "The two of you aren't just asking this in passing... How much of an interest do you really have?"

Estan traded looks with Dewin. Hers told him to keep his mouth shut, but he wasn't entirely sure. Having someone out there, a trusted source to many, that knew just a fraction of what they did... It didn't seem like such a bad idea. He did trust Dewin's judgment, however, so he compromised with a, "Maybe another day, we'll find something to haggle over. Today, I'm feeling a little talked out. Flayers aren't exactly an everyday occurrence."

"That's as true a statement as I've ever heard," Tak said. He seemed to mull things over a bit longer before he finally got up the nerve to say, "If you don't mind my asking just one more question before I drop the subject..."

"Go ahead and ask. No guarantees whether or not we'll answer," Estan said, softening his answer with a smile. The trader already knew they were hiding something at this juncture, but there was no reason not to be friendly about it.

"What's with your horse?" Tak asked.

Both Dewin and Estan began laughing while Catapult snorted and flicked his tail irritably. "That, my friend, is a question only the gods can answer," Estan chuckled.

JARELTON'S STONE WALLS loomed over the horizon, stretching along Mytana's border as far as the eye could see. Estan wondered what it was Mytana had been guarding against when they built the fortress city. In all his years of study to become a knight of Taymahr's temple, he had never come across that particular bit of history. Whatever the reason for the wall, Jarelton's somber mass of gray stone created a bleak sense of foreboding every time he saw it. Whether the sun hung in the sky or not, the air above the city echoed the essence of the dismal, dull stone.

Maybe he had just been on the road with Khiri for too long, Estan mused. He had been reared on Temple Row in the great city of Seirane. The last time he had been inside of Jarelton, it hadn't seemed so terrible. Granted, he'd gotten poisoned the last time he was in the city. Remembering that, Estan fought the urge to ask Taymahr if it were really necessary for him to return. His patron was the High Goddess of Protection and Loyalty. She wouldn't send her avatar, a wanted man, back into the thick of things without reason.

Dewin had negotiated for a trade of clothes as they'd passed through Illesdale; a process helped by the clothier's recognizing her as one of the strangers that had helped save his village on the eve of Petora's festival. They were both wearing soft, well-hooded cloaks, travel-worn but thick enough to keep the wind off. With his hair having been seared down to the roots and the protections afforded by carrying a goddess within him, Estan wasn't sure the hoods were necessary. But it was foolish to take chances.

Checking to be sure that Tak was out of hearing as their feet crunched against the pebbled road, Estan asked Dewin in hushed tones, "Perhaps it's a little late to bring this up, but wasn't there a reason Corianne and Evic sent you out of the city? I mean, they didn't tell me anything specific, but it occurs to me that it had to be something big if they knew Khiri was being hunted by the Venom Guild and they still sent you with her rather than having you stay."

"It's sure to have blown over by now," Dewin replied, also glancing at Tak's slow progress toward the ever-approaching wall. "I surely didn't mean anything by it, and I'll be bound if they meant me to be running the whole of me life from a misunderstanding."

Estan's shoulders started to itch. It was a sense of danger, like someone was approaching his back with a knife. He'd only experienced a premonition of this sort twice before; it had been with him the day that he overheard High Priestess Shalora chortling about the way the Gray Army had infiltrated the temples, and again when Lord Rethos had led them through the city of Harish.

"What sort of misunderstanding?" he pressed.

"The Queen may still be believing that I betrayed her, runnin' the blind for a couple of wags what had it in mind to drop her an' knick her crown," Dewin mumbled, dropping her gaze from the information trader in front of them to the wagon-scored road. "None of it were my own doin', and never would I have betrayed her had I thought that's we'd been about. They tol' me I was following orders. Never occurred to me they might've been from someone other than the Queen."

His bad feeling traveled from between his shoulders to the pit of his stomach where it began threading its way firmly into his gut. Dewin, in all likelihood, still had the Queen of Thieves looking for her and they were walking straight into the Thieves' Guild's seat of power. It was as foolish as Estan walking straight into Seirane, expecting the temples to just ignore his presence because he hadn't *meant* to uncover the subversion of the Gray Army.

"Dewin..." his voice quivered with both concern and anger. There was no way she could be so naive as to think that her return would go unnoticed, let alone unchallenged. Recalling the way Resmine had reacted when Dewin announced her intentions to come with him, Estan suddenly felt a deeper understanding for what had passed between the two of them. Memories of Syara, her sudden death arranged by an enemy too big for one knight and the squire that loved her, echoed through his being. "Resmine knew about this, didn't she?"

A tear fought its way out of Dewin's eye, racing down her cheek before she wiped it away with a dusty hand. "I can't stay away forever, Estan. Running away from the Queen when all there was to lose was a year or two, that was one thing. It's different now. I can't not come back when the world's about to erupt. Knowing what we know... it's different. *His* waking, it changed everything."

Reading her features, Estan understood something else that hadn't occurred to him before. Dewin was one of the only people that ran with Khiri that was still close to her family. Ullen had been alone for ages, he and Resmine were orphans that had been raised by the temples, and Khiri would have been separated from her parents even without the exile. Estan was unsure about Kal's past, not that he cared much to find out. Catapult... well, Catapult was Catapult. The blue roan had been a mystery before he became avatar to a mischievous goddess. If things were reversed, would Estan risk the ire of the Queen of Thieves to say goodbye to his loved ones?

When the Flayer Mage was on the loose, angry guild queens and assassins did seem to fade into the shadows. Unfortunately, that was where those sorts of problems thrived.

10

~Irrellian~

IRRELLIAN STEPPED OUT of the shadows of the Demon Realms into a small courtyard, surrounded by torches, candles and mirrors. No average Flayer could accidentally stumble into this place. It was so surrounded by light that almost no shadows were cast.

In the twenty years that Irrellian had been absent from the world, the Venom Guild had acquired a new leader, Arad Rhidel. Irrellian was familiar with Arad from before. He'd barely joined the Venom Guild when Irrellian had last used the services of an assassin. Still, Irrellian had recognized the thirst for power and seething within the young man's soul. It didn't surprise Irrellian in the least that Arad hadn't just risen in the ranks, but taken hold of the guild's reins.

The Flayer mage would expect no less from a man that had seen a potential for Flayers outside of an occasional menace or a major hazard. Much like Arad's predecessor, the late Col Kimlan, the new Head Assassin knew the value of savage creatures that could be turned against one's enemies. Unlike the unfortunate Col, Arad was much more cautious about closing the snake's cage behind him. Or perhaps, more likely, he was this cautious *because* of what happened to his late master.

But as long as Irrellian knew where he was going, there was little that could prevent his entering any arena he wished.

Aside from the mirrors and the assortment of flames, the courtyard held very little of interest. There was a small fountain built flush against the wall so that it couldn't hide an assailant with anti-poison runes carved directly into the stone stem of the water spout. This was where Irrellian's sliver of darkness had deposited him. Stepping over the fountain's lip, Irrellian shook what water he could from his boot. He could've dried himself more easily with a spell, but as thoroughly as the yard was protected, the use of magic would likely set off a series of alarms.

Treading softly over the cobblestone pavement, Irrellian stepped over a tripwire, crossing his arms so that his cloak fell no lower than the hem of his robe. It wouldn't project the proper image if the all-powerful Flayer mage managed to alert the Venom Guild to his presence by clumsily setting off a tripwire he'd already stepped over.

The purpose of Irrellian's visit was too important to leave in the hands of the Gray Army. Irrellian hadn't even made his followers aware of his return yet. Not that he hadn't looked in on things. He'd found his believers in about the same shape as he'd expected: too devout to question, or too greedy to be useful. All tools had their place. For this job, he required someone with finesse and bought loyalty. Bought loyalty had a certain degree of flexibility.

Arad seemed to be out at the moment, but Irrellian could wait. It wasn't as though he was in a hurry, after all. His enemies were quite adept at keeping themselves busy.

11

~Khiri~

SWEATING DESPITE THE humid chill that clung to her skin, Khiri sliced into the meaty, mottled arm as it swung at her through the fog. The Flayer belonging to the arm bellowed in frustrated pain.

Throughout the foggy terrain, no less than ten other Flayers were tracking her group and Horis' team. After Horis and Ullen had discussed Horis' current mission, which involved the hunting down of armored Flayers, Ullen had told the dwarven captain a very abbreviated version of the events that had led to Harish burning and the waking of Irrellian Thornne. Horis had agreed that they should make all haste to Taman, capital city of Eerilor. As soon as they left the mountains, they encountered a Flayer fog, full of creatures equipped with random bits of high-end armor.

Khiri grabbed onto the wrist of the Flayer as it punched at her again, allowing it to drag her forward when it withdrew. Swinging her legs in, Khiri rode the momentum into the creature's chest jumping from its arm to its neck as soon as she was close enough. Her father's dagger, an enchanted piece he'd gifted to her before she'd left home, found its way into the thing's flesh. The sharp metal sank into the demon creature's arteries, just above the collarbone. She rolled off of the Flayer as it hit the ground, narrowly avoiding a face full of steaming demon blood.

To her left, Khiri heard the voice of Horis, Captain Aldash outside of private quarters, barking orders to his people. Even in the fog, they functioned as a unit, fighting back to back as the Flayers came to them through the clinging mists. Ullen, having taken up his role as prince, was lucky to be allowed to join their formation. They'd wanted him to hide in the center of their platoon, if not inside the cook's wagon. He had reminded them of a long history of royals that led charges alongside their men, but he'd left out the long record of battles he'd participated in as a civilian. Horis had argued it would only make the ranks uncomfortable to think of their prince as an average bloke.

Khiri still didn't entirely understand the distinction of royal blood. After Horis had returned to his camp, Ullen tried to explain it again, but Khiri had waved him off. Something happened a long time ago in Eerilorian history that Ullen's ancestors had found intolerable. They had taken up arms and won, joining many of their supporting clans into an army. Those clans had become nobility. Nobility was led by royalty. Thus Ullen's clan had become what they were already, leaders, only not quite. Special leaders that didn't really do the fighting any more. Despite being elevated for that skill in the first place. The elven woman shook her head to clear it of the baffling logic.

Battle cries brought her attention back to the fight at hand. Flayer fog was dense enough that moving through it too quickly was hazardous. One could end up fighting an ally as easily as an enemy. Barely able to make out her hand when she extended her arm fully, Khiri made her way forward cautiously. She listened for signs of Resmine and Kal, both of whom had been near her when the fog rolled in, but she hadn't seen or heard from since.

"I'm here," came Kal's mental assurance.

"Where's here?" she attempted to send back. She wasn't certain if talking to Kal mentally was any different than talking to Micah or Imyn.

"If you try, you should be able to feel my presence, along with anything that's near you," Kal told her. *"Just imagine you're reaching out with an arm that stretches beyond your actual reach. Keep stretching until it hits something."*

Touching Micah's bow for reassurance, Khiri attempted to stretch an invisible arm out into the haze. She struggled for a moment, not trusting that she was actually feeling anything. As soon as a fuzzy shape registered only a few feet to her right, she began trying to see through the mist with her eyes again.

"Close your eyes. It will make things easier," Kal instructed.

The last thing Khiri really wanted to do in the middle of a Flayer fog was close her eyes, and she said something similar to Kal in less than honeyed terms. *"Are you a damn fool?"*

Rather than getting upset with her, the Odlesk mage's voice chuckled in her mind. *"I've got my eye on things. If anything gets too close, I'll alert you. I know this sounds like I'm asking a lot, but there's no greater teacher than adversity."*

Khiri clenched her teeth. This seemed like a horrible idea. *"Can't we try this some other time?"*

"We can practice again later, in a safer arena," he assured her.

"I'm also watching out for you," Micah told her. *"This is just like learning to jump from the stairs of the Life Trees. Your senses are going to lie to you, tell you that the ladder is the only way down, but once you try it, you may find it to be more effective than the old way."*

A wry smile played over her lips. Trust Micah to know just how to cajole her into something... Khiri well remembered that day, on her fourth hunting trip with her father, when Genovar had turned and told her she was only allowed to come if she made the jump the way he did. He wouldn't have a daughter that needed someone to accompany her on every trip just to make sure the ladder was stashed after she left. Closing her eyes, Khiri chose to leap off of this new set of stairs.

This time when she felt the fuzzy shape to her right, Khiri resisted the urge to open her eyes. Instead, she wrapped her perception around it, recognizing the shape as Resmine's slight form. Resmine was advancing slowly, sweeping her whip in a large forward arch, using it as her eyes. Moving further forward, Khiri sensed a Flayer her friend would encounter in only a few more steps. Trusting in Resmine's abilities, Khiri moved her awareness out past the two of them, still seeking Kal. A gang of five filtered into her awareness before she found him, but she could hardly ignore a clump that large. It was time to get back to the fight.

Kal's hand fell on her shoulder. Wincing, Khiri realized her mistake. She had only been searching in front of her. "Time for that later," Kal said. "Right now, we've got bigger things to deal with."

Pulling Micah off her shoulder, Khiri nocked an arrow and brought the string back to brush her cheek. She closed her eyes and reached out with her new perception, then let the arrow fly. The piercing sound of a Flayer death cry announced her success through the thick mists.

"One down," she grinned.

Rewarding her with one of his rare smiles, Kal shot a fireball into the group she had just weakened. That was when the remaining three charged them.

REGROUPING AFTER THE fog had dissipated, Khiri lent her hands to the healers wherever she could. Resmine had sprained her wrist, and Ullen had gotten injured when a Flayer blindsided one of his guards. Prince Ut'evullen Dormidiir leapt to his bodyguard's rescue, taking a deep stab wound, meant for the man's heart, solidly in the meat of his bicep.

"It's not as bad as it seems," he struggled to keep his princely voice intact around his obvious pain. "I'll be up in the thick of things again in no time."

Searching Khiri's face, Kal bent without a word and fired up his staff. Slowly, the pain creasing Ullen's features lost its hold on him. The wound itself began to fade, gradually becoming little more than a star of silvered-pink scar tissue before vanishing altogether.

"Many thanks, lad," Ullen breathed, his muscles twitching in response to their sudden release. "Though I'm sure there are others that could use a bit of relief, if you're up to it."

Khiri squeezed Ullen's hand as Kal turned with a muted sigh and some semi-sincere grumbling about getting himself involved with the welfare of others. Kal was a better person than he realized and it was starting to show through the cracks. Eventually, he wouldn't be able to hide it from himself any longer. Ullen, seeming to follow Khiri's thoughts, returned her squeeze with his own, "Go on, lass. Every healer needs an assistant."

It didn't take long for the camp to be up and running again. Most of the injuries were abrasions, sprains, or bruises; they'd taken no casualties and only one of Horis' team had taken a worse blow than Ullen. Despite Kal's abilities, the lady dwarf stubbornly refused to allow the Odlesk mage to do more than stop the bleeding. "What do I need a second eye for, anyhow?" she protested. "If you fix it, the lads will just feel bad when I fight beside 'em. Can't keep up with me as it is."

Horis beckoned Khiri to lean down so he could whisper a most un-captain-like comment, "Sad thing is, Solancia's probably right."

Turning back to the gruff dwarven woman, Khiri felt a growing respect for the soldier as she pulled an eyepatch out of her own belt purse. Highly decorative embroidery, a pattern of bright purple flowers Khiri recognized as blooms of nightshade, covered the black fabric. "Always suspected I'd be losing an eye someday. Had a bet running with Radley on just how long it'd take."

"You owe me, woman!" Radley, the camp cook, called from his seat on the lone wagon.

"Pull it out of your own purse, then!" she called with a laugh. "Boys, do you see how he treats his lovin' wife? Who'll be comfortin' me with a shoulder to cry on then?"

There was a good-natured mood to the banter, making light of the wound and the brush with death. A dark undercurrent was present, though. Knowledge of what may have been lurking out on the battlefield for one or both of the spouses couldn't help but tint the conversation, adding an ominous flavor to the otherwise friendly barbs.

"Alright, alright," Radley sighed. "I'll come give ya a hug, iffen it'll make you shush." With a great show of effort, the cook bent to place his hand on the wagon's seat and launched himself off of the wooden slab, down into the tacky soil that couldn't decide whether it was more mud or dust. His height bespoke the presence of some human ancestry, causing Khiri to feel an odd sort of kinship with the cook, though they had barely spoken before. Brushing past several onlookers, Radley threw his burly arms around his equally burly wife. His short, blonde curls mingled with her long, auburn waves as they exchanged an affectionate head bump that seemed more intimate than any kiss that Khiri had ever experienced. She found herself longing for that kind of shared closeness.

Telgan Korsborn, the voice inside of her almost felt smug, as though her pang of envy translated into a caress. A momentary lapse in judgement on her part could provide the *thing* she was connected to with a foothold. She ducked away from the open display of affection between the warrior woman and her husband, before it could remind Khiri any more of what she would never experience.

Running into Kal's chest, Khiri felt tears fall from her cheeks as she pushed her way past him. If the mage had resisted at all, she wasn't sure she could have found the strength to fight the pull of his arms. There was a heat between them she couldn't quite ignore, stronger even than the lapses she'd experienced with Estan. Kal was part of her problem, why her situation with Telgan Korsborn was even more intolerable. She wondered if this had been what pushed Genovar Fortiva to the edge... Had he feared his soulmate? Loathed her? Did her name physically revolt him? To sever and bind new soul-names to her mother and the-elf-who-had-been-Leyani, despite what it would do—had done—to the rest of Arra... It was enough to make Khiri feel, for the first time in her life, that she very much didn't want to be her father's daughter. She would fix things.

She had to...

Out on the edges of camp, she found Resmine, looking every bit as glum as Khiri felt. A bandage was wrapped around Resmine's sprained ankle, though Kal's efforts should have put it well on the mend. Resmine spared a damp smile for Khiri as the elf approached. Sitting in the damp dust, Resmine's dark, reinforced leather armor was coated with an almost buttery layer of yellow-brown sludge.

"Are you okay?" Khiri asked, already knowing the truth. Still, when approaching someone who had obviously been crying, she didn't know what else to say.

"Do you regret not going with Estan?" Resmine asked. Her lips dropped the smile they had been struggling to hold up. "If you two truly never see each other again, are you okay knowing that you let the chance to be together slip away?"

Khiri sat next to her friend in the mucky soil. Rearranging Micah so that he was safe from the moist dirt, mostly so he wouldn't complain at her later, Khiri studied Resmine's profile in the gray, overcast afternoon light. "I'll miss Estan," she replied. "But I don't think my decision was the wrong one. He kissed me, that night, before he left. It wasn't unpleasant, but it cleared up any lingering doubts."

A wistful sigh escaped Resmine's lungs, "It must be nice to be so certain. When Syara died, I was sure, in the depths of my soul, that I would never... Could never... feel that way again. So when Estan and I ran into your party, when I saw her again, I thought it wouldn't change things. Dewin could only ever be a fling. Someone who could help me pass the time, so that I wouldn't miss Syara so strongly... I never thought... I never wanted..."

Putting her hand on Resmine's shoulder, Khiri felt an echoing sense of her own predicament. At least, in this instance, Khiri knew that one of them could be happy. "Resmine, I don't think Syara would want you to spend your life half-dead. You didn't die when she did. I know a piece of you went with her, and that part of you is with her forever. But, if you never see Dewin again, are you really okay with the way the two of you left things?"

"No," Resmine shuddered. "When she left, the last thing I said was 'Syara would fight for me.' I as good as told her she'd never measure up. I may as well have shouted that I didn't love her in her face." With tear-bright eyes, Resmine searched the ground in front of her for answers. "What must she think of me?"

Trying to send as much warmth and comfort through her grasp as she could, Khiri remembered Dewin's face as she had turned to depart. The expression had been sad, resigned, but no trace of anger or latent hostility. "I believe she thinks of you as she always has," Khiri said truthfully. "As a person she was lucky enough to meet, even if you never felt quite as she did."

Resmine gave out a rough chuckle, "By Locke, it's no wonder she and Estan get along so well. They have similar misfortunes when it comes to choosing their love."

"Not entirely, it would seem," Khiri retracted her hand, sensing that Resmine no longer needed it. "When do you leave?"

Startled, Resmine glanced back at Khiri, the denial in her eyes dying before it ever reached her tongue. She rocked forward, resting on her knees in the slick clay and offered Khiri a hand so they could pull each other up. "I suppose I should get packing," the former squire said.

This time, Resmine's smile was tinged with genuine warmth.

12

~Estan~

STREET NOISE FILLED every nook of Jarelton's stone roads. Every major throughway was packed with farmer's markets, cloth vendors, spice merchants, fishmongers, farriers, weaponsmiths and tinkerers of all shapes and sizes. Thieves kept a wide berth, recognizing Dewin's seal as the mark of the guild. Smells, both pleasant and putrid, assaulted Estan's nose with equal enthusiasm. Unwashed bodies crowded through the spaces left by the merchants as people tried to make their way through the city with their coin intact between the tavern and their homes.

"WHY IS IT SO CROWDED?" Estan didn't want to shout into Dewin's ear, but the sounds of the city made it impossible to be heard otherwise.

"DON'T RIGHTLY KNOW!" Dewin shouted back. "WE'LL HAVE TO ASK IN A SPOT WHERE WE AIN'T GOT SO MUCH TUMULT ABOUT US!"

Tak was still with them, though Estan was curious how much longer the unusual trader would feel the need to stick around. There wasn't much profit to be gained from travelling with the former thief and a knight errant. Granted, they'd avoided telling Tak that they were both wanted fugitives from their own people. Fighting the urge to fidget with his hood, Estan kept his grip on Catapult's reins tight.

It occurred to him, rather too late, that they had done nothing to disguise the large roan. The warhorse stuck out like a wart on a nose; impossible to miss no matter how hard one tried not to look. Catapult would be a dead giveaway to any hunters sent out by Temple Hill. Estan cursed his lack of forethought. If he'd left his horse with Khiri, Catapult would've been well tended and cared for. *Taymahr's tits, Resmine has probably spent more time with my horse than I have!*

*"**I beg your pardon,**"* Taymahr's tone was colder than hoarfrost.

Estan begged his goddess for forgiveness while cursing himself for a fool. It was just like him to step around one pile of horse dung just to sit in another. It hadn't occurred to him that she could hear even his idle thoughts. Taymahr eventually told him to leave it be. She could hardly hold it against him when he was one of her truest followers left.

*"But don't think for **one moment,**"* the goddess warned him, *"that my leniency this time is permission in the future."*

Assuring his goddess that it wouldn't happen again, Estan let a sigh out through his nostrils. Having just offended Taymahr, he didn't feel it was the best time to ask her advice on what was to be done about Catapult. He looked back at the warhorse and found he was holding the reins of a sorrell plow horse. Staring at the reins in horror, Estan turned to search the crowds for someone making off with his blue roan, trying to imagine how someone could have switched his horse's harness while neither Dewin nor himself had noticed.

The soft chuckling nicker drifted into his ears despite the noise and settled his nerves, though it made him uneasy in a different way. This plow horse was Catapult. His big, deep brown eyes were the same, and when Estan patted him, the hair stuck to his glove was still that of a roan. Like his human counterparts, Catapult possessed divine gifts. And the horse had found it more entertaining to wait until Estan was looking away to change his appearance... Estan couldn't remember if he'd ever felt such a strong urge to punch a horse, but it was there. His nerves were so frayed in this mass of humanity, it was all he could do to let out a sigh and keep moving.

Dewin suddenly veered to the right, ducking down an alley Estan hadn't noticed until the thief disappeared. Tak stood to the side, ushering Estan and the disguised Catapult into the shadows. Estan wasn't entirely sure about trusting Tak at their back, but the alley was wide enough for the warhorse to have a clear kick at anyone looking to jump them. And he did trust Dewin.

"And here I am, thinkin' me life's all plunders and feathers, when out of the sky ya land like a great pigeon ready to roost," a familiar voice said. The playful cadence carried down from near roof-level.

"I'm back, Corianne," Dewin said, a defiant note carried from her speech into her stance. Estan got the impression Dewin was ready to fight her sister if Corianne tried to dismiss her again.

Dropping off of a small awning Estan didn't think was large enough to fit one person, let alone two, Corianne and Evic landed with the ease of much practice. Even with the street noise folding away from the alley's mouth as though sensing it was unwelcome, the two thieves seemed to move with a preternatural sense of stealth. They were the essence of danger, out for a stroll.

"Aye, I be seein' that you're back, and none too shy have you been either... Prancin' about as though ya think yer forgotten. ya better hope I not find ye've done summat to the one we sent to guard ye. And this one," Corianne turned her gaze on Estan, "we send after the pair of ya. Did that poison ya danced with dry up what sense ya had? You're both as crazed as a hawk what thinks he's found a mouse the size of a cart horse!"

"Perhaps," Evic's dark eyes, no less angry than Corianne's, seemed to take in more than his sister's torrent of words allowed to filter in, "we should escort this sad little reunion to better quarters, before we draw the cats to see whether we make a decent dinner."

SITTING WITHIN THE walls of the Talon Acre Inn, Estan remembered his thoughts the last time he had passed through: wondering what to expect of Genovar's daughter, battling the poison in his veins, meeting Ullen-the-unfortunate-bard who turned out to be Ullen-the-unlikely-prince. He'd barely stepped foot into Jarelton before things had started to get out of hand, and this trip was proving to be no less eventful. Estan sent a brief prayer to his goddess, asking her protection against a second bout of poisoning.

"We'll see," Taymahr said, her tone still bitter. The knight had nearly forgotten his earlier misstep with his goddess. Seeing the ire flashing toward him from Corianne's deeply brown eyes, Estan resolved to stop talking altogether. If he didn't say anything for the next twenty years or so, maybe he could avoid making anyone else angry with him.

"Well, go on then. The quicker yer about the tale, the sooner we can plop you out again." Corianne crossed her arms, her black shirt nearly blending with the black leather of her bracers, and tilted her head. Her jet black hair, tied into a loose knot, fell behind her head, forming a halo of dark curls that made her seem like a vengeful goddess in her own right.

"I have to admit a certain sense of curiosity, myself," Tak said. The information trader was sitting at the end of the table, balancing on the back legs of his chair. Even though Estan still viewed the man as an outsider, Corianne and Evic knew him well. Tak continued to tag along on the strength of their invitation. "I thought I detected a family resemblance, but I couldn't for the life of me figure out what a sister of yours would be doing that close to Grimson's Pass even with such a charming travel companion."

"We're not..." Estan began to protest.

"Maybe had you not been makin' eyes at Khiri so fast, love," Dewin winked at him. "And had I not found Resmine's company a might more pleasin'." The former thief had her elbows propped on the table, and seemed to be trying her best to throw off her sister's mood by being as larksome as she could.

"Grimson's Pass?" Evic cut in; he seemed to take his sisters' feuding in stride, which made Estan feel slightly more at ease.

If only Estan hadn't found himself in the center of their current fight. He tried to ignore the smoldering looks from Corianne's side of the table and Dewin's flirtatious wink. Estan wasn't sure why Dewin was pretending to flirt with him, except that it seemed to bother Corianne. A lot. Which was odd. He'd never had an actual sibling though, so maybe he wasn't meant to understand.

Evic asked, "What were a pair o' birds like you doin' down by the pass? Whatever happened to Khiri an' Ullen?"

Suddenly as serious as she had been silly, Dewin let out a deep sigh. "I'd rather if we didn't have to tell you, loves. I'd really rather not... but it seems as though we're not to be given the chance to keep the story to ourselves. Adari's breath–" she said, alerting Estan to just who had instructed her sudden mood change "–here it goes."

She launched into her narrative; starting from when she and Khiri's group had been found by Estan, Resmine, Ullen and Catapult, Dewin told them about the interrupted festival at Illesdale, Micah's tragic fall, discovering that Fennick had taken Khiri and ending with the story of the Flayer mage's awakening. Corianne, Evic and Tak sat in silence, just listening. When Dewin was finished, it was still several minutes before any of them spoke.

"Well," Corianne blinked, "that's a right muddled soup of troublesome."

"I left out a detail," Dewin said. "Estan, Khiri and the rest of us have been tapped by the High Gods. They've got us runnin' errands and any bit o' footwork that they can't be doin' themselves. It was on

Taymahr's orders that Estan had to return, and Adari's word that you lot were to be told. No secrets at this table tonight."

"If the Flayer mage is back," Tak said, setting his chair down with a thunk, "it's good the High Gods are on our side."

"So now, the query becomes what's the bother about Jarelton for a tough the likes of Taymahr to have just one bloke wander into town?" Corianne traced a finger over the lines of wood grain that traveled across the table. "Also, we still be stuck in the alley on what's to be gone and done with Dewin and the queen."

Dewin shrugged, seeming unhappy. "I'm sorry, Corianne. This may be more than a small bit o' bother to you and Evic. I know that bein' members o' the Court, my being back will pull the two o' you in the fire. But I have to go to Dothernam Square."

Silence fell over the mostly empty taproom for the second time that evening. Estan found himself at a loss, being the only one at the table unfamiliar with certain parts of the city. "Where is Dothernam Square?" he asked.

Evic took a deep breath and let it out through his nostrils, "Nothing like starting off a family reunion with a little cross and bother... Dothernam Square is blocked off, but for major events such as Lady Ilamar's speeches, festivals, the changing of nobility. Part of the Guild charter what keeps the Guard off our backs states specifically that we ne'er enter the Square. Place o' safety for the average citizen. Can't rightly think why the Goddess o' Greed and Guile would be wantin' you in such a place."

"I can't say," Dewin said. Her fingers were woven together and her elbows were on the table. She was leaning so far forward that she was hanging over the bench more than she was sitting. Estan had thought only Resmine could get Dewin to this level of frustration. "It's imperative that I get in there, though."

Corianne and Evic exchanged helpless looks, having a conversation with facial expressions that was nearly vocal. If Estan was following them correctly, he thought that Corianne was pulling for them to risk it and Evic was trying to remind her that their sister had enough trouble without the two of them helping her break even more regulations. Dewin had mentioned in the past that her sister was almost as devout a follower of Adari as Estan was Taymahr's; he guessed that meant Corianne would follow the goddess' orders even against her queen.

"I can get her in," Tak said. Every head at the table turned toward the information trader. "I'm welcome at the Thieves' Guild, but I'm not a member. I do business with Lady Ilamar and her sons often. There's one catch."

"What catch, love?" Dewin and Corianne asked together. The sisters turned to face each other, raising the same questioning eyebrow. Despite the situation, Estan found himself coughing to keep from laughing. They turned equally disdainful looks his way, which didn't help him regain control any faster.

"You'd have to renounce any remaining ties to the Guild and sign on as my apprentice," Tak told her. "Without the tattoo, we wouldn't fool anyone."

"Renounce my Guild... I'd never really thought about it before, but..."

Dewin looked up at her older siblings, both of whom were suddenly very interested in the table, ceiling, their hands, or anything else that was not their younger sister. Dewin's voice shook with emotion as comprehension weighed in on her. "The two of you made me leave hoping I'd do just that. Forsake our father's legacy, and never come home."

"The Guild's a rough and tumble lot," Corianne said. "It's taken me and Evic years to carve out a bit o' dirt what's ours. We did hope you'd find summat better."

"If I didn't have so much other to deal with, I'd be very annoyed at you right now," Dewin sniffed. "You two always act as though you're so much older, but Evic's only got five summers on me and you're younger than him."

"Still older than you," Corianne muttered, sticking her tongue out when her sister wasn't looking, only to return to studying the ceiling before Dewin could catch her.

Ignoring Corianne, Dewin exchanged a brief glance with Estan, inviting him to comment. The knight shrugged, having no real insight into the Thieves' Guild or Tak's trade. If accepting Tak's offer meant they were able to move freely throughout the city, or more freely, anyway, it seemed a decent option. But it was Dewin's decision to make. Seeing no objections, Dewin turned to Tak.

"Alright, I'm in. Teach me to trade."

13

~Khiri~

ESTAN HAD TOLD KHIRI about Eerilorian engineering and some of the things that had been developed through their mix of rune magic and technical experimentation, but nothing had prepared her for her first walk through Taman. Khiri remembered conversations about lamp posts with flame runes charged by a steam pipe system; no one had said these posts were everywhere. Every street corner, in the middle of each city block, adhered to buildings; an ornate steam pipe holding two caged glass globes at the very top would cast its light in a dancing circle, overlapping and merging with other circles of light, until the Taman glowed like it'd been set ablaze.

Water condensed into droplets at the tops of the globes, but Khiri didn't see any vents. It seemed like the pressure of all that steam should've caused the entire system to explode. Since she was sitting on the bench of the cook's wagon with Radley, Khiri asked him about the lamps.

"Gotten a might used to them meself," Radley chuckled. "'Tis a bit beyond me knowin', honest, but I know they've somehow rigged it so that each series o' lamps is all powered off o' the next. One set o' runes heats the water, steam runs back through the pipe, heats another rune, and that rune heats the water and so on. Whole city only needs a couple o' barrels every year to keep it goin'."

Architecture in Taman was also vastly different from the cities that Khiri had witnessed within the borders of Mytana. Jarelton had convinced Khiri that buildings made of stone felt lifeless and dull. Taman breathed life back into the rock. Each street flowed like a river between buildings. Store fronts and homes looked as though they'd grown in place rather than been built. It wasn't that they looked like plants or trees as Khiri knew them. More like the stone had achieved its purpose and chose to remain in place. Elegant, colorful surfaces of smooth granite, basalt, and soapstone wound into intricate, curly webs of windows and doors. Some of the structures stretched as high as four stories above the ground.

Arched walkways laced their way through the city, connecting one side of the street to the other, in a way that was reminiscent of the board and rope constructs of Harish. Taman was on a whole different level of finesse, though. In Harish, the bridges, and half of the city, had appeared slap-dash and hazardous; on the streets of Taman, bridges jumped like playful rainbows from one level to another with the occasional spiraling ramp that rose all the way to the highest roof tops.

Small shapes darted from one building to another, glinting in the lamp light like tiny gems. Khiri watched them in puzzlement, before Radley took pity on her and told her that they were rune-powered messengers. If a shop owner or tradesman found themselves unable to pull away from a project, they could send for a tavern to deliver food. Or they could send for the city guard, or a healer. Each message was color-coded and the name of the sender was etched onto the jewels, which were called "flits". Khiri watched as one of the flits narrowly avoided running into a group of children that were climbing the railings of one of the highest walkways.

"This place is amazing," she whispered. "I'd never imagined anything like it could exist."

"Taman is one of a kind, lass," Radley said, breaking into a wide grin. "Not another city like it in the whole o' Arra, not even in Eerilor. The flits and the lamps, sure, they be sprinkled about the kingdom, but we take a might o' pride in the capital."

"Just you wait, Fortiva," Solancia said, gripping the wagon seat with one hand and swinging herself up beside the elf. "The capital's pretty an' all, but the palace! Now that's a gawker."

Khiri had been spending more and more time around the couple since Resmine's departure. True, when she had first left the Life Trees and her party had consisted of Micah, Fennick, and herself, Khiri hadn't cared that she was sharing camp space with two men. Things seemed different with Kal and Ullen though. She and Micah had shared a history, but there had been no pressure once their bond dissolved, and Fennick was, at best, unconcerned with Khiri's presence. At worst, he'd envisioned her death daily in his ambitions to unchain the Flayer mage. Unlike Micah, she and Kal had heat, and unlike Fennick, Ullen got nosey and protective.

When she had to get away from Kal's overwhelming aura, or Ullen was becoming a bit of a mother hen, Khiri would seek out the warrior woman and her husband. They reminded Khiri of her parents, or what she imagined her parents would have been like when they were younger. Often, they would play cards with her or, on one memorable and catastrophic occasion, Radley tried to teach Khiri to bake a pie. Seeking to keep her mind on more pleasant things, Khiri glanced back to watch a purple flit darting from a doorway over a series of walkways. It rounded a curve and flew past a tall, skinny figure that made the blood in her veins crystalize like ice.

Between one breath and the next, she leapt over Radley, off of the cart and was pelting up the walkways. Finding herself at the apex of her chosen ramp, she bounded off one hand rail and caught hold of a different ramp with her fingertips. Using muscles honed by growing up in the Life Trees, Khiri hoisted herself up the side of the upper ramp without losing her breath. She could hear her name being shouted from below, but she had to catch up with that figure.

"Khiri, slow down. Be cautious. If it is him, what are you going to do? In all likelihood, it's a trap!" The panic in Micah's voice finally cut through Khiri's need to catch up to the figure she'd been certain was Arad Rhidel. *"He's never been shy before. If he's running now, catching up is not going to be to your advantage!"*

"I know." Khiri's breath was coming hard, not with exertion but frustration. *"I just... I want... I want..."* Hot tears started to well up in her eyes as Khiri realized that what she wanted was to sink her blade into his chest. Before Fennick had forced her hand, Khiri had never taken a life that hadn't either been game or a Flayer. She hadn't desired to kill Fennick. No matter how she tried to phrase it, or deny it, she craved the death of the Venom Guild leader. The more she thought about it, the more she wanted a bath.

"I'm here," Micah told her. *"It'd put an awful strain on my curve to hug you, but if you wish it, I'll make the attempt."*

Khiri managed a damp smile as she turned to rejoin the paused progress of Horis' team on their way to the palace. She hoped she wasn't making a mistake, leaving the question of Arad Rhidel's presence in the city unanswered.

As she rejoined the scouting unit, Khiri hoped she'd be able to pass a discreet warning on to Kal and Ullen, but her sudden flight into the city had caused too much commotion. Several of Horis' soldiers wanted to spread out and scan the streets for the suspicious figure, but Horis would brook no more delays to the palace where he was to report to Queen Di'eli Dormidiir.

"She will not be happy that we've found nothing pointing to the mysterious benefactor of the Flayers," Horis muttered, with a slight shake of his head. "Though perhaps finding her second son will put her in a better mood."

Khiri nodded absently. She wasn't sure why it felt wrong to tell Captain Aldash about Arad Rhidel, but she couldn't bring herself to mention that she suspected the head of the Venom Guild was loose in Taman. The probability of increased security for the royal family was already high and Ullen seemed unhappy about his current allotment. Maybe that was it. Maybe it wasn't that Khiri feared someone else would go after Arad Rhidel themselves... Though Khiri could tell she was kidding herself. If someone else pursued the assassin, they would get themselves killed, or they would succeed and Khiri would never have the chance to face Arad herself. Neither of those options appealed to her.

Khiri's thoughts halted when the home of Eerilor's royal family came into view. In a city composed like a gorgeous symphony of stonework, the palace stood apart in unmatched splendor. Flame rune lamps surrounded the parameter of expansive yards that separated the palace from the streets, creating a clear line between royal grounds and those of the common Eerilorians, though the yards were open for public use. Another row of lamps lined the palace gates, delicate webs of gold and iron that surrounded a mountainous, glittering blue stone dome. It looked like a large chunk of the night sky had been ripped from the heavens and placed upon a hill. Slightly removed from the dome, sharp, crystalline edges tore into the air, creating six towers, softened only by the rounded balconies and scrolling trim worked in friendly green striations of malachite. The six towers looked to be connected to the dome at its base level with tubular hallways of crystal or glass.

"It's only pretty on the outside," Ullen warned her in a low voice. "Brace yerself, Khiriellen Fortiva, because we're about to get an Eerilorian welcome."

QUEEN DI'ELI DORMIDIIR sat in a throne room every bit as opulent as the outside of the palace had hinted. The galaxy of a ceiling had been inlaid with a golden sun and silver moon; constellations depicted with brown goldstone glowed against the deep night blue goldstone. Khiri had seen small samples of the created stone before—she knew it was made by folding flecks of copper into clear crystal or glass. The amount of it used in the palace of Eerilor would've beggared the whole country of Mytana. Columns melted from the ceiling into the floor, which had more brown goldstone inlay displayed in a simple alternating squares pattern. Malachite and gold flowed up the far wall, forming both dais and throne.

In such a setting, Khiri would have thought that the dwarven queen would have a hard time standing out, but Queen Di'eli didn't seem to care what Khiri thought. Dressed in a crimson velvet gown, she wore a single teardrop ruby suspended in silver at her throat. Her once raven hair, threaded with the silver of age, flowed over her exposed shoulders. Though she possessed the stockiness inherent to her race, the air of majesty lent her height. The queen's voice held a thin veneer of civility, but it was impossible not to feel the layer of ice lurking beneath the surface, "So, after fifty summers have passed, our son returns. And what news has he brought me? I should dearly love to hear what has kept our beloved Prince Ut'evullen away."

"I would dearly love to trade barbs with you, your majesty," Ullen said, kneeling at the bottom of the dais. Khiri and Kal knelt to his right and left, the scouting contingent spread out behind them. Having come straight in from the street with days of road dust and sweat clinging to their skin, Khiri realized that they made a rather motley display in the midst of all the grandeur. "But I fear the news that brings me back into your gracious presence is too important to delay it a moment longer."

"Is that so?" Queen Di'eli looked largely unconcerned. "What could possibly be more important than the return of my long absent heir?"

"I'm not your heir, your majesty. My brother, Prince Hon'idar, is next in line for the Eerilorian throne, as he was in the past," Ullen said, his voice weary. Khiri could feel how heavy her friend's shoulders had become in the space of one response. The queen had started fresh on an old argument.

"If I were to name someone else my heir, who would oppose me? It is my right as queen to choose my successor. Now that you've returned, you will accept your place as heir," Queen Di'eli's voice had barely risen at all, but Khiri could feel the command intensify. She fought against her impulse to breath harder. The last time she had been the presence of this sort of personality, she had been alone in a cave with Irrellian Thornne.

"Your majesty, I have no more interest in being a ruler now than I did then. I returned with urgent news. The Flayer mage has awakened. It's only a matter of time before he makes contact with his agents and forms an army that could swallow his first. I came to you in hopes that you would call a summit and spread the word. We need to be ready when Irrellian makes his move." Ullen rushed to get his explanation out before his mother interrupted again.

Both of Queen Di'eli's eyebrows rose, an incredulous lilt to her ruby colored lips displaying her disdain. She practically purred, "Poor Ut'evullen, the great big world out there must have been fretfully dull for you to feel the need to try and impress me in this fashion."

"As witness, I bring with me Khiriellen Fortiva, daughter of Genovar Fortiva. Call forth your rune-thrower or mage, whomever you currently employee, to verify my claims. Your majesty, I guarantee you..." Ullen looked up, meeting his mother's eyes. "...This is in earnest."

Leaning back in her throne, the queen held up a hand to silence the chatter that had started amongst the scouting party. She considered Ullen, as though he were a puppy that had just performed a rather amusing trick. "If I were to call this summit," she said, "I would do so only to introduce the world to the heir to the Eerilorian throne, posed to lead our armies against the Flayer threat."

"Enough, Mother!" a new voice broke in from the entry of the throne room, behind where Ullen and his entourage knelt. It echoed off the celestial ceiling and bounced around the columns. Khiri glanced under her arm and caught her first glance at Ullen's older brother, Prince Hon'idar.

Taller than Ullen by only inches, Hon'idar held the same presence as his mother, making him seem to tower over the room. His long hair, tied back into a thick tail, was a warm pecan shade, whereas Ullen's was closer in color to the queen's. Also, compared to Ullen, Hon'idar's facial hair was extremely understated. Both mustache and beard were clipped short, fashioned into sharp lines along his jaw. He had the same hook to his nose and chiseled cheeks as his younger brother. Rather than ornate decoration and plush fabrics, Hon'idar wore a fine chain mesh laid over a black leather tunic. His leggings appeared to be made of studded leathers, with plated boots. "Enough," he repeated. "Does it mean nothing to you, that you chased my brother away with talk like this fifty years ago? He pledged then, that he would rather renounce his blood than stand against me as heir. You know he does not care for power, and still you persist in this charade. If my brother speaks truly, as I believe he does, send for the others! Call the summit, dammit!"

"I've made my decision, Hon'idar. Remember that you are not elevated to my position yet, and you are not free to speak to me in this manner!" Queen Di'eli sneered. "Only once Ut'evullen agrees to my terms will I notify other countries of his news. As long as you're here, see to getting these people a place to rest. They are grossly in need of grooming. Especially if I am to throw a proper feast for the return of Ut'evullen." She rose and exited through a door hidden behind her throne.

With a sigh, Hon'idar turned and gripped Ullen by the arm, hoisting him to his feet. "I'm happy to see you back, my brother," the older prince said. "But I know you'd only have returned if the need was dire. As you can see, our mother has only gotten worse since Father died."

Ullen turned and motioned for Khiri and Kal to get to their feet as well. Captain Aldash and his men slowly stood as well. "We can't be seen to move against her," Ullen said softly. "It will be much as it was when I left."

Clapping his hand on Ullen's shoulder, Hon'idar made sure that Ullen was looking him in the eye. "Despite the complications you've brought on your heels, I am glad to know you are well. I've missed you, little brother." With that, he yanked Ullen into a hug.

Politely looking away, Khiri couldn't fail to notice a single tear trailing down her friend's cheek.

14

~Estan~

DEWIN REACHED UP TO scratch her new tattoo for the third time in a handful of minutes. Estan grabbed her hand and scowled at her. The two of them were hiding between a blocky granite pillar and a brick wall, trying their best to stay in the shadows until Tak reappeared in the doorway across the street.

Theoretically, Dewin's new mark meant she should be accompanying Tak, but the ink was too raw. Maybe if Ullen had been present, his time spent as a tattoo artist would've made the process smoother. The first time they'd punched the design into Dewin's flesh, Corianne had used one of her runes to heal the red and puffy skin. Instead of merely reducing the swelling, the rune pulled the ink back out of the flesh, making it necessary to etch the mark into Dewin's neck all over again.

Dothernam Square was unusually active when they arrived. Tak remained to investigate the commotion, while Estan and Dewin found somewhere to wait until the trader signalled them that it was safe to return. Estan checked the sack of supplies that Dewin had insisted on once more; rope, chalk, a bottle of blessed wine, a single candle, a chisel and mallet, and a small bag of salt. It reminded him of the ritual kits that the priestesses would use to set up an altar or perform a cleansing. What Dewin needed it for in Dothernam Square, he wasn't certain. It was the inclusion of chisel and mallet he found most perplexing.

A pair of guards passed by, not paying much attention to a normally empty street. Even if the Guild hadn't made an agreement to stay away from the square, there wasn't much in or around it. Most of the vendor stands in this section of Jarelton were taken down or stripped when there wasn't a festival. The choicest locations were all next to the city's gates or near food vendors. One lonely pub was stationed near the square; a rundown hole with watery ale and rat on a stick that was called "Sherman's" by regulars, despite its sign which read *The Peppered Barrel*. Even if the ale was really pond water, Estan felt that he would gladly chug a pint or two if he and Dewin got through this. He let out a breath of relief once the guards had passed.

As Estan felt his tension easing into boredom, Tak popped his head out of the long-watched door. Summoning the knight and former thief with one hand, the information trader glanced up and down the street to make sure no one was watching. Estan shifted his grip on the sack and hurried behind Dewin, attempting to keep his weight on his toes.

"What in blazes are you doing?" Tak asked, his voice low as he chuckled.

"I was sneaking," Estan hissed. "Try running with this thing without clinking and see how you do!"

"Not now boys," Dewin said, taking the sack from Estan and setting it down gently on the ground. She turned and examined the open expanse of ground. Cobblestones, polished by the passing of generations of feet, reflected the generous stream of moonlight the gods had granted them for this escapade. Arched door frames lined the southern wall, the entryways for commoners during events, while only a handful of smaller doors were carved into the eastern and western walls. There were two raised platforms; one in the very center of the square that was obviously the main stage, and the other ran along the northern wall. Two more exits were built into the north wall on either end of the longer platform. Large, arched windows lined the wall well above the height of an average man. Estan doubted they could be seen through even when one stood on either of the stages. The interior of the courtyard was open to the elements, though the walls themselves were protected by some semblance of a roof.

"Seems simple enough, let's get to work," she said, digging out some of the chalk.

"What exactly are we doing here?" Estan asked. He looked around the space dubiously. It seemed rather poorly designed, having no real functionality outside of what the city already did with it.

"...Creating a temple," Dewin said. "Only... We can't finish it."

"So, we're starting a temple, here, in the middle of the night, for a deity whose primary followers aren't allowed to enter the space, and we can't finish it, because..." Tak trailed off, seeming to hope that Dewin would finish the thought for him.

Dewin ignored the probe and began dragging her chalk over the cobblestones.

"Good to know I have the respect of my new apprentice, for whom I've already greased a few palms."

"I can't say," Dewin said, not looking up from her work. "Not because I think you'll gab, or nothing. Adari's not told me why she's wanting it done. Only that we can start it, but to finish, a god needs a holy act grand enough to stamp their seal, and we haven't the ability. So, we're here doin' our lot, and just trustin' to fate and time that things... Things'll happen."

With a shrug of surrender, Estan squatted near the end of Dewin's chalk line and asked, "So what do you need us to do?"

"One of you, keep a lookout, and the other... Grab yourself a chisel. We need to be sure that these lines aren't to wash off should it happen to rain," the former thief said, biting her lower lip. For the next few hours, she let her chalk do most of the talking.

The hazy edge of dawn was invading the sky when Dewin finally called for the bag of salt and began spilling it along the finely chiseled lines that marked the entire square. She had Estan follow in her wake with the wine bottle, not yet pouring any, but chanting a ritual blessing. In a normal temple, the sanctifying march was done by the Head Priestess and one of her attendants. Adari likely considered Estan an appropriate substitute due to his status as an avatar. Estan thought his goddess might protest his part in creating a temple for her divine sister, but Taymahr seemed to have no qualms with her knight aiding in this endeavor.

"Naturally not," Taymahr said. *"The power of the High Council is shared power. Anything that helps one of us will help all. If one of us is hindered, we are similarly hampered."*

Dewin stopped as she reached the origin of her path and held her hand out for the wine bottle. Estan handed it to her and stepped away from the circle. Taking out her knife, Dewin popped the bottle open. Immediately, the pungent aroma of soured grapes tinted the air, sticking to the back of Estan's tongue. A bit of the cork floated around in the dark burgundy liquid, only to be poured out on the stones with the rest of the wine. Stepping back, Dewin examined their handy work.

"Is it safe to leave a nearly-sacred space just lying about?" Tak asked. "What if it becomes defiled?"

"It becomes normal, again," Dewin said. "Can't kill a man what never shows. Can't defile something's almost holy. Like as not, nothing will come of our little project, but can't say no to a goddess what's in your head."

A cry rising through the streets made the three of them rush to the nearest door, Estan pausing only long enough to grab the lightened sack of equipment. Tak leaned out into the street and motioned the others forward. Crowds of people, all looking forward, not paying much attention when more onlookers joined their ranks, were all flocking toward the city's main throughway. Bells were clanging, guards were clapping their pikes to their shields and criers were shouting over the noise. The cacophony was enough to make Estan's teeth ache. Craning his neck for a look over the crowd, the knight saw a wagon coated in livery being dragged in the wake of the clamor. Hissed whispers ran through the onlookers, confirming his suspicions.

"Lady Ilamar has died," Estan said, too low for anyone to hear. He turned to Dewin and Tak, feeling a deep sense of regret weigh in his chest. They'd recognized the livery too, and looked concerned and pensive. Estan hadn't met the woman, but she'd been well loved by her people; even the criminal element had seemed to regard her as a respected rival. He wondered who would be her successor.

"She died without naming one," Taymahr informed him. *"You must convince her youngest, Orin Treag, to become the next Lord Ilamar."*

"What?" Estan was startled enough that he barely realized he'd raised his voice enough to be heard over the crowd. His companions looked at him with varying degrees of curiosity. *"How am I supposed to convince him to do that?"*

Taymahr did not choose to continue the conversation. She had given him a task. Now it was up to him to perform it. Biting back the urge to hurl curses into the air or at random passersby, Estan turned on his heel.

His thoughts were centered largely on getting back to the Talon Acre for food and a bit of shut eye before tackling this latest quandary, when his head snapped to the side, almost of its own accord. Dewin narrowly avoided plowing into the knight from behind.

She tried to follow Estan's line of sight. When she spotted what he was looking at, she seemed puzzled, "Is that..."

"An elf," Tak confirmed.

"Genovar Fortiva," Estan sighed. "And if he's recognized me, he's probably wondering where his daughter is."

"Well, this should be fun," Dewin said, though there wasn't a glint of humor in her eyes.

GENOVAR WALKED INTO the Talon Acre Inn almost twenty minutes after Estan and Dewin had returned. Tak had left them in the street, explaining that there was too much following the death of a noble that he had to know in order to ply his trade. Not only would resting during such a momentous event take coin from his pocket, but his absence would raise suspicions in certain circles. An information trader had to be where the information was. He offered to take Dewin with him, but she declined on the basis that her tattoo was still too pink around the edges.

Ducking out of his large, brown travel cloak, the elf looked much as Estan recalled him from their last encounter. His long, silver-white hair was twisted into a simple braid that hung down his back. The warrior's eyes, a fathomless blue withholding countless secrets, missed nothing as he swept them over the uncrowded barroom.

One of the owners, Madam Adela Lysira, immediately came out to welcome him to her inn. He thanked her as an old friend would, though Estan could hear snippets of an introduction pass between the two. Requesting a full meal and inquiring after their wines, Genovar slowly made his way toward the table where Dewin and Estan were already seated. His motions were so deliberate and graceful that Estan found himself checking to make sure there really were other tables still in the room.

Without preamble, the elf sat across from Estan, "Last we met, Sir Estan of the Protective Hand, I believe we agreed you would guard my daughter while I arranged forces to meet your hidden conspirators of the Gray Army. I've been monitoring your people for a few days, and from what I've seen, I don't believe Khiri is with you."

"You would be correct, sir," Estan said. He didn't feel that he was being chided, exactly. A hint of reprimand carried through Genovar's tone, but his body language spoke only of weariness. Estan wondered if the elf had been on the road ever since the two of them had parted ways in the early summer. It was late harvest now, tiptoeing its way into winter. For someone who had likely thought himself retired from the life of a soldier, it was a long stretch away from home.

The elf gave Dewin a slight smile and inclined his head, "My apologies, we've not been introduced. I am Genovar Fortiva."

"Dewin," the former thief tilted her head back and crossed her arms, making a show of being unimpressed. "We ran with Khiri all the way up to Eerilor, 'fore she went one way and we went the other."

"Eerilor?" Genovar sounded troubled. "Has her search for her Destined led her so far?"

Estan opened his mouth to answer, but his voice seemed reluctant to leave his throat. All at once, he realized Genovar Fortiva still lived in a world where the biggest worry his little girl had was finding someone with the right name so she could go home, where Micah Ulimani still breathed, and a creature named Irrellian Thornne still slept. When Estan had run into Quinton Ilyani, none of those things had changed yet, assuming Quinton had succeeded in finding Genovar.

"She's been distracted as of late," Dewin interjected, sensing that Estan needed a moment. "Should be plenty safe, though. Ullen, Resmine, and Kal are still with her."

Mention of Kal made Estan tense. How was he supposed to explain the decision to partner with a former member of the Venom Guild? One of the very same team that had succeeded in killing Micah, no less? Originally, bringing Kal along had been Khiri's decision, but Estan was very aware he was the one responsible for unbinding the mage. In the heat of the moment, it had made sense. But would Khiri's father see it that way?

"Ullen..." Genovar repeated, interrupting Estan's worries. "Is this Ullen a dwarf that braids red ribbons into his mustache and has an incredibly long list of occupations?"

Estan nodded. "Unless there are two such dwarves in existence, it sounds like the same Ullen."

An odd shadow passed over Genovar's features. He didn't seem angry, but something about Khiri being in Ullen's company had definitely discomfited him. "It seems that you have yet another story to tell me, my friend. How did the lot of you end up running with one of my former companions?"

15

~Resmine~

MAKING HER WAY THROUGH the mountains on her own, Resmine regretted letting Dewin and Estan leave without her more than ever. She hadn't realized how much she'd come to rely on companionship over the last few months. Staying in the hidden cave for one night without the sounds and snores of her friends, Resmine felt lonelier than she had since Syara's death.

"I am with you," Locke reassured her.

"I'd almost stopped believing in the gods, you know," Resmine admitted.

Flames sizzled as her dinner dripped fat onto the coals. She'd been lucky to find the grouse poking around in the brush earlier in the day. Roasting it would last her a few days if she was careful with her portions. Resmine wasn't the best hunter, but she was good at surviving.

Of course, surviving wasn't the same as living. It was a lesson that Resmine was finally starting to understand. If she listened hard enough, it felt like she could still hear the argument with Dewin bouncing off of the walls.

"I know. I can see it all here within you. The old anger. The new pain. I know."

"I'm sorry you got saddled with a headcase like me," Resmine said, poking at the bird to test its firmness. "Taymahr got Estan. That's probably like living in a palace for a god, right?"

The silence lasted long enough that Resmine thought Locke may have decided to ignore the question. She nearly jumped when Locke's voice started to speak again.

"Belief or faith doesn't equate to living space within the being of one's vessel. It doesn't hurt, but it doesn't help as much as you may think."

Resmine mulled that over a bit. "Do you sleep when we sleep? Are you bound to our bodies? Why did you choose me? Was it just because I was raised in your temple?"

Locke chuckled, seemingly amused at the onslaught. *"We don't really sleep at all. Until something large enough happens to grant us a door back into our realm, we are bound to this plane but not necessarily your bodies. I didn't choose you merely because of our previous connection, but it was a factor."*

"Something large enough?" Resmine asked.

"A surge of faith. The face of Arra shaking. A volcano erupting. A star falling from the sky. We were called out of our plane by an imbalance. It would take something equally powerful to allow us to return."

"That's... concerning," Resmine said. "What happens if nothing that powerful occurs?"

"Things will change," Locke said, his tone grim. *"But things are in motion. It will not come to that."*

Resmine prayed he was right. She felt a small flare of heat in response. Her waning ember of faith was glowing brighter than it had in years. It rivalled her cookfire. And she could feel it.

"What—" Resmine started to ask something, but she wasn't sure how to word it.

"We are bound, Resmine. As your faith feeds me, I champion you. I am the God of Battle and Beauty. I wouldn't accept just any avatar. While I was with you before, we are now forged. Wield me."

With a curt nod, Resmine accepted the mantle Locke had placed on her shoulders. She was done running when things got hard. Locke was with her. The loneliness burned away like cobwebs.

The smell of charred meat brought Resmine back to the task at hand. Removing the grouse from the spit, Resmine set it on a rock to cool. It took some digging through her pack to find the sheathed cooking knife she knew she'd plucked from the shared supplies before leaving Ullen, Kal and Khiri. Dividing the grouse into three portions was easier said than done. The third helping was barely a meal, but it gave her time to forage for supplements. Hopefully, the forest would provide more in the way of food than the mountains had done.

Feeling more confident with her god than before, Resmine still hesitated to ask the one question that had been with her ever since Locke had appeared in her head. "What happened to Syara?"

"She was one of mine, Resmine. She went where the children of Locke go when they fall in battle."

"Will I see her again?"

"One day, yes. If you should still wish to, you will see her again."

Resmine started to protest, but the unvoiced objection died on her lips. She wanted to see Syara again, but Resmine no longer knew if she wanted forever or merely a chance to say goodbye. Until she knew which, it would be foolish to make promises with a god.

16

~Khiri~

HON'IDAR LEFT THEM at the stairwell of Ullen's private tower and continued walking with Horis and his unit to wherever it was that the soldiers bunked. Despite the camaraderie she'd shared with the soldiers on the road, something about their relationship with Hon'idar filled Khiri with misgivings. She tried to push the feeling out of her mind as she turned and followed Ullen up into his past.

Though the outside of the palace and the interior of the main dome were one uniform stone, each of the towers were lined with their own unique themes. As the stairs ascended into the heart of Ullen's spire, the midnight tones were replaced by gentle gray, white, and stormy blue lines that ebbed and crashed much like the grain in malachite.

"Lace agate," Ullen said, noticing the focus of Khiri's attention. "Is the least garish of these thrice-cursed towers. Though, the red jasper in Hon'idar's is not too bad, I suppose. My mother surrounded herself with raw emerald. Honestly, not sure what our ancestors were thinking, but still, they coulda' just made the entire thing of gold and had done. Woulda served us right, practically handin' out the invitations to invade."

"Your mother..." Khiri started to ask.

"She was never quite right," Ullen said, leading the way into a door that opened out into a very spacious sitting room. "This'll do for a moment. We need to have us a chat away from the others, and once we get all the way to the top, they'll be wantin' to bathe and fancify us 'til we're pink in the teeth."

Kal, unbidden, raised his staff. The golden dust of his anti-spying spell tumbled into place and Khiri found herself taking a deep breath of relief. For the first time since Captain Horis Aldash had run into them outside Grimson's Pass, it felt as though things were normal. Khiri wasn't sure she wanted to contemplate what that said about her life during the last few months. It was getting harder and harder to remember what she'd been like before her Name Breathing.

"You were a bit less complicated, but you were still Khiri," Micah told her. *"You've never been dull."*

Giving Micah a friendly mental shove, the elven woman turned her attention back to the dwarven prince and the Odlesk mage. Once Kal signaled the all-clear, Ullen brought his attention back to Khiri. "What in Earth's name possessed you back in the streets? I'd thought you'd seen the Flayer mage himself."

"Close enough..." Khiri shuddered, the memory of her desire to see blood causing her skin to prickle. "I'm pretty sure I saw Arad Rhidel."

Ullen's gaze immediately swung to Kal. Whatever the dwarf had meant to say, whether accusation or query, went unsaid. The former assassin seethed, achieving a level of anger Khiri had never seen in the mage.

"Say it." Kal spat. "I know the knight told you to keep an eye on me, never to trust me, for *her* sake. Make whatever comment you like about my easily shifting loyalty. Just remember, before you do it, I was weighed by the same divine beings that the rest of you bear. They did not deny me!"

"Easy, lad," Ullen said, making the same calming motions that Khiri had seen Estan and Resmine use to quiet Catapult during thunderstorms. "I'm not about to throw out all I seen ya do just because the lass might've spotted yer old employer. Ye've just the best knowledge about what it might mean, if he is here."

Taking a deep breath and letting it out slowly, Kal made a visible effort to calm himself. An uncertainty still hung about him, and he refused to look at Khiri. "If it was Arad Rhidel, and it may well have been, he wouldn't have let Khiri spot him by accident. He's declared war on her, which means he has the entire Guild on alert. There's not a city connected to the Demon Realms he won't have agents in. It's one of the biggest reasons the Venom Guild hires so many Flayers... Easy transportation. Ever wonder how they find people like you, out in the wilderness, so far from the main roads?"

"Not really, lad," Ullen said. His mouth twitched into a humorless grin. "I fought in the Great War. Things I saw, they'd bleach yer bones clear through yer skin."

Kal paused, searching for some hidden insult. Satisfied nothing deeper was being implied, he continued. "I recommend we assume Master Rhidel is in Taman. With Khiri's display of athletics, he's aware we've seen him. I was hardly one of his most trusted minions, so outside of my personal theories, I'm not going to be much help when it comes to deciphering his motives. He could be trying to lure Khiri away or distract us while someone else sets up a trap. Master Rhidel may simply be toying with us..."

Khiri grimaced. Trying to piece together her encounters with Arad Rhidel over the summer, it struck her once more how odd it had been when the Guild hunted Fennick to the trunk of the Life Trees. They'd completely forgotten about the treacherous man once they'd chosen her as their target.

Back in the Flayer mage's cavern, some of the pieces had fallen together. She knew Fennick was behind the Guild's initial interest; however, she still couldn't make heads or tails of the head of the Venom Guild declaring war on a single person for the slaying of two Flayers. Tightening her hold on Micah, Khiri fought against the on-coming headache.

"Do you trust me?" Kal's voice brushed her mind, more quietly than she had ever before heard it.

"...Yes," she sent back. Her answer was just as soft. Khiri had understood Kal's hushed tone meant he was afraid of her answer. This mental speech made it much harder to lie, and the mage wasn't certain he was ready to hear her truth. Still, he had asked. *"Yes. I trust you,"* she repeated, sounding much surer.

"I won't let Master Rhidel harm you," he assured her. *"Not if it's at all in my power to prevent him."*

Ullen, unaware of the silent exchange, continued on with his own thoughts. "Not that the Venom Guild is ever a small matter, but I was wantin' to broach summat else before we're missed. The problem is these equipped Flayers what's being flung about from somewhere within these borders. This'll be a delicate business, bringing other countries into the fold quiet enough so Mother doesn't find out until she can't do a damn to stop it... Especially with us still being at war with Mytana. If they catch wind o' such a thing before Eerilor manages to do aught, our position becomes much more suspect. I'll need the two o' you sittin' at the table tonight, but after... I can handle things here with Hon'idar and Horis. Can I trust the two o' you to stop up that leak?"

"You want the two of us to investigate where those Flayers are getting their equipment in a strange country, when the official parties involved haven't gained any ground whatsoever?" Kal asked, his mood swinging back into its usual wry humor. "Life certainly hasn't been dull since the lot of you tied me up and draped me over a horse."

"Do as Prince Ut'evullen asks," Imyn said. The goddess's tone was more urgent than Khiri had heard it before. *"Eerilor will be pivotal to future events."*

Foreboding welled up in Khiri's chest. The last time that she had received instructions from a deity she'd been told to "ignite the darkness," which had ended with her waking Irrellian Thornne. The same move had freed the High Ones from Irrellian's prison, but they were weak from twenty years of absence and neglect. Their light was an ember, glowing in a maelstrom. Even so, Khiri had made a bargain. She was bound to follow Imyn's instructions when asked.

"I'll do it," Khiri said. "We need that summit to work. If we want a chance against the Gray Army, we've got to have allies. Eerilor must not fail."

"Indeed," Ullen agreed. "In that vein, I've some letters that need writin'. May the gods guide us all."

AFTER THE QUICKEST bath Khiri had ever taken, an invasion of maids came into the room and began primping and polishing the stunned, naked elven woman. It seemed as though there were hundreds of them, though every time Khiri managed to count she only found three. Those three managed to be everywhere at once. Her auburn hair was twisted, brushed, pulled, braided, undone, redone, pinned, unwoven and pinned again. Several dresses were produced, all of them far too big. One of the garments was declared the closest in size. It was tightened and hemmed, all in the space of an afternoon. It was a relief when the ladies, all dwarven, were quite willing to accommodate Khiri's desire to retain her weapons. If anything, they seemed pleased by her attachment to them.

At the end of their efforts, Khiri was escorted to a full length mirror, framed in delicate vines of malachite, at the end of the bathing chamber. Festoons of curls and braids tumbled down the back of her neck, seemingly careless of their beauty, though she knew how hard the maids had worked to achieve the effect. Her bright blue eyes were decorated with some sort of smoky shadowed powder and her lips were subtly enhanced with stain like she had eaten a sweet plum. Khiri was startled to realize that in the flood of gowns, the final dress was the same brilliant azure hue as her Name Breathing robe had been all those months ago. A sleek, form fitting, silk bodice, cut in the same bare-shoulder style as the queen had worn, flowed into a skirt of silk and light blue chiffon layers.

"I did tell you that it was a good color on you," Micah sounded wistful, as though he was also remembering that fateful day.

"Regrets?" Khiri asked.

"Well, if I could do it all over again, I'd probably try harder to stay alive," Micah said. *"I owe Kal a punch in the jaw."*

"What? Why?" Khiri was genuinely puzzled. Over the last few weeks, the mage and her bond-brother had seemed to be getting along as though they had been friends for years. She hadn't noticed that they had been fighting. Not they would have necessarily told her.

"Well, I punched Estan. Now he's not here and someone needs to punch Kal for me. If you do it, it defeats the whole purpose," Micah tried to explain.

After several minutes of trying to wrap her head around all of the necessary punching that she couldn't do, Khiri let it go with a shrug. It was the first she'd heard about Micah hitting Estan, and they'd seemingly gotten along as well. Micah did things she couldn't comprehend sometimes. It was best to just leave them be.

Kal was waiting in the hall. His pale, reflective skin was still highlighted pink from his scrubbing. Two plaits of his gray hair were swept back into braids tucked behind his ears, while most of his tresses still hung loose on the back of his head. The faded robes that he'd worn ever since they'd first discovered him were replaced with a long silk tunic that matched his hair, overlaid with a black velvet jerkin. His black trouser legs were swallowed by black leather boots of the same shade.

"Well, well," Kal said. His warm, welcoming smile didn't hold a trace of derision. "You're a sight for a sore mage."

Despite the amount of bare skin around her neck and shoulders, Khiri felt as though the cool stone halls had suffered a heat wave. Feeling the color rise in her cheeks, she welcomed the arrival of Ullen.

Her friend looked distinctly uncomfortable in his finery. New ribbons had been woven into his freshly braided mustache. Ullen's clothing was laced more tightly than Khiri had ever seen him wear it. He seemed to think the high-collared black velvet jerkin was trying to strangle him. A soft, red silk tunic covered his arms, matching his mustache ribbons. Unlike Kal and Khiri, Ullen's clothing had gold embroidery winding its way around his shoulders, as though the thread was creeping up behind him. A small band of gold lay over his ears and across his forehead, but that he plucked off his brow and threw down the hall.

"Let's get this farce over with," he grumbled.

They made their way down to the banquet hall, which was located within the main dome. Steam-charged rune lamps, designed to look like sconced torches, lined the walls. The flickering light over the blue goldstone reminded Khiri of the many campfires she and her friends had shared under the stars. An odd ache, like homesickness, formed in her chest. She wished that she was back in her armor. *I'll be back in it tomorrow,* she reminded herself. True, her large group was down to her and Kal...

Warmth flooded her cheeks again. She glanced toward Kal as they flanked Ullen through the palace, staying a step behind as though they were his entourage rather than equals. It was just like her to agree to such a hunt without thinking over every aspect. Khiri had an inkling as to why Micah wanted to punch the Odlesk mage. Not everything was done because someone deserved it; sometimes, they might deserve it later.

As the three companions entered the banquet hall, Khiri's mind was forced back onto more pressing issues—namely, the room packed with courtiers and food. Row upon row of guests, tables filled with dishes that Khiri didn't recognize, and the queen, seated on her throne and grinning like a hungry cat at the head table. "Rise! Rise and greet my son, the next King of Eerilor!" Queen Di'eli radiated smugness.

Ullen's answering smile held absolutely no warmth. "I welcome you all as my mother's son, but I am no one's king."

Before the queen's face could finish its transition from prim satisfaction to outright rage, Hon'idar rose to his feet with a mug in hand, "To Prince Ut'evullen's long awaited return!"

"Prince Ut'evullen!" echoed off the walls and down into the corridor.

Through the forest of raised cups, Ullen's mother watched her returned son with intense calculation. Khiri wasn't sure what the queen was planning, but it was obvious the queen's ambitions weren't going to be dashed easily.

17

~Estan~

AFTER SEVERAL DAYS of scouting the city, Estan resorted to asking Tak for help. The trader discovered, after a brief afternoon's questioning, the best way to encounter Orin Treag was to frequent a tavern called The Legend and The Knave in the West District. Practically against the wall of Jarelton, the place was very popular with local craftsmen. According to Tak's informants, the majority of the tavern's regulars had no idea "Ory" was at all related to their city's late ruler, and Treag usually came in around sunset.

Nursing a pint of some home-brew that one of the regulars recommended, Estan tried not to dwell on the conversation he'd been wanting to forget. After he'd told Genovar about Khiri's journeys, the elf had dropped a few coins on the table for the innkeeper and walked out the door, not saying a word. Three days later, Genovar had reappeared. Apologizing for his behavior, he'd explained to Estan that it hadn't been a reaction of anger. It had been a necessity.

"There were messages to be sent, and people that I had to see." Genovar had seemed sincere in his regret. "I know Irrellian Thornne in a way that few others can. Even with the lead you gave me, I'm still playing a game of catch up. I... I can tell you care deeply for my daughter, which will make what I ask of you now all the more difficult."

"What do you ask of me?" Estan asked. The apologies etched in every line of Genovar's face had warned the knight to keep his guard up.

It wasn't enough, because Genovar's request still hit Estan like a punch in the gut. "If my daughter comes to you and begs you to help her, refuse. It is imperative, I repeat, imperative that you refrain from aiding her at that juncture."

"Why..." Estan's features must have shown his shock, his fury, that Khiri's father would make such a request.

Genovar had held up a hand, urging the knight to let him speak.

"I've walked with the gods, too, dear fellow. There is a larger plan in place than the two of us can realize. I was told one day I would have to deliver such a message, under certain circumstances, and now I have done as I was asked. It pains me that those circumstances have come to pass." The elf's shoulders were heavy as he turned to go. Estan didn't even hear Genovar's footsteps as his childhood hero disappeared into the night.

Over twenty summers prior, the gods had known Genovar would have to ask someone not to help his daughter. Estan chugged down the remainder of his ale and half-heartedly called for another. He needed to stop dwelling on the encounter with Khiri's father and concentrate on what he would say to Orin Treag. It was unlikely that he could open with: "Hello, condolences, but the gods want you on your dead mother's seat. All done."

Gulping down the dregs of foam left in his second tankard, Estan came to the conclusion his errand wasn't going to go well if he slurred as he introduced himself. He was in the act of standing up when people behind him started shouting greetings.

"Ory!"

"Good to ya, Ory!"

"Pull up a pint, stay awhile."

"Is there something I can say that will make him more receptive to hearing me out?" Estan pleaded with his goddess.

"You could try buying him a drink," Taymahr suggested, her tone almost matching the sarcasm and mockery Estan normally associated with Kal.

Disliking the brief parallel between his Goddess and his rival, the knight scowled and cursed himself. Taymahr took pity on her avatar and explained, *"I cannot tell you specifics. We are bound by certain restrictions that mortals aren't. We can guide you toward these moments, but we cannot be active participants."*

Estan took a deep breath before turning to tackle the problem at hand. Dust, alcohol and roast beef flavored air, anchoring Estan's thoughts on something solid and mortal. It was somehow reassuring to him that it wasn't within Taymahr's power to tell him exactly what to say, but she still trusted him to get the job done. While Estan was very aware he might stumble in his attempts to convince Orin to follow the will of Taymahr, that didn't matter as much as Estan taking initiative. Unsaid words were the ones he would regret most, after all... That was why he'd told Khiri how he felt. No regrets.

Orin Treag, the youngest of the late Lady Ilamar's offspring, was about as average looking as a man could be. He didn't appear muscular, overweight, or incredibly slender... Just... Average. His dark hair was brown—not chestnut or auburn, but a shade that was too dark to be blonde and too ashen to be black—peppered with gray in his sideburns. Orin's skin was a soft tan that could've been achieved by too much time in the sun or wind as a younger man, or could've been his natural coloring. It wasn't that Ory brimmed with charisma either. A word here, a smile there, and people were satisfied that he'd noticed them, but they forgot they'd been interrupted a moment later. Estan couldn't tell what it was that made this particular man necessary to the gods as Lady Illamar's replacement but for Estan, placing his trust in his goddess was second nature. Even when the temple had turned on him, Estan had kept his faith.

Estan turned back to the bar and ordered a third tankard, more to have something in his hand than because he wanted another drink. Considering Taymahr's advice, sarcastic as it had been, he ordered a second tankard and made his way across the room to Orin.

Clapping the mug into the nobleman's hand, Estan gave the man a friendly smile and invited Orin to join him at an empty table. The knight would've prefered something more private, off in a corner, but the only empty table available was next to an almost constantly swinging kitchen door. Traders and craft workers called for service or hailed fresh arrivals, growing louder by the second, as The Legend and The Knave entered the busy portion of its day.

"I'm sure you're wondering what this is about," Estan said. A self-conscious effort to smile made him puff his lips. He wished he'd left his armor at the Talon Acre. The occasional glances his way told him he looked a bit like an out-of-work mercenary.

Orin scanned Estan with a measuring look. Nothing about the calculation behind that gaze matched the nothing-but-average persona that had waded through the taproom only moments before. It was the look of someone who had grown up in a world of politics and mistrust. "Have you ever noticed that when someone asks if you're wondering why they're there, it's generally because they either have bad news or they're not really sure either?"

Estan tapped on his tankard with one finger, watching the bubbles spiral to the surface. He bit his upper lip and nodded. "That's fair. Especially considering that I have very little idea of what to say. First, I'm truly sorry about your mother."

With the slightest twitch of his eyebrow, Orin said, "Thank you, both for the thought and confirming my suspicions. Now that we've established that you are in possession of my identity, perhaps you'll tell me who you are, and what you're after."

"I'm..." Estan glanced around, suddenly conscious of how open the nobleman was being in such a crowded tavern. He began to lean in, when Orin made a staying gesture.

"We're safe enough. As long as you don't act like you have secrets, no one here cares what we might say. For all these people know, you're a friend that I just happened to ask here, or you're trying to commission a piece of sculpture for your front hall. No one knows, no one cares. Until you try to hide something, you're invisible. So, friend, who are you?"

"My name is Estan, I was a Knight of the Protective Hand. If the temples knew I was here, they'd do away with me before you could turn your head and sneeze. A certain mage recently woke and would like nothing more than to see the world burn. The temples are run by officials from his former army, which angers the gods. Those gods sent me here. They want you in your mother's seat. You need to step up as Lord of Jarelton," Estan said. Taking a swig of his dark ale, he set the mug down hard. He'd meant to use the thump as punctuation, but it was swallowed by the noise of the crowd. "Blunt enough?"

Taking a swig from the drink Estan had brought him, Orin flashed an anti-poison rune at Estan from his other hand. A surprised laugh jumped out of Estan's throat. Orin answered the laugh with his own grin, "Can't be too careful. My siblings have tried to take me out before, and the story you just told me would make anyone reach for their cup. You're taking an awful risk, trusting me, if all you say is true. So, it is with the deepest respect that I tell you I cannot do what you ask..."

"But—" Estan had no idea what to do or say, but he was driven by the need to do something. Failure was not how he intended to serve Taymahr!

"...Unless you help me with a little problem." Orin seemed pleased with Estan's reaction. "I can see I have your attention, so I'll be brief. I cannot, will not, rule a city that is in severe upheaval. Especially if what you say about a certain mage is true. I need you, and whoever is with you, to help the Thieves' Guild regain control of the criminal element."

"What do you mean?" Estan asked. His mind flashed on Corianne and Evic, who had seemed out of sorts when he'd last seen them. He'd assumed Dewin's return to the city was the cause, but they could've easily been apprehensive over any number of things going on with their guild. He hadn't bothered to ask about the uprising they'd been dealing with during his last stay in Jarelton.

"Currently, the thieves of Jarelton are in trouble," Orin confirmed. "If I were to take power, I'd have more than my fair share on my shoulders. Soon, this entire city will be at war. As a law-abiding member of the nobility, I can't *legally* choose sides. 'They should all be in prison or hanged,' or whatever justice demands any particular day. That said, I don't want Ysinda deposed. She's damned fair at keeping the peace in the streets, normally, and she understands the importance of balance. The new people don't."

Orin took another long pull from the clunky wooden tankard in front of him and stood. Like he was putting on a pair of slippers, he eased back into the guise of the-most-average-man that had first entered the tavern. "If you find those terms acceptable, you know where to find me," he said. With a wink, he made his way back up to the bar.

Taking one last swish of sudsy, hops-laden foam, Estan fought back a sigh. "Aye, I know where to find you," he agreed. "Now I just have to broker peace with the lawless."

MARCHING INTO THE TALON Acre Inn, Estan searched the taproom for any signs of Dewin or Tak. Ren, Madam Lysira's husband and cook, came out of the kitchen, rubbing his hands on a towel. "Master Estan, what's on your mind?"

"You and your wife, the two of you once told me you were close to Ysinda... You don't happen to know where I could find her?" Estan asked. His mind was working, but it felt like he wasn't getting anywhere. "No, I'm sorry. I just–I need to find Evic or Corianne. I—"

Ren looked as though he were growing more and more concerned, "You haven't been poisoned again, have ya? You're lookin' a bit green."

"Not unless it's extremely slow to activate and is triggered by slowly sinking into a pit of madness," Estan sighed. One glance at the large-set cook told Estan that the man was in danger of taking him seriously. "Truly, I'm fine. I'm just dealing with something that I knew would be complicated, but I had no idea *how* complicated."

"Well, lad–" Ren tucked his towel into his belt and clapped Estan on the shoulder "–if the problem involves the Thieves' Guild, there's no way it'd be simple. I've a fresh bit of cobbler coolin', if you'd like to wait while I send for someone."

Estan let himself be prodded into a chair while Ren placed a large bowl of fragrant, tartly sweet, sugar-crusted cherry cobbler on the table. A large dollop of whipped cream, also fresh, was slowly melting into the cracks of the cobbler's crust, creating pink swirls of syrup that oozed across the bowl's ceramic glaze. It was hard for Estan to retain his sense of urgency in the face of Ren's baked goods. As soon as the cook was convinced that Estan was content, he ambled back into the kitchen. Estan could hear as the stairs to innkeepers' private rooms creaked with the large man's tread.

Alone with his thoughts for the first time in days, Estan's mind took the opportunity to roam back to Grimson's Pass. His first kiss with Khiri had turned into his parting kiss, and now her father had effectively asked Estan not to interfere with her further. If she had come to Jarelton, Estan may have been more inclined to reject Genovar's plea. But Estan held a great deal of respect for the elven war hero. He held even more for the divinities that had originated the plea. Though it cut him to the quick, circumstances and distance made it clear it was time for him to push away his dreams of Khiri. She'd never really been more than a dream for him, after all. There had been moments, but they'd always ended with that pained expression of sadness Khiri wore when she thought about her soul mate.

Her *Destined*.

"Excuse me–" a soft voice said.

Looking up from his largely empty bowl, Estan saw the shapely silhouette of a woman standing in the door of the Talon Acre. She was short for a human though still too tall to be an elf or a dwarf. As she stepped into the light, an angelic sort of innocence radiated from her pale features, glowing from the tip of her button nose, racing along her smattering of freckles, up her round cheeks to the ends of her ear-length honey blonde hair. Her emerald eyes were expressive and wide. The stranger timidly extended a delicate hand to the nearest chair, resting there before she spoke again. "Have you seen Ren or Adela? I was told they sent for me."

Estan stared at her dumbly, his brain demanding that he speak while heart struggled to find its rhythm. He almost felt guilty about having such a strong reaction to someone on the heels of his thoughts about Khiri, but the guilt didn't find steady footing and soon tumbled out of his mind.

"I...uh...Sorry," he rasped. "Ren's... He's in the back."

"Oh," the newcomer said. She took two steps toward the kitchen door before pausing, a shadow of disappointment sweeping over her features. "I don't suppose you'll mind my company while I wait?"

"No, no, please!" Estan kicked the bench opposite him out at his table, wincing inwardly at his lack of finesse. "Have a seat. I was just finishing..."

"I can smell Ren's cherry cobbler. It's pretty impossible to resist," a bittersweet smile curved the young woman's soft lips. Estan's skin seemed to tingle in response. His heart started hammering hard enough that he thought she'd hear it when she slid into the place across from him. "Only two things in this world are half as good, but I won't tell you what they are."

"Adds to the mystery?" Estan felt his own smile forming and sent a quick prayer to Taymahr that he didn't look too foolish.

"Oh, good," Ren boomed, the kitchen door swinging behind him. He carried a second bowl of cobble, as though he had anticipated his visitor's wants. "I was hoping you'd be around tonight. Adela's out, visiting her mum, and my friend here said he needed to speak with Evic or Corianne. Figured you'd know where to find 'em. Estan, this is Ysinda. Ysinda, I'd like you to meet our friend, Estan."

Choking on his last bite of cobbler, Estan felt surprise stretching his features into a mask of their normal shape. "This... you... you're Ysinda?"

"You wanted mystery," the Queen of Thieves said, flashing Estan the world's most mischievous grin.

18

~Khiri~

SILVERY CLOUDS WHISPERED across the path in front of Khiri's feet. She reached for Micah for reassurance, only to find that she was unarmed. Mostly. Her father's dagger was still at her side but, for some reason, she felt certain the enchanted blade was sheared in half.

Before she could dwell on it, a voice called to her through the fog. "Come to me," it beckoned. A voice... The voice... His voice.

Khiri wanted to fight the pull, to ignore the compulsion of that voice. It wasn't the same as when she was controlled by Fennick's runes; this was deeper. Less like an intruder, more like a traitor. More primal. A part of her being. She could see the outline of Irrellian Thornne's lithe, onyx form—a shadow in the shimmering mists.

"Come to me, Khiriellen Fortiva. Meet your destiny."

With a gasp, Khiri woke in the palace of Eerilor. She was drenched in cold, clammy droplets of sweat. The large, round bed was a twisted mess of sheets and fur-lined blankets. Her sleeping robe and undergarments were in need of replacing. Shoving off of the enormous bed, Khiri made her way to a chest of drawers she'd seen the maids stuff with similar sleep clothes. Fresh garments weren't going to make things better, but they were a start. Moonlight fell from the sky and bounced off the polished mineral floor of the balcony outside her room, allowing her to pick out new drawers and a night shirt.

Micah was resting. She could tell because when she tried to send to him all she received was a contented sort of buzzing. Warmth rose from the stone base under the mattress, but it failed to comfort her the way her friends sleeping nearby would have. Even if she couldn't bring herself to admit the Flayer Mage was somehow her Destined, it would've been nice to have someone with her when Irrellian Thornne called to her in her dreams.

Khiri sat back down on the edge of the bed, propped her knees up under her chin and brushed a tear away from her cheek. She had almost convinced herself to try easing back into sleep, when a hushed tapping sounded at the door.

Wearing the gray silk shirt and his soft, black breeches from the feast, Kal looked much less kempt than he had at dinner. His jerkin and boots were missing. Khiri got the impression that he hadn't been dressed before coming to her room. In the dimness of the night, with the torches out, Kal's luminous skin gleamed with the starlight flooding in through her balcony. He leaned against her door frame, his large pupils fully dilated, shining like two small moons.

"I heard you call," he said.

"I didn't—" Khiri started to protest. The brisk autumn air was no longer the only thing causing her skin to pinch into barbs.

"You did." A sly quirk of his mouth told her Kal recognized the effect he had on her. "But if you'd rather I go, I can leave."

Breaking herself from his gaze, Khiri turned away but left her door open. She didn't want him to leave, but she couldn't bring herself to invite him in. The name of *Telgan Korsborn* thrummed darkly in her mind, angry and jealous. If Kal stayed, it wouldn't be silent, but if he left, she would be alone in the dark with only the name of her Destined, her enemy, for company.

Kal's arms wrapped around her from behind. Their warmth shot through her, from floor to fingers, like an electric pulse. Her lips trembled in response as a shock of emotion rippled through her, composed of both grief and desire.

"I can't..." she pulled away from Kal's embrace. "The one I'm bound to... I can't. He... I'm drawn to him in a way I can't fight."

Kal placed his hands on Khiri's shoulders and turned her toward him. His voice was full of its usual wry humor, but there was something deeper beneath it as he said, "It may be hard on me, in more ways than one, but all I'm offering tonight is comfort. A hug. We can do that, yes?"

Biting down another sob, Khiri nodded. She let herself sink into his arms, accepting his offer of comfort. Slowly, he lifted her and placed her back in her bed, while he sat on the edge. He made no move to join her, but took her hand in his and waited for sleep to come back to her.

When Khiri woke again the next morning, she found a note on the dressing table: *Maybe next time.* Shaking her head, Khiri felt herself smile—a true smile—for the first time in what felt like ages.

KAL MADE NO MENTION of the night before when she met him in her newly cleaned armor. The Army of Three, as Khiri had taken to calling her maids, had brushed and buffed the leather until it looked almost as new as the day Fennick equipped her. Kal was still wearing the silk tunic and black trousers from the night before, but his boots were on and he'd donned a belt.

"Ullen's already been dragged off by his brother, so it's on us to begin this task you volunteered for," Kal said. "Where would you like to start?"

Considering it for a moment, Khiri suggested, "Let's go find Captain Aldash or someone from his unit. Maybe they'll be able to tell us something and we won't be starting from scratch?"

"Fair enough." The Odlesk mage planted his staff against the floor and leaned in toward Khiri's face, stopping at the thinnest edge of her comfort zone. "I'm with you, *laska*."

Khiri swallowed, suddenly finding her throat parched. "What does—"

"Another time," Kal said, shaking his head. "Turns out, we're in a rush. Before he left, Ullen said he'd try to give us until the solstice. We've got two months, at most."

They made their way to the bottom of Ullen's tower without encountering any of the castle staff. Since they were supposed to be avoiding attention, Khiri figured it was better that the halls were empty; however, finding their way into the barrack yards unassisted proved to be a challenge. All of the doors leading outside the palace were watched by guards.

As Khiri was about to suggest they allow the guards to see them exit, a dwarven noblewoman walked through the adjoining hallway. Her chestnut curls dripped with pearl accents and bobbed around her tawny, gold cheeks. The lady's dress was a surprisingly simple wrap of burgundy silk under a heavily embroidered, plum overcoat. For the briefest of moments, the woman's eyes met Khiri's, so quickly Khiri wasn't sure it had actually happened. Upon approaching the door, the noblewoman addressed the two guards, "I require an escort into the city. You two will follow me."

"Forgive us, Lady Terilles, but we can't simply—"

"You would have the prince's betrothed leave unaccompanied?"

An awkward hush fell over the two guards as they exchanged a look and a shrug. Soon, the lady departed with the two guards in tow. Khiri felt certain Lady Terilles, whatever her agenda was, had just intentionally helped the companions of the long-lost prince escape the palace.

Unlike the palace, the barracks were made up of stone longhouses and smaller office huts, divided by grass courtyards and walkways.

Fountains popped out of the ground and hedges blocked certain paths, making the barracks feel as though they'd been stuffed into a garden maze. As frustrating as it was to find their way around, Khiri couldn't help being grateful for the sunshine. Something about the interior of the palace felt like being trapped underground.

Captain Horis Aldash was out, briefing his commanders on his recent venture, but Solancia spotted Khiri and Kal on their way from the captain's office to the dining hall.

"Fortiva!" the warrior called. "I'd thought they'd tie you up with tales o' yer pa for a spell or two. Guess ya busted free, what with the queen all in a tizzy over her boy comin' home, though. What're the two o'ya about today?"

Khiri looked around to see who might be nearby to overhear as she trotted to catch up with Solancia. The burly woman had a new eye patch, one an even larger nightshade flower than those sewn into the first, surrounded by leaves.

"Why nightshade?" Khiri asked, taking a moment to indulge her curiosity.

"Named for it. My pa told 'em I was gonna be beautiful and dead-ly. He was pretty near the mark. I'd be easier on the eyes if I cared much for it. Best I can muster is a bit o' poisoned flowers on me fin-ery. One doesn't have to be a beauty to get a lad's attention though," Solancia gave Khiri a wicked, conspiratorial smile as her remaining eye flicked up toward Kal. "Not that I'd need to give you tips there, I wager."

As the blush rose in her cheeks, Khiri hurried to change the sub-ject. "Kal and I wanted to start our own investigation into the Flay-ers, where they're coming from and who's equipping them. Was there anything you could tell us about what your team found out in the field?"

Solancia was quiet for a long moment, her lips pursed as the three of them walked through the courtyard. Khiri could almost feel herself being weighed and measured, like a sword or long bow. "Officially, I can't say much. Across enemy lines, covert and discretion and all, but unofficially, there ain't much that goes on in Eerilor that don't get noticed by merchants. If I were parta a small team what's not drawin' a lotta attention, I'd start askin' about those shops what carry armor," Solancia said. "Ya know, unofficially. Armies, though, they don't think like that. Go kill the problem, hope the river o' bodies leads to the source."

"Spirits," Khiri sighed. "I feel like I should have thought of that without bothering you."

Giving Khiri a fond pat on the back, Solancia grinned. "S'alright, lass. Too much time on the road makes ya stop remembering that society's just its own kind of forest. First shop I'd try, were I goin' about it, Shielded Thoughts. It's on the east end o' town, run by a Master Ian Vort. He's known for takin' on five to six apprentices at a time."

Khiri thanked Solancia for the tip. The warrior woman gave Khiri a friendly punch and continued on toward the grub hall. It was time to head back into Taman.

Brisk winds chilled the autumn morning, though the sun was attempting to burn through the cold. Flits buzzed through the air, dodging through pedestrians as they made their way through the city. It was less crowded than when the scouting unit had arrived the day before, probably due to the earlier hour.

"MAKE WAY!" The urgent cry echoed through to sculpted streets, interrupting the peaceful morning routines. "Beg pardon! Coming through!"

Kal yanked Khiri to the side of the road as an odd contraption—two tree-trunk thick wheels affixed on either side of a small, suspended chair with a basket propped in front of it—barreled through the streets. A young blur of a dwarf with dark brown skin and a leather helmet with goggles raced after the thing, calling for people to move out of the way. Catching hold of the oddity with one hand, the dwarf pulled a rune out one of his many pouches and held on for dear life. It came to a stop only a hair's breadth away from the nearest wall. Across the back of the dwarf's light brown jerkin, the words *Purple Wren's Tavern* were painted in big black and purple letters.

"Must be one of those rune-tech inventions I've heard about," Kal said. "I'll give them that the lighting is innovative enough, but that seemed rather hazardous."

"Looks fun," Khiri replied, her eyes bright with excitement. "Do you think he'd let me have a try if we caught him?"

"I'm going to pretend you didn't just ask that." Kal rubbed his temples with his long fingers. Only a brief glimpse of a smile betrayed that he was exaggerating for effect. "Like as not he's on a delivery anyway. I imagine those violet flits belong to the Purple Wren, so we may be able to track him down before we leave town."

Shielded Thoughts was housed inside a basalt building with orange doors and matching shutters. Runes were etched into the stone along the threshold, but unlike those of the nearby buildings, no magic seemed to be shimmering off of them. The merchandise windows of Shielded Thoughts were still shuttered, despite most of the neighboring stores being open. Everything about the place seemed off.

Kal walked across the street to chat with the vendor of a clothing store housed inside a soapstone building.

"Excuse me, sir. I don't mean to interrupt your day with questions about your neighbors, but my friend and I were referred to Master Vort for a special commission, and he seems to be absent. Is it normal for him to arrive later in the day?"

The clothier, an older human man with parchment pale skin, auburn hair and kind aqua eyes, seemed concerned. "In all the years we've worked near each other, Ian never once has been late where he could earn a coin. Isn't like him... Not at all," the clothier said, scratching worriedly at his scruffy beard. "Don't have a personal flit for him, but I might be able to send my girl to his place in a bit."

Kal thanked the clothier before returning to Khiri's side

Khiri had been examining the basalt store front. On a whim, she tested to see if the store was locked or barred. A gentle nudge with her fingers and the door creaked inward, giving absolutely no resistance.

"I don't like this," Kal told her, switching to their shared mind speech.

"I'm with him," Micah agreed. *"This stinks of wrongness."*

Before Khiri could respond, she heard a pain-filled groan inside the deep shadows of the armor shop. Without hesitation, Khiri rushed into the darkened store, dagger in hand.

Blood. The copper-laden air stank of it. A lot of it had been spilled here recently. She recognized another stench threading its way through the thick smell of death. Decay. Flayer. Realizing her mistake, Khiri sensed rather than saw the demon-bound rise from the darkness behind her. *"Blood..."* it hissed. *"Coursing... dripping... running... pumping..."*

Falling to the ground, Khiri rolled away from the Flayer's arm as it shot through the space her chest had previously occupied. Kal spouted a line of syllables that Khiri didn't understand and tossed a globe of light into the room. Bodies littered the room, those of the unfortunate apprentices that had been beginning their daily tasks when an unseen threat had sunk its talons in from behind. The Flayer facing Khiri slipped into the shadows and out of sight.

As Khiri started for the exit, a mortal moan reminded her why she'd entered in the first place. Changing direction, she charged toward the source of the groans; a lump on the far end of the room whose chest was still rising and falling with uneven, labored breaths. She reached him just as an all-too-familiar chuckle echoed off the Shielded Thought's walls.

"Oh, no..." Khiri felt her stomach knot as she met the gaze of Arad Rhidel.

"We really should stop meeting like this," the tall, bald rune-thrower strode out of the back room, which was probably normally used as an office. His deep-set eyes were hard with hatred. "It's how rumors start."

Khiri glanced from the leader of assassins to the dwarf she knelt beside on the cool, black basalt. Now that she was next to the injured shop owner, there was little she could do. Administering first aid would open her to attack, but if she didn't stabilize his wounds soon, the dwarf would die.

"Is this your work?" she demanded.

"Technically, no. But the guilty parties did so under my command, which I'm sure amounts to the same thing to you. It is rather moot, at this point. Dead is dead."

Kal cleared his throat, none too subtly. Magic was flowing from his hands into his borrowed staff, offering almost as much light as the orb he'd launched into the room.

"Well–" Arad's gaze flicked toward Kal, "–some things do die better than others. Remind me, should we meet in another life, I can't trust you to finish off my leftovers."

"Remind me why I haven't killed you yet," Khiri snapped. The hand holding her dagger ached with the need to sink into the man's heart, but she held herself between Arad and the dying dwarf. If only...

"You have the power to heal him," Kal told her. *"I can distract Master Rhidel long enough for you to stabilize the wounded, but a full healing... That would drain you, so please don't risk it."*

"How?" Khiri sent.

Suddenly, the knowledge of how to heal opened inside of her mind like the blooming of a flower. Layers of technique and theory cascaded into understanding and Khiri had to blink away the fuzziness of what felt like a blow to the head.

"Sorry," Kal said. *"I've never done that before. It kicked harder than I thought it would."*

Without warning, Kal flung a fireball at Arad Rhidel's smug face. The leader of the Venom Guild had to tumble out of the way. Arad answered Kal's attack with his own volley of runes. Splashes of blue and violet fire burst against Kal's shield. Keeping one eye on the exchange, Khiri reached back with her free hand and grasped the dying dwarf around the wrist. She felt a strand of golden thread connect her life to his, mending bruised lungs and knitting together several large gashes.

Seeming to notice that the fight was only between two people, Arad Rhidel tossed a rune in Khiri's direction. Unable to move without severing her connection and leaving the prone craftsman to his fate, Khiri watched the rune float toward her like a moment paused in time. She tucked her head into the crook of her elbow and braced for whatever came next.

"Khiri!" she heard Kal shout, half warning and half alarm. A small tap registered on the skin of her forearm. Tiny clatters followed the progress of the rune as it bounced away.

Half convinced the rune was a dud, Khiri began to lower her arm just as the shivers set in. Lines of frost began to trail up the stricken limb and out toward her fingers. As they climbed, the icy crystals grew, gaining in weight as well as size. The cold made her bones ache, but she fought the despair that was attempting to claw its way into her being. Riding a surge of anger, Khiri slammed her freezing fist against the stone floor. Ice and frost fell like fall leaves in a torrential rain, steaming into nothingness like a dying Flayer.

Arad Rhidel's look of surprise was quickly replaced with a vicious smirk which tugged at his tight lips in a way that made Khiri's fists clench. "That was unexpected, but then you do so often surprise me,

Fortiva. I didn't really come here to play, though. I came to give you a message."

"A shop full of dead merchants? Is that your message?" Khiri hissed.

"Temper, temper, dear woman. My message, or errand if you prefer, is to let you know that *He* awaits you. Our war has been put on hold."

"What?" Even though Khiri's body was no longer freezing, she felt an icy grip ensnare her heart.

"Though, if you were to die before I managed to give you that message, I could hardly be held responsible. Just look at the carnage here... It looks as though the Flayers broke free of my control in their blood lust..." Arad stepped into the shadows, pulled a rune from his pouch and shattered it against the floor. Smoke swallowed his form as five, six, seven Flayers stepped through a rift between realms.

Kal rushed into the room, extending his shield to encompass Khiri and the unconscious dwarf at her feet. She was fairly certain the victim was Master Vort, and not one of his apprentices, but there was no way to confirm that until he was awake. If he awoke. The rising number of Flayers didn't swing things in her team's favor.

"The flits!" Khiri said, inspiration striking her. "Do you see them?"

Kal didn't seem to hear her. He was already muttering in his arcane language as the markings of his staff glowed with a deep red light. Several balls of fire shot toward the oncoming Flayer mob, taking out two, but three more seemed to rise in their place.

"I can't just burn this city down," Kal gritted his teeth. "Tempting as it sounds at the moment... Any thoughts?"

"We need to get to the flits," Khiri repeated.

"To what purpose?" Kal asked. Three Flayers were now at the barrier, pounding against it as though it were a wooden door. Sweat began to form on Kal's forehead and the staff markings turned white as he switched his focus to holding the shields around them.

"Trust me," the elven woman said. "I've got an idea."

19

~Estan~

ESTAN FELT HIMSELF staring. He knew his mouth was hanging open, but he couldn't seem to process his thoughts. This vision, this angelic being sitting in front of him, was the cold hearted, ruthless Queen of Thieves that threatened Dewin's life? When he had imagined the woman Corianne and Evic served, he'd imagined her more like...

His mouth shut itself of its own accord. He could never tell Resmine he'd imagined the Queen of Thieves looking like her. Resmine would never let him live it down. And she would hit him. Hard.

"So what's this all about?" Ysinda leaned forward, toying with her spoon. She took a deep whiff of the steaming cobbler, coming close to dipping her nose in the cream. "Ren's pretty careful about who he introduces to me. I'm known to have a bit of a temper."

"I... I'm not entirely sure where to begin. You already know that I'm acquainted with Evic and Corianne," Estan said, finally finding his voice again. "I assume that you also know that I travel with their sister."

"Ah, yes... Dewin..." A frown passed over Ysinda's soft features. Estan caught his first flash of the woman that reigned over the seedy underbelly of Jarelton. "It's not that I really believe she was responsible for what happened, you know. I just can't afford to be soft on those that aid my enemies. I sliced the throat of my predecessor out of necessity. He was leading our guild right into calamity, raiding only the wealthy districts and targeting the city guard. That looks good in novels, but the reality is that behavior earns a ticket straight to the gallows for any thief unlucky enough to get caught with their hand in the baker's window. I couldn't have that for my people. Now, someone is trying to take my seat. Whether it's because they think a woman can't lead or they're just greedy, it makes no difference. There's no stepping down in this business. I can't just let your friend walk."

"That wasn't really what I needed to talk to you about, but since you are here and I've already brought it up..." Estan leaned forward as he threaded his hands together and placed them on the table, close enough to Ysinda's bowl to feel the warmth emanating from it. "What is the Guild's relationship with Tak Anverin?"

"He's a trusted ally. In exchange for his cooperation, we offer him autonomy. He has access to places my people can't go and his information-gathering network is without equal... Save for maybe the Venom Guild or the former Gray Army," Ysinda answered. "Why do you ask?"

"If Tak had...taken on an apprentice, would that apprentice be afforded the same protections?" Estan prodded. Even as he waited for her answer, he found himself falling into the depths of her emerald eyes. He blinked, reminding himself to stay focused.

"I would have to." The Queen of Thieves directed her attention to her cherry confection, scooping a large tangy-sweet mess into her mouth. She looked like she had reached a moment of pure ecstasy as she slowly drew the spoon back out. Heat rushed away from Estan's brain and tried to relocate to a region much farther south. Ysinda opened her eyes as though nothing had happened. "Tak is too valuable to us to risk offending him by attacking someone he's taken on."

Clearing his throat, Estan studied his hands, trying hard to think of something less provocative than Ysinda's obvious pleasure in her dessert. The image of what the Queen of Thieves would do to Dewin if she found her cooled his desire enough for him to focus. "So, if Dewin were to renounce her place in the Guild and Tak took her on, would that be enough to buy her a reprieve?"

Ysinda considered the knight, tapped her spoon against the edge of her bowl, and straightened her spine. "I've been pretty open with you, since you've impressed Ren enough to actually call me here and risk Adela's ire, so level with me. This isn't a hypothetical situation that you've concocted just to test the waters and see if I'll let your friend live, is it? Tak really took her on?"

"He did," Estan said, still wary.

Without warning, Ysinda fell over sideways, disappearing beneath the edge of the table. Estan jumped to his feet in concern, knocking his bench over in his haste. The door to the kitchen swung open as Ren bustled into the taproom, alarm creasing his normally jovial expression into worried wrinkles. Whatever he saw on the other side of Estan's table calmed him, and the cook ambled back into his own private world of spices and herbs. Sounds of mirth rose from the opposite bench, finally reassuring Estan enough to allow him to rearrange his seat.

"I'm sorry," Ysinda chortled. "I'm sorry... I didn't mean to startle you... It's just, it's such a relief! You can't know... Corianne and Evic are two of my best, though they don't know it. I *hated* that their sister ended up in that mess... But, well... Her or me, you know? The Court would've dropped me faster than mouse in a gnorel den, if I just let her walk..." Her face was blotched with red streaks across her cheeks when she sat up, making the rest of her even paler by comparison. "It's not even funny, but I've been so worried. If I did catch Dewin, as loyal as they are, Corianne might even make a play herself. I'm so, so happy right now!"

Unsure of what to say or do while Ysinda regained her composure, Estan wished Ren would come back in the room to refill the cobbler in his bowl. Eating was a distraction from Estan's current awkwardness.

"Alright, you did say that Dewin's situation wasn't the real dilemma, so why did you call me here?"

Taking a deep breath, Estan debated whether to start at the beginning of his story or stick with telling her about Orin Treag's request and nothing more. His original intention was to let her know he wanted to help with the reunification process and leave it at that. Having actually met Ysinda, Estan wanted to prolong their conversation. If she felt he was wasting her time though, she might not accept his help.

"It's a long story," the knight said, finally deciding to leave it to the Thief Queen's curiosity. If she didn't want to know, she didn't have to ask. Estan really hoped she'd ask. "It ends with me asking Orin Treag to take his mother's place as Lord Ilamar, and him asking me to help you regain control of Jarelton's underworld."

"That does sound complicated." Ysinda picked up her spoon and resumed chasing cherries onto its concave surface. "Perhaps you should start at the beginning. That will give me time to convince Ren to part with the rest of his cobbler."

"I heard that!" Ren called from his service window. "And I'm already makin' a second, ya minx!"

Doing a dance of celebration in his imagination, Estan started with the discovery of the Gray Army within the Temple of Taymahr. He was tempted to try and downplay his attraction to Khiri, but it wasn't worth muddling the story. Too many of his decisions were based on the fact he rarely thought with his head before throwing his heart into something. Resmine often chided him for it, but she'd probably be surprised to know how much Estan actually agreed with her. But that was why they complimented each other so well as friends. He thought with his heart all the time, while Resmine rarely got out of her own head long enough to act on her feelings.

Estan was just finishing his story when Dewin and Tak strolled in, discussing what had apparently been Dewin's first outing as Tak's underling. She had a knack for it, Tak had said when he'd suggested giving her the tattoo, Estan recalled. They both froze as Ysinda rose slowly to her feet. The friendly, innocent aura the Queen of Thieves had displayed for their entire conversation dropped like a robe at her feet and a wall of cold flooded the room.

"Your majesty..." Tak's hand shot out and caught Dewin before she could sink into a full bow. "This is quite unexpected."

"Isn't it?" The chill in Ysinda's voice startled Estan. He could hardly reconcile this as being the same woman that had been giddy with laughter when he told her about Dewin's apprenticeship. His eyes darted from his friends to the Queen of Thieves, and he wondered if he had been mistaken to trust her. "I thought it was made clear, I never wanted to see this one breathing, again."

"Apologies, highness, but—" Tak began, but he was interrupted by the shaking of Ysinda's shoulders.

The tremors moved down into her chest and Ysinda let out a full bellied laugh. Tak's expression was curious if bemused, but Dewin looked thoroughly spooked. If anything, the laughter of her former queen seemed to have shocked her even more than find Ysinda waiting in the taproom.

"Your friend here told me, and it's not as though I can't see your tattoo. Oh, Goddess Adari, but I couldn't help myself," Ysinda choked out as her chuckles subsided. "It just feels good to laugh. I haven't had a chance to let myself relax in a very long time."

"So... You're a right love, then?" Dewin asked, still wearing a look of incredulous disbelief. "I'm safe?"

"From me," Ysinda said. "Assuming you follow the rules that make Tak so very valuable, I can afford to turn a blind eye just this once. I trust this is a one time arrangement and you'll remain as selective in your apprentices as you've been in the past."

Raising his hands, Tak stepped away from the queen as though to indicate that he wouldn't dare interfere with her justice again. With a nod, Ysinda turned and resumed her seat across from Estan. A brief silent exchange between Tak and Dewin ended with them joining Estan and his guest, albeit uncomfortably.

"Estan has been telling me quite the tale," Ysinda said, playing with the syrup-and-cream residue left in her bowl. Whether she was drawing something or watching the swirls of pink form, Estan was uncertain. "Quite frankly, I'm of the opinion that you're a little too open and trusting with this information. You told me, after having known me for all of half a batch of cobbler. And you told Orin Treag. I'm guessing that you told my lieutenants, based on Dewin's kinship and the fact that you seem to be old friends. But in the first few sentences, you admit to being a fugitive of temple justice and being pursued by the Venom Guild. If I were inclined to do the Venom Guild any favors, I'd rat on you myself."

"She's got a point," Tak agreed, tapping his fingers against a knot in the table's surface. "I make my trade in something you keep giving away each time a taker asks. I'd never apprentice you, charming as you are. Well, that and Vesk would kill me if I started lugging around someone that handsome."

"Who's Vesk?" Estan asked. It was the first time Tak had mentioned the name, but the trader said it with such affection. Tak often spoke a lot without saying anything worth mentioning. The glimpses into his private life were few and far between.

"Runs a rune shop on the Firinian border. Also happens to be my husband," Tak shrugged.

"You're married?" Estan asked, surprised. The man was such a flirt, Estan hadn't imagined that Tak might have someone waiting for him back home. It hadn't even occurred to Estan that Tak might have a permanent residence.

"Happily."

"That being said, I believe you were asking me if there was some favor you might perform to help me regain my hold on the city." Ysinda's honey blonde eyebrows wrinkled into a vexed line, which Estan couldn't help but think of as cute. The Queen of Thieves just brimmed with cute. "I think I have an idea of how you may be of service."

"What did you have in mind?" Estan asked.

For a few moments, Ysinda said nothing. She set down her spoon and pushed her empty bowl onto the table behind her. Oil lamps and torches scattered throughout the barroom chatted and hissed, offering the only constant counterpoint to the silence. Even the city outside seemed to be waiting for her answer, things were so still.

"Have any of you heard of a man called Rothan Haud?" she asked.

Estan and Dewin both turned to Tak, expecting the information trader to talk business. They were disappointed when he said, "Only what I've heard since arriving in Jarelton this trip."

"That's the problem," Ysinda said. "Right there. Most challengers, you can hear them coming. Rumors of this young hotshot that wants to make a name, hearsay of this thief that has new ideas, or someone that just doesn't like the way you're running things. This past summer, I've been running my people ragged trying to track this tough the normal way; taking down his sympathizers and seconds, feeling out his network, trying to find his rat hole... I thought I'd found the ring leaders when we hunted down Reldan Jack, Tyronian Shedson, and Steward Jels, but as soon as we had them, three more sprouted. This bloke's got a silver tongue, no mistake, to keep taking on my people with no sign of a lair."

Ren popped out of the kitchen with fresh bowls for Estan and Ysinda. He'd brought two more for Dewin and Tak. While Ren deposited cobbler, everyone at the table seemed to fall quiet aside from murmurs of thanks or appreciative smiles. Picking up the empty bowls, Ren excused himself with apologies for the coming noise from the kitchen as he was about to prepare dinner.

"That's Ren for, 'I'm going to try not to eavesdrop,'" Dewin said, licking her spoon. "He's a right love, he is."

"Anyway, I think Rothan Haud has infiltrated my Court, which means I need someone from outside to make any headway. The way he's come out of nowhere with his resources, I think he's got backing. If you could prove that he's in it for some outside force, like say the city guard or the Venom Guild, that would convince those in the watch wings that he's no friend to the Thieves' Guild. Then I could find the snake's head."

The cruel smile that crooked Ysinda's lips this time was in no way cute.

20

~Ullen~

ULLEN HOPED HIS FRIENDS were having a better morning than he was. He was three meetings into the day, and no closer to getting his mother to agree to ending the war with Mytana. The only upside was that the castle cooks had remembered to include his favorite stuffed sausage buns when they'd provided breakfast trays to the council rooms.

"If we concede the river, then Mytana will see that as a sign of weakness and they'll try to take Eswayne next year," Queen Di'eli said. "I have no interest in letting those thugs take the kingdom from me. However..."

Here we go, Ullen sighed inwardly. Every time his mother had uttered an *however*, it ended with the same ultimatum.

"...If you'll agree to become my heir, I'll abdicate in your favor and you can do as you wish."

Well, the abdication offer was new. It surprised Ullen enough that he didn't respond as quickly as he normally did to his mother's traps. He was about to voice the same protests he'd been using all morning when Hon'idar stood and slammed his hands on the table. "Mother! We've been over this so many times that it's beginning to wear down on our scribes! I saw the one behind you sigh!"

Turning her head to lock her eyes on the unfortunate individual pointed out by Hon'idar, Ullen was certain his mother was about to breath actual fire at the man. The scribe in question looked up in dread and shook his head frantically. "It was merely a yawn, your Highness! I had a late night! I meant no disrespect to your Majesty!"

"He's a right to sigh if he chooses," Ullen interjected, drawing the room's focus away from the scribe before the man could get himself fired or worse. "This farce is getting old, Mother. You have an heir in Hon'idar. If you are tired of leading, hand your crown to the son that wants it. I'll advise him the same as I have you. The Flayer Mage is back, which means we need allies."

The interest in Queen Di'eli's eyes seemed to fade as Ullen spoke. There was only one thing he could say that held any interest for her and that was to accept the throne. It wasn't a concession Ullen was willing to make. He'd rather the whole world forget he was ever even a prince and die as an uninteresting, untalented bard. Or any one of the other occupations he'd tried his hand at.

"It wouldn't be horrible for the ruler of a prominent nation to be able to sympathize with the common citizens," Tharothet said.

"Don't you start," Ullen thought back. *"It's one thing to argue with my mother, but you* could *order this of me. That's what it would take and you know it."*

"I do know it. This isn't an order, merely an observation."

Ullen grimaced. He recognized that tone. Tharothet wasn't going to order him to take the throne of Eerilor *yet*, but it was something his deity was considering. If Ullen didn't make some progress soon, his mother might get her wish.

Hon'idar wouldn't stand idly by if Ullen decided to take the offered crown. Even the affection they currently shared was starting to strain under the pressure of their mother's desires. There was no way it would withstand the pressure of a god's command.

A SOFT KNOCK ON ULLEN'S door startled him out of a nap he hadn't meant to take. The morning's meeting had taken a toll on him mentally, so he'd come back to his quarters intending to write another letter to Genovar or possibly Quinton Ilyani, another of the seven generals of the last war and a member of Estan's knighthood. Former knighthood?

Perhaps it was time to write Estan, Dewin, and Resmine as well. Ullen missed his young friends. All the more since he'd sent Kal and Khiri away.

The knock repeated. It was still gentle, but this time was a bit louder. "Ut'evullen?" Hon'idar's voice sounded as hesitant as his knock. "If you don't want to see me, I understand. Mother's putting a lot of pressure on both of us right now. I just thought you might like to get out of the palace for a bit. Take a walk into Taman with me and we can stretch our legs!"

Ullen rolled off of his bed, knocking a pillow to the floor in his eagerness to get to the door. "I'd like that, Hon'idar! I think the door's open if you'd like to join me in here while I get ready!"

Hon'idar eased the door open and walked into Ullen's quarters. His piercing gaze took in the state of the room at a glance.

Ullen had been making an effort not to fling clothes all over the place, but they still seemed to accumulate near his changing screen no matter how careful he was. Otherwise, there wasn't much to see. The room was huge, as were most rooms in the palace towers. Unlike the guest rooms, Ullen's personal suite didn't have a balcony. He hadn't cared much to have an opening to the outside this far from the ground. It was decorated with a few decorative rugs and reading chairs, but it lacked the opulence displayed in the rest of the palace.

"This place hasn't changed much since you left. Mother had the palace staff keep it tidy, just in case, but it looks like you've not been assigned a proper valet if you're answering your own door," Hon'idar observed.

"Not much used to them anymore," Ullen shrugged, struggling to pull on his new boots. He tried to remember his courtly tones, but it was hard when he was alone in the room with Hon'idar. Hon'idar had been his idol growing up. The perfect big brother. While their father was busy with the minutiae of running a kingdom, Hon'idar had been the one to teach Ullen how to fish, how to hunt, how to talk to women about something other than court politics. "I suppose Captain Aldash might know someone less formal."

Hon'idar laughed. An honest laugh, deep from his gut. "He might, at that. I know the two of you got a chance to catch up on the road. I would've invited him along for your sake, but I really hoped this would be our chance to set aside politics and be brothers for a while. Away from court and our mother's demands."

"I'd love to trip down to our old drinking bench," Ullen said. Despite the awkward interactions with his mother, perhaps getting to see Hon'idar was worth coming back. "Think they still have it taped off for us?"

"They'd better!" Hon'idar grinned. "I still sneak down there from time to time!"

"Do they still have that dent in the bar from the time you dared me to do a backflip off of the stool and I missed?"

With a laugh, Hon'idar clapped Ullen on the shoulder. "I'd forgotten about that! If it's not there, let's go make another!"

21

~Khiri~

IT FELT LIKE ENTIRE seasons passed while Flayers hammered against the dome of Kal's protection. Kal inched the shield forward and Khiri dragged the unconscious artisan along. A row of flits gleamed in sconces along the back wall near the office, tantalizingly close and agonizingly distant. As the shield pushed its way into the mass of Flayers, more and more of them began to thrash against it. Even after several days full rest and many decent meals, the Odlesk mage was beginning to flag with the effort of holding a barrier against so many demon-bound.

Khiri dropped the dwarf's arm and sheathed her dagger. Pulling Micah from her back, she knocked an arrow and began loosing missiles into the Flayer ranks. For each demon-bound she dropped, a new adversary waded into its place.

"I hate to spoil the fun, but I'm not sure how much longer I can keep this up," Kal said through gritted teeth. Sweat coated him, making his silk shirt cling to his toned frame. "It's like I'm attempting to lift Catapult with my head."

"Is it easier to maintain than it is to move?" Khiri asked.

"Much," the mage said. "This particular spell is earth-based. Fire, water, wind, even spirit, they all appreciate movement. Metal can be flexible. Earth doesn't like moving and fights against it. If I'd known we wanted to wade through the Flayer army, I'd have used a different spell."

"I'm sorry," Khiri said, letting another of her arrows fly. The unlucky Flayer on the receiving end caught the projectile in its eye and began thrashing wildly in its pain. Flinging one arm violently into the chest of another, the injured Flayer managed to take a second down with it. "Next time, I'll let you know I'm planning to ask some Flayers to dance."

Kal managed a labored grin. "You do that. Assuming we make it to next time."

"We'll make it," Khiri assured him. They were in the midst of the work tables now, with only one row between them and the back wall. Measuring the distance between the surface under the shield and the flits, Khiri calculated the route she would have to take. "I need an exit."

"What? There's no way..." Kal started to lower his staff, but the sheen of their protective layer buckled and he had to break off to regain his concentration. "I can't let you—"

"Either I take the risk, or all three of us die here!" Khiri snapped. "I'm not about to let that happen. Either give me the exit point, or I'll make my own!"

Unhappy silence passed between them like a physical thing; the gnashing whispers of Flayers couldn't penetrate it any more than they could tear down Kal's spell.

"Where do you need it?" Kal asked, his expression dark.

If the circumstances had been less dire, Khiri may have felt worse about making him unhappy; however, during the current crisis, all of her energy was keyed into the task at hand. She envisioned the spot she wanted weakened and passed it mentally to Kal. Being neither small nor fast enough to clip through the shield the way her arrows did, she had to be careful not to give the Flayers an opening. Strapping Micah back into his place on her back, Khiri unsheathed her dagger, settling it into her grip as she mustered her courage. There would only be a few seconds between landing and fighting for her life.

An unhappy sigh accompanied Kal's nod. The spot would be ready when she gave the signal.

"Go!" Khiri yelled, leaping to the top of the work bench and diving through the section she'd asked Kal to drop. For an instant, a small hole in the glowing blue gaped above the heads of the Flayers almost within reach and they surged eagerly toward it. But it didn't take them long to recognize that one of their intended prey was loose outside the impenetrable dome. Hungrily, they turned on Khiri.

Rolling to her feet, Khiri came up right beside the nested jewels. She plucked one from its sconce and let it fly, hoping that there was no magic word or phrase needed to activate it. As soon as it started to drop, the flit began to shine with an inner light, hovered and then darted toward its preordained destination.

"Do you even know who you called?" Kal demanded, his mental voice rising over the den of the Flayers.

At that moment, the first Flayer reached her, a large once-woman that probably would have been able to best Estan in arm wrestling. Ducking under one of the Flayer's brutal claw strikes, Khiri came up behind the thing. Her ragged brown hair provided Khiri with a handhold to climb up the unwieldy creature's back, even as several others reached her flanks. Catching the claws of another with her dagger, the elf perched on the big Flayer's shoulders. Her mount thrashed and flailed, reaching back as it strived to pry Khiri off of her chosen position. The elven woman held on for all she was worth.

"I called for help!" she told Kal, unable to concentrate long enough to use her silent sending.

Other Flayers were getting sick of waiting for the large one to dislodge its guest. They were not patient by nature and what little politeness they could manage had ebbed. In their frustration, they began tearing at Khiri's mount, ripping her apart a piece at a time.

As the large Flayer cried out in pain beneath her, Khiri leapt off the dying Flayer and clung to another. This one managed to catch hold of Khiri's leg and attempted to throw her to the ground, but a second Flayer stabbed its claws into her new mount's arm, causing the first creature to lose its hold. Khiri fell against the nearest work table and rolled off onto the floor. She thanked the spirits that they were in an armor shop instead of a weaponsmith armory. Even so, she would be a mess of cuts and bruises if she survived to see the next day.

Sparing a glance toward Kal's dome, she could see that only half of the Flayer tide had left to pursue her, while the others continued their work at Kal's shield. The barrier was buckling more often now, bending inward at their blows instead of bouncing them away. Kal's focus was on her rather than his own safety.

Dodging under a workbench to her left, Khiri kicked the feet out from under the Flayer on the other side and stabbed it in the neck almost casually. She and Kal were grossly outnumbered. The only hope they had was riding along with that small purple gem.

Almost as though her thought had summoned it, there was a call from outside that made her spirits rise.

"MAKE WAY! MAKE WAY! OH, SWEET MERCIFUL MOTHER!" The exclamation was nearly lost in the collision as the two wheeled contraption smashed through the wall. Large chunks of rock and small chips of shrapnel exploded into the room. Two Flayers flew back into their brethren as the vehicle plowed into the work table nearest the door. Armor rained down from the ceiling, causing many remaining Flayers to flee back into the Demon Plains, convinced that some sort of war machine had interrupted their promised feast.

The delivery dwarf jumped to his feet, disentangling himself with remarkable ease considering the mess of wood, stone, leather and metal that surrounded him. "Someone called for Purple Wren Tavern? I've a meat pie and a nice cask... somewhere... in..."

Seeming to look around for the first time, he trailed off before looking at a bleeding and dirty Khiri who was pulling her dagger out of the last Flayer's chest. He glanced wide-eyed from her to where Kal was consoling an awakened Master Ian Vort, taking in the number of bodies and carnage between them.

"Demon spit," the delivery dwarf said. "That does it. I'm telling Jev tomorrow—I quit!"

RELOCATING TO THE PURPLE Wren, in the company of both the young delivery dwarf and Master Vort, Khiri and Kal asked for a private table and a bowl of hot water. The bartender, Jev Tanerd, took their request in stride, along with his delivery boy's resignation.

"You were the one that insisted on that...thing...you created. Can't say I'm all shocked by its causin' ya trouble," Jev shrugged. "Just glad you ain't hurt."

"You made that device?" Kal asked. "I'd assumed it was the invention of an engineer."

"I am an engineer!" The young dwarf scowled daggers at the Odlesk mage. "I may not be old enough to rightly pursue my certifications yet, but I've more talent than any of those so-called 'inventors' on the waterfront. As though a real engineer would allow something like water rights stop them. The future is paved with runes! Mages will soon be obsolete!"

Khiri tried to hide her amusement at Kal's pursed lips. When the hot water arrived, the Odlesk took the rag from the bowl and started to gently doctor Khiri's cuts and scratches. He was trying hard not to snap at their unlikely rescuer. He was also likely holding in a good word or two for Khiri concerning her harebrained gamble–risking her life to call for a food delivery. Never mind that it'd worked. It was a little out there, as plans went.

"Not that I'm not grateful for your interference," Master Vort interjected, "because I truly am thankful to be alive. Especially given... Given what happened. I do have families to notify and arrangements to be made, though. So whatever you wanted to speak to me about, please be brief. I lost six of my finest proteges today. Esky's work would've outdone mine one day..." The craftsman let out a sigh that ended in a sob.

He seemed down enough that Khiri hated to broach the subject of Flayers and equipment, but he was still the best lead they had. "We were coming to ask if you knew anything about some unusually large orders of armor."

"During a war?" Vort said with a sniff. "That's pretty ambiguous. The army can hardly keep up with its own equipment, so there's been an upward spike of orders everywhere. If you're looking for someone specific, maybe you could give me a bit more to narrow it down."

"Flayers," Kal said. His voice was hard, without its usual hint of humor. Khiri started to turn toward him, but he held her still with a deliberate but soft touch on her shoulder. "They're being equipped with high end leathers. We were directed to begin our search with you."

"...That's very troublesome," Master Vort responded, his voice soft and sorrowful. "How high end are we talking? Most of what I sell is made by apprentices and journeymen, with only a scrap here or there of my own work. Mass production of master quality... I could name those capable of such a thing. Four masters and any one of them could have arranged what just happened to my shop. We all know each other, you see. Shouldn't be too hard to narrow it down if they're trying to keep the rest of us quiet, either."

Khiri waited, unwilling to push a man that was obviously already beginning to grieve. Kal's tense silence was less forgiving, but he was keeping his head down. She felt a warmth trickling its way up her arm. Healing magic, though he was getting close to being tapped out. Despite Khiri's subtle attempts to tug her wrist out of his grip, the mage stubbornly refused to let go.

"Kal, stop. You'll knock yourself out," she sent, concern flowing through their link.

His response consisted of emotions and images rather than the usual mental vocalizations she was used to. A tumble of reds, purples, anger, passion, helplessness, her face, his want, an older human man—his grandfather, blackness, jealousy, Estan, her being flung by a Flayer, him being blocked by his own shield, a shield fading to fire, short bursts of yellow... It all crashed through Khiri like an avalanche, too big for her to comprehend and too quick for her to sift her way into it.

"I owe it to my apprentices to cooperate. The masters you're looking for: Kivian Threshler, Thomas Illesan, Elsina Rorsband, and Rory Task. If I think anyone capable of the murder involved, I'd recommend starting with Thomas. He's never been what you'd call ethical. Now, I apologize, but there's little more I can do for you right now. Jev knows where you can find their shops, and if you like, see me before you head out and I can see about giving you some better equipment. Those leather scraps are obviously inferior Mytanan stock." With a jerky bow, Master Ian Vort made his way out the door, leaving Khiri and Kal with just the young former-delivery boy for company.

Despite the quiet, the young dwarf seemed quite content to sit in a human-sized chair and swing his legs back and forth. "So do you two do this often?" he asked.

Khiri, not sure how to answer such a question, just gave the dwarf a weary smile. He was young enough that his beard hadn't sprouted, but his brown skin was taut and free of baby fat. Guessing at his age, given the long lifespan of dwarves, she estimated the boy to have almost ten summers on her. It was odd to think that someone so much older could be so much younger.

"My name's Rigger. Well, not really. But you can call me Rigger," he said.

Kal's irritation at the young dwarf was starting to rub against Khiri's arm like sharp nettles, surrounding and abrasive. Before the mage could snap, she requested, "Rigger, could you perhaps give us a moment? Kal needs to tend my back, and I'm rather shy."

"He needs to... oh. Oh! Right... I'll just, I'll go check on Jev. He may want... something before I..." Rigger trailed off as he walked out of the private dining room, shutting the door behind him.

"Kal?" Khiri tried to look at him, but Kal again stilled her with a touch.

"We never talked about it before," he said. The sounds of cloth dipping into the water bowl and dripping trickled through his words, somehow lending his voice the soft warmth of a bath. "When you were fighting Fennick, just now with the Flayers, and I'm sure there will be more scenarios in the future... Estan would try to promise to protect you, to make you promise to be careful. That's not me... That's not you."

Plunge. Squeeze. Drip. Drip. Drip.

"I know you, *laska*. You're impulsive and fierce. Being careful is not in your nature and it wouldn't do a bit of good to ask you to be otherwise. That doesn't make it easy to watch you jump through a barrier that could protect you. I'm not..." Kal hesitated. The cloth stopped moving.

Clearing his throat, Kal sighed, his words continuing to pour over her. "I don't think of others first. My grandfather...he raised me under duress. My mother died giving birth to me. She loved my father, I'm told. Loved him more than she could stand. My father, pure

Odlesk, couldn't travel far from water, and my grandfather was not a tolerant man. He named me, you know. My name... Kal... It means silt, water trash. He took me away from my father's lake, unwilling to let his daughter's son be raised by an Odlesk, despite my nature. When the mages came for me, it was a relief for both of us."

Plunge. Squeeze. Silence.

"I'm not entirely sure why I'm telling you this," Kal admitted, his voice rough with emotion. "It has no bearing on anything. It was a long time ago... Just, watching you plunge into danger, I keep putting my faith in you to come out of it. I have to trust you to survive. And I don't—I've never trusted anyone. Except you. Khiri, I trust you. Please..." Slowly, his arms wrapped around her middle, careful not to brush against her injuries. His warm breath tickled as it caressed her ear which was already tingling with the inward flow of Kal's magic."...don't let me down."

"Kal, I..." Khiri's heart ached. She felt the spot where *Telgan Korsborn* pulsed unhappily in her head. What was she supposed to do? She'd been raised to believe that the soul name was her destiny, but something about Kal's touch felt so *right*.

"Khiri," Micah's voice flowed into her thoughts. *"I know who you're bound to. Do you really want to save yourself for your enemy?"*

Thoughts of her father's past, her mother's past, and her current predicament rushed to meet the question. How could she defy the same forces that had swept her into the maelstrom her parents had started?

"Which is worse?" Micah argued. *"Risking too much, or regretting that you never took the chance?"*

Khiri felt herself lean into Kal's embrace, not ready to answer Micah's question, but not ready to pull away. "Kal, I can't make promises," she sighed.

"I know," he said, and Khiri felt something like a kiss against her hair. "I'm not asking for promises. Promises get broken every day.

I'm not pressing for anything more than you're willing to give. Just... There are times when you seem to think you've got nothing left to lose. I want to convince you there's something here to live for."

"Not yet," she whispered. Khiri paused, not sure she should encourage him. Yet, she yearned to give in. "But... Is it too much to ask you to keep trying?"

She could feel his wry smile curve through her hair, his body rocking softly with a chuckle he didn't vocalize.

"I can do that, *laska*. Nothing could stop me."

22

~Estan~

LEADING CATAPULT IN circles around the small stable yard for exercise, Estan considered the events of the past few days. After Ysinda charged his group with discovering everything they could about Rothan Haud, Estan began spending more time with the roan. It seemed as though Catapult's personality was getting too playful for Adela and Ren's stableboy. Even Estan found the warhorse trying at times–especially as it seemed Catapult's ability to alter appearances wasn't limited to his own being. At least twice, Estan had tried to sit on nonexistent hay bales.

"Any advice on how to find a rogue that doesn't want to be found?" Estan asked the horse. Catapult's response was to leap into a canter and make the knight either let go or jog in a circle.

Estan imagined Catapult was restless. It was hard for a horse to walk around on his own through the city. Even disguised as a cart horse, Estan couldn't take him on fact-finding missions. Horses didn't belong in taverns.

Catapult nickered, swinging his head back and forth, and began rearing, kicking at the air with his front hooves.

"What's the matter, friend?" Estan asked, yanking hard on Catapult's harness. No matter how empty the yard seemed, letting a warhorse rear unchecked was unwise. With his hooves level on the ground, the horse started twitching his back muscles, clearly unhappy about something. That was when Estan smelled it. Smoke. And it was close. Too close.

Estan opened the gate to the stable yard and sprinted around to the front of the Talon Acre, certain that he'd be able to see where the smoke was rising from the main throughway. In his hurry, the latch for the stable yard bounced off of its catch and he could hear the war horse clopping after him. With any normal horse, Estan would've turned around to fix the situation immediately. But Catapult was a fellow avatar. Depending on the situation, backup was nothing to scoff at.

Before Estan made it to the street, a hand caught him and pulled him back into the alley. Dewin, her features drawn in sharp lines of worry, held a finger to her lips, urging him to be quiet. The front of the Talon Acre was surrounded by a mob of torch-wielding protestors.

"We got wind of it before they got here," Dewin said softly, her tone full of anger and bitterness. "Got Adela and Ren out in the nick of it. These people ain't just random swayables. They were picked for the purpose; Rothan's looking to send Ysinda a message, a right foul one."

"So we're just going to let them tear the place apart?" Estan felt his rage boil at the very thought. "What of their living? What of their home?"

"That lot is foul, Estan, no doubts. But they are still people. We can't just wade in like they be Flayers and drop the lot!" Dewin hissed. "We'd have the guard on the Thieves' Guild like a nest of hornets on a bag of sweets, never mind we ain't rightly affiliated. These lot, they're after violence, and you're wantin' to give it to them. It wouldn't save the tavern, and like as not, we'd be in a thick heap of it comin' out the other side."

Harsh cries were being raised and jeers were being hurled at the building. Estan realized that the crowd was unaware they faced an empty building. The knight glanced at Catapult who was huffing at Estan's shoulder. Dewin looked equally unhappy despite her arguments.

"If they want a fight, I'm inclined to give them one. But let's give them one they're not expecting," Estan said. "Catapult… I feel odd asking this of a horse, but I've got a plan and I'm hoping you're clever enough to pull it off."

Estan turned to Dewin. "Go find anyone you can that's willing to help out. We're about to shock these people into the Demon Realms."

SOMEONE SCRAWLED 'FRIENDS of the False Queen' across the door with something that looked an awful lot like blood while the mob chanted for the tavern owners to come face justice. Frustrated with the lack of response, someone in the crowd of Rothan's sycophants picked up a rock and hurled it at the Talon Acre's window. The shattering glass elicited a cheer from the others, who scurried to find their own projectiles. A torch flew through the air, smacked against the building's face and landed tip down on the steps.

Before any more missiles were launched, a wind that no one felt blew the crowd's remaining torches out. A few of the more cautious members of the mob attempted to point out the oddity to their neighbors. Those with more mob practice weren't so easily deterred, however. Soon people were yelling, "Eerilorian sympathizers! They raised the Blood Queen! Let them burn!"

Estan, masked from sight by the horse at his shoulder, snuck into the mob. Catapult waited at the back of the group disguised as a small tow-headed boy holding a puppy. The boy tugged on the shirt of one of the people nearest him. Since the horse couldn't affect actual matter, Estan assumed his horse had bitten the man's sleeve.

"You want in on the fun, sonny?" the man asked, offering the boy a rock.

Catapult's disguise shook his head and then let out a very horsey whinny. The man's eyebrows rose into his hairline, his face a mask of confusion. The small blonde child pulled back a fist and hit the man in the gut, sending him careening into Estan's arms. Using the man's momentum, Estan yanked him over his invisible hip, making it appear as though the child had floored the man with one blow.

A gang of street urchins formed at one end of the street, screaming against the mob of adults.

"Leave Aunt Adela alone!"

"That's Uncle Ren's place!"

"Go away!"

Estan grinned, even though no one could see him. He felt the agitators' annoyance at this development. It was one thing to try and pick a fight against a building full of adults. But a group of kids standing between them and the tavern turned them into the bad guys, no matter what reasons they gave for being there.

"Run home, kids. This has nothing to do with you. You don't want to get hurt," one of the larger aggressors said. He was flipping a rock into the air and catching it with the opposite hand. "I ain't above hurting youngsters."

"But do you rightly think we're above hurtin' you?" one of the kids, a young girl with thick black curls that sounded an awful lot like Corianne asked. She brought her fingers up to her lips and let out a sharp whistle. At the sound, the urchins rushed forward, meeting the adults with blows that were far stronger than their size would've suggested.

A woman with a mop of matted, filthy copper tresses pulled out a pair of knives. "I won't be done in by a lot of snotty twigs," she snarled. The child she faced looked an awful lot like Dewin. Her blade was met by what looked like a doll but clanged like metal.

Mid-swing, the knife-wielding woman found her hand caught by the end of a long, braided cord of leather. Resmine's expression brooked no mercy. Rage burned around her like an aura of fire. Even Estan, who had known the former squire of the Battered Iris for most of his life was taken aback at the sight of her. The wild knife wielder dropped both of her blades and began shrieking as she ran down an alley to escape from "the rage demon."

The large man that had claimed not to fear hurting children got sat on by the blonde boy with his puppy. Men and women dropped their torches and rocks, along with whatever else they felt would impede their get away. Estan threw punches at the few mob members still lingering, either wanting to finish what they'd started or pick up the pieces others threw down.

When the only agitator remaining was the one that Catapult was sitting on, the roan dropped the illusion so a group of thieves and fighters were seen making their way into the damaged tavern. Dewin threw her arms around Resmine and the two began kissing so ardently that Estan turned away, blood flooding into his cheeks. She might not be his blood, but Resmine was his sister in every way that mattered. Watching her reunion with Dewin was more than a little uncomfortable. He mumbled something about it being good to have her back, before hurrying away to gather the unconscious prisoner from under his horse's rear.

Once inside, the captive was taken from Estan's hands and slammed against one of the tables. A member of the Thieves' Guild that the knight hadn't met took a dagger and stabbed the table in front of the instigator's face, twirling the blade back and forth.

"Tell me what I want to know and maybe I don't run this like a carving knife down the sides of your cheeks," the strange thief purred.

Corianne grabbed her guild mate by the scruff of his neck and tossed him off of the big man like the thief was no heavier than a bracer, "Go on then! You ain't right in the head, Dagan. If the Queen hears that you be spilling blood in a tavern what bears her mark, you'll be a right slice of saddle soap and pudding. See to dispersal, I'll converse with the corpse."

"Corpse?" Estan asked, his eyes widened slightly. "Isn't that a big extreme?"

Giving him a sad, contemplative glance, Corianne did nothing to dispel Estan's obvious disapproval. She answered his question with one of her own. "If he were a spy of the Flayer mage, would you pause before droppin' the bit?"

Estan started to deny it, but his mind flashed to Fennick's rugged jaw and tanned features. Had he known that Fennick was a member of the Gray Army, he didn't know if he would've killed him. Probably. Especially if he'd anticipated the danger to Khiri and his other friends. Estan felt ill. Killing someone in a fight was much different than looking at someone as they lay helpless on a table, living and breathing, and seeing them as a dead body.

"I don't like this," the knight said. "This is not why I asked Dewin to go for help."

"You've been named friend to the Guild," Corianne told him. "Sometimes, that'll throw you in with our lot and you'll be wadin' in our waters. We're a rough sea, with harsh rules. If you be makin' eyes at our Queen, you can't be so... Khiri... about things."

"Making eyes at...?" It made Estan uncomfortable that Corianne knew about his feelings concerning her leader. He wasn't sure why it should bother him, but he didn't like how casually she'd tossed it out there. Something to think about later, perhaps.

"Dewin's my sister, and while she was never much use at nippin', she's always been a right keen observer," Corianne said. "And now what with your pokin', there's no chance this one'll be anything but a corpse. May have managed just to clip his tongue, but now..."

"The Queen's rather sensitive about her privacy," the thief called Dagan said, reentering the room from the back door. "All out and I'm about dust. Wanted to tack a board on the window, make sure the glass was cleaned up."

"Out!" Corianne's tone brooked no argument. She leaned against the large instigator while Estan bound his wrists, but her attention was on Dagan's wiry form as he sauntered out the front of the building. She shook her head at Estan's raised eyebrow, indicating that now was not the time for more questions.

She turned to their captive and yanked him up by the front of his shirt until they were breathing the same air. "You and I, we're going to have a chat, love. By the end of it, if you haven't nicked the skinny, you're gonna wish that I'd given you to Dagan. Solid?"

"As ice," the man hissed. Unfastening a strap from around her wrist, Corianne grabbed a towel from behind the bar. She wadded the towel into a ball, stuffed it between the prisoner's teeth and tied the gag in place with her wrist strap.

Tossing him back to Estan, she beckoned for the knight to follow her out the back door and continued to lead him down the alley. They turned three corners—down one street, back up another, and through a new alleyway that smelled of ancient hay and urine—before they reached an old, abandoned storefront. Corianne led Estan into the back room; a musty, dimly light workshop with manacles hanging from the ceiling and nasty stains soaked into the limestone floor. The coppery tang of old blood flooded Estan's nostrils and burned the back of his throat like an acrid belch.

"String him up for me, like a love. He's a might tallish or I'd be on it myself. I won't ask you to stay. Some aren't meant for things outside their sphere. As a friend, I thought I'd point ya to a side o' things that I doubted you were seeing," Corianne said, her dark brown eyes glittered with what little light crept into the abandoned building. "Queen Ysinda's a much different creature when her back's to the wall. Ren and Adela bring out her best. This here's only a sliver in the grain of her being."

"I didn't know it was in you, either," Estan whispered.

Pulling her strap free, Corianne gave the knight a sad smile and casually smacked the large stranger across the face with the thin leather wrap before twining it back around her wrist.

"Not that I don't find talk about your personal lives fascinating, but could you spare me the melodrama and get to the actual questioning?" the large man snarled. "If you two don't stop wagging your tongues, I may just forget everything I know out of sheer boredom."

"You're a right friendly one!" Corianne said with a smirk. She pretended to study her nails, then brought her fist back across the man's face, causing him to spit blood. "Rothan Haud. Who is he?"

As he began backing out of the hidden torture room, Estan paused at the sound of the prisoner's laughter. He leaned against the frame and waited to hear what the large man would say.

"You want to know about Rothan Haud? No one knows Rothan Haud. He only works through agents. Demon spit, if you dragged me all the way out here just ask about him, you could have saved yourselves time and effort by dropping me in a gutter along the way!" the man cackled.

"Still an option." Corianne turned and met Estan's eyes. "You're a love, Essie, but you're sure not wantin' to be here much longer."

Estan hurried away from the old building, certain screams would chase him all the way back to the Talon Acre Inn. Still, something inside him preened at Corianne's nickname.

Again, something to think about later.

23

~Irrellian~

TRAVIN ESK HAD BEEN one of Irrellian's top generals during the Great War. Watching the man from the shadows, the Flayer Mage could see lines of age withering the complexion of his subordinate. Twenty years had not been kind to Travin, who'd seen thirty-odd summers when Irrelian had recruited him. Back then, Travin Esk's stern beige complexion had been enhanced by a chiseled jaw and mahogany hair. Travin's mustache and beard had been trimmed into thin lines with precision every morning. If Travin had trimmed his graying beard in the last decade, Irrellian couldn't tell. There was a softness to his jaw now and a paunch to his gut which indicated he'd taken to drinking too much ale.

But Travin's age was not relevant to Irrellian's current task. The Flayer Mage needed to know how much of his army was still faithful. He'd interrogated a handful of servants, two knights, and one priestess to confirm what he'd already suspected—Travin was the linchpin holding the entire Temple Hill organization together. If Travin remained loyal, Temple Hill could be invaluable to Irrellian's plans. If Travin had lost sight of Irrellian's vision, Temple Hill would have to make itself useful in other ways.

Irrellian stuck his foot out of the shadow portal and placed it on the flagstones of Travin's office. Before he could emerge the rest of the way, the office door flew open and Shalora, High Priestess to the Temple of Taymahr, rushed into the room.

"Travin! We must speak! That little git Estan still lives! And I've received word that Genovar Fortiva has been spotted all over Mytana!" Shalora threw a handful of letters down on the map Travin had been pouring over for the last twenty minutes.

"I told you to deal with Estan years ago. It was dangerous to make the boy into a true believer. It was dangerous to pull him off the front lines and back into the temples. It was dangerous to label him a traitor and put a bounty on his head," Travin said. His voice was every bit as soft and measured as Irrellian remembered. If one didn't listen closely, it was easy to miss the layer of molten rage simmering beneath the surface. "If the boy lives, you know what must be done, Shalora."

"It's too late for that! We have reason to believe the High Gods are back!"

For the first time since Shalora entered the chamber, Travin looked up from his desk and met the woman's eyes. His brown irises held a ring of red in the center, as though his pupils were outlined with blood. "Tell me."

Interesting... Irrellian paused. The return of the gods wasn't news to him, but a lot could be revealed by witnessing how his followers reacted to the news. *I think I'd like to see how this plays out before I reveal myself.*

As the High Priestess reported the destruction of Harish, a town Irrellian hadn't heard of, and the discovery of Irrellian's empty cavern, Travin's expression barely shifted.

"And what of our master?" Irrellian's general asked when Shalora's report reached its end.

"Missing," Shalora said. "No one has reported seeing him. Could the gods have taken him somewhere? Why hasn't he returned to lead our people?"

"That is a question unworthy of one in your station," Travin said. "Watch your tongue if you enjoy your seat. There are plenty to replace you. Have Knight Commander Jersal round up the other Knight Commanders and summon the rest of the High Priestesses. It's time we had a council meeting."

Irrellian decided he could wait to take in a council meeting. He withdrew his foot from the flagstones and back into the shadows.

24

~Khiri~

THOMAS ILLESAN RAN an armor shop on the far side of Taman. Jev told them Thomas Illesan and Ian Vort had been rivals for many years.

"I wouldn't take anything that old Vort says about Illesan at face value," the bartender's voice was a base grumble, like a mountain packed into mortal flesh. "They were rivals long before they wore apprentice sashes."

With a shrug at Kal, Khiri thanked Jev for all he'd done for them. She left a few of the coins Ullen had given them from his palace account. She'd never been the one dealing with the money before–the Life Tree clans operated on more of a barter system–but since she no longer intended to return to her people, she'd been attempting to learn more about the value of money. Judging from the look on Jev's face, she'd over-tipped again. Without a word, he handed one of the gold stamped pieces back and cleared his throat. Her cheeks going a bit pink, Khiri slid it back into her purse.

Almost a block from the Purple Wren, Rigger caught up with them. "So where are we going?" He was huffing with the effort, despite having jogged such a short distance. The young dwarf's legs were smaller than Ullen's though. He was only as high as Khiri's armpits or Kal's waist.

"We, Khiri and I, are going to investigate whether Master Illesan is involved with Flayers," Kal said. "You should go home."

"That's not very friendly toward someone who saved your skin not but two hours ago," Rigger responded, not seeming put out in the least by the mage's disdain. He tugged on Khiri's arm, reminding her of Micah when they were children. "Want to see my latest invention?"

"It's not that thing that crashed into the front of Shielded Thoughts, is it?" Khiri asked. When Rigger shook his head, she found her curiosity piqued. "How big is it?"

"Why are you encouraging him?" Kal's sending was heavy with irritation.

"I find this rune-tech stuff interesting," Khiri sent back. *"I've always really enjoyed learning. Why do I encourage you to teach me magic?"* She had the urge to stick her tongue out at the mage. He hadn't seemed this out of sorts with anyone since Estan had left.

"Why, indeed?" His response elicited a trill of warmth down her spine. Surprised at her own reaction, she shoved him away mentally and tried to turn her attention back to the young engineer.

Rigger was pulling out a book with several runic locks, which he pushed down with his fingertips. "It's still in development, so I haven't put together my prototype yet... I haven't actually been able to get my hands on this rune right here..." As the book popped open, he pointed to a sketch of a rune that had arrows pointing to a spot inside the drawing of another contraption. Khiri wasn't very skilled at identifying runes, but one aspect of the drawing did catch her eye.

"Are those wings?" she asked, tracing one finger along the edge of the picture, careful not to touch the actual page.

Despite himself, Kal's attention turned to the drawing as well. "Suspension delivered by wind runes and then this one here," he tapped the rune that Rigger was pointing at, "provides the balance and steering. Like the rudder of a ship?"

"Exactly!" Rigger said. "If I could just get my hands on a…"

"Grounding stone," Kal inserted. "They aren't all that rare. I mean, if you wanted, you could substitute a chunk of hematite or…"

"I did think about that, but see the way I have the energy flowing back out here? Hematite would need to be replaced as the stone wore down. The rune's structure would be reinforced by the wash off," Rigger said.

"You're right," Kal nodded. "It would be a better fit, but if you moved these two to this back section…"

They continued talking about the flying contraption until something that Kal said reminded Rigger of a different sketch he had elsewhere in his book. The two of them began discussing the merits of speed runes versus force runes to generate movement in an object. After reaching an agreement, they moved on to whether a storm rune or lightning rune would produce more harnessable power. Khiri listened to Kal and Rigger with more curiosity than understanding, but a sudden change in the atmosphere around them caused her to drop out of the conversation.

People in one neighborhood were smiling, nodding their good days, content with their corner of the world. As suddenly as if they had crossed an invisible border, there were no smiles. The beautiful stone streets were quiet and empty. A feeling of desolation haunted this section of the city.

"This is the soldiers' district," Rigger said, noticing Khiri's inattention. His expression melted from eager enthusiasm to heart-wrenching sadness in the space of one sentence. "A good many of them that lived here aren't coming back. We didn't figure to be fighting Mytana for so long…"

"I thought the army had barracks behind the palace," Khiri's voice was soft. It seemed hard to raise her voice here. It felt like being in the Burning Valley, after she'd realized the ashes had once been people.

"Only a few scouting factions and maybe a handful of other units. Most of our army is out in the field. Jev says it's only a matter of time before they pull 'volunteers' out of their normal jobs and put swords in their hands. He says it's happened before, during the War of the Burning Valley. A lot of them didn't come home either." Rigger's sorrow was palpable.

Khiri's hand rose to Micah's grip, as it often did when she wanted the comfort of his presence. She hesitated, remembering the period of time in which she didn't have the ability to communicate with Micah, despite having the bow beside her. Who had Rigger lost to the war with Mytana?

The young engineer stopped talking, seemingly absorbed in his own thoughts. He absently flicked through the pages of his sketchbook, his eyes not really focusing on any particular point. Concern urged Khiri to reach out and pat his shoulder, but she wasn't sure Rigger really wanted to share his grief with a complete stranger.

Before she could decide, the rank, rotting smell of Flayer assaulted her nose and magic tickled at her ear tips. The hard glint in Kal's eyes assured her he sensed something too.

"I'm not sure if water based shields will be strong enough, but given this morning..." Kal raised an eyebrow, as though measuring the likelihood that Khiri would jump through his shields again. "I'll keep things flexible. After you, *laska*."

Khiri sprinted toward the source of the smell, keeping her eyes peeled for any Flayers lingering in the nearby shadows. It wasn't surprising to find herself at the door of Master Thomas Illesan's shop—the Flexible Helm. Though the reek of Flayers still clung to the brisk autumn breeze, there were no signs of life in the pink granite shop.

Creeping her way into the storefront, a growing sense of unease gurgled up from her stomach. It was the second time in less than a day she'd encountered a silent shop instead of the expected bustle of industry with students bending over workbenches, their fingers stained with dye.

Shaking her head, Khiri tried to snap herself out of the threatening moroseness. It wouldn't do to have her mind elsewhere when trouble started. As she began to enter the Flexible Helm, Kal placed a restraining hand on her shoulder.

"Use your senses, like we did in the Flayer fog," Kal instructed.

Khiri struggled to focus when the urge to rush in was pressing so firmly on her instincts, but she knew Kal's way was the safer option. She couldn't help anyone if she died doing something stupid. Expanding her magical perception as far as she could reach, she swept the workbenches and shelves, leaving no shadow of the shop untested.

Kal's power followed along behind her, reminding Khiri of her earliest solo hunts. Her father would tag along behind, watching to make sure she didn't stumble into danger, not even masking his presence from her.

Once they'd established the building was clear of Flayers, they walked in and Kal set a shield over the shop's walls.

Unlike Shielded Thoughts, the Flexible Helm had opened its shutters for the day's business. If the shop had been located elsewhere in the city, somewhere where the streets weren't deserted, maybe the staff would've been able to call for help. There were no groans coming from these bodies. Rigger stood frozen in the doorway, his lips quivering with unuttered grief. As Khiri approached the first body, the bile of unease reached up into her throat and she found herself fighting to keep down her breakfast. These weren't fighters or soldiers, out to defend their lives, homes, or loved ones on the battlefield; they were people about her age, learning about a craft. They had friends, families, dreams outside of this desecrated pink store. None of that mattered to them now. They were in a place beyond those dreams.

In the back of the store, a body with a master's knot verified Thomas Illesan's identity as one of the victims. A roster of his apprentices on Illesan's desk confirmed Khiri's suspicions there had been customers in the storefront at the time of the tragedy. Collapsing his shield, Kal wandered over to the sconced flits.

"Which of these will alert the guard to the scene?" he asked Rigger.

"...Red," the dwarf said. His lower lip wasn't trembling anymore. Instead, Rigger's expression had shifted into anger and determination.

Kal pulled out the red flit and tossed it into the sky.

"We should go," Khiri said. "We don't want to be here when the guard comes."

"My... I know a place nearby," Rigger suggested. "I'll want to pick up some things if I'm going with you."

"You aren't coming with us," Kal told him.

"How close is it?" Khiri asked, ignoring Kal's objection.

"He's not coming with us," Kal repeated.

"This way," Rigger said. "It's only a few blocks north and up a few levels."

Khiri fell into step next to the dwarf. It was hard to keep herself from running and she had to work even harder to restrain Rigger. Even though they had nothing to do with the deaths, strangers to the city would make excellent suspects if they were found hovering over corpses.

"WHY IS HE COMING WITH us?" Kal hissed a sigh out through clenched teeth.

"Because we could use someone that actually knows Eerilor," Khiri said. It was the third or fourth time the mage had asked the question since they'd left Rigger's tiny, one room apartment.

Ahead of them, Rigger toyed with his dagger. The knuckle guard unfolded and separated so the point of the blade could be used as a drawing compass when a catch was released. It had the potential to be a great asset when Rigger was struck by inspiration, but Khiri wondered if it wouldn't also be a liability in the hands of someone that didn't use a weapon very often.

Khiri wondered why the dwarf had been living alone. His one room had housed a bed, a stove and a privy closet. Very efficient. Very quiet. Very stark. There hadn't been the usual paraphernalia of a functioning home. No pots, no trinkets, no artwork or notes hung on the wall. Nothing. Even the smell seemed off. The room hadn't smelled much like Rigger. While gathering his meager possessions, Rigger had talked about how the sewer system worked in Taman. She hadn't objected to the subject, since it was another of the oddities of rune-tech she hadn't seen anywhere else, but she couldn't help feeling that Rigger was trying hard not to talk about his circumstances.

"He needs something to focus on," she sent, not wanting Rigger to overhear. *"Can't you tell he's lonely?"*

"Alright, I'll stop complaining. I can tell you've already adopted him... You trust far too easily," Kal said, sighing again for effect. His sardonic grin was creeping up at the corners of his mouth, though, so Khiri knew she'd convinced him.

"That's why you're still here," the elf shot back.

"You wound me deeply, *laska*." The mage cupped an overly dramatic hand over his heart. Despite his teasing, when his enigmatic eyes caught hers, a flush of warmth washed through her system. "What's our next destination?"

"Jev told us that two of the other names are close to Tenising—out on the western border—while Kivian Threshler was somewhere near Elmesh, which I think was...north?" Khiri squinted as she tried to remember if she'd ever seen an actual map of Eerilor. Her shoulders relaxed almost immediately as they exited the soldiers' district.

"Isn't that why you wanted to bring an Eerilorian?" Kal scratched his chin as they walked, trying to look as though it were a casual question.

"Good point," Khiri said. "You can talk to him about it while I talk to Master Vort about new gear."

Shielded Thoughts' shutters were still closed, but light showed through the awkwardly hanging door Rigger had popped off its hinges earlier in the day. Loud hammering sounds echoed into the street from inside the shop. Khiri pounded her fist against one of the shutters, not trusting the wounded door to survive the impact. In the middle of her third swing, Master Ian Vort admitted them into a partially-revived store.

"I had doubted whether you'd take me up on my offer," Vort said, his perpetual frown pulling into his beard. "But I set aside a few pieces I thought may be of interest to you."

Khiri waded into the pile that Vort had made for them, occasionally pulling out a piece for Kal or Rigger to try on. Rigger began helping Master Vort hammer up boards and repair sections of floor and workbenches that had been chipped or cracked. The Odlesk mage knelt at the door. He said nothing, but his staff began to glow, indicating that enchantments were probably involved.

Most of the equipment Khiri had piled next to the mage went back to the benches untested. "Armor tends to inhibit my connection to magical forces. I may be able to ignore a very sleek set of bracers, but never a breast plate. It dampens my energy too much."

"I always thought the whole no armor thing was because mages worked out their minds and not their bodies," Rigger snorted.

Kal gave Rigger a pointed look and poked the young dwarf in his paunchy belly as he ambled by. Rigger scowled, but didn't retaliate enough for Kal's liking. The mage asked, "Just who do you think crafts those runes you like to fiddle with?"

"I don't fiddle," Rigger argued. Khiri felt like she was missing something about this byplay. Rigger acted more fond of Kal after the chiding. He even offered the mage a swig from the water bucket when he went to fill it from the nearby city fountain.

When they emerged from Shielded Thoughts, Khiri had a complete set of new armor: a walnut brown chest plate with gold etching around the collar and kilted sleeves, black braided pants that were lined with rabbit fur—nice and warm, good for traveling now that the breath of winter was closing in—and matching bracers and boots embossed with oak leaves. She even came away with a new bow sheath for Micah and a fur-lined cloak that only hung down to her elbows.

Kal had accepted a long midnight cloak of his own and a pair of gloves. Rigger refused to accept anything from Master Vort unless he was allowed to pay, protesting his part in the rescue hadn't been an act of heroism but accidental vandalism.

"I'm really not comfortable being rewarded for being accident prone," he told Master Vort, sheepishly rubbing his hands together. Even so, the dwarf walked away with a masterwork buckler, boots, and a dagger sheath for his weapon for much less than they probably cost a normal customer.

"How far is Elmesh from Tenising?" Khiri asked.

"Never been, myself," Rigger said. "But my... I've heard that it's maybe a week between the two. Elmesh isn't too far away from here though. Traders make the trek from there to Taman pretty regular. It's three, maybe four, days to the northeast."

Checking the position of the sun, Khiri estimated that they could make maybe a quarter day's travel before the light gave out on them.

"Time to get going," she said.

25

~Estan~

A LEADEN LUMP SETTLED in Estan's gut as he descended the steps into The Dusk and Dawn, the current seat of the Thieves' Court. It was his first time seeing Ysinda since Corianne had educated him on the darker side of guild matters. Also, it would be his first time seeing Ysinda in an official capacity. Estan would have preferred to continue seeing her at the Talon Acre, with its relaxed atmosphere and easy rules. Even with Tak's protection, Dewin couldn't join him here. But Resmine could. He was insanely grateful to have his bond-sister back, watching his flanks as they descended the darkened staircase.

"Nice place," she said. "Cozy."

Estan fought against the smirk pulling his lips out of his carefully-arranged serious expression. He knew he could look dangerous, as long as he didn't smile. Dewin had told them dangerous was a good thing to be in the Court.

The Dusk and Dawn was divided into two different levels. The ground floor was home to the normal combination taproom and pub, offering simple foods and a variety of ales, lagers and cider, depending on what was available in the market; whereas the lower level was behind a door disguised as a broom closet. Because they were expected, the door swung open after Estan rapped with his knuckles only once.

Just past the door, two holes had been carved out of the wall with just enough room for a bear of a man and a woman about Khiri's size to watch people as they edged down the stairs. "Mind yer step, love," the woman purred. "Wouldn't want ya to take a tumble."

Estan fought the urge to stare as he recognized her as an elf. Short silver hair, sky blue eyes, and pointed ears. Tattoos marked her forehead and left eye, with two bars in black raked across them. An exile, condemned for murder. Despite her counterpart's size, her gaze sent shivers down Estan's spine. He could feel the exile's eyes burning into his shoulders as he continued into the pit.

Limestone lined the walls and floor, reminding Estan uncomfortably of the room where he'd left Corianne with a prisoner. Stained cushions were strewn about the floor and stacked on benches surrounding a long table in the center of the pit. Estan couldn't bring himself to think of the lower level as a room. Reddish-purple splotches clung to every surface. Either a lot of wine or a lot of blood had been spilled in this place.

Though there were quite a few thieves and vagabonds leaning against the soiled walls and draped across the benches, the knight was under the impression there were many guild members absent. Evic acknowledged Estan and Resmine with a slight nod, but didn't push off of the wall to join or greet them. The normally-friendly thief's discretion made the knot in Estan's throat double in size.

At the far end of the pit, there was a dais holding a grand, backless chair. Estan got the impression the Throne of Thieves had been chosen to remind the current monarch of the guild there was no such thing as safety. It was a chair that left the leader open to backstabs. Ysinda looked completely at home as she lounged with one arm over one of the massive armrests and one foot tucked up underneath her.

Ysinda's green eyes and honey gold hair were no less bright in this den than they had been in the friendly tavern light of the Talon Acre, but here her face was cold. The lips that had quirked so warmly in her childhood home carried no such smiles in the Court. Her demeanor, which had been relaxed on their prior meeting, was one of practiced poise and quiet menace. Estan expected the change to quench his passion, but when their eyes met desire quickened his blood as thoroughly as it had on their previous meeting.

His quest for Ysinda hadn't progressed much since the incident outside of the Talon Acre. Dewin and Tak were still out looking into... Something. Estan wished he had more to report, but it was unlikely Ysinda summoned him here for a briefing. He hadn't the slightest what else this meeting could be, though. It seemed out of line with her earlier desire for someone unconnected to the Court to be her investigator.

"Not many outside of the Court are ever called here," Ysinda said. The smooth arc of one golden eyebrow lifted as though she were issuing a challenge to someone, anyone, to contradict her. "Only those that have proven themselves to be a Friend to the Court can be offered the invitation, and even then... Well, we're not exactly a hospitable bunch."

A rough murmur of chuckles ran through the onlookers.

"Do you accept responsibility for the events at the Talon Acre yesterday?" Ysinda asked, seeming almost bored. Estan wished he knew what was going on in her head. Her voice betrayed nothing of her motives.

"Possibly," he said. "Are you referring to the mob's actions or the efforts to drive them away?"

"And the other attacks on my people? Have you any insight?" The Queen leaned forward in her makeshift throne. Shifting her attention to her fingernails, she began to study them with a feigned interest. When she pulled out a knife and began digging at the imagined dirt, Estan realized she was warning him. Any wrong moves and she would be forced to act. Something was very wrong in the Court.

"What other attacks?" Estan asked. "I hadn't heard anything since I left Corianne with the big fellow that was heading the crowd outside Talon Acre. She was about to interrogate him in one of your safe houses, and she told me to go. I was patching up the tavern with Ren all night."

"My lieutenant never made it back." Ysinda dropped the news like a brick over Estan's head. "The last anyone saw of her was when she ducked off with you and the captive."

His legs buckled underneath him. Despite the danger of showing weakness in a den of snakes, Estan fell to his knees. Resmine was at his side in an instant, hauling him back to his feet. The knight was still having trouble standing when he felt the pit's atmosphere change. Though he had just had the wind knocked out of him, the edge of danger had dulled with his reaction. Evic stood on his other side, clapping a steadying hand on the knight's shoulder.

"I do believe he's innocence itself, highness," the thief said. "No charlatan would dare eat the dirt in here; they all know where it's been."

"Do any here still doubt him?" Ysinda asked.

No one in the room said anything, though the man Corianne had referred to as Dagan the previous day was glaring at Estan with such loathing, the knight held no illusions about their eventual friendship. "But what of Corianne? Are we going to go find her? What might have happened..." he sputtered.

"Corianne came wanderin' home fit as a raven what's snatched a scrap of tin," Evic assured him. "She were testin' you. Seein' if you were a right fine love or just full of piss."

Shaking his head, Estan looked at Evic and then up at Ysinda on her throne. "I don't understand."

She gave him a cool smile, though he could see warmth in her eyes. This was part of what Corianne had tried to warn him about. The warm woman that had spent an evening with him inhabited the same existence as the mocking and aloof Queen. Ysinda wore her title the way he had once worn his Knight of the Protective Hand armor; it stifled as much as it defined. Little wonder he felt a kinship with her. But Corianne's point wasn't without merit.

"We had to know we could trust you. Half of my Court is gone today. Those that remain, are my loyal subjects. Those that left us, we will strike down. Your task is no longer secret," Ysinda told him. "Would you swear that you are a true friend of this Court?"

"I would," Estan replied. Resmine, still holding his arm, squeezed a warning at his elbow, but he didn't understand what she was worried about.

"Are you an alley of sympathetic nobles?" Ysinda inquired. Her eyes, still revealing hidden warmth now held a thread of eagerness. The knife she'd pulled out as a warning was being used to dig a hole in the arm of her throne as she balanced her palm against the butt of the pommel.

"Not openly, but I do have an understanding with someone," Estan answered. He tried to pull his arm out of Resmine's grip, but she was latched on as though her fingers had become cat claws. She wanted him to stop answering Ysinda's questions, but he couldn't understand why. The immediate threat had passed. Though Dagan's dislike of the knight would have to be dealt with at some point, Estan didn't think anything would be resolved by refusing to answer Ysinda's questions.

Raising her gaze from Estan to the rogues and thieves scattered about the pit, Ysinda gave them a wry grin. "Very well put, no? He's passed the test of loyalty, he's sworn the oath, and he's allied with those that would benefit our cause. I hereby decree that Friend Estan is given the title of Queen's Consort and granted all the rank and privileges due him until such time as he can no longer... *perform*... his duties."

Estan fought the urge to fall to his knees again. If Corianne's disappearance, false as it was, had been a punch in the gut, this sudden betrothal to Ysinda left him in a river of rushing water. He didn't even remember stepping into the stream, though apparently Resmine had sensed it coming. Maybe it was some sort of Thieves' Guild thing that she and Dewin had discussed, or maybe Resmine had read the situation better than he had.

Either way, Estan had been proclaimed Consort in a guild he'd never wanted to join.

"As custom dictates–" Ysinda stood as she spoke, holding out a hand to Estan. "–I'll be taking my new consort into the royal quarters. We'll make things... *official*." The way her tongue licked her teeth as she rounded off the last letter of *official* almost pushed Estan's annoyance out of his head. He followed her through a hidden door, the seams of which were worked into the limestone behind her throne.

Estan had assumed that there would only be one stuffy room behind the wall of the pit. Instead, he found himself in a corridor with two cot rooms branching off to the right and left.

"I suppose I should give you the tour, you being a ranking member now and all," Ysinda grinned. Her manners had changed now that they were alone. She seemed friendly and flirtatious, more like the Ysinda he'd met in the Talon Acre Inn. "This is where the Court makes berth when the guard is riled or if we feel our homes and hideynooks are compromised. Off to the left, we even have a kitchen and a fully equipped bath chamber. No one wants to be stuck down here for days on end with fifty sweaty, ale-soaked rogues. Off to the right, there's two emergency exits—both are one way—and my personal quarters."

Dragging him down the right hand passage, Ysinda paused next to her door and pulled a rune out of her pouch. Placing it next to a piece of the wall that looked just like the rest of the limestone, a thin panel slid open, revealing three colored stones that she touched in some sort of key pattern. The panel slid shut and a second slot appeared. Ysinda slid her knife in up to the hilt and gave it a quarter turn. Her door popped open with a small hiss, as though a spell had just released its energy. She yanked Estan inside with a playful grin and leaned against the door until it clicked shut.

Before Estan could push any of his questions past his lips, she clapped a hand over his mouth and gave a slight shake of her head. She spoke loud enough to be overheard, though still within reasonable conversational volume. "It's nice to finally have you here, lover."

She tilted her head and used her eyes to indicate that they could move farther into the royal chambers of the Thieves' Guild. Despite knowing the Guild was as old as Jarelton itself, Estan was impressed. There was no limestone visible in the Queen's home. The walls were lined with warm wooden panels, and shelves were sunken into every available surface. An odd assortment of impressive weaponry and armor was displayed along with glass baubles and stuffed toys. Picking up a stuffed horse which looked a lot like a fat, fluffy version of Catapult, Estan cocked an eyebrow at the Queen of Thieves.

"What?" She mock-pouted, taking the horse away and placing it back amongst its friends: a glass dog and a frighteningly large mace engraved with the name *Nutcracker*. "I like cute. And deadly. Sometimes together."

As he perused the collection of daggers, glass flowers, swords, stuffed cats, books and other oddities, Estan felt his mind touch on Khiri. He couldn't help but wonder if she would like these rooms, gather a similar collection of baubles, get along with Ysinda. It was the first time he had given her more than a passing thought since he had met the Queen of Thieves. Odd how his infatuation with Khiri had evaporated after such a short time. He'd really thought himself to be in love. This thing between him and Ysinda wasn't love. Not yet. Maybe not ever. But he was powerfully attracted to her, and it seemed to be mutual.

He finally made it past the shelves and into the next room. Estan found himself standing in a small kitchen with glazed mugs of sunset pink, teal-rimmed white, and amber hanging from pegs along one wall. The cupboards and pantry were white-washed, practically glowing in the steady light of several discrete skylight vents. In the dim atmosphere of the pit, Estan had nearly forgotten it was still morning. Ysinda picked up a fire rune from a stack next to the stove, whispered the activation word and placed it under a copper tea kettle.

"I never get to drink this in public, but since you're my Consort, you get to find out my biggest weakness in the whole of Arra is peppermint tea," Ysinda grinned.

"Peppermint tea, cherry cobbler, cute things, all culminating into the Queen of Thieves," the knight said. "You're a complex woman, Ysinda."

He pulled a ladder backed chair out from the round polished cherry table in the center of the kitchen. The sound of the legs scraping across the floor boards seemed oddly homey. If he could forget the Court was waiting outside, Estan could see himself living in these quarters with Ysinda in a normal way, like Ren and Adela running their inn. Watching Ysinda move around her kitchen, it was as though he had momentarily stepped into a world where he didn't have to worry about the return of Irrellian Thornne, and she didn't have to worry about Rothan Haud usurping her guild.

"Lemon, cream, sugar?" she asked as she pulled down a pink mug and an amber one. Neither mug clinked as they were set down, a gentle reminder the woman in front of him was a creature of stealth. It was almost a relief to hear the hot water trickling into the cups. "I didn't dream about this life as a child, you know. When Ren and Adela took me in, I really thought I wouldn't go back to the streets."

"Cream, please." Estan accepted his cup, his fingers brushing against Ysinda's. Her gaze was soft, unfocussed. He'd seen that far away look before, when they had spoken in the Talon Acre. "What happened?"

"It hardly matters now," Ysinda said, pushing away her thoughts and turning her attention on him. She handed him a mossy green jug and set a matching sugar bowl on the table, where she began spooning lumps into her own tea. "This is what I chose. I can't waste time with regrets when my kingdom's on the line."

"So what's this really about?" Estan asked. "I'm getting the impression bedding me wasn't your motivation for declaring me your consort." He poured a touch of cream into the minty warm liquid. Clouds billowed in his cup.

"Maybe not my sole motivation, but don't dismiss the notion." Ysinda gave him a playful half-smile and leaned toward him over the table. She touched a finger to the front of his mail shirt and traced it up until she was drawing a line over his neck. A shudder of desire coursed through him, reflecting in her beryl eyes. "I'm used to getting what I want, you know."

"I'm starting to get that..." Estan managed, though his voice was a bit rough.

She eased back in her chair holding the cream jug, she grinned slyly at him from behind her honey blonde bangs as they drifted over her forehead. "Good."

Her ease melted into seriousness as she poured cream into her tea. "As for what this arrangement is really about... The old plan of secrecy and investigation is out. We found out Rothan Haud's background, and who he works for."

"And that made no difference to your people?" Estan asked.

"I overestimated the grand tradition of our honorable organization," she frowned. "It's bad, Estan. Talon Acre was not the only tavern they hit. People have died. My people and the innocent. Marks are being dropped in alleys as we speak and aside from your friend Orin, outsiders don't know my people aren't responsible."

Estan swallowed a large gulp of his tea. What should've been warm and refreshing tasted sour in his throat. "Who–"

"Rothan Haud is apparently a high ranking assassin," Ysinda said. "The Venom Guild wants my city."

26

~Khiri~

CHARGING IN WITH A relatively knife-shaped stick, Khiri aimed for the cleft between Rigger's neck and shoulder. The dwarf was not a fighter, despite his fancy dagger. After the first sparring match on the road, Khiri had gone out into the forest and made two practice daggers out of fallen branches that were roughly the right size and shape. Kal had protested, telling her that the practice sessions were wasted on the boy. In one match, Rigger nearly stabbed himself in the foot as he fumbled drawing his blade from its new sheath. The young engineer also had a habit of turning his back to his opponent when he got flustered.

Rigger rewarded her by meeting her attack with a shaky-if-effective block. She'd only been teaching him for two days, but he was showing a great deal of improvement. Every time they broke for a rest or to set up camp, he would practice the basic movements Khiri had shown him. Once the sun peeked over the horizon, they would set up a sparring ring while Kal monitored the camp boundaries. Rigger wasn't a natural fighter, but through dedication and practice, Khiri thought he could become an adequate one.

"Adjust your grip," she advised, breaking away. With a hop to his right, she brought her practice blade into his guard and poked him lightly in the ribs, "And watch your elbows. If you keep them in, I'll hit that buckler of yours instead of your vitals."

Taking a step back, Rigger panted. Sweat was dripping down his forehead. "I don't understand how you make this look so easy," he grumbled. "Don't you ever need a rest?"

Khiri shrugged and tossed the practice blade to Kal, who stuck it in their shared pack. Aside from the practice blades, it held some dried fruit, two loaves of rye, a gloriously sharp head of cheese, a long rope and two thin, waxed blankets. Between Kal's spells and Rigger's runes, their campsites remained warm and dry despite the frosty mornings. Khiri supplemented their food supply with fat squirrels and the occasional unlucky pheasant. She wouldn't hunt big game on such a short journey.

"I've had a lot of practice," Khiri said. "If you wish to return to your old life, you still have the option. We can part ways in Elmesh and you can find a trader to escort you back, or wait for us to come through again."

"No," Rigger shook his head. "I don't want to sit around in my... In the..."

For a moment, Khiri thought Riggere was about to close up again, the way he did any time he came close to revealing something personal. Instead it all poured out of the young dwarf in a flood. "It was my brother's apartment I was living in. My mother, a big war hero in our family, wanted him to follow in her footsteps. She retired when she met my pa because he wanted a quiet life and during the Burning Valley, she'd lost use of her left arm to a Flayer attack. But retirement never set right on her, so she pushed Liev into the regiments as soon as he was of age. Just a few weeks ago, we got word... Liev died his first time on the lines. My mother, she went quiet for a day or two, and then she started in on me with all the stuff she used to say to him. 'Got to uphold the family honor' and 'It's part of your heritage.' Not a word of remorse, no visible grief... Just on to the next son, regardless of any dreams I already had, or of anything I was working toward."

Taking a deep breath, Rigger shut his eyes as though he could erase the past if he just concentrated hard enough.

"I left the day I came back from my apprenticeship to find that my ma had my master and an officer waiting for me to change over my papers from engineering to enforcement without even consulting me. The only sticking point was Eerilorian law doesn't let parents sign contracts for those within three years of majority. Liev had been protecting me from her most of his life, and I hadn't even known about it," Rigger sighed. "When I refused to sign the contract, my ma kicked me out. Liev gave me a key to his place before he got sent to the front. He probably knew what my ma would do better than I did. I got a job with Jev because my old master wouldn't take me back. Said he didn't want ungrateful sons rejected from their own families muddying up his workshops."

Khiri took one of Rigger's callused hands in hers and squeezed. "I'm sorry you lost your brother. I know how important it is to have one watching over you."

Micah's presence in her mind was comforting but he stayed silent. In this moment, they were both aware of the emptiness caused by his physical absence.

"That's all very unfortunate, but I don't understand why that made you want to come with us," Kal stood, shouldering the pack. The mage was still unhappy about Rigger's presence, though he was more accepting when Rigger produced a new sketch. Then Kal would spend hours with the dwarf, discussing the value of one rune over another and placement of energy lines. "You certainly aren't going to fulfill your ambitions out here on the road. The things Khiri has been going out of her way to teach you... Aren't they more in keeping with what your mother wanted for you?"

"I can't go back," Rigger said. "No engineer in Taman will take me."

Kal exchanged a look with Khiri. She suspected he had other motives for trying to push the dwarf away, but he was making a lot of sense, too. Everyone else she'd traveled with had been aware of the danger, or driven into her party by something more dangerous than overzealous matriarchs.

"What if we found you a new apprenticeship in Elmesh or Tenising?" she asked.

"What about finding the Flayers? I don't want to distract the two of you," Rigger protested.

Khiri picked Micah up from where she had perched him for the sparring match and slung him on her back, double checking the buckles on the sheath. It was a mark of how nervous she was about the conversation. Every piece of her equipment was an extension of her body once she'd hung it in place. Micah, doubly so. He could tell her if she'd missed a strap.

"We don't have a lot of time between the investigation and the solstice," Kal reminded her. "But I follow you in this, *laska*."

Prior to leaving the Life Trees, she hadn't had a lot of people enter and exit her life. Micah had been her Destined and her best friend. Her mother and father were gone for a few days at a time with hunting or trading. Nothing had prepared her for the constant ins and outs of the world.

"Breathe, Khiri," Micah said. *"Think of it as his Name Breathing. We would've moved on after your ceremony. It's a coming of age tradition. He's got to move on."*

"I hate it when you make sense," Khiri sighed.

Falling into step next to the dwarf, Khiri gave him a one armed hug. "We'll get you a new master for you to finish out your apprenticeship, even if I have to twist their arm off to convince them."

ELMESH WAS A SMALL town, by Eerilorian standards, meaning that it was smaller than Jarelton but far larger than Harish or Illesdale. Taman was much prettier. Walking into Elmesh, Khiri almost thought she was back in Mytana. Two differences made it obvious she was still over the border: the number of the dwarves and the presence of rune lamps. The streets were cobbled, and so were the buildings. Pebbles and dust lined the edges of the streets.

"Is Taman the capital because it's prettier or is it prettier because it's the capital?" Khiri mused, not really expecting an answer.

"Oh! You mean the ancestral stoneways? Taman was where the dwarven ancestors returned to the Stone, back when my people still did that. Something about our rune craft and modernizing the lamps and sewage systems interfered with Arra's magics though and now we follow the human ash scattering rituals." Rigger didn't seem bothered by the fact his people had effectively lost access to their ancestors.

Imagining the Life Trees abandoned for the sake of advancement sent chills down Khiri's spine. It would be like permanent exile for all the clans. No, worse. Even exiles returned to Arra in some form. Micah had sprouted into a bow, but he was still Lifewood. Did the human gods look after the dwarves?

Those that ask us to, Imyn said. The voice of the goddess nearly made Khiri jump. It had been so long since Imyn had last spoken, Khiri'd nearly forgotten the goddess was within her. Nearly.

"Khiri, over there," Kal pointed. "Isn't that our destination?"

Khiri followed the line of Kal's finger with her eyes and felt a sinking feeling in the pit of her stomach. "Oh, no..."

The shop was boarded up, from the large windows under their copper awnings to the large, splintered oak door. There was an official notice pinned over the boards, stamped with a wax seal. Moving as quickly as she could, Khiri had to restrain herself from yanking the parchment off of the building.

"'Attention Citizens: Due to the tragic incident at this site, this building is barred from public access until the official investigation has been closed. Upon such a time as it has reopened, all properties previously held by Master Kivian Threshler will be relinquished to resolve any outstanding debts. Anyone with knowledge pertaining to the investigation is welcome to bring it to the office of the guard between sunrise and sunset. Sergeant Kari Peplar,'" Khiri read. "This is not good. Ullen wants us to do this as unofficially as possible. We can't just go talk to the guard."

Glancing up and down the street, Kal touched the boards and gave them a test yank. He then tapped on the door, pressed against it and felt along the edges. "Swings inward. If we remove the bottom board, you and I can sneak in underneath," he said. "Sneaking into places is one of the few things I was good at in my last profession."

"What were you before?" Rigger asked.

Kal cleared his throat and Khiri pretended not to hear the question. She tugged on the bottom plank, wishing she'd picked out her own pair of gloves. Dwarves and humans never seemed to have the same sensitivity to wood-crafting as her people; which made sense, given that humans had their gods and dwarves were people of the stone. Or, they had been. Ullen still swore by it, so maybe they were both of stone and gods? Thoughts for another time. The plank felt as though it had been harvested in pain. Its wood was too fresh for the timber to have settled into its death. A sharp snap echoed down the street as it popped out of place.

Rumbling through a spell, Khiri noticed Kal's staff remained dark and lifeless. She raised a questioning eyebrow at the mage as the door swung quietly inward.

"I did study on my own before I acquired this magnificent arcane tool," Kal reminded her. "Granted, I'm stronger now. I used to require components to do something this small."

"Rigger, if someone comes, don't wait for us. Just get out of here," Khiri said.

"But I–" Rigger protested. "–I thought I was making progress. You don't trust me to watch your back?"

"It's nothing to do with how much I trust you," Khiri said. She waved Kal to duck into the store before her. "If we get caught here, we may get arrested. I promised you I'd do everything I could to get you an apprenticeship. I can't do that if they catch you breaking in with us."

Concern wrinkled Rigger's dark brows into almost a solid line. He opened his mouth to argue, but Khiri cut him off. "Be our lookout. If we get caught, we'll need an escape. I'm counting on you."

Drawing himself up, Rigger gave her a tight nod. She still didn't know if he'd run if he saw someone from the guard coming, but she trusted Rigger to do what he felt was best. She sent a small prayer to the spirits that nothing requiring the young engineer to risk his dream would happen while he was helping them out. She knew what it was like to lose dreams of the future. Khiri kept her eyes on him until she was forced to duck into the door.

Once inside the storefront, Khiri felt like she was going to be ill. It took all she had to close the door behind her instead of leaving it open to let fresh air in. Flayer musk saturated the air like they had been stuck in a stove and been made to sweat in their own foul stench for several days. Copper threaded its way through the pungent cloying air and raked itself through her lungs. She'd seen two of these attacks already, but this one was the worst yet.

"Spirits," she uttered. "Why is it so bad?"

Breathing through his sleeve, Kal offered her a shrug before he turned to begin looking over his side of the room.

Master Kivian Threshler's shop was coated in blood. Merchandise, floor, workbenches. Every surface held blood and old bits of body that hadn't been large enough for the burial crews to worry about. Though it seemed pretty obvious the attack was the same as the other incidents, they had to be sure before they left town. A good tracker didn't assume one set of prints only meant one animal, after all.

By the time she met Kal in the office, the mage had already had time to rummage through the armor maker's desk drawers. The Odlesk was wearing a deep scowl of consternation.

"What's wrong?" she asked.

"All of the papers are missing," Kal said. "That could mean that the guards investigating this mess didn't want to peruse the stack in this funk, or..."

"Or this was all staged," Khiri finished the thought. "Great, that means that we have to visit the guard office anyway. Have you broken into one of those before?"

Before Kal could answer, there were the sounds of a scuffle from outside and the cracking boom of a thunder rune exploding. Khiri and Kal both dropped behind the desk, readying their weapons automatically.

"Guard!" Khiri heard Rigger call from the door, and then the sound of his pelting feet. She only had moments to be relieved that he had taken her advice before the sound of planks breaking apart and the door slammed into the wall.

A tall human woman of significant girth strode into the room like she owned it. Her nose was hooked and crooked, as though it had been broken many times in the past, and her hair hung down her back in long, brown, curled braids. Her uniform was crisp. Not a single stitch dared to break its lines. Hazel eyes darted over the main room, searching for alterations to the crime scene. If Khiri and Kal had been looters, she would have spotted them in those first few seconds.

"Camouflage?" Khiri asked Kal silently. They only had a few seconds in which to disappear from her sight, or she would notice that the desk had some extra legs.

"Wouldn't work," Kal replied. *"She would feel a spell working. I've already felt her probing."*

Their time was up. The guardswoman was walking toward them, full of confidence and resolve. "Drop your weapons and come out with your hands above your heads!" she demanded. "I've got guards at every exit and archers at my side. Any attempt to resist can and will result in your death. I do *not* tolerate the looting of the dead in my town, and I do *not* tolerate murders. Being in this building where someone already flouted my jurisdiction puts me in a *very* bad mood."

Khiri wasn't about to shoot the commander for doing her job. She dropped her dagger and hoped they wouldn't take Micah strapped to her back as a threat. Following her lead, Kal let his staff slip from his fingers. It landed with a hard clack on the cobbled floor.

"They can't see me unless I allow it, as long as you don't draw me," Micah assured her. *"I have some abilities similar to the Life Trees. I gave my life to protect you. Can't do that unless I'm with you."*

A wave of relief swept through her. She wouldn't be defenseless.

"At least we'll be well guarded," Kal's mental voice was dripping with his usual brand of humor. *"Imprisonment means you get your rest."*

27

~Estan~

MINTY FIRE CLUNG TO Estan's lips as Ysinda claimed his mouth. He couldn't remember when the conversation had melted into passionate playtime. The last few hours were a blur of desire, need, and euphoric release.

"What? Again?" Estan laughed. "I might be able to manage in a minute or so."

Ysinda pouted playfully and traced the lines of Estan's muscles as she snuggled against him. "Maybe I should've found a lover with more stamina."

"Perhaps," Estan said, running a finger along her side. "If I haven't lived up to my duties, I suppose you could dismiss me."

"It's a possibility. But I think you earned a few days reprieve with that one thing. I've never encountered *that* before," Ysinda murmured, a dreamy smile drifted across her lips.

Estan was glad the room was getting darker as day slid into evening. It made it easier to hide his blush. The particular thing Ysinda was referring to had been a suggestion from Taymahr. In the heat of the moment, Estan hadn't thought much about it. Basking in the aftermath of successful love making, remembering that moment was extremely embarrassing.

Recalling one moment led his thoughts to another. Relief rushed through him again as Estan remembered yet another thing to add to his list of boneheaded decisions. He'd asked about potential pregnancy after they'd lain together the first time. When Ysinda pointed out the protective enchantments carved into her bed frame, Estan had nearly cried. He couldn't imagine raising a child within a thieves' den.

Perhaps that didn't bode well for how long this union would ultimately last.

Between his embarrassment and the cloud of doubt boiling up in his thoughts, Estan suddenly found he was no longer in a love making mood. He rolled to the side of Ysinda's bed and started looking for his trousers.

"Leaving so soon, Consort?" Ysinda asked. "By my reckoning, we still have a few more hours before anyone expects us to come up for air."

"I'd love to do that several more times," Estan told his lover. He wasn't lying. She was a beautiful woman and her touch drove him absolutely wild. For as long as this thing between them lasted, he wanted to stay the course. Other things weighed on him though, and he was first and foremost a creature of duty. "But if what you said about Arad Rhidel being the man behind your guild's trouble is true, I think I need to check in with Treag."

Ysinda made a face of disgust, and rolled out of the bed. "Alright, you have a point. But if anyone asks, I kicked you out for skunk breath and told you to come back later."

They got dressed together in mostly amicable silence; handing each other discarded boots, an assortment of belts, and other gear Estan couldn't remember shedding in the early rounds of kissing and petting. Once Estan was fully dressed, he was ready to set out. Hesitating, he suddenly wasn't sure what Ysinda expected of him as her Consort. Was this like a marriage? Did she think he was supposed to move in with her?

"Should I return here after I see Treag?"

Ysinda considered the question for several heartbeats longer than Estan liked. He couldn't tell if she was angry with him for asking or simply measuring all her options. "Best if you don't come back tonight I think. I have other matters to look after as well, while people think I'm busy."

Leading Estan through a back entrance to her quarters, she did give him a keyrune and instructed him on how to locate the door again. "You are my Consort. I trust you not to abuse this knowledge."

One last kiss and his thief queen vanished into the shadows. Estan turned toward the street and made his way to The Legend and The Knave, hoping Orin Treag would be there.

The first night Estan had spent in The Legend and The Knave's taproom, things hadn't been quiet. It had fluctuated between less rowdy and more rowdy, with varying levels of rowdiness in between. Things were very quiet as Estan strode into the tavern. One of the regulars that had happily suggested the home brew nodded in foggy recognition, but there was little cheer to be shared.

"What happened here?" Estan asked the bartender as he signaled for a pint.

"Owner's kids went out for a plate of iced cream. They didn't come back. Damned thieves are out of hand." The tender grimaced as he placed a foamy tankard in front of the knight. Estan felt the last of his bliss with Ysinda bleed into a puddle, much like the one being formed by the trails of foam his beer wept over the rim of his tankard.

"Why would thieves take children?" Estan asked, trying to wrap his head around this latest turn of events.

Remembering the scene outside of the Talon Acre, Estan's throat went dry. He had started this, fighting fire with the illusionary urchin trick. The Venom Guild were using children against the thieves for the same reasons he'd thought to disguise adults as kids. Make the enemy look like the kind of monster that moves against children.

Estan rubbed his eyebrows, remembering the last time he'd rushed into a fire like a moron. Maybe Taymahr should have left him scarred, as a reminder that he needed to think more before he acted. But how could he have predicted this outcome?

"Have there been any ransom demands or..." Estan let the question die off, unasked. He wanted to press the subject, to find out as much as he could and solve things. The burden of guilt was already heavy on his shoulders.

"No bodies," the bartender said, answering the question Estan hadn't asked. "Almost worse, not knowing."

Nodding absently, Estan removed himself to one of the nearby tables. Very few people were ordering food, so even the table near the kitchen was much more somber than his previous visit. Even when Orin Treag arrived, there was little in the way of greetings being called.

For the first few minutes of Ory's arrival, Estan wasn't sure the nobleman had seen him. As during Estan's previous visit, Orin worked his way through the subdued crowd: a word here, a comforting hand here, sad smiles shared across the room, and a sense that he belonged here, every inch the common man. Until he plopped himself down into the chair across from Estan, the knight thought he may have to go and fetch Orin from the crowd.

"I gather that it's not going well," Orin said without preamble. "Instead of things calming down, it seems that there is less safety than ever on these streets. I trust you heard about Van's kids..."

Giving a grim nod, Estan hid his face in his mug. Orin was too observant not to notice the ashen quality to the knight's features.

"So why are you here?" the nobleman asked. "I was pretty clear that I would not lead a city at war while facing another outside my walls."

"It's the Venom Guild," Estan said. "They are the ones behind the rift in the... behind the threat to Ysinda. We thought you'd want to be informed."

Orin Treag let out a deep sigh and rubbed his eyes.

"Which either means someone with deep pockets is funding them, or they've aligned themselves with the Gray Army," he surmised. "As much as I wanted to stay out of this, it stinks of one of my brother's or sister's schemes. If my father had ever bothered to rein either of them in, we'd already have a new Lord or Lady Ilamar. Instead, he's proclaimed that he's going to give the decision to my mother's council. If the decision isn't made by the winter solstice, the title will go to our oldest cousin... She's only sixteen and has never even been to Jarelton."

Estan's jaw dropped.

"Exactly. My mother's council members aren't stupid, but my brother and sister are not above making threats. If it gets out that they've been employing the Venom Guild and they've something to do with these kids getting abducted, the council will just let the time lapse. I've never been considered to be much of an asset because I've always kept myself out of the arena, so now I've got my work cut out for me. I can't let my cousin stand up there and try to claim the title with my siblings watching. She'd be dead in a week," Orin said, though it was more like he was visualizing the situation out loud than he was talking to Estan. Contemplating the shadows on the surface of his cider, Orin let the quiet creep over their table.

After a few moments, Orin's focus returned to Estan. His mouth was pressed into a grim line. "I'm going for it. All you have to do is help me stop them. I still want Ysinda to be working on the other side when this all shakes down."

NIGHT HAD FALLEN WHEN Estan finally returned to the Talon Acre Inn. He thought he might fall asleep on one of the tables before he could drag his weary body upstairs. Resmine and Dewin were playing a game of cards against Tak and Evic. Corianne was watching from the end of the table as her fingers twisted absently through a few sleight of hand exercises. Five runes, none, three, two, five again, one, none.

"The Consort's not going to stay the night with his Queen? What will people say?" Tak tsked at him as he wearily plodded forward.

"Don't pay him any mind, love," Dewin smiled. "The boys are just sore that Resmine and me are trouncing them right proper." She slammed her cards down with a flourish and a whoop. "And there's the sweep!"

"That's my girl," Resmine's eyes practically caressed Dewin. It struck Estan in that moment that his bond-sister was in love again. He'd known her fondness for Corianne and Evic's little sister had grown, but he hadn't really thought she'd let herself fall in love. Syara had been a friend of his, too. A very hard act to follow. Estan's estimation of Dewin, already high, rose a bit further. His heart felt a bit lighter as he took in the domestic scene.

It couldn't last. He had to tell them about the missing children.

Estan blew a breath out through gritted teeth. "I dropped in on Orin Treag. The owner of The Legend and The Knave has children missing. Apparently, it's happening all over Jarelton, missing kids. I think we started this."

Corianne's fingers stopped moving. She got to her feet without meeting anyone's eyes, practically running by the time she reached the door. No one else at the table moved, but Estan's shoulders felt mountains lighter. If anyone could find where the kids were being stashed, he was certain it was Corianne. Unlike him, she was also smart enough to come back for reinforcements once she did.

"I'm about to fall asleep on my feet. I hope the lot of you find some rest this evening."

He ascended the staircase to a chorus of muted good nights and sleep wells.

Placing his armor and equipment on the chair in the corner, Estan rolled into bed and was asleep within two breaths of his head settling onto his pillow. The knight didn't know how long he floated in the peaceful sea of nothingness, but he couldn't fight it when the dream seized him.

Walking into the clearing, Estan felt as though he should know this place, though he had never seen it before. Emerald grass grew before him, each blade the exact same height. Seven flowers, each a different species but all the same shade of holy blue, grew in a divine circle within a perfect copse of trees. It was too orderly, too precise to belong to the mortal plane. His familiarity was likely residual from sharing a body with his Lady Taymahr. The urge to explore was overwhelming, but Estan's legs wouldn't respond to his directives. His body deposited him behind one of the heavenly blooms.

Something tugged at his core, like when sweaty skin stuck to a leather saddle was pulled away but worse. It began somewhere in his chest and coursed through his extremities. It was painful, but not unbearable. At the peak of the sensation's intensity, Taymahr became a translucent being of light on the opposite side of her flower. Estan was reminded of the first time he'd heard Taymahr's voice. Despite never having seen her face before, he knew, beyond reason, this was his Goddess. Taymahr stood tall and regal, radiating her holiness. But it was more than that. She was Beautiful. Flawless. No mortal could compare. Her rich brown skin, almost ebony, glowed with golden highlights along her cheekbones, while her eyes glowed a rich, deep amber. Wearing a simple, white robe and a copper breastplate, her hair was a lovely festoon of finely crimped black hair with strands of gold and copper woven into occasional braids. At her side, a divine golden blade hung on a corded belt.

One by one, the other avatars arrived in the clearing and the other High Ones drifted into the circle where their translucent forms appeared—Khiri with Imyn, Kal with Shydan, Ullen and Tharothet, Dewin with Adari, Resmine and Locke, and Catapult standing behind Numyri. Estan knew each of the High Ones as he knew his own name, and if he had control of his own body, he would've fallen to his knees in awe.

"Time grows short," *Shydan stated into the silence. His eyes were as black and deep as the starlit heavens, while his skin was porcelain white. Rich auburn hair, nearly burgundy, rolled down his back in one long braid. The God of Death and Dreams held no weapon, but thin wisps of black smoke trailed from his fingers, almost blending with the darkness of his robe.* "If they do not succeed in opening the portal by Midwinter—"

"We have little choice," *Taymahr spoke.* "These were the ones that freed us. If we should trust in any mortal—"

"It was my avatar alone that freed us. She barely survived the encounter. What should we do if they fail?" *Imyn, her raven silk hair hanging past her golden tan shoulders in waves, raised an eyebrow at Taymahr. Goddess of Power and Change, Imyn wore a silver chest plate over a bronze robe that shimmered with moving shadows even when she stood still. She reached out for Shydan's hand, pulling toward the death god as much as she was able. It seemed as though the gods could not move far from the flowers they used to separate themselves from their avatars. Estan was hit with a momentary pang of jealousy as he noticed Khiri and Kal exchange a meaningful glance, but the memory of Ysinda in his arms consoled him. He shifted his focus back to the inner circle as Imyn continued.* "The heavens shake with the sound of war as it is."

"I say we trust in 'em as they would us, were they able." *Numyri reached back to scratch Catapult behind the ears. Her copper hand shimmered as it reached over the line created by the holy flowers, and she pulled it back with a sigh.*

Numyri and Adari could've been twins, both having thin, nearly elven, olive toned features. They both adorned themselves in thief-like garb and had silver tipped daggers strapped over their chests in bandoliers. The biggest difference between the two of them, visually, was Numyri's hair was a deep brown threaded with golden blonde highlights, while Adari's hair was copper with golden blonde highlights. Adari, Goddess of Greed and Guile, nodded her agreement with her sister, Goddess of Mirth and Mayhem.

With a melodramatic wave of one dark hand while the other rested on the hilt of a silver twin to Taymahr's blade, Locke, God of Battle and Beauty, gave the lot of them a smirk that included the avatars as well as his fellow deities. His bald head gleamed as though it had been oiled, and he wore the most magnificent set of silver plate armor Estan had ever witnessed. Even amongst his divine brethren, he was breath-taking. "I'll just give the reigns over my lovely Resmine, and she'll have it all sorted within the week. We clashed with the foul Thornne creature once and plummeted the fiend into darkness. Once we rise again, we'll just do the same as we did before, only this time we'll do it from our place in the Heavens as we should have last time."

Locke's cockiness seemed false, as though he were trying to lighten the mood. An unsubtle wink in Numyri's direction seemed to verify Estan's suspicions. The God of Battle and Beauty's gray eyes were troubled, despite his flair.

Tharothet, God of Seeking and Knowledge, watched the whole exchange with his scarred arms crossed against his chest. His hazel eyes missed nothing. No nuance was too small, no gesture too great. His skin held a weathered quality Estan had never imagined amongst the deities, but it made Tharothet no less striking than his peers. It seemed fitting that a god for wisdom seekers would show more age. Estan wondered how the God of Seeking and Knowledge had acquired his scars.

Did the other High Ones have hidden scars? Tharothet met Estan's eyes and a knowing smile curved the god's thin mouth. He said, "I feel that luck was with us in our choice of avatars. In the heart of each lies a great wealth of bravery, a good deal of curiosity, and much fortitude. As we set ourselves in the hands of mortals twenty years ago, let this lot prove their worth."

"The real question is: Does Irrellian know how pivotal opening the portal is? If he learns of our true goal in all of this, he'll stop at nothing to ensure the Keystone will fall," *Adari said. Her grimace was echoed on every High One's face. Estan felt his own features pulling downward, even though he was at a complete loss when they spoke of portals and Keystones. Prior to this meeting, he hadn't been aware the Heavens were at war.*

"Events are in motion that should propel us forward," *Imyn frowned.* "Let us hope they aim true."

28

~Irrellian~

IT WAS AS HE'D EXPECTED. The once proud generals of the Gray Army considered Irrellian to be little more than a childhood monster, used to keep their underlings in check. Ambition and power had robbed them of perspective. This was why he'd contracted with the Venom Guild before seeking out his former followers. Greed was reliable.

No matter how tried and true someone seemed, they almost always had a price.

Every rule had its exceptions. Irrellian's current task was to find the outlier. One of his underlings must still be a true follower of his original goals. He needed someone to face off against the forces Genovar Fortiva was building.

But he also knew that examples needed to be made.

Too many double-crosses. Even those aware that their master had returned to the world were plotting to take what he'd built two decades ago and squander it on their petty power plays. None of them remembered his ultimate ambition would make the current face of Arra obsolete.

A thousand factions of humans, elves, dwarves, his people, and others. Everyone united against a common foe: Flayers and Gods. That was his dream. To end the cycle of suffering. To make a better world. Not everyone would conquer death. But those that did would join him on the other side and make their march into the heavens. Mortals would become immortal and the gods would be cast to the surface. The Hell planes would run dry.

Telgan Korsborn sneared somewhere within the depths of Irrellian's soul. The demon thought very little of Irrellian's plans, but a deal was a deal. Irrellian had worded his wish too well. If there'd been a way to break free of the mage, Irrellian was certain his captive soul would've broken free a long, long time ago.

His other half's grumbling did lead Irrellian's thoughts toward the connection he'd forged with the Fortiva girl. Attempts to follow that bridge had met with a significant amount of resistance as of late. Other than being able to place her within the borders of Eerilor, Irrellian couldn't sense much. It did make him curious, though. What was she after in the dwarven kingdom? Perhaps it was worth a look.

Perhaps... Perhaps Irrellian felt the beginnings of a new plan. He would have to see what pieces were in play.

29

~Khiri~

WAKING FROM THE DREAM of the High Gods, Khiri's chest felt heavy. The gods said something about a portal and Midwinter, which was also when she and Kal had to be back in Taman with the results of their investigation. The timing seemed unlikely to be coincidental. Khiri had suspected the human gods had their own agenda. After all, Petora had warned Khiri about the war in the heavens well before she'd reached the Burning Valley.

Kal stirred in the cot below hers. She wasn't sure what the gods expected of them when both Khiri and the former assassin were imprisoned outside the city of Elmesh. Their cell, barely wide enough for Kal to lay down in, was enclosed with special bars that cut off the mage's link with his magic. For Khiri, who had lived most of her life without recognizing her magic, it was like her sense of smell had been cut off. It seemed much more dramatic for Kal. He'd screamed when they threw him into the small, barred room, flailing as though he didn't recognize Khiri when she had attempted to calm him.

The mage hadn't settled down until Khiri sent her thoughts to him, despite the magic restrictions. Khiri hadn't been certain it would work, but her contact with Micah hadn't been affected. It seemed to comfort Kal, so they'd talked long into the night using the unspoken words.

Now that he was awake, Khiri sent to him again. *"Was that real?"*

"No reason to believe otherwise," Kal still sounded shaky. He'd likened the absence of magic to having his eyes plucked from their sockets.

Khiri rolled off the upper bunk. There wasn't actually a mattress, but a skin stretched over an iron frame. It was anchored into the cobbles of the wall and provided no warmth at night.

Sitting on the edge of Kal's bed, Khiri took his hand in hers and stroked it with her thumb as he had done for her in the Eerilorian palace. His reflective skin was pallid and clammy, but his lips twitched in recognition. "I'll be alright, *laska*. It will pass."

"I hope so." She reached to his forehead and brushed a few strands of his gray hair from his pale forehead. "I don't like to see you in pain."

"So I *am* making progress." He tried to smile up at her, but he couldn't keep the pain out of his large golden eyes. "Good to know."

When they'd been arrested, Khiri thought Kal would get them out of it. The guards had gathered their weapons and walked them through town, toward what Khiri assumed would be their prison. Once they had entered the office of the guard, Khiri's dagger and Kal's staff had been tagged and placed in a large closet with several shelves of weapons—all tagged.

Sergeant Kari Peplar, acting captain of Elmesh's forces, had made a few scribbles on a parchment as she'd informed them they would be confined for two days before she bothered to question them.

"I've got my priorities and there's a war on. I'm sending you two to my holding cells on the outskirts. You shouldn't be able to cause any trouble there." She'd given Kal a pointed look with that parting remark.

Khiri and Kal found themselves in this building less than an hour later: six cells, all with magic blocking enchantments and thickened bars to deter the use of brute strength. Khiri was surprised the cell had a window, even though it was high enough on the wall that even Kal wouldn't have been able to reach it. Khiri could probably climb to it, but it was too thin to fit through. After she'd comforted Kal, Khiri had searched for any weakened metal, loose cobblestones, crumbled mortar, anything that might provide an easy escape. But the city guard of Elmesh kept its cells well. Nothing was out of place.

They'd fallen asleep the night before, despondent and frustrated. Now the trust of the High Ones weighed heavily on Khiri's weary shoulders as her gaze drifted over the dreary prison cells, uncertain of what to try next.

Something was intruding on her reflections. A sound, teetering on the edge of her awareness. It was tickling her hunting instincts, telling her the wind was changing. Letting go of Kal's hand, Khiri drew closer to the wall with the window. It was too high up for her to see anything, but she could hear through it just fine. An odd clomping sound was drifting through the city. It would pause for a few seconds, a few smaller shuffling clomps would follow, and then the hard clomping would begin again. Puzzled, she looked to Kal. He'd sat part way up and was resting on his elbows. The mage gave her a partial shrug.

As the clomps grew louder, Khiri climbed up to the small opening to see what was causing the clamor. Fresh air from outside the chilled iron bars slapped her in the face as she drew up to the window. It was a pleasant change from the stuffy air inside the prison. Even with the window, smells lingered.

What she saw was nothing like anything she'd ever encountered. A gigantic barrel-shaped boulder on two bird legs of wood, stone and metal tromped through the city as though it were an actual bird looking for food. It ran from one side of the city to the other, not even pausing when arrows bounced off its thick outer skin. Then it turned to face the prison. Though it had no head, Khiri sensed it had caught sight of her somehow. It charged toward the prison, its massive barrel bobbing up and down over the city' roofs as it loped closer.

"What is it?" Kal asked as Khiri jumped away from the window.

Without pausing to think, she flung herself over Kal, protecting his head with her body as the oddity smashed its way through the wall. Chunks of stone and mortal pelted her in the back. Dust washed over her face, threatening to choke her as it coated her lungs. The creation began pulling on the bars with its metal talons, demolishing their prison cell with a single minded focus. Khiri pulled Micah off of her back, ready to fight this thing to the death.

"Calm down, Khiri," Micah urged her. *"It's not a threat."*

A wind that was not a wind rushed past her ears, causing them to almost go numb with the force of magic building up behind her. The void caused by tossing a mage into a place that magic couldn't flow was filling with the force of a thunder clap. Kal screamed, his skin glowing through his thin silk shirt as his staff often did. Trusting Micah to be right about the bird-thing, Khiri rushed back to Kal's side and took his hand. She had no direction for this, but she grabbed onto the magic surging through him and yanked it into her as well. Calling out to Kal mentally, she urged him to hold onto her through the storm raging through them.

She felt his mental grip, weak at first, strengthen as they held each other through the powerful surge that was electricity and water, fire and wind, all and nothing. It ripped at their souls even as it coaxed them with promises. Through all of it, Khiri and Kal bobbed as though they were floating in a great, terrible ocean, uncertain they would ever see the sun again.

As it ebbed, Khiri became aware of a callused hand on her shoulder. She looked up into Rigger's deep brown eyes and sheepish smile.

"Sorry, I guess I forgot to factor in the backlash of the anti-magic runes when I made the thing," he said.

"When you made..." Khiri repeated, feeling as though she had just woken from a very tiring dream. She gazed past him, not quite understanding, until she saw the bird-thing's barrel torso leaning down over the hole in the wall. It was open, the lid laying at Rigger's feet as though he had tumbled over it instead of setting it down.

Kal groaned beside her as he sat up. He squeezed her hand in gratitude and then hoisted himself shakily to his feet. The mage closed his large, owl-like eyes and seemed to be going through some sort of calculations or catalogue as he regained his bearings. After a few moments, he seemed to be back to normal. For him.

"No permanent damage," Kal assured the dwarf with a lop-sided smile. "I just hope you thought of a less obvious way out than you used to get in."

"Not really less obvious," Rigger said. "But faster. We just need to get back into this thing's compartment."

In a rush of gratitude, Khiri wrapped her arms around Rigger in a hug she usually reserved for her parents or lifelong friends. The dwarf harrumphed a few times, waiting for her to decide to let go. When the elf leaned back, she saw that Rigger had gone a little pink around the edges. "No offense, Khiri, but you're really not my type."

She coughed a laugh back, but couldn't fight down the urge to grin. They still had to get out of the prison's remains before the guards caught up with Rigger's latest contraption, but she was giddy with the sense of being alive. Everything around her seemed to glow with renewed vigor.

"What is your type?" she asked.

"I don't really know," the dwarf admitted. This close to the bird-thing's torso, Khiri could see that it was actually large enough to fit all three of them, though it would require them to sit down and Kal's legs would be invading her personal space. She was glad that he wasn't wearing the robes he'd favored when they had first met.

"So what type am I?" she asked, more out of curiosity than any true desire to try and woo the dwarf. Between her soul name, Estan's attempted courtship and Kal's... Kal... she didn't really need another suitor. She pulled herself into the bird thing and settled into as small a ball as she could.

"Taken." Rigger left her to help Kal settle into place while he grabbed the lid.

Kal chuckled, sounding a bit hoarse. "I think I'm beginning to like you, Rigger."

"Don't you start," Rigger said.

With his two passengers loaded, Rigger squeezed himself into the front of his contraption and sealed the lid. Khiri had imagined they would be sitting in the dark as the thing bounced and trundled its way out of the city. Instead, large disks of polished quartz were worked into the sides like blisters. As they lifted into the air, the quartz pieced together a panoramic view of their surroundings. Runes of various colors and shapes glowed throughout the patchwork frame of the creation, visible from the interior in a way they'd not been from the outside.

"Brak and silt, how did you manage this overnight?" Kal asked, echoing Khiri's thoughts almost exactly.

"I had a bit of help," Rigger admitted. "Honestly, I thought I dreamed it. But it was still there when I woke up, and I didn't think to question it after I got in." His hands moved with a smooth surety of purpose as he dug out three or four runes and switched them with others, flipped a few more and turned yet another three-quarters around. "You may want to hold on to something."

Khiri was trying to puzzle out who'd helped the young engineer and why, when the contraption lunged into motion. The sudden rush of forward momentum threw Kal against her. The quartz disks revealed a group of guards bearing down on the broken building, but they were too late. The bird legs were tucked up under Rigger's contraption and it zoomed across the landscape like a drunken hummingbird.

"BRACE FOR LANDING!" Rigger warned them. He was already manipulating the runes in front of him, turning one here and flipping two there, when all three of them jolted to the right and smacked against the rounded stone.

"Sorry, sorry... I think I hit a tree..." the dwarf said.

Kal braced against Khiri as another sudden impact threatened to throw them against the left side. He seemed a lot less shaky and his skin was no longer glowing with barely contained power. *"You seem to be feeling better."*

"You're looking much closer to normal, yourself," he commented, sending her an image of what she had looked like after joining hands with him during the magic surge. Her blue eyes, always bright, were practically stars, while her coppery olive-toned skin flared to life like the sun itself. Khiri couldn't help but think of the throne room from Eerilor's royal palace, with the sun and moon glowing side by side in the vastness of the blue goldstone galaxy.

She shook the image out of her head and attempted to extract herself from Kal's grip.

"For safety's sake, you'd better stay put until we're on the ground," the mage remarked as the stone barrel slammed against its own clumsy legs as it landed. Khiri wished Rigger had been able to place handholds or cushions against the sides, as grateful as she was to be freed from prison.

"Where exactly are we headed?" she asked as the contraption waddled its way to a stop. Each step the thing took threw them from one side to the other. The experience reminded her of being on a thin tree limb during a windstorm.

"Well, I told you I thought I dreamt I'd built this thing and I had help," Rigger said, his voice breaking up with the back and forth movements of the container. "We're going to the place I built it."

As though they'd crossed an invisible barrier, the barrel bird contraption came to a halt and toppled toward the ground. Rigger fell against the lid, causing it to pop free. Khiri and Kal rolled forward, scrambling to either side of the dwarf as they attempted not to stand on him. Stiff and sore from the jostling, Khiri started to ask who Rigger was hoping to find when she heard a throat clear from behind them. An older woman with dark hair and eyes, taller than Khiri but tiny for a human, stood at the edge of the clearing. She wore a simple blue tunic, brown trousers, a heavy smith's apron, and a very stern expression.

Khiri's breath froze in her chest. She recognized this woman, though Khiri had only seen her once in a vision of the past.

Shydan's avatar from the War of the Burning Valley. One of her father's generals.

30

~Estan~

ESTAN WOKE WITH A START. The reality of the Gods' meeting faded with the realization that he was not alone in his room. Whoever was keeping him company was eerily silent. It wasn't Ysinda. Wishing he hadn't left his sword next to his armor the night before, he thanked Taymahr he was wearing pants. There was nothing worse than facing the unknown without trousers.

"Who's there?" he asked groggily.

Resmine and Dewin had both been within the dream meeting, meaning they couldn't be watching him from the shadows. If it had been Corianne or Evic, they would've announced themselves as soon as he woke. Tak would have started laughing—he'd made a game of sneaking up on Estan as they'd traveled, which had given the knight a sense of what to expect from the trader. This heavy, contemplative silence was not it.

"So this is the infamous Estan. Youngest elevated Knight of the Protective Hand, Consort to the Queen of Thieves, and traitor to the Temples of Seirane... Did I leave anything out?" the shadowed figure asked.

The loathing in that voice sent shivers down Estan's spine. The knight kept his eyes on the figure. If he could make it to his sword, propped up against the chair across the room, he might have a fighting chance. Estan attempted to roll onto the floor to put the bed between him and the menacing shadow.

Attempted, but did not succeed. As soon as he moved, he discovered he'd been tied down while he and Taymahr had been distracted.

"But at least I made sure you were wearing pants," his Goddess said with a hint of sarcasm.

"What do you want?" Estan demanded. He struggled against his bindings, which a distracted corner of his mind noted were oddly soft. Leather or sheepskin. Breathing deeply in and out, he reined in his growing fear. He used the rise and fall of his chest as a focus point, not wanting to stare at his captor any longer. Look at the shadow, he told himself. If he could just identify the intruder, he could figure out what to do from there. For a wild moment, he thought it might be Irrellian Thornne.

"It is not the demon-bound mage," Taymahr said.

"My Goddess..." Estan began a prayer he'd used once or twice before, while on the front lines of the Eerilorian war over a largely insignificant river. *"Will I die today?"*

Taymahr was still for what felt like hours though Estan's chest had only risen three times. *"You might,"* she said.

It wasn't meant to be comforting, but it did help.

The figure moved out of the shadows, though he was still covered in a hooded cloak. A chill ran through Estan as he recognized the unofficial uniform of the Venom Guild. His eyes darted over the rest of the room, searching for the other two squad members. Then he remembered the anti-Flayer runes carved into every doorway and window of the Talon Acre. He was safe from being fed to the demonbound, at least.

"What I want... That's a loaded question," the man said. His frame and his voice were distinctly male, though Estan couldn't immediately place either. "I'd like to drive the Thieves' Guild out of this city to start. From there, well... That's really not your concern."

"Rothan Haud," Estan hissed, throwing the name out as though it were an accusation.

Chuckling as he shook his head, the figure paced toward the window and turned, just before the light could dip into his cowl.

"Rothan Haud," the intruder laughed, but it wasn't a happy sound. "Suits me as well as any other name you might call me. We don't all have the brass to stride about town with our true faces telling our names to any who might listen, Estan of the Protective Hand. Did you forget the Temples have a contract out on you? Or did you just assume Jarelton was safe, what with the thief queen and her little friends running the streets?"

Despite Estan's efforts to fight it, fear was weaving its way through his heart up into his lungs. His breathing was becoming more shallow, more rapid, as though the fear was greedily consuming air before it could reach his lungs.

"I think that it's time I send the queen a message. Since you so enjoy putting yourself in my way, you may as well play messenger for me." The sound of a long blade scraping against its sheath rang through the small room.

Estan struggled harder against his restraints, but his wrists were bound around the bed frame. Each time he pulled against one side, the other became tighter. His legs could barely move at all.

"If you are Rothan Haud, what are you doing with the city's children?" Estan tried to make it sound like a demand despite the shivers working their way into his jaw. He didn't feel brave. He wanted to cry.

The man chuckled again, as though he found Estan's struggles amusing. Annoyed, the knight yanked at both of his wrists, hoping to suddenly break free. But the most he managed was a strained muscle in his left arm. Estan's fear was beginning to thaw as the flames of failure turned inside his gut.

Either because he wished to watch Estan's reaction, or because he believed Estan would soon prove no threat at all, the cloaked man answered the knight's question. "The city's children are alive, mostly. Their minds are more malleable, easier to shape. There are those that pay well for such molds. I believe you're well acquainted with one such repository."

As Estan digested the implications of this revelation, the man brought his arms over Estan's chest.

"Enough. Your path ends here."

A curved dagger, almost long enough to be a short sword, gleamed in the rising light of the morning. Any minute, his friends would expect Estan to descend the stairs and join them for breakfast. They may even still be down the hall, not quite awake from a sleep that had been hijacked by their deities. They might be dead.

Raising the dagger over his head in both hands, the man's hood was thrown back. Estan's eyes widened with recognition and his jaw worked, trying to form the syllables to name his murderer before the knife dropped. A slow grin of triumph crept up the man's cheeks as he plunged the dagger into the knight's chest.

Shock was the first sensation that rode through Estan. He watched blood pool around the dagger. His blood. A scream still rang in his ears. His scream.

As the shock ebbed, it was replaced with pain. Absolute agony flowed out from his chest and into his arms and legs. A rush of fresh hell overlapped the last wave of torment as the blade twisted on its way back out. Continued waves of pain pushed and dragged him into the darkness, promising an oblivion that would free him from the cares of the world and those in it.

He fought the blackness as he had his restraints, with similar results. Ysinda. Khiri. Resmine and Dewin. Ullen. Catapult. Evic. Kal's smug grin. Even as he was dying, Estan wanted to hit the mage. Maybe he'd get his chance. In the next life.

The last face to filter through the growing darkness was Cori-anne's. Estan wasn't sure what it meant, if anything... He'd have to think about it...

Later...

31

~Resmine~

WAKING FROM THE MEETING of deities into her lover's arms, Resmine smiled. Things were still chaos everywhere they looked, but she'd found someone to spend the mad times with. She still wasn't sure she deserved Dewin's love. It didn't seem to matter though.

Dewin nuzzled her nose into Resmine's chest, hiding her face from the light and making sleepy mutterings. If not for the gods and thieves and Estan's dumb ass, Resmine would've been content to spend the entire day forgetting the rest of Arra existed. Leaning her chin on Dewin's hair, Resmine absently ran her fingers through the inky locks, drinking in as much of her love's essence as she could before setting out on the day's work.

Estan would probably be mad when he came down and found that Resmine had left before breakfast, but she needed to meet with Evic and Corianne without a lot of gawkers. The only way to manage that was tracking them down on her own. Her first stop was The Dusk and Dawn.

Resmine's attempts to corner Evic for a word at The Dusk and Dawn were hampered by his pulling the Life Tree exile away for a job. They could call it what they liked, but Resmine had been forced to observe many such interactions during her time as a stablehand.

Thwarted in her attempts to talk to Evic, Resmine looked around the room to see who might be able to help her find Corianne.

The elf's companion from the day before was climbing up the stairs into the main barroom. Resmine decided to do a little digging.

As large as he was, the burly thief didn't shoo anyone away from a favored table or chair. He lumbered over to the nearest empty stool and eased himself into place. Without ordering, he was brought a goblet of wine and the serving woman smiled at him warmly. Looking past his girth, Resmine realized he wasn't unattractive. Estan and Evic both were a fair bit prettier, as men went, but this man's soft blonde hair and sapphire blue eyes could still garner a glance or two. His sandy complexion wasn't marred by pocks or acid. Maybe a scar or two, but Resmine had known a few women who liked that sort of thing.

Introducing herself to the big man, who went by Shiv, Resmine learned that the elf's name was Risk.

"Are those two an item?" she asked.

"I'm not supposed to say," Shiv said. The big man spoke slowly, but his diction was heavily pronounced–Shiv had undergone some extensive formal education at some point. He didn't seem bothered by his teammate's absence, even though the two of them had looked like a pair when Resmine and Estan first entered the thieves' den. "They do spend a fair deal of time together, though."

Filing the tidbit away, Resmine shrugged. "Not really my business anyway. I'm just a good friend of Evic's sister."

"Yes, I recall," Shiv chuckled. "I was there the night you two met."

No use getting embarrassed, Resmine thought. It wasn't like she and Dewin had ever been anything approaching discrete with their attraction. "I was hoping to talk to him about something concerning that, actually. Corianne, too."

Shiv weighed Resmine with his gaze. "Not a thing we normally do here, give away locations. Generally, when the Thieves' Guild wants to find you, we find you. We're all about staying hidden."

Resmine nodded. She hadn't really expected someone to hand her an address. Estan's status as Consort was probably the only reason she'd been let into the lower level of The Dusk and Dawn unmolested. Though she hadn't been proclaimed a Friend of the Court directly, Resmine had been treated like one thus far. She didn't want to press things with Shiv and wear out her welcome.

"I understand. If you see either of them, please let them know I was looking."

There was a thoughtful look on Shiv's face as he leaned back, sipping from his goblet. "I hate to turn you away empty handed. Tell you what... If you'll share a drink with me, we'll ask for the Knives and Nobles board to be brought out. We can make a few wagers and if you win, I'll tell you where to find your friends."

"If I lose?" Resmine asked.

"A secret for a secret," Shiv said.

With a laugh, Resmine asked, "What secrets do you think I have?"

Resmine was well aware she had secrets. Very few people went through life without hiding something. The question she was really asking was what Shiv thought was worth knowing. Resmine would guess the Thieves' Guild was curious about Estan, but she'd been wrong before. Unfortunately, a flat rejection of the proposal would be suspicious in its own right. She had to play this very carefully.

"I'm sure there's something," Shiv shrugged. "Shall we play?"

RESMINE LOST TRACK of time while focused on the Knives and Nobles board. She hadn't played in ages, not since before her time pretending to be a slow-witted stablehand. It was odd how easily the game came back to her.

"Not that odd. You're the avatar to the High God of Battle," Locke reminded her.

While that was true, Resmine was still amazed to see patterns and strategies unfold in front of her eyes. A knife here meant two nobles were in danger of capture in three turns. A note there, and the knife would fade into darkness. Removing a peasant from play could possibly wreck her opponents entire game plan.

Shiv yielded after they'd been playing for over an hour. "Well played. I thought I'd be earning myself three or four secrets before taking pity on you. It isn't often I find a competent Knives and Nobles opponent."

"You make this offer often?" Resmine asked. She helped him clear away the pieces into a concealed compartment on the bottom of the gameboard. They were well-worn, the dingy enamel chipping off of corners. Resmine wondered if this was a personal set Shiv kept at the bar, or if he was merely the most frequent player.

"Not often. Most people aren't so difficult to read."

He was trying to bait her. "You lost. I believe we had a wager."

Shiv chuckled and slugged back what was left of his current goblet. "We did. Aye, we did."

When the barmaid came by to retrieve the Knives and Nobles board, Shiv asked for an inkwell and parchment scrap. The items were brought, Shiv made a few scribbles and tucked the parchment into Resmine's hand. "Memorize it and burn it. I'm not responsible for your safety should you enter unannounced."

Resmine memorized the address and made sure to throw the parchment in the fire while Shive was watching her. She didn't want to risk the wrath of the Thieves' Guild because she'd not followed the large man's instructions.

SOMETIME AFTER NOON, Resmine returned to the Talon Acre Inn. While Shiv had given her Corianne and Evic's address, Resmine still hadn't managed to track down either of Dewin's siblings. It wasn't surprising that tracking two of Ysinda's lieutenants was nearly impossible, but it was frustrating.

Dewin met Resmine at the door. Her expression immediately put Resmine on high alert. Something was wrong.

"Thank Adari you're back, love..." Dewin hugged Resmine tight. "Catapult's a right mess. He near about pulled a beam down, aimed a kick at Tak, and he won't listen to the lot of us. I've been trying to rouse Estan, but he's not budged all mornin'. I don't know what might be wrong, but the gods have gone quiet on it."

"Locke?" Resmine tried.

"I'm not permitted to say."

A lump lodging in the pit of her stomach, Resmine took the stairs two at a time on her way to Estan's door. Something told her this was the real problem. Catapult was a warhorse, trained to protect his rider. Swallowing her fear, Resmine slammed her fist against the door and hoped her gut was wrong.

32

~Ullen~

IT WASN'T THE FIRST meeting of the High Ones Ullen had attended. During the War of the Burning Valley, those dream conferences had been crucial while fighting an enemy that could send messengers through shadows. This meeting had been much more cryptic with its talk of keystones and portals.

Of course, during the last war, the gods had come into things as a last resort. Officially, the new war hadn't started yet. Lines were being drawn and forces were being rallied, but no battles had yet been fought. Historians would likely argue Eerilor and Mytana's continued struggles over the water rights between their borders was the beginning of the Second Great War, but Ullen knew in his heart the real war was still on the way. He had to make his mother concede to peace with Mytana. Both countries would need every soldier they could muster soon.

Ullen allowed his attendants to help him dress with limited patience. He wouldn't yell at the servants for doing their jobs, but he hated the fussing. Ullen hadn't had a chance to find his own valet yet. The price of having been away so long was not having his own servants on retainer any more.

Ullen considered if he'd be more inclined to stay under his brother's court. He had no such intentions, but it was a more tempting prospect than serving under his mother. After all these years, it was upsetting how delusional Queen Di'eli's ambitions were. Her servants wouldn't switch to Ullen's side on her deathbed. One didn't inherit loyalties like that.

Loyalty was earned. And Ullen was the runaway prince.

The only servant still on his side seemed to be the head of the kitchens. Once again, Ullen found a table of his favorite breakfast foods when he entered the meeting hall. Lavender honey cakes, spiced fruit, sausage rolls, three kinds of eggs. For a breakfast meeting, it bordered on too much. But the household staff were free to eat their fill from any food the nobles left, so perhaps the kitchens were indulging while Queen Di'eli was preoccupied with her son.

Many of the courtiers in attendance made a point of exchanging greetings with Ullen as well as Hon'idar. The longer their mother dragged this out, the more the courtiers hedged their bets. When Ullen had first arrived, he'd gotten a few curt nods from some of the more civil minded nobles. This wasn't a good sign.

Everyone had filled their plates and seated themselves around the grand table by the time Queen Di'eli was announced. Rising from his seat with the others, Ullen risked a glance at the queen as she entered.

During the last meeting with the courtiers, Di'eli had threatened her sons with abdication. Despite the stacks of lavender honey cakes and sausage rolls, Ullen's appetite abandoned him. His mother had a new plan. She wore an expression far too smug for this meeting to be about his petition for peace with Mytana.

"Please, sit, eat!" Queen Di'eli smiled at the gathered nobility. Her tone was nauseating with its sweetness. "We can begin soon enough."

"I'm sure our courtiers have plenty on their plates besides breakfast, mother," Hon'idar said. The frost in his voice was enough to cool the room by several degrees despite the number of bodies in the room.

"And I'm certain their business will still be waiting for them once the meeting has been called," the queen said, her tone tighter than before but still dripping with honey. "Now, Hon'idar, dear... *Sit down.*"

There was no reasoning with their mother when she used that voice. Everyone in the room immediately turned their attention to their plates, not wanting to risk the queen's ire. Ullen sighed as he stuffed a lavender honey cake into his mouth and chewed without pleasure. He'd have to tell the cooks to stop making his favorites for these meetings. As much as he appreciated the gesture, his mother had a way of making everything taste like ash.

After what felt like hours of silent chewing, the last noble pushed their plate away with a belch of appreciation. Queen Di'eli nodded at the complement to her kitchens and the platters were cleared away.

"As you all know, my sons do not agree with me on the matter of my successor. Prince Hon'idar feels the crown is his due. While Prince Ut'evullen is my chosen heir, he continues to deny he has any desire to lead."

Pausing to make sure all eyes were on her, the queen sighed a dramatic sigh. "While I would well be within my rights as the ruler of Eerilor to simply demand that my boys bend to my wishes, I've decided to make things a bit more interesting."

The doors on the far side of the meeting hall swung open to admit a young dwarven noblewoman. Ullen recognized her the moment their eyes met. How could he not? She was the reason none of his relationships lasted more than a fortnight. His first love, Lady Jaspar Terilles... Her violet eyes, chestnut ringlets and flawless golden skin were as beautiful as Ullen remembered.

"Mother? Why is my betrothed here?" Hon'idar asked.

Ullen's stomach shriveled like a raisin in the sun.

"My daughter was promised to the future king of Eerilor," Earl Tolen Terilles said, his voice gentle but firm. "I told your mother in private conference that her insistence on changing the heir would force me to withdraw our house from the agreement. This nonsense is a breach of trust."

"I heard your concerns, Earl Terilles. My proposal is such that it should ease your worries concerning your daughter."

What little breakfast Ullen had forced down threatened to come back up. No one had informed him that his first love and his brother had been engaged. He didn't like where this was heading at all.

"Whichever of my boys woos Lady Terilles will be my heir. Your house will be joined to the next ruler, which fulfills the contract, and it takes the pressure off my shoulders to determine my heir situation. The Lady Terilles is to announce her choice during the Solstice Ball. Which you've already agreed to, haven't you, my girl?"

Jaspar dipped her head, not meeting anyone's gaze. "Your majesty made it hard to refuse."

"So I did," Queen Di'eli said. "Now, I believe Hon'idar said everyone had plenty of other business. You're all dismissed."

"Mother, please!" Ullen stood. "Mytana..."

"If you care so much about this Mytana business, you'd best start courting the next queen." Not even looking back into the room of courtiers, Di'eli left through her private door.

As soon as the door was shut behind her, the room erupted into turmoil. Hon'idar was yelling at Earl Terilles while several other nobles restrained him. Earl Terilles looked equally unhappy but wasn't backing down to Hon'idar's onslaught. Several of the nobles had immediately surrounded Jaspar, demanding to know how the queen had talked her into such a scheme. Ullen had a crowd forming as well, asking if he'd known about this, demanding he immediately withdraw from candidacy, and other things. He knew better than to respond. Anything he said in this room would be twisted into a thousand different agreements he'd never intended to make.

Hon'idar's gaze fell on Ullen as the crown prince finished his tirade at the Earl. Ullen had never seen his brother so livid. It was fair to say they wouldn't be sharing another beer anytime soon. During their brotherly trip, Hon'idar had talked at length about his upcoming nuptials, though he'd never quite mentioned Jaspar by name. Just that he thought Ullen might or might not remember his "little honey duck." They'd both been very drunk by the time it was brought up. Hon'idar had insisted Ullen go first, and relating his own adventures had taken them almost eight pints of good brew. Wishing he'd stayed in Jarelton, Ullen stood and made his way out of the room.

As he passed Jaspar, neither of them spoke. But a whiff of her perfume nearly tested his resolve not to take the crown. They'd been so careful back then. How had his mother known? How was Ullen supposed to choose between his brother and the love of his life?

33

~Khiri~

"YOU MUST BE KHIRIELLEN," Shydan's former avatar said. Her short hickory brown hair was almost black, only showing its true color in the glowing rays of the sun. Light caught her irises just enough to reveal they were slate gray rather than brown. Some sort of grease or oil was smudged over her face, apron and sleeves. Her apron pockets were heavy with tools. Khiri thought she could see the outline of a rune satchel at the woman's hip.

"Y...Yes," Khiri stammered, accepting the woman's extended hand.

"I was a friend of your father's many years ago," the woman said, squinting at Khiri as though she could read Khiri's soul. "But I imagine you know that."

"I...know your face," Khiri admitted. After the woman began to pull Rigger to his feet, Khiri belatedly turned to help Kal. "I'm afraid I don't know your name..."

"Vess Lorrei," the woman said. "Welcome to my home. Rigger and I have already met, though I did wipe his mind after the work was done... At his insistence. He said there was a danger of being captured."

"I asked you... Oh..." Rigger tapped his head. "Right... I guess I would've. You know her, Khiri? I thought she was something I made

232

up when I was trying to figure how I would've rigged this thing without a workshop."

"You made it in my workshop," Vess said. She gestured behind her, where a small cabin poked its roof up out of the surrounding trees. One end of the cabin was little more than a roof on support beams, opening out into the clearing. A long workbench ran the entire length of the large covered porch, while the wall next to it was covered in pegs that held various sized hammers, wrenches, chisels, rune pouches and an assortment of other tools Khiri couldn't even begin to name. Rigger's mouth hung open with a look of awed glee.

"You've got a lot of talent, Rigger. I'd like to speak with you about it later. First, I believe Khiri and I have some planning to do."

"I need to get back into Elmesh," Khiri said. "They took my dagger and Kal's staff... and we need to look for some papers in the office of the guard."

"You would be Kal, then." Vess offered her hand in greeting to the Odlesk mage. Kal accepted it with one solid pump.

Khiri's cheeks flushed. Introductions were a basic common courtesy and she was failing keeping up with that much. It seemed ridiculous that her friends kept looking to Khiri for leadership when she barely knew how to talk to people.

"It's alright, laska," he told her. Kal was facing Vess, but Khiri could tell his smile was meant for her. *"I'm harder to offend than that."*

"Down to business. You have to sneak into Elmesh's office of the guard, correct? After we poked the ants' nest by freeing you in the first place?"

Khiri nodded.

Vess ushered them over to a small fire ring surrounded by wooden chairs and stone stools. Sitting in a chair of elm, Khiri felt as though she were lounging against the trunk of one of her favorite hunting trees near the base of the Oak Wood Life Tree. She met Vess' gaze in surprise.

"Trick of the trade," Vess told her. "I'm one of the few living masters in the engineering craft. I have to guard my secrets closely."

"Would you like an apprentice?" Khiri asked.

Rigger tensed visibly at the question. His desire to work with a master was written on his face, and his stance was both eager and defensive. Vess studied Khiri for a long moment, before turning her gaze on the younger engineer. For a few moments, Khiri was worried she'd over-stepped herself. She still hadn't thanked the woman for aiding Rigger. Not the best start.

"I had intended to bring it up after we had spoken, but it seems that you have your father's temperament," Vess said with a soft smile. "Rigger, I would like to formally offer you a position as my apprentice, under the jurisdiction of the Engineering Authority. As is tradition, once you have passed my tests, I will sponsor your application to the Academy of Trades. Do you find these terms acceptable?"

"I...I... But..." Rigger looked from Vess to Khiri and back again. "What about the..."

Khiri stretched out her hand and took Rigger's calloused fingers in hers. "I told you that I would find you a position with a master, didn't I? Here's your chance. Kal and I will be okay. We're built for this sort of thing... and I know Vess can help you with your fighting as well as your creations," Khiri told him. "She's a veteran of the Burning Valley."

Rigger squeezed Khiri's hand, gratitude shining in his chestnut eyes. He turned back to Vess and nodded his acceptance of her offer.

"I'll get the contracts out once we're done here," Vess said.

When Vess turned back to Khiri, her expression was deadly serious. "First, let me tell you what you need to know about getting in and out of Elmesh under our Sergeant Kari Peplar's nose."

KHIRI SQUATTED IN THE alley behind the guards' office as the sun began to set over Elmesh. The day shift was making preparations to head home, according to Vess' information. Soon, it would be time for Khiri to move.

The mud beneath Khiri's feet reeked of urine. A drunk patron of one of three nearby pubs decided at some point during the night to mark his resentment of the law on the wall, rather than seeking the privacy of a privy. Maybe several drunkards. Or one in possession of a particularly foul bladder. The man might need a healer... But Khiri was losing focus. Unable to see the front entrance from where she stood, she was counting on Micah to count for her. Shifting carefully away from the pungent dirt, Khiri checked in with Micah to make sure he could still sense how many people were in the guard house.

"Four guards remain," Micah said. He sounded tense, though Khiri could hardly imagine why. His part in the plan was very small: make sure no one snuck up on Khiri. As if he'd read her mind, Micah grumbled, *"No small feet at all, keeping you out of trouble. Just be careful, Khiri. I believe Vess knows what she's doing, but this is still risky."*

"Riskier than anything we've done yet?" Khiri asked.

Micah didn't bother to answer her. *"Three left."*

Khiri reached out to Kal's mind, feeling his touch like a caress along the back of her neck. Nothing took the heat out of linking minds like the stench of a drunkard's piss. She was almost grateful to the inebriated stranger. *"It's time,"* she sent Kal. *"Are you ready?"*

"I'm not sure how I let you talk me into this," the mage replied. *"Take care, laska. They'll be distracted, but you'll still only have so much time."*

"You be careful, I'll be quick," Khiri said, trying to keep her tone light. She wanted to say more, but she still wasn't sure how much she could trust herself to vocalize. Thoughts and feelings ran together in a jumbled mess, which the elf didn't want to risk sending Kal all to-

gether. There was no way to know if he'd read too much into it, or not enough. Instead, she ended with a simple, *"Be safe."*

His smile warmed more than her cheeks. Khiri edged farther away from the suspect mud, not wanting her memories to be tainted by the smell.

"Stand ready," Kal warned.

From the far north end of Elmesh, a booming crash, followed by a rolling clatter. An alarm began trilling within the guard office, making someone near the door curse loudly. "What in the Demon Realms is it now? Intruders in the Flayer hole, prisons getting ripped apart... It's getting too interesting around here..." the voice started to trail away.

"All clear," Micah informed Khiri. The elf took a deep breath and crept out of the alley. In their haste, the guards had left the front wide open. Vess had warned her that even if it looked clear, she needed to tap the rune key first. Like a spider web, the place was rigged with pressure gages. Anything disturbing the strings would alert the spiders, or guards, and then they'd rush in and capture her. But not to suck her blood. The metaphor broke down at a certain point. Khiri pushed it out of her head and tapped the rune code Vess had made her memorize.

Only months before, the system had needed to be renewed—some of the oldest runes were drained of energy, which was causing a strain on nearby runes as the older ones sought a source of magic when careless guards still attempted to use them. Vess was the engineer they'd called on to fix things.

Foreseeing a future need, Vess had taken the opportunity in hand and given herself a private set of codes. Tapping in one of these codes, Khiri ducked inside the enemy's stronghold as soon as the runes' magic blue glow turned green.

Khiri's first task was to get inside the weapons closet. It would be a bit more complicated. Two people were normally required to open the thing. She had to stand in the right spot to activate the pressure plate while the rune to open the closet was well out of her reach. Pulling Micah from his sheath, she stood with her toes on the edge of the plate and touched the bow to the far side of the door, narrowly missing the wrong rune with the first tap. Gritting her teeth, she willed more strength into her wrist.

"Please don't drop me," Micah said, straining her concentration.

"Micah..." Khiri warned.

"I'm sorry... Just...Don't," he sounded nervous. She sent an image of donkeys chewing on branches at him, and he quieted instantly.

A quiet pop and the closet door swung open. Khiri scurried to get at the weapons shelves. Her father's dagger was soon sheathed at her side, and a tremendous weight lifted from her shoulders. Some people had good luck charms. Khiri had a dagger.

Life was complicated.

Kal's staff was on a higher shelf, but Khiri was able to retrieve it with minimal climbing.

Her second objective—the papers from Master Kivian Threshler's desk—would be easier to get to, but harder in that Vess hadn't been able to give her much information about the filing system. She'd only known the files had very little in the way of magically enhanced security. Shifting Kal's staff in her grip, Khiri walked up to one of the desks and flipped through a few parchments. She only found lists of check ins and minor complaints.

"How's your distraction going?" she asked Kal.

"Oh, you know... Destroy a statue of a town hero, get chased over a few rooftops... Disappear into what turns out to be a dress shop... I am hiding in a fitting room with a very frilly lavender and periwinkle disaster. How's the infiltration?" Kal responded.

"I've got the weapons, but there are too many papers in here that have nothing to do with what we need to know," Khiri told him as she shuffled through another stack of parchments on a different desk.

"It's part of an on-going investigation," Kal said. *"The way this Sergeant Kari seems to operate, she seems rather hands on. I'd go straight for her personal files."*

Wincing at her own oversight, Khiri thanked Kal and wished him luck on getting out of the dress shop. His silence wasn't promising, but Khiri had her own work to do. There was only one space in the whole office possessing the pomp of a captain's position; a desk twice the size of anyone else's, divided from the rest of the room by a long swath of empty floor. It looked as though there had once been a wall between the other desks and this one, but that area had been paved over with extra mortar.

Rifling through the stacks of parchment, Khiri found a large envelope that was labeled *Kivian Threshler's Effects.* She started to open it, but the sound of someone approaching the front door was echoed by Micah's hurried warning. Dropping to the ground, her back pressed against the knobby desk drawers, Khiri hugged the envelope to her chest and hoped whoever it was didn't notice the staff laying on the floor.

"...not half as weird as that one night five years ago," a male voice was saying. "We had to arrest two hundred people that thought they were receiving commands from gods, demons, and ancestors to do the craziest shit. Painting other people's houses, gluing fur to peoples' skins..."

"Oh, right! The mushroom incident! I heard about that from Stephans last year," a female voice replied. "Did they ever find out who was responsible?"

"No more than we did tonight," the male was inside the door now. The room immediately felt much more crowded, like the air had somehow gotten thicker. Khiri felt her breathing steady, the way it did when she was out hunting and had sighted a deer. Steady movements, deep breaths, soft hands. Nothing sudden, nothing extreme.

This was the contingency, the reason that she and Micah had done this part rather than the distraction.

"Can you really do it?" she asked.

"We're about to find out," Micah said. *"Now let me concentrate."*

She was alert to the presence of the two guards, carelessly flirting in the non-serious manner Khiri still found difficult to comprehend. Because she and Micah had grown up together, Khiri never indulged in casual flirtations, though she had been aware that some others in her age group had seen nothing wrong with telling someone they looked pretty, or handsome, or shot well while giggling and touching. It never amounted to anything more than a smile or an eyelash flutter to her knowledge... Then again, she hadn't been aware her mother was really a human, either. How much of life within the Life Trees was really the way she remembered it? She stowed it away as something to mull over later.

"Okay, I think that did it," Micah announced. *"Stand up."*

"I can still see myself," Khiri protested. *"What if I stand and they see me? We may not be as lucky the next time we need freeing. Vess and Rigger..."*

"The only way to know if it worked or not is to test it. I know it's risky, but sometimes it's worth it," Micah insisted.

"Sometimes it's worth it..." Khiri echoed. One last deep breath and she rose from the cobbled floor, carefully keeping the staff from knocking into anything. There was a brief pause in the conversation between the two guards, but it started again after a moment. Relief flooded Khiri's senses as she crept along the wall and back out into the lantern lit streets of Elmesh, toward the designated meeting point where Kal should be waiting for her.

When she saw him, she had to stifle a giggle. He was wearing what could only have been the lavender and periwinkle disaster he had mentioned before. The skirt was alternating layers of the two colors: chiffon, lace, taffeta, silk, and... canvas? The bodice of the thing was a violent shade of purple with sickly yellow-green flowers embroidered on at random. His hair was curled and primped with various colored ribbons woven in a style that may have been called bold by some, and whimsical by others. To Khiri, it was the masterwork of ravens building a nest.

"Not one word," the mage warned her. Khiri nodded, not trusting herself to speak. If she unclenched her teeth, she feared she'd never stop laughing.

"I've had enough of this place for two lifetimes," Kal muttered as they hurried down the road that would lead them out of Elmesh.

34

~Genovar~

GENOVAR WRAPPED HIS arms around Leyani, pressing his lips to hers in a kiss both passionate and tender, fueled by his many long months on the road. He wished he was meeting her in their home in the Oak Wood Life Tree, but there wasn't time for him to travel the whole distance and make it to Taman by the solstice. Even at his quickest, he'd never been able to outrun the growth of the Gray Army.

"It makes my heart ache to see you. I wish I could stay," he said as Leyani pulled away. Khiriellen had so much of Leyani about her, Genovar couldn't bring himself to look into his wife's eyes for very long. Too much of what Khiri faced was his fault, and he knew it would only get harder for her as the war broke over the world like a plague. "Things are not going quite the way we'd hoped."

"Your message was very vague, my love." Leyani sat across from him at a table in the Tilted Donkey. He'd never asked her to come here before, but it was one of the few inns left anywhere near the Life Trees that he still trusted at this juncture. He and his generals had left things in place that should have ensured the safety of the world. With every stop he made, it seemed like more of those plans had fallen apart.

"It's not going well, dear heart. Mytana has fallen apart in recent years. It's barely a country. Jarelton and Seirane have basically become city states. There is war between Eerilor and Mytana... Really, it's between Taman and Seirane. Neither side has made a real push since the war has started, almost as though they are trying to thin the ranks of fighters–" Genovar stopped, his eyes widening slightly.

"Almost, huh?" Leyani quirked an eyebrow at him. "What of our other allies?"

"There's talk of Eerilor calling a summit. I need to be there..." Genovar paused, wanting to tell his wife what he had learned, but he couldn't find the right words. "...To speak against certain factions."

Leyani studied her husband for several minutes, tapping her finger against the grain of the wooden table, not saying a word. For over twenty summers, they'd shared meals, secrets and a bed. There was little Genovar could hide from her, but there was little that she chose to pry about when he omitted things. She chose to let him keep his secrets now, which made him feel even worse.

"It all sounds bad, but why did you call me all the way out here for this sort of news? There must be something you need me to do... Speak with Vess or Lirya? As I recall, you were always a bit nervous around those two."

Genovar shook his head. "I had another vision."

Gripping his hand, Leyani sat up a bit straighter. The last time he'd told her about a vision, the War of the Burning Valley had erupted. They had scoured the countryside for six potential avatars and carried out a promise made the night she had become Leyani Ardair, not... He tried to remember her old name, but it was hardly important. She'd been Leyani, his Leyani, for so long, it was hard to remember her as being someone else. Too many other things were on his mind. "Go back to the Life Trees, convince as many as you can to go with you to Illesdale by the southern route. It is crucial that you are not seen leading our people away from their homes."

"How much time do I have?" Leyani asked. No explanations required, just complete and utter trust in her love's abilities.

With a sigh, Genovar caressed his wife's hand with his thumb, tracing the old scar in her palm, touching to one that matched it in the cup of his own hand, "Maybe a month after the solstice at most. The sooner you get people out, the better. The Life Trees are no longer the bastion of safety they once represented."

"You can count on me, Gen," Leyani's voice broke as she used his old nickname, the one she hadn't uttered since they had climbed into the Oak Wood Clan so many summers before.

It felt as though that life, their life, had been nothing but a pleasant dream and she, like him, could sense the coming of the dawn. He rose and took her in his arms once more. They had loved each other enough to defy the gods... But what of their daughter and her role?

Genovar hoped one day his daughter would know a love like her parents shared. But if his suspicions were correct, Khiriellen was doomed. Because her father hadn't known how to let go.

35

~Estan~

GASPING, ESTAN SURFACED from the dark space he'd been inhabiting like he'd spent too long underwater. Partially dried blood still coated his chest. The tackiness of congealing red had permeated the mattress beneath his back. There was way too much blood outside of his body. Sunlight and a brisk autumn breeze were running in through the open window, creating an oddly cheerful backdrop to the grisly death scene... Only he didn't seem to be dead.

"*Did I...*" Estan's mind was stuffed with wool. No matter how hard he tried, he couldn't remember the last few hours.

"*You died.*" Taymahr's presence asserted itself, steadying his nerves as no other being could have at that moment. "*You seem to have improved drastically.*"

"How...?" he blinked. There was a film over his eyes, like he had been sleeping for a very long time after imbibing a barrel of ale. Breathing was difficult. His chest protested every breath. He struggled to sit up only to find he was still bound.

"Flayer spit," he hissed, struggling against the restraints. Estan felt a tide of panic sweep over him as he finally recalled that moment of futility as the jagged blade came down...

"*Easy. Calm,*" Taymahr said, her voice soothing. "*You'll be fine. It was lucky that he only pierced your heart. If he'd taken it, even my gift of healing wouldn't have brought you back.*"

"*Oh...*" It was far from adequate, but it was all Estan could do to respond. Focusing on his breathing and little else, the knight forced himself to stop struggling against his bindings. He needed to get out of here eventually, but first he had to think.

Rothan Haud; Estan knew who the man was, and he now thought that Estan was dead. That could be a major advantage, if Estan kept his wits about him. Calling out for help while the window was open to the street would give him away. As uncomfortable as it was to lay in a pool of his own blood, he had to wait for someone to come find him. But the delay would give him time to plan.

By his figuring, it was midafternoon when a series of frantic knocks pierced the silence of his room.

"Estan!" Resmine's voice was barely muffled by the thick layer of wood. "Estan! Open this door! Catapult is wrecking the stable! Are you in there?"

It required real effort on the knight's part not to respond to Resmine. He didn't like making his oldest friend worry, but given who their enemy was, someone was probably listening. Estan's door was locked but not barred, because he didn't often worry about barring the door when he was inside the Talon Acre. With Catapult watching the back and Ren, Adela, or one of his friends in the front, he'd never given it much thought. Not a mistake he was likely to make again, though he couldn't come back to the inn as long as Rothan Haud was watching.

There was muffled conversation, followed by the scratches of lockpicks.

As the door swung open, Estan watched Resmine's face change from worry to shock to absolute horror. "Mighty Locke!" she rushed to his side and then screamed when he moved. "Gods above! Estan! What..."

He motioned for her to come closer, hampered by the restraints. Resmine made a stifled sob and came up beside him, only to give Estan a solid punch to the arm.

"How dare you," she hissed. "Is this your idea of a joke? Is this funny to you?"

"Not at all," he whispered back. With his healing ability still working on his last wound, he was pretty sure that blow would be a solid bruise within the hour. "This isn't a joke, Resmine. Rothan Haud was here. He stabbed me through the heart. I died. I need you to help me, now. Dewin, too. The two of you have to be the only ones that know I'm still alive. We're going to have to move quickly; I don't know how much time I've already wasted."

Resmine's gaze was hard, but she nodded. She touched the tacky blood trails and studied her stained finger, tears forming in the corners of her eyes. "You died," her voice sounded hollow. She hit him again before she got up. "Don't do it again."

Once Resmine had retrieved Dewin from the hall, it was obvious that the former thief had been warned, but even so her eyes were as big as dinner plates.

"Sweet Adari's tits," Dewin breathed. Estan couldn't help but wonder if Adari took as much exception to the phrase as Taymahr. He could feel Taymahr scowling at him just for mulling it over.

"We've only got a few minutes before it becomes suspicious no one has gone for the ashkeeper," Resmine said. "So what's the plan?"

"First, if someone could unstrap me, that would do a lot for my sanity," Estan said, keeping his voice as steady as he could. "Then, Dewin... That gift of yours with the body doubles... Can you do that to other people?"

"I... It'll be a shot in the dark, love, but I'm willing to give it a go," she said, still standing back and gazing at the dark rivers across Estan's creamy brown skin. She walked slowly over to him, as though she were approaching an actual corpse.

Resmine knelt beside the headboard and pulled out a small knife she kept in her boot. Working it through the straps next to the mattress, his oldest friend tried not to look at the bloody body as her lover took the real Estan by the hand and moved with him across the room. The knight fought his own gasp of astonishment as he realized Dewin had pulled him through the restraints Resmine was still working to remove.

"There's a limited range on the ability," Dewin whispered. "Get too far from the image body, and you'll be visible again. You bump someone, you'll be visible again."

"We've just got to get me down into the stable yard, and then Catapult will be able to handle keeping me out of sight," Estan told her.

"So what's the rest of your plan?" Resmine asked. She was still talking to his other body, the one laying in the puddle of blood. From his new vantage point, Estan could see why it had taken her until he moved to realize he was alive. He could barely see the rise and fall of the decoy's chest, and the eyes, his eyes, were glassy and unfocussed.

"After I am...disposed of, I need the two of you to get Corianne, Evic and Tak to meet you in the stable yard in two to three hours time. I'll try to talk to Ysinda if I can. I'll go over the rest once we get there," he said. "Now, one of you needs to go get Ren or Adela. And both of you–" he gritted his teeth, knowing the next few hours would not be easy on any of them. "–will need to pretend I'm really not coming back from this. We need Haud to believe I'm out of action for good. Estan is well and truly *dead*."

KEEPING SILENT WHILE he watched the innkeeper and her husband react to his body was one of the hardest things Estan had ever done. Not only did he have to stay quiet, but he had to be careful when he timed his breaths. The decoy had no heartbeat. That was probably beyond the boundaries of Adari's gift... but it matched his breathing. Adela was holding his false hand and murmuring things about how he'd been such a sweet boy. Ren took one look, sighed a deep sigh, and headed out to fetch the ashkeeper.

Tak watched with the grim expression of someone who had lost a lot of people in his life. Even though Estan thought he could trust the information trader, he still didn't know much about the man's past. He wished that he could pat Tak's shoulder and reassure him.

Resmine was quietly sobbing in the corner while Dewin held her hand and gazed sadly on the still form. If it hadn't been for their earlier conversation, Estan would have been convinced that they believed him dead. Several times, he nearly believed it himself. He had to remind himself he hadn't dreamed coming back; the soreness persisting in his wounded chest helped. Estan didn't know for certain, but he didn't think spirits felt pain.

Walking the body double out of the room was nerve wracking. A veritable crowd gathered in the room as the ashkeeper and his two large sons placed the false body into a bag and carried it down the stairs. Somehow, Estan was going to have to replace the fake before it got placed in the burning coffin. Estan followed the ashkeeper and his sons down through the taproom and into the kitchen. A large smoked pig was hanging on one of Ren's meat hooks near the stove. Veering toward it, Estan looked around to make sure no one would accidentally bump him. He hoped he was still invisible as he headed out the back door.

Holding the pig, the knight hurried to stay behind the ashkeepers. No one said anything to him, or seemed to notice a blood covered man with no shirt carrying a pig carcass. Estan felt safe assuming he was still not visible. Catapult began following Estan. He wasn't nosing the bag, but leaning his head over Estan's shoulder, careful not to touch his knight.

"I need them to drop the bag, boy," Estan told the horse.

Displaying his rare intelligence, Catapult trotted up the bag and began tugging at the burlap. "Horse wants to say goodbye to his master," one of the two sons observed. "We let horsie say goodbye?"

"Alright, Sellan," the ashkeeper said. "But only for a moment."

The ashkeeper's voice carried a softness usually reserved for children. Estan realized his son was slow, and Catapult had noticed. Sometimes, the roan was downright scary. Trusting the horse to cover the alteration, Estan slipped the knot off of the body bag and shifted the pig into the burlap. As he tied the bag off, he backed against the wall of the Talon Acre Inn. There was no need to follow the bag any further. All he needed now was to be left alone with Catapult so he could come up with a new identity.

"That's long enough, Sellan. We need to get this unfortunate lad in the burner so we can go pick up others waiting to meet the fire," the ashkeeper told his slow son. "The horse needs to leave his master to dream the next dream."

Estan waited for the ashkeepers to pass. Once they reached the main road, a small group of mourners began following them. It was normal for friends and family to escort the body to the door of the furnace room. Resmine and Dewin were resolutely following his request to make his procession seem real, while Tak, Adela and Ren followed in a wake of true grief. Estan hoped one day he'd be able to set things right with the innkeeper and the cook. He'd make a start by replacing the pig he'd borrowed while they were gone.

Catapult meandered back, ears forward and nosed Estan in his invisible ribs. The first thing the knight needed to do was scrub the blood off of his chest. He grabbed a bucket and a towel from behind the bar and brought it out to the stable yard.

As he started scrubbing, he thought over everything that would need to be altered or replaced. His armor was pretty average. It was probably due for an upgrade anyway. His sword was the last remaining piece of equipment he had left from his days as a knight of the temples. It had been his badge of office, the symbol of his Knighthood, his link to the past... Maybe it was time for that to be left behind as well.

"Alright, Catapult, here's what happened," he said. The warhorse had displayed a very deep understanding during the riot in front of the tavern and again during this latest encounter, so Estan decided not to mince words. "I was dropped early this morning by Ysinda's nemesis, who happens to be someone we know: Arad Rhidel."

He paused to see if Catapult was following. The way the horse's ears suddenly flattened seemed to confirm he was understanding the knight all too well. Estan cleared his throat and continued, "Obviously, I survived—came back—but I don't want him to find out. I need your help. Can you make an illusion that would stay with me even when you aren't around?"

Catapult huffed through his nostrils, blinking slowly. Estan waited, unsure of what to expect. There were times that he wished the horse could communicate as well as he seemed to understand. It would save a great deal of time, and possibly frustration. As he waited for the roan's reaction, Estan started to dip his towel into the water and nearly jumped at his reflection. He was looking at a female version of himself, from the short, tightly curled hair to the soft brown skin. The only difference aside from height was that his reflection was wearing a breast band.

"Very funny." His reflection's rose petal lips curved down. "But I think the voice would give me away... and I'm sure my twin sister showing up out of nowhere would be a little obvious."

With an amused snort, Catapult nuzzled Estan along his shoulder, giving the knight a horsey hug. Estan patted the warhorse on his thickly muscled flank, appreciating the sentiment. Estan assumed Catapult was telling his knight he was happy Estan was alive so the horse could play his pranks, but it was only a hunch.

"Alright, alright," Estan said, fighting back the lump in his throat. "Now, if you would... Something a little less obvious?"

Watching the reflection in the cloudy red water bucket, Estan saw his features slowly melt back into the masculine. His coloration altered so he was no less brown, but the undertones were copper rather than leather. The hair in the reflection straightened and his nose acquired a bend, as though he'd broken it a few times. His belly grew flabbier, his muscles less defined, and his lips thinned. It pleased Estan's vanity to note he still wasn't hideous, though he doubted he'd win anyone over with just a wink and a smile. Catapult left Estan's eyes alone, but the knight didn't recognize himself at all.

Estan raised his head to tell Catapult this creation was more to his liking, when he jumped back, startled out of his skin. Instead of the blue roan Estan was expecting, a woman stood in front of him; copper hair, copper skin, and golden eyes. "Too much?" she asked.

"What... Who...?"

"I'm your horse, dunce," she smiled. "I figured out how to create a voice. Harder than the looking bit. Numyri taught me. I has words now!"

"I have words now," Estan corrected automatically, not quite listening to himself. He was still staring at the petite woman who claimed to be his horse. "But... yes... too much."

The hair went darker, shorter, while the skin became a pale shade, close to Kal's without the reflective sheen, and the frame became a big burly man comparable to the mountain of flesh that worked with the exile in Ysinda's Court.

"Still no?" Catapult asked with a grin.

"Still no." Estan shook his head, trying to come to grips with this latest development. He had just been thinking how much easier life could be if the horse could communicate. Estan hadn't thought of how much harder life would be. "Try to be subtle."

The pale mountain of flesh raised an eyebrow. Estan had to admit the current image did seem pretty close to what Catapult would look like if he became a person and retained his horse coloring. "Subtle..." the horse echoed. He morphed into someone that was a combination of Evic and Tak, probably the two most subtle men Catapult had ever encountered. "This is subtle, yes?"

"Close enough," Estan sighed. "I'm going to go grab a shirt, you imagine yourself some clothes, subtle clothes, and we'll go grab a pig before our friends get back."

"We are planning?" Catapult asked. "Vengeance?"

"Something like that," Estan agreed. "We're going to save this city, which to someone like Arad or Rothan or whoever, will amount to about the same thing."

"I like it when they go squish," the warhorse-as-a-human informed Estan as the knight headed back into the building to grab something indistinct from his wardrobe. While they found a pig, he'd also have to see about new armor and the price of a good sword. Maybe he'd be able to borrow the coin from Ysinda.

Ysinda... He needed to let her know he was still alive. *Nothing like letting your partner think you're dead to put the strain on a new relationship,* Estan grimaced. Surely the Queen of Thieves would understand.

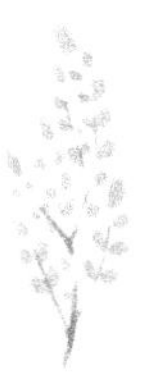

36

~Khiri~

"I DON'T UNDERSTAND," Khiri said. She flipped through the documents she'd pulled out of Sergeant Peplar's desk for what must have been the thousandth time. "These have nothing to do with Master Kivian Threshler's work, orders, or staff. Why would there be nothing in his desk but—"

"Love letters," Kal finished for her. He held back a branch for Khiri to pass, since her hands were busy with the letters. "Six love letters to a mystery recipient that were never sent. Seems rather like a false lead, if you ask me."

"What do you mean?" Khiri asked.

The sun was little more than a bright dot attempting to pierce a haze of cloud stretched from one horizon to the other, coating the hilly landscape in a veil of shadow. Khiri and Kal pushed their way out of the treeline surrounding Elmesh. Another day closer to Tenising, where maybe they'd find some answers. Having left Rigger with Vess prior to the guardhouse heist, Khiri felt an odd sense of imbalance. With Kal as her only *corporeal* companion–Micah, Imyn and Shydan being somewhat less substantial–the road felt different. More confined. Like they were back in her chambers at the royal palace, where she didn't invite him in but neither had she shut the door.

The mage walked along the solidly packed road, completely oblivious to her dilemma. Or, ignoring it. Giving her space. It drove her crazy that she couldn't read him the way he seemed to be able to read her.

Pausing, Kal slipped the letters out of her grasp with a deftness she hadn't expected. With a scowl, Khiri tried to clear her head. "These seem to have been planted at the scene precisely to make people wonder what you're wondering. Why are there love letters instead of business documents? It's a much more intriguing question than 'Where are the business documents?' and it sidetracks whomever comes along to do the research."

"...because they want to follow the mystery..." Khiri scowled again. She didn't need the mage's presence to drive her crazy. She did a fine job of it on her own.

"Exactly!" Kal rewarded her with the wry upturn of his mouth. Her heart thumped in response. She made her legs keep moving, even though her knees were threatening to betray her.

Khiri needed a distraction. That was the main difference between when she and Kal had companions and when they were alone. Distractions. Khiri decided to practice her ability to reach out with her magical senses as opposed to her physical. She shut her eyes, listening to Kal's feet ahead of her as they strode over the relatively even surface of the road.

Relaxing into the magic that made her ears hum, Khiri reached out and saw without her eyes. She was in an entirely different landscape. The green of the grass became black, like the glistening soot of the Burning Valley.

She couldn't feel Kal in front of her anymore. The sun, once hanging over her in the dimly lit sky, had vanished from her sight. There was no sense of the road. Darkness over the ground blended into the pitch of the horizon. Above her, the sky was as black and blank as an overcast night during a new moon. Darker... Blanker... It was a void.

"I wondered if you'd meet me here." A voice, *his* voice, flowed over her skin like cold water. The looming figure of the Flayer mage stood before her. Khiri wondered how she could have missed his presence, even in a place like this. "But I see you haven't truly arrived. Plane shifting... Not uncommon for an initiate. But intriguing. You do have some odd gifts, Daughter of Fortiva."

"What do you want?" Khiri demanded. An odd echo sounded when she spoke, as though her words were being said in two different places by the same throat. The idea made her deeply uncomfortable, but she didn't think it was far off the mark. Plane shifting was not a term she was familiar with. Kal would know about it. Khiri wished she knew how to get back to him.

Irrellian Thornne walked toward her, silently flowing over the shimmering black sands with the grace of a predator. Hypnotic, strong, deadly. *Telgan Korsborn*, the name inside of her greeted the otherness within him.

"What I want..." His onyx features reflected whatever light it was that Khiri could see by. It occurred to her suddenly that the Flayer Mage had never been human. At least, not entirely human. He actually bore a rather strong resemblance to Kal. She made a mental note to ask Kal about his people at some point. "I want the same thing I've always wanted... A better world."

"Is that what this is?" Khiri felt a flare of anger build within her. A righteous, burning, *stupid* anger that was determined to provoke the Flayer mage. Part of her wished she would hold her tongue, while the other part of her urged her to keep going.

A laugh erupted from Irrellian's throat. It wasn't a noise of joy, but derision. "My dear, this is not my vision. You've traveled into the Demon Realms. You're lucky that I'm the first being you encountered here."

"Why?" Khiri gritted her teeth. Irrellian Thornne was still walking toward her. Fighting against some mental impediment, Khiri tried to move. Her feet were frozen in place. She was trapped, as surely as if she had been bound and gagged.

"Because I actually want you to live," he purred, touching her face with one onyx hand. "I want you to come to me of your own accord. It will happen one day. I've seen it."

"Never." Khiri tried to lean away from the hand on her cheek, but her body betrayed her. It leaned into the caress as though she were a kitten seeking attention from a kind stranger. The name within her mind, with its heavy iron aftertaste, trilled its satisfaction.

Irrellian withdrew his hand, giving Khiri an amused smile. "You will. You will be at my side as I tear Arra down and build her anew. We are bound, you and I."

Tears tumbled their way down her cheeks when Khiri felt her eyes opening, though she'd been certain they were open already. Blurry images, as though she were rushing through a great distance, flowed past her in a whirlwind of color, smell and sound. Kal's hands were on her arms, shaking her. She was laying on the ground in the center of the road. All she recalled was the nearness of Irrellian Thornne and his nearly clear blue eyes holding her transfixed as he had promised her that she'd come to him, eventually.

Throwing his arms around her in a fierce hug, Kal was the most frantic she'd ever seen him. "Sweet river waters, Khiri... I thought you'd... I couldn't sense you!"

Khiri felt wetness smack against her neck. If she hadn't been so distraught herself, she would have been absolutely shocked Kal would cry over her.

"Plane shift?" Khiri couldn't quite find the words for everything she wanted to ask, so she trusted Kal to pick up the question.

"It's a mage's ability to travel through the realms of being. Uncommon, because most mages find it safer to stick to mortal paths.

I tried sensing for you in the neighboring dimensions, but you were too far away," Kal sighed. He still hadn't released her from his embrace, but his grip was less urgent. Khiri felt the shift from panic to something warmer. Deeper.

"Kal..." She pushed him away and crawled to her feet. After her experience, only moments ago, with Irrellian Thornne, she needed the freedom to move. The sensation of the Flayer mage's caress still burned against her cheek. She felt tainted by the touch.

Kal didn't fight when she pushed him, but his eyes still held the smolder of ignited passion. It was almost enough to cleanse her of Irrellian's touch, but not quite. She had to tell him. Maybe then he would understand why she was so reluctant to be with him, so restrained when he offered her affection, so... torn.

"I encountered the Flayer mage in the Demon Realms," she said, hugging her arms to her chest. Khiri began walking in the direction they had been headed before things had gone haywire. Judging by where the sun had drifted, she had already cost them almost an hour of travel time. Walking also gave her an excuse not to look Kal in the eyes.

Kal was silent as he walked beside her. She could feel him watching her, but aside from the occasional tap of his staff against the packed dirt or the crunch of a rock beneath his boots, he offered no comment. Khiri was grateful that it wasn't Estan in the mage's place. The knight would have demanded to know if she was alright, plied her with questions of where and how and why, and then made some sort of promise that he would find a way to fix things. With Kal, she could tell him without having him jump to conclusions. He wasn't one to make vows that could only end badly.

"I wasn't trying to go to him," Khiri said. "I was trying to practice the sight-without-seeing thing that you taught me on the way to Taman. As soon as I released my senses, I found myself in a place of darkness and black ash, and he was there. I... He may have come to me, or I may have gone to him. The... My..."

With a sigh, Khiri worked to find the right words, but she wasn't sure where to start. She wasn't even certain how much Kal knew about her people. "Do you know about the Name Breathing and the soul names of the Life Tree Clans?"

"I know the elven people are born knowing who their ideal soul-mate is—your 'Destined,' I believe is the term. It's a rather different process than the Odlesk, and very odd how the two interact," Kal answered, his tone neutral. Khiri was pretty sure if she looked at him, she would see him smiling at her, but it didn't flow into his voice. "I've gathered that there was something unusual about your Destined."

"The name of my soul bond changed on the day of my Name Breathing. I grew up thinking it was Micah," Khiri felt old tears mix with some of the new ones. She thought she'd moved past the pain of the exile and all her old dreams. It was still a relief not to be pretending the wrong sort of affection with someone she'd never really loved. But Micah—her best friend and bond brother—was on her back as a bow instead of being at her side, and she was bound to someone that made her skin crawl.

Worst of all, she did feel a pull every time Irrellian Thornne was near. She had to admit it, if only to herself. Something, whether she was soul-bound or just drawn by curiosity, drew her toward the Flay-er Mage. "I was sent out in search of either my new Destined, or a way to reverse whatever had happened. Micah came with me, and we discovered that we didn't want to change things back. We didn't like each other *that* way. And then I... I found my Destined. That day you and Estan came to save me... When Fennick died. My Destined had been asleep for a very long time..."

As they continued along the road, the dimming sunlight matched Khiri's bleak mood. She wasn't sure what Kal would do, but now the truth was out there. Her heart ached. He may choose to give up on her. Shydan might want him to leave her side. Maybe Kal would think she was a liability, and he'd choose to leave on his own.

"It's funny," Kal said into the growing silence. "I don't know if you realized it, but you being bound to Irrellian Thornne is no great revelation to me. Before we encountered the Flayer mage, you were looking for something. You had been looking for something when I tracked you as an assassin and you continued to do so even as far as Harish. Every new person you set eyes on, you searched."

Khiri's heartbeat thudded in her ears. She'd been so scared to tell anyone, afraid they'd somehow blame her for her bond.

"I watched you as we scouted together in Grimson's Pass, you know. You weren't searching anymore. The longing, the seeking... It was replaced by a guardedness and no small amount of fear. I've known the name inside your mind for almost as long as you have."

"But... You..." Khiri started to protest, not understanding. "If you knew, then why..."

Kal stopped her with a hand on her shoulder and tilted her chin up so she could look him in the eyes. "Khiri, do you think I care? Irrellian Thornne, Estan, Micah... It doesn't matter what name is linked to your mind. I only care about the one linked to your heart."

Before Khiri processed what Kal had said, before she could back away, before she could run from her feelings, Kal's mouth came down to hers and lightly pressed against her soul. Golden sparks swirled in her vision and her breath caught in her chest as his hands clasped her arms. The last vestiges of Irrellian's touch flaked away from her skin in the embracing fires of Kal's inferno. The name *Telgan Korsborn* pulsed unhappily behind her eyes, attempting to assert itself, claim its territory in the slag and mush that Khiri's mind had become. All of her previous protests were indistinguishable from the rest of her mental landscape. Nothing seemed to matter aside from her desire, her *need*, to press into Kal's lips, to feel his tongue rush into her mouth, to let his touch scorch away the icy burn of the Flayer mage's presence.

This time Kal pulled away, leaving Khiri dazed. He tugged her back toward the path. Khiri noticed the sun hadn't moved. She'd expected the clouds to have burned away, or the sun to be setting. Surely, Arra herself had just shifted.

"Did you know that the Odlesk are also bonded to soulmates?" Kal asked.

"No..." Khiri said. She was giddy with golden sparks still flying across her vision, but something about the question brought back some of her doubts. Something about needing to know more about the Odlesk. "How does it work with your people? Did you know my name?"

With a shake of his head, Kal gazed down at Khiri with his large, golden eyes. His lips twitched in amusement. "We know them when we see them."

A lingering worry tangled its way into Khiri's thoughts. With enough time, she hoped she could work it out.

37

~Estan~

ESTAN SLIPPED INTO the hidden entryway and tapped the rune code Ysinda had shown him. Catapult remained two streets away, amusing himself by browsing the merchant stalls and letting the vendors pitch their wares to him. The warhorse was practicing his new speaking trick, using the merchants as an audience; he didn't seem to have the hang of keeping his voice at a constant pitch yet. Maybe Estan should have told Catapult to pose as an adolescent. They usually had pitch control issues naturally and thus the squeaks and bobs of the false voice would've garnered less attention.

Not seeing Ysinda within her quarters, Estan sat down at the kitchen table to wait for her. Estan had forgotten he currently wore the face of a stranger and Ysinda wouldn't recognize him, until he was plowed out of his seat by a seething blonde ball of rage.

"I don't know who you are, or how you got here, but you'll not live to long regret your mistake!" Ysinda's dagger was inching its way toward Estan's throat. He'd only managed to get his arm between the attack and his face because years of training had moved his muscles before his brain even recognized the threat.

As he struggled to keep the dagger away from his jugular, Estan choked out, "Ysinda, calm down. It's me!"

Confusion played over her features, but Ysinda didn't let up on her attack. She was a predator whose den had been infiltrated. Again, he'd rushed in without thinking about the consequences. He'd leapt into the same damned fire like a fool, thinking maybe it wouldn't burn off his eyebrows this time.

"Who are you?" Ysinda demanded. "Speak quickly, because one slip and you die."

"Estan, Knight of the Protective Hand, your chosen Consort," he said. He managed to get his hand around her wrist, prying it back from his unprotected skin. Estan wasn't sure he'd come back if he died twice in the same day.

Being the Queen of Thieves, Ysinda did not take him at his word. She kneed him in the ribs, barely missing the tender center of his chest, and shoved forward with her dagger. The point was digging into his flesh as she hissed, "Prove it."

"You like cherry cobbler and mint tea with sugar. You like cute almost as much as you like deadly, and you originally asked me to investigate the identity and whereabouts of Rothan Haud," Estan sputtered.

Recognition cooled Ysinda's features, enough so that Estan detected the traces of tear trails over her dusty freckles. "Estan?" Her voice quavered ever so slightly, and she drew her dagger away, though her grip on it never faltered. "But you're dead."

"Rothan Haud paid me a visit," Estan said. "Because of my bargain with Taymahr, my death was a little less final than he would've hoped. I know who he is now."

"Who?" Ysinda demanded. Her aura of innocence faded as a growing promise of death radiated from her gaze. It struck Estan in that instant that Corianne had been right about how different Ysinda could be when push came to shove. Even the cocky, confident woman he'd seen sitting on the throne inside the pit, her Court, hadn't been enough to really drive home what Ysinda was in her heart of hearts: a killer.

"You really are the Queen of Thieves, aren't you?" he asked, trying to sort out his feelings during this moment of revelation. "I mean, I knew you were the Queen of Thieves, but I didn't really understand..."

"What are you talking about?" Ysinda snapped. "Estan, if you know who Rothan Haud is, I need to know. If you don't, I don't have time for this. Since I'm done mourning you, I need to get back to work."

"I'm sorry," Estan said. He eyed her dagger as he scooted himself out from under her, forcing himself to move past the moment. She had been ready to drop him. No hesitations. No qualms. No second thoughts. He recalled the guilt he still carried from his time on the front lines of the war against Eerilor, and wondered if she would've felt anything later. "It's been a long day for me, too. Maybe I'd make more sense if I could get off the floor?"

Ducking her head, Ysinda put both of her hands on her thighs, drawing herself up onto her knees. She pushed herself to her feet and held out her hand to help him up. "I didn't mean it," she said. "I mean, I am busy, but..."

Estan watched her transform back into the woman that he had first met, the one she tended to be when he was the only person watching her. She was very like her collection of weapons and stuffed animals; soft and fluffy one moment, sharp and deadly the next. "I... I just don't know that I really saw you before," Estan admitted. "Do you enjoy the torturing, the murdering, and the danger?"

"I told you before. I chose this life, Estan. It's all a part of who I am. As much as I like you, if you can't deal with that, we'll part ways now. I'll do my best not to hold it against you. Either way, I need that name," she sighed. Even though her words stung, Estan couldn't help but notice how she clung to his hand. She didn't want him to go. She had cried for him when she thought he was dead. He didn't want to lose her.

"I... I'll try," he said, drawing her into a hug, trying to ignore how the flattened blade of her dagger pressed against his back. "As long as you don't ask me to participate, I think I can manage."

"Deal," she whispered into his chest. "Name?"

"Arad Rhidel," Estan told her.

She tensed, drawing away from him enough to meet his eyes. "The head of the Venom Guild?"

He nodded, letting her turn from him as she began to pace. The threat identified, Ysinda was trying to work out how best to fight it.

"I knew the Venom Guild wanted Jarelton, but Rhidel being here in person is a much bigger problem," she muttered, patting the flat of her dagger against her empty palm.

"He's selling the children of Jarelton to the temples of Seirane," Estan continued. "I think I have an idea of how to stop him. If we pull it off, it will slow him down."

"What did you have in mind?" Ysinda asked. "I'll see about lending you some muscle."

"But..."

Ysinda held up a hand, "I'm not going to tell them who you are. I can already see why you came disguised, though how you managed..."

"Catapult," Estan shrugged.

"Your horse?" she raised a delicate blonde eyebrow. Estan felt a sudden urge to kiss her, but restrained himself. It was hardly the time. Instead, he inclined his head in a slight nod.

Giving a shrug of her own, Ysinda didn't question the matter further. "I have two enforcers in mind. I'll assume you've already involved Evic and Corianne. Even if the other two guess your identity, they won't betray us."

"Then have them meet us in the stable yard of the Talon Acre Inn," Estan said. "I still need to find new equipment and a new place to stay."

"You're my Consort," Ysinda said. "I can save you some time on both counts."

YSINDA HAD DONE BETTER than fund his new equipment; she'd taken it out of her own collection. His new sword was a good blade: flexible, light, sharp edge, tapered point. Not quite as short as his old sword, but he could adjust. The one-and-a-half-hand hilt was wrapped in soft buck hide with a solid knob of burnished steel and an unadorned hand-guard. Estan couldn't quite remember how long ago he'd started traveling with steel at his hip, but he felt naked without it. A sword hanging at his side was comforting, even if it wasn't fancy.

The Queen of Thieves' selection of armor had been very limited. Ysinda only kept three piecemeal sets outside of her personal gear, and only one of those had been his size.

"I only keep what I like," she'd shrugged when Estan made the mistake of inquiring. The knight tried not to think about who'd originally owned his new gear while strapping on a black leather chest plate with brassy studs. His pants were now a reddish brown, thick with padding and studs. New gloves, much more decorative than the rest, with braided patterns burnt into the dyed blue leather, made him feel a tad silly. He'd tucked the gloves into his new pouch rather than wear them. Once the true bite of winter settled in, Estan knew he'd be happy to wear them no matter how decorative they were.

"*Are you certain you were a member of the knighthood?*" Taymahr asked.

"*Of course I was, my Goddess,*" Estan replied, hurt and confused at the question.

"*But you didn't feel the full ceremonial plate was too much?*" She almost sounded amused.

Rather than allowing his Goddess to bait him, Estan blew a sigh out his nose and continued down the street. Catapult fell in beside him, not saying a word but huffing his horse breath into Estan's ear. A rather disconcerting sensation when the person walking next to him looked like an average person.

"What's next?" Catapult asked. The voice he used sounded oddly familiar. Estan shot the horse a dirty look when he placed it: *Kal.* "Do we have a plan?"

"Stop it," Estan scowled. "He isn't here, and I don't want to deal with any part of him."

"But he's easier to do than this one," Catapult complained, switching into a gruff imitation of Ullen's voice. "And you're using your voice."

"They aren't using their voices?" Estan asked.

"Not here," Catapult mumbled, doing his best to look petulant.

It struck Estan that the warhorse was probably missing his friends every bit as much as the knight did. Maybe even more so when it came to the mage. Probably more so. Definitely more so. Estan still couldn't stand the man. He started to relent, when something else occurred to him.

"It's probably not a good idea to sound too much like someone that was once an assassin," Estan cautioned the horse. "Someone may notice."

Standing straighter, the disguised horse tilted his head in such a way that Estan could sense that his ears were pivoting the way that they did when he was on alert. "Understood," Catapult said. "So I should blend them the way I do faces?"

"Not a bad idea," Estan said. "Our next step is back to the Talon Acre, and from there... We'll talk more about that at the meeting."

As they wandered through the streets, Estan contemplated his plan. He wondered who Ysinda was planning on sending him. He knew she trusted Evic and Corianne more than the majority of her

Court. They had always struck Estan as very genuine. If they were a tad on the rough side, it wasn't without reason. He hoped that Dagan wasn't on the list of Ysinda's trusted enforcers. The wiry thief rubbed Estan the wrong way. Recalling the way Corianne had ordered the man out of the inn when they'd been leaving, he was pretty sure he wasn't alone in the sentiment.

Estan and Catapult arrived at the stableyard first. The horse dropped his disguise and returned to his stall as though he'd never left. Climbing into the hayloft, Estan waited for the others to arrive. Adela and Ren were the first to return. Neither of them looked up to see the knight, but Adela gave Catapult's nose a soft, sad pat as they ambled into the building. Estan swallowed back words of comfort to relieve their suffering. One day, he promised himself, they would be repaid for all they had done for him. They deserved far better than this charade.

Resmine, Dewin, and Evic all arrived together, and it was only another ten minutes before Corianne came in, dropping down from the rooftop. "Let's nick the skinny of it right in the jaw," Dewin's elder sister said. She sounded angry, angrier than Estan had ever heard her. He couldn't see her face, but her voice was hoarse. "What's this I hear about Estan bein' dropped? First I sees of him, he's speakin' down a mob, then he's got himself poisoned and now he's bein' carted about by the Sweeps."

"It's a long story," Resmine said. Her eyes were still red from the crying she had been doing. Watching her, Estan felt almost as bad as he did when he had seen the owners of the Talon Acre. She knew he was alive, but he'd still put her through hell. Considering Syara's death, Estan nearly punched himself. Of course Resmine was upset, finding him the way she did. It probably had sent her right back to the dark place. He was such an ass.

Estan was about to descend and announce his presence, when a voice spoke from behind him. "I imagine this one may know a bit about it, Cori."

The knight jumped, nearly falling from the loft in his haste to get away from whoever was up in the hay with him. He hadn't sensed their approach. Recent memory flashed the image of a curved dagger right before it was thrust into his heart. If the person behind him hadn't caught him, Estan would've fallen into the stables and likely broken his neck. Having died once earlier in the day was more than enough for him.

Pale, short, silver hair and the barred clan tattoo of the Life Trees. The exile was grinning her deadly, maniacal grin. Her gigantic companion shifted himself out of one of the stalls and stood below Estan, silently extending his arms. With an insincere, "Oops," the exile pushed the knight out of the hayloft and into the huge man's waiting grip.

"Estan!" Dewin and Resmine rushed over to help him down.

"The Queen's dead consort?" The large man's tone was more assessment and less confusion. "Interesting..."

Resmine looked up into the giant's face and said, "Please, put him down, Shiv."

"I knew you people had secrets, but I may have underestimated you," the giant, Shiv, said.

"What're the two of you doing out of Court, Risk?" Evic asked. "And... Estan?"

"Knew Shydan'd leave his gloves off you," Corianne grinned, not seeming to notice he didn't look anything like himself. It wasn't until she got closer that Estan could see the redness in her eyes. Combined with the hoarseness in her throat, he could tell she'd been crying hard earlier. She wrapped her arms around the knight in a hug. "You're too entertaining."

Estan squeezed back, trying to hug all of the grief he could out of her. "I'm sorry I made you worry."

Tak entered the yard, shutting the gate with a clack, and paused to take in the scene before him. Estan, still disguised, was the only one that appeared to be a stranger to the information trader, but Tak didn't seem perturbed by the group of thieves. Just curious. "Are we going to drink him into the next life together, or am I missing something?" the trader asked.

"It's me," Estan said. "Catapult's keeping me out of sight, but..."

Before he got more out, Tak joined Corianne in giving Estan a huge hug. Grinning, Evic wrapped his arms around the three of them and squeezed. Estan's chest protested the attention.

"Alright, enough of that, lads and ladies." Risk jumped from the loft with the grace only someone raised in a tree could possess. "We left our post for a mission. I'd very much like to get back to Court before it snows."

38

~Khiri~

TENISING WAS PRETTIER than Elmesh, but still nothing like the stone confection that was Taman. Streets were lined with large red and brown stones, much smoother than the rough cobbles of Elmesh, while large expanses of greenery had been left to grow around the stores and homes. Pine trees were everywhere. While the occasional oak or elm peaked out from the needles, they were stripped naked of their leaves in preparation for the coming cold. The buildings were amalgamations of brown timber and flint, while those with a second story were covered in a creamy plaster to keep out winter's drafts.

Winter was worse here than in the Life Trees, and Khiri was happy she wouldn't have to stay long. At the same time, she felt a growing sense of curiosity about the city where her parents had met.

Her first priority, of course, was to find the armor masters and finish the investigation. Assuming she and Kal could manage not to get arrested while they were in town, there was no reason she couldn't also ask around for someone who knew her father. Or maybe her mother... and what she was like before she began her new life as Leyani.

What if her mother still had family in Tenising? It had never occurred to Khiri to wonder about extended family before. Her father's parents were very unattached and inattentive to their son and his daughter. Much like Micah's parents had been. Maybe that was the original reason that whatever force it was that assigned the elves their Destined had brought Khiri and Micah to each other. Her father understood what Micah had gone through in a way that she never could, because Genovar and Leyani had always been loving and attentive parents.

"I think we found one of the shops." Kal pointed to a very simple black-paint-on-whitewash sign that read: *Rory Task's Armor House.*

Khiri followed after the mage with mixed feelings as they approached the two-storied, mostly wood and plaster workshop. Only two apprentices were visible, working diligently on their projects. They didn't even look up as Khiri and Kal entered the door, despite the chime that floated a delicate jingle through the shop's interior. Unlike the other armor shops Khiri had been in, this one did not have piles of armor haphazardly stacked in center tables for easy perusing. Chest plates and shields were mounted against the walls. The only things stacked on the center table were the in-progress pieces of the craft master, who seemed to be in the middle of a complicated bit of matching armor and horse livery. No one wearing a master's knot was in the front, but she could hear someone clomping around upstairs.

"Be right with you," a heavy base reverberated down the stairs, thick and earthy. It was easy to imagine the owner of such a voice was a gruff, no nonsense sort of person. Khiri swallowed, and reminded herself that she wasn't here to waste time.

Even though the apprentices had already been busy when Khiri and Kal had walked in, they bent over their work with greater determination. Rory Task tromped down the stairs, each step deliberate. This master was a perfectionist. Everything from his spotless, tan leather boots to the top of his recently shaved and oiled head was immaculately manicured. His skin was as smooth and brown as an acorn's shell, not a trace of blemish or scarring. The only stain on him was the obvious darkening around his fingernails that a leather crafting master tended to accumulate over a lifetime of working with dyes and oils. His broad nose flared as his penetrating, brown eyes locked onto the two strangers that had entered his shop. "Your equipment looks to be in fine repair. Master Vort's work if I'm not mistaken. What brings you to my shop?"

"We are investigating a delicate matter. Unofficially," Kal said, his usual hint of humor missing from his tone. Rory Task was not a terribly large man, seeming average to most of the tavern patrons Khiri had observed, but he demanded respect. It was hard not to give it to him. "The arming of Flayers by someone of master work capabilities in mass quantities. Your name was mentioned, so we wanted to ask a few questions."

"Ah." Master Task's lips pressed into a sharp line as he made sure his apprentices were focused on their work. "Tryger, you have the floor. I'm only to be interrupted if absolutely necessary."

He led the elven hunter and the Odlesk mage up a small flight of stairs, then across a room filled with bolts of leather, scraps of metal and several large wooden vats. Much of the upper work rooms were clean, but not as carefully maintained as the store front. Rory Task still seemed like a stickler, but maybe he wasn't quite as overbearing as Khiri had initially imagined. All the same, she kept her grip firmly on her hilt in case he was leading them into a trap. Too much had happened in the other shops for her to discount the possibility.

What Master Task led them into looked a lot more like an office than a trap.

"Normally, I'd ask on whose authority you feel you have the right to ask me anything. Unofficially or not." Rory Task eased into what was obviously his chair behind a solid oak desk.

Like his sign outside, his chair was as basic as it could be: sturdy, rounded corners, no scroll work, no etching, finished but not painted. Serviceable. His chair and the two facing him were similarly serviceable. It seemed like a good word for most of his office, Khiri decided. This was not a man dedicated to *pretty*.

Master Task gestured for Khiri and Kal to take the remaining seats while he continued talking. "But just two nights ago, I had Flayers beating on the doors and shutters of this establishment. Tryger, Oster and I were trapped in here overnight, until the guard managed to drive them off the next morning."

Sliding Micah and her pack off her back, Khiri kept her brother close at hand. While Rory Task certainly noticed Khiri's reluctance to shed her weapons, he didn't protest.

"Elsina Rorsband and I have been rivals, friendly ones, for well over twenty years. She... She was not as lucky. Flayers tore her shop to pieces. Three of her apprentices were murdered, while Nillian, her newest—a former scout from the front lines—grabbed a leather knife and the bracer he'd been working on. Nillian is the only reason Elsina made it out alive. The guard hasn't cared to investigate, so I'm willing to work with someone who is. I don't have a lot in this world, but those two down there are under my care. I will not just stand by while my livelihood, and their lives, are in jeopardy."

"We'll do what we can to find answers," Khiri said. "Every other master of your craft has been attacked as well."

"All of them?" Rory Task raised an eyebrow. "How can we all have been attacked?"

"Thomas Illesan, Kivian Threshler and Ian Vort lost all of their apprentices, and we only know for certain that Ian Vort is alive. He was in bad shape, and if we hadn't arrived when we did, he might not have made it," Kal said. He was watching Rory with his large, unwavering eyes, waiting for the master craftsman to react.

When Rory Task did react, it was not the way they were waiting for. Khiri had been half expecting a violent outburst, demands to know why they suspected him, fierce denial, or maniacal laughter followed by something along the lines of "You found me!" She hadn't been prepared for the slow deflation of a man receiving heart wrenching news. Her suspicions had been resting on Master Task. Not only was he one of the last leads they had, but his shop and those working there hadn't been destroyed.

"Why is it that the Flayers didn't get in here?" she asked.

"Anti-Flayer charms," Task answered absently. "Most shops don't bother with them, because, well, how often do Flayers attack businesses other than inns? Anti-theft and trespassing charms don't actually do much to the demon-bound. Flayers tend to avoid crowds and main throughways unless there's a Flayer fog, and the Flayer fog demons are usually too weak to get in through shadows. But I live here. My gran used to scare us with stories about living alone, waking to find a Flayer gnawing on your toes, so I've always been cautious about keeping charms renewed."

"Would it bother you if I took a quick peek at your recent orders?" Kal asked. He was already standing up, as though he expected an affirmative. Task motioned to a small set of drawers in the back of his office, still seeming distant. Khiri stayed in her seat, watching the armor master for signs of irritation or smugness. Anything that would indicate he was misleading them.

"How well do you know Kivian Threshler?" Khiri asked on a hunch.

Task looked at her in confusion for a few moments, then he seemed to snap out of his haze. "We were friends during our days in the Academy. Never best friends, mind, because our tastes were never that similar, but we ran with the same crowd. We exchanged letters once or twice a year, visited each other when we traveled, that sort of thing."

"Was Threshler the type to write love letters and never send them?" she inquired. Kal continued to rustle through papers behind her, though Khiri could feel his awareness intensify. Either he had found something, or her line of questions was particularly interesting.

"Love letters?" Task frowned. "Never in the time that I knew Kivian. He was much more likely to put it all on the line and ask in person rather than write anything. Kivian would've preferred not to pick up a pen to keep records, if he could've avoided it. Didn't much care to read either."

"*Khiri, I found something, but I want your opinion before we say anything.*" Kal's mental voice sounded both upset and excited all at once. "*Switch places with me.*"

"That's very odd," Kal said aloud. He pulled out the envelope Khiri had stolen from Sergeant Kari Peplar's desk and handed it to Task, "This was all that was left in Kivian Threshler's desk when we arrived there. What do you make of it?"

While Kal settled himself back into his chair, Khiri stretched and stood up, pacing back to where Kal had left an order side by side with one of Task's records. It was obvious the one Kal wanted her to look at was not Task's. Rory Task was as deliberate and measured with his penmanship as he was with anything else. His order forms were as precise and detailed as a scribe's hand. In fact, Khiri suspected he went to a copyist each time he was running low on his parchment. The one next to it was hastily scribbled and had none of the delineated sections describing what was being ordered, who was ordering, when it was expected to be finished, or where it was to be sent. It merely stated a location on the far side of Tenising and a date.

The parchment on its own would have been suspicious, but the seal at the bottom and the signature next to it made Khiri's blood chill within her veins. "*I don't think it's Task,*" she told Kal. "*He never would have left it where you could see it. He doesn't strike me as that sloppy.*"

"*No, but someone definitely wants us to get that impression,*" Kal replied. "*I don't think the source of the crafting is our biggest concern.*"

Khiri agreed with that sentiment wholeheartedly. *"This is dated for tomorrow; we should make sure that we're there. We need to verify—"*

"Slow down," Kal sent. *"I agree, but we need to be careful. There are too many coincidences here. I have a very bad feeling about this. We need to go speak to Elsina Rorsband, just to be sure that we're not reading Task wrong. If anyone will tell you about someone's faults, it's a rival."*

ELSINA RORSBAND REGARDED them with a cool stare from across the smoothly polished pine of the tavern table.

"I ain't gonna tattle on Rory Task for doin' naught wrong," she said. Master Rorsband was every bit as gruff and forthright as her rival, though as a dwarf, she was almost a quarter of his size. Khiri was getting another sense off of her as well. Elsina Rorsband was harboring a deep attachment to her rival. If it wasn't love, it was something very similar. "He's a good man, and there ain't enough of those."

They'd arranged to meet her in a local tavern. Task had assured them the place was nothing special as far as food or drink, but it was well known for its attention to cleanliness. Even its name, The Sparkling Cider Glass, was a nod to its reputation. From what Khiri could see, it was a reputation well earned. No cobwebs lingered in the rafters, not a dead fly or speck of dust lingered in any of the windowsills, and the mugs in front of them appeared brand new. Khiri felt ten times grubbier sitting on this tavern's bench than she'd felt when entering the palace. *Not a great start when meeting someone already inclined to glare at me like I've got a whole radish hanging out of my mouth,* Khiri grimaced.

"We just wanted confirmation he wasn't likely to work with someone that's been equipping Flayers meant to be released into neighboring countries," Kal assured her. "If you think it's unlikely, we'll take you at your word."

"Then ya ain't too bright, are ya?" Elsina Rorsband spat. "You go around takin' everyone at their word?"

"Hardly," Kal grinned, a touch of his wryness shining in his eye. "But we've already met with him and someone else is supposed to meet us here very shortly. They'll likely be much more cooperative."

Khiri didn't break her gaze from Master Rorsband, though she didn't remember making plans with anyone else. The tavern door swung open and Tryger, Task's head apprentice came through the door. Elsina Rorsband's face tightened as she gazed at the young dwarf, who looked surprised to see her there.

"And what's he going to tell you, other than Task's a great deal fairer than his old master and twice as gifted!" she demanded.

"Actually, Master Rorsband, I was here to tell you that Master Task is wanting to give you a spare work bench until you get your shop up again," Tryger gulped, bowing his head and ducking out the tavern door.

"I thought you said..." Elsina Rorsband scowled at Kal, then at Khiri. She looked annoyed and slightly confused.

"As I said," Kal grinned. "We'll take your word for it. If you were working with Task, I doubt Tryger coming here would have been a surprise to you. He's already vouched for your character. We seem to be at a dead end, so we'll be leaving tomorrow morning. Thank you for your time."

Master Rorsband hustled out the door, muttering about time wasters. Khiri shifted in her seat on the bench. She felt compelled to follow Elsina Rorsband in order to ask more questions, unrelated to the current investigation. Master Rorsband had lived in Tenising for many years. Decades, possibly. Khiri looked at Kal and silently asked, *"Tomorrow morning?"*

"Just in case someone is watching us," Kal said. *"We have to appear to be disappointed, like we're giving up. What's going on? You seem restless."*

As quickly as she could, she sent him what she knew of her mother and father's past, and all that she had thought of concerning her mother's family and what she hoped they might be able to find while within the city of Tenising.

Kal sighed. With a nod, he said, "Alright, we still have tonight. Let's see what we can come up with. Where do you want to start?"

39

~Estan~

ESTAN'S PLAN WAS VERY straightforward. "Haud doesn't know I'm alive, right? So what if I joined the Venom Guild like this, and then lured him into a trap where the rest of you could jump him?"

Resmine punched him on the arm in the same place she'd bruised early. "You moron! Really? You spend half a day coming back from the dead and that's the best you could come up with?"

"Ow!" Estan protested. "I'd like to see you come up with something better..."

He tried not to take it too personally when Resmine did come up with something better within moments of his challenge. It was easy to forget how smart Resmine really was when she wasn't distracted with Estan's own latest blunder.

"Catapult can disguise us as kids again," Resmine said. "Like he did for you during the riot out front."

Even though Risk and Shiv were not present for the occasion, they didn't seem surprised at the revelation of the warhorse's abilities. During the attempted riot, Estan had been careful with Catapult's identity, but it had been impossible to conceal someone within their group possessed the talent to craft illusions. He wondered if Ysinda had trusted Risk and Shiv enough to inform them, or if someone like Dagan had told them about the encounter. Either way, they nodded as though it weren't a shock.

"Corianne, did you have any luck finding where the children were being kept?" Resmine asked.

"I found a few likely dens, but no luck baggin' the foxes. They've likely camped a spread to keep from an easy smoke."

Resmine's nose scrunched as she absorbed and translated Corianne's answer. She looked around the room, making some rapid calculations, weighing their group against the task at hand.

"Here's how we'll do this: in groups of two, we'll head into the six major sections of the city and act like children until the Venom Guild comes to collect us. They can't have given up assassination contracts entirely. It's their main source of income and they've got to keep feeding their pet Flayers. That means they're unlikely to maintain more than one base per district."

"How far away can we move before Catapult's ability falters?" Risk asked, directing the question at Estan. The knight still found her to be the most unsettling member of their group. When she wasn't actively trying to intimidate him, or anyone else, she had an unflappable sort of calm about her. There was a sense that she felt superior to anything someone else might try. It was similar to being in the same room as Genovar Fortiva, though his presence was warmer, more feeling. Ysinda trusted her, but Estan wasn't certain if Ysinda trusted the exile's loyalties or merely her abilities. Given that Risk knew his true identity, he hoped it was both.

"Honestly, I don't know," Estan said. "Catapult?"

The horse trotted out of his stall, nickering proudly and tossing his large head. He chattered at the group, turning this way and that, as though he were taking a great deal of pleasure in telling them exactly how he would fulfill all of their needs. A few of the others in the group were starting to shoot Estan and Resmine worried glances as Catapult continued to shuffle and whinny. Estan let out a huff and patted the horse on his flank. "Enough, Catapult, we'd like to get moving tonight."

Blowing out his soft nostrils at the knight, Catapult melted into his disguise as a tow-headed child holding a small black puppy. "I think I can hold your images as long as you're within the city," the horse said, borrowing Khiri's voice for the small child. "I just place the image and it rides you. I don't have to watch. It stays unless you do something to make it go away."

"Any idea what would make it...go away, love?" Dewin scratched at her chin. She was obviously amused at addressing Catapult as an equal. Sharing a look with Tak, she rubbed her tattoo. He smiled and rubbed his own tattoo in response. They had been spending a lot of time together since the trader had taken the former thief on as an apprentice, but it had never occurred to Estan that they'd develop their own set of inside jokes and communications. He blamed his recent distraction with Ysinda. Estan hadn't been paying near enough attention to his friends. Something he should rectify, assuming they all came out of this scheme alive.

"Please, Goddess, let us all come out of this alive," he prayed.

Catapult seemed to be contemplating Dewin's question, or maybe he was discussing it with Numyri. His disguise was stroking the imaginary puppy, which was panting and wagging its tail. The horse was becoming better with details, more in tune with what his human companions noticed. "If I am not around and you do something that makes it not seem right, it may fall off," the horse said slowly. He frowned, and tried to rephrase it. "People may see through it."

"In other words, act like children or people will see the real us," Resmine said. "Fair enough. Who wants to team up? And who's most familiar with which city districts?"

ESTAN GLANCED AT CORIANNE and wondered how she felt being stuck with him. Catapult had imagined her as a girl of eight or nine summers, but she was still recognizable—same copper skin and raven curls, same sharp eyes. Estan had assumed Evic would want to be with one of his sisters, and Dewin opted to go with Resmine. Instead the male thief and Risk had chosen each other. While Estan had looked to see who else was surprised by this, he saw Resmine nod and whisper something to Dewin. Shiv approached Tak, seeming completely unconcerned that his normal partner was leaving with another. Tak agreed, leaving Estan, Corianne and Catapult to form the last team.

"The last time I came this way, it was with Tak and Dewin," Estan said.

"You're a right different piece o' fluff than I took you for, *Erdan*," Corianne snapped, referencing the first time she had met him. He had been attempting to be covert, but in retrospect, it wasn't a very good attempt. Corianne's vehemence caught him off guard, though.

"We're kids," he reminded her.

"And you don't think kids fight?" she demanded, balling her fists and stamping her foot. He hoped that some of what she was displaying was for effect, because he had no idea why she was so angry with him.

"You seemed happy earlier," he said. As hard as he tried, he couldn't think of what he might have done. "You gave me a hug."

"I was happy earlier, you lunk. Now, I'd be happy to make a right smear of you myself. Gave you a warning, solid as stone, what you were in for, and ya go and get all truss and fluffed anyhow," she gave him a shove. Estan couldn't help but wonder how the tiny girl shoving a very heavy-set and tall boy of ten summers looked to anyone around them. "Can't believe how easy you shuffled off your morals like you got a new set o' drawers. Can't last... She won't change."

"You... you're upset because.."

"Kids," Corianne reminded Estan.

It was timely; a group of adult workers were walking by, smiling and waving at the trio of urchins, one even warning them not to stay out too late. Either the workers hadn't heard about the recent abductions or they didn't believe kids in this neighborhood were in danger. Judging by the smell coming off of them, they may have been too intoxicated to care.

"Because I decided I liked *her* anyway?" Estan finished with a foot stamp of his own. He felt his own ire growing in response to Corianne's anger. It was ridiculous for her to react this way about his relationship with Ysinda. Just because he hadn't listened when she warned him away. Unless... "Cori... Are you jealous?"

"Now I know you're a lunk," she said. Estan didn't miss the hint of blush creeping up her temples, but Corianne didn't give him a chance to interrupt. "I ain't brooding over our might-have-beens, love. I'm concerned for a friend. Do you know what happened to her last...friend?"

"No," Estan admitted. "We haven't really talked a lot."

"Three friends, and I can't tell ya where to find a one of 'em anymore," Corianne said. "All dropped or missing within months of becoming her... friend. She's a right decent leader. I'll do what I can to keep her there as long as I can, but that don't mean I want to see you, or anyone else that I've taken to, fallin' 'neath her blade nor the knives of her admirers."

"Her admirers?" Estan echoed.

"How dense can a bloke get!" Corianne sighed. "You think you're the only tree baskin' in her sun? There's several that was waiting to maybe get tapped, no matter the success of her priors. Always a lunk, such as yourself, who thinks they're immortal."

Estan wanted to respond that he was closer to immortal than most, when he noticed Catapult had fallen behind. Stopping to check that the horse was still behind them, Estan met the tow-headed blonde's eyes much closer than expected. Opening his mouth to ask Catapult why it sounded like he'd stopped walking, his breath was suddenly close and stuffy as his vision went dark. Burlap scratched against his cheeks. A muffled cry from Corianne notified him that he was not the only one caught unaware.

"We got three for the warehouse!" A raspy cackle threaded its way through the sack around Estan. "Back up the wagon. This lad's heavy!"

"Probably been stealing this one's food. He's light as air," another voice said.

Ah, Estan thought. That's why the horse had hung back. Estan's disguise accounted for a bit of his weight discrepancy, but there was no way a small boy of six summers could ever be as heavy as Catapult. Catapult's disguise must have some added layer to it that the abductors didn't seem to notice they were carrying a man-shaped sack and a completely empty sack. Perhaps Estan could ask his horse about it later, when they weren't in the middle of the operation.

It took two of the captors to toss the captured knight onto the wagon. Smacking the wood hard with his chest and his face, Estan discovered his chest was still not fully recovered as the pain sent him into a fuzzy dark place between sleep and death.

DIM, HAZY LIGHT FILTERED into Estan's vision. He was cold and damp. His body lay against hard wooden planks. Lack of motion meant either he was on a floor or the cart had stopped. Carefully, he opened his eyes and pushed himself up. There was no longer a bag over his face. He was no longer on the wagon with Corianne and their abductors, but as to where they had put him...

It was a small wooden cell, only about as long as he was tall. In the dull light, he could tell the ceiling was not made for his height, though Khiri or Risk could probably stand comfortably in such a tiny room. Ullen most definitely wouldn't have had trouble, though his shoulders were broad enough he would've had a hard time turning sideways. Estan barely had room to sit. There was a small door with bars in the window and a feeding hatch. His disguise appeared to be intact, judging from the small pudgy arms he could make out in the darkness.

Estan shuffled toward the door on his knees. Only now, within the holding cells, did it occur to him to worry he and Corianne might not get taken to the same warehouse. What if he was stranded inside of a prison he'd voluntarily walked into? He really was the lunk Corianne kept accusing him of being. One of these days, he'd actually remind himself to listen to her. Trying the handle, the knight was unsurprised to find it locked, but it was worth testing.

"Cori?" he hissed through the bars.

There was no verbal confirmation, but a knocking on the wall on his right alerted him to her presence in the next cell. He wasn't aware that a knock could sound sardonic, but Corianne managed it. *She'd probably get on well with Kal,* he thought with a sigh. No way he wanted to be there for that introduction.

Conversation carried down the corridor, heading toward Estan and Corianne's cells. "...don't know how many you want directly from the lot," a male intoned. He had a polished voice, with a bit of a foreign lilt. Chulithan, if Estan had to guess.

"Oh, I trust your judgment. You know that," a woman answered.

Estan stopped breathing, as though the air in his lungs would give him away. Backing away from the door, he laid down in roughly the position he had started in, trying to be as silent as he possibly could. The woman's voice was one he knew very well; it had been one of the formative voices of his childhood. One of the strongest advocates for him becoming a Knight of the Protective Hand. On the day he'd left the temples, Estan thought to never hear the voice of Shalora, High Priestess of Seirane's Temple of Taymahr, again.

"These three just arrived," the male voice said, tapping Estan's door as they passed. "We'll see how they fare in the next few days."

"How many total?" Shalora's voice was beginning to taper off as their footsteps reached the end of the hallway. Given how close they'd sounded to start with, Estan estimated there were maybe ten rooms on this side of the hall. They had turned toward him, and the steps were turning away now which he reasoned put Corianne and him on an outer wall.

The response was hard to make out, but Estan thought he heard, "I can promise you about thirty from this warehouse, and another forty between..."

At least thirty from this warehouse alone; the numbers made Estan feel sick. How many had already been shipped to the temples? How many kids were left in Jarelton? What was happening to them once they arrived in Seirane? He wished he could coordinate with the others to find out where they were, share knowledge and keep someone on the inside all the way to the city of his youth. But there was no way Catapult's abilities would stretch that far. Catapult had only been guessing about his ability to cover them as long as they were inside Jarelton's walls.

All of these thoughts rushed like a torrent through Estan's mind as he heard the sound of his door unlocking. Afraid that Shalora's guide had returned to perform some sort of orientation, Estan continued to feign unconsciousness.

"Well, don't just lay there, you great lunk. If we're goin' to evaporate into the haze, we've got a night of it."

Corianne's voice had never sounded sweeter.

40

~Ullen~

AT LEAST HIS MOTHER'S proclamation about Lady Jaspar Ter-illes meant Ullen didn't have to find a way to stall the Court until the Solstice. Things were pretty much stalled on their own. Hon'idar wouldn't speak to Ullen until Jaspar chose to remain engaged to him. Jaspar was currently refusing all visitors, though Ullen had heard that in the kitchens rather than seeking to visit her himself.

Ullen couldn't blame Jaspar for refusing his brother entry to her quarters. Hon'idar was livid with his betrothed for agreeing to Queen Di'eli's latest scheme.

Jaspar...

It had been such a long time ago, but Ullen still remembered the first summer Jaspar had come to the palace. He'd been a young man, only entering his twenty-second summer. The Earl Terilles had been exchanging a warm greeting with King Dormidiir, Ullen and Hon'idar's father. Hon'idar hadn't been there that morning. The Crown Prince had gone with his regiment to do field exercises. Ullen had wished fervently for his older brother to arrive before the Earl Terilles. Hon'idar, with his golden hair and beard, looked the part of a prince. Prince Ut'evullen had often been accused by the courtiers of appearing too surly or stand-offish. The court ladies had found him charming, but nothing to his brother. Ullen had always been okay with Hon'idar's being the better liked. He'd never minded hiding in his brother's shadow.

While the king and the earl had stood in the morning sun, talking about the length of the journey and the banquet to be thrown later that evening, Ullen had suddenly been glad his brother was miles away. She'd hit him like the wind of a storm, and Ullen had felt his legs were suddenly made of steam. Despite years of etiquette training and countless drills, his jaw had worked to produce sounds that refused to exit his throat. Her chestnut curls had framed those widely-set violet eyes and her golden skin had been dusted with freckles. Ullen had tried not to stare at her pert nose and a strong jaw. She'd worn a dark green travel dress, but she'd carried herself with the grace of a queen all the same.

"Prince Ut'evullen, I presume?" Jaspar's voice had sent trills of pleasure down his spine, tickling like the tiniest of fingers.

"I... Uh... I mean, that is..." Ullen had glanced at his father for help. His father and Earl Terilles had still been talking though, his father pointing out the new barracks being built in the back yards and talking about his plans for a university in the front yards.

"A little shy for a prince, aren't you? Well, we'll have plenty of time to get acquainted. I think you'll be my escort to the ball this evening. My father brought me here for the suitors to get a good look, but he can hardly complain if I spend the night dancing with a prince."

"Suitors?" Ullen's first actual words to the Lady Terilles, and he'd been asking about other men. It had embarrassed him then, and truth be told, the memory of it still turned his cheeks pink.

Jaspar had given him a mischievous smile and winked. He'd never stood a chance. In that moment, his heart had been irrevocably stolen by Jaspar Terilles, to do with as she willed. What had followed was a summer of stolen kisses in the corridors, long rides taken separately to meet away from prying eyes, and Ullen's first... Everything.

Earl Terilles and his daughter had left the court in good spirits. Both of them had been certain a proposal was going to follow them home. The proposal the Earl Terilles had expected was not the same one his daughter had anticipated, however. While Jaspar and Ullen had been courting in secret, the earl had been working with King and Queen Dormidiir on a more fortuitous alliance for Eerilor. Ullen hadn't noticed, looking at the world through the goggles of young love, that a number of neighboring countries had been sending their heirs to visit Taman.

When Ullen had petitioned his parents for the right to propose, he'd been informed Lady Terilles was meant to wed foreign nobility, to forge ties with neighboring kingdoms. That had been when Ullen first began his plans to run away from court life. He'd been plagued with nightmares of Jaspar's nuptials. Before he left, he'd sent her a letter of apology. How she'd managed to go from a bride promised across borders to Hon'idar's betrothed, Ullen had no idea. It seemed impossible to him that she'd managed to stay unwed this long.

"Prince Ut'evullen?"

The voice came from outside his door, but with the torrent of memories Ullen had been reliving, he doubted his senses. "Jaspar?"

"Please, hurry. Before someone sees me out here." It was Jaspar's voice. Despite the urge to hurry, her voice was steady and unbothered. A proper, bored tone. Nothing worth noticing to passing ears.

Ullen wished Kal was still in the palace. His spell to prevent eavesdroppers was invaluable for these kinds of intrigues. Checking to make sure his valet was still absent, Ullen opened the door to his chambers and beckoned in his former lover. While the valet had been recommended to him by Captain Horis Aldash, Ullen didn't trust the man. Until Ullen left his mother's palace, he wasn't sure he'd trust anyone again for a long time.

There were exceptions, of course.

"What are you doing here?" Ullen asked as soon as the door was sealed.

Even with a pulled up cloak concealing her face in shadows, Ullen couldn't imagine anyone mistaking Jaspar for another, lesser, woman. Nothing could conceal her natural sense of grace and poise. He longed to reach out and pull her toward him, but he'd learned a lot about restraint in their years apart.

"It's been a long time, my prince. But I'm obviously not here to exchange pleasantries. I came to let you know to get ready for a fight. I intend to choose you, when the time comes," Jaspar said, lowering her hood.

"Not you, too," Ullen sighed. "I've no interest in ruling, Lady Terilles. As I've told my mother, time and again—"

Cutting him off mid sentence, Jaspar shook her head. "I know you don't want this, and I am sorry to do this to you. This isn't about what you might want or even what we might have once been..."

An expression flitted over her features so quickly, Ullen thought he might have imagined it. Pain, regret, an old wound broken open. His heart pulsed in his throat. A traitorous flame of hope flared to life. Had she been nursing feelings for him as long as he'd been longing for her? He tried to push the emotions back down. The crown was too high a price, even for two people's happiness. Ullen's voice was thick with emotion as he made himself ask, "Then what is this about?"

"Your brother isn't the man you think he is," Jaspar said. "If I were to confirm him as Eerilor's next king, this country, *our* country, would suffer for it."

"You're here to appeal to my patriotism? Am I not the runaway prince?" Ullen laughed, more harshly than he intended. He'd imagined a thousand different ways his reunion with Jaspar would occur over the decades. This wasn't going at all as he'd hoped. It was pretty close to some of the worst case scenarios he'd come up with, though.

"Hon'idar seems much the same as I left him. He's a good man who'll make a good king. When we last spoke, he told me how excited he was to marry. I think he bears you genuine affection. Between what he sees as your betrayal and the trials our mother has thrown at him...Well, I believe it would wear down anyone."

"A runaway is better than a tyrant," Jaspar said. "You've seen Hon'idar's deterioration since you've arrived. He's not wearing down because of your mother's antics. I was in his confidence until your mother's announcement. Your brother was certain you'd be gone in a matter of days. His friendly facade was for your benefit. The rest of us know what's waiting for us the moment he's crowned."

It was impossible to keep the skepticism off of his face. "My mother has been plaguing me for the benefit of Eerilor?"

Jaspar actually laughed at that, shaking her head. "By the Stone, no. Your mother is a mad woman, playing games against a gnorel with an unlocked cage. It's only a matter of time before he opens that door. I'm probably mad, too, agreeing to this latest scheme of hers. Hon'idar grows angrier by the day. If I don't assuage him soon, I'm likely to be in as much danger as the queen."

"Please," Not caring about decorum, Ullen found himself across the room and gripping Jaspar's forearms. He knew he was begging, but he didn't care. "Don't ask this of me. You don't know how much I've wished... Jaspar, don't put yourself in danger for this. Surely, it can't be as bad as that. Hon'idar's always been hot-headed, but he was always quick to cool down as well. Are you telling me there's nothing left of the brother I knew?"

Pressing her lips together, Jaspar didn't have to say anything for Ullen to read the answer on her face. "You've been gone a long time, Prince Ut'evullen. People change. Not always for the better."

Extracting herself from his grip, Jaspar began adjusting her hood. "I hope your friends made it out safely. I did my best to clear the way for them. I wish I could let you go as easily, but, Ullen, you're Eerilor's best hope."

She was gone before Ullen realized she hadn't called him by his royal name.

41

~Khiri~

"OF COURSE I REMEMBER Genovar Fortiva!"

The bartender treated Khiri and Kal to a closeup version of the same disgusted sneer he'd been skewering them with since they'd entered his establishment. Even though a bath sounded heavenly, Khiri was relieved they wouldn't be staying overnight at The Sparkling Cider Glass. She doubted the dubious bartender would wait ten seconds after they left to begin scrubbing away all signs of their presence. "It was before all that Gray Army, Great War nonsense started. He began lurking around town with that awful lady of his. He took up with some young thing, and next thing we knew, all three of them had left Tenising together."

"Did the 'young thing' he left with have any family?" Khiri asked. She tried to ignore the disdain in the bartender's eyes and focus on her enthusiasm. It wasn't much of a link, but it was more than she'd had only moments before.

"They're all gone now... Big family back then. Her father died not long ago, and good riddance. Didn't come in here. Wouldn't dare. Never was a nastier piece of work in this city. Rumor was he beat the kids savage every time he lost at cards. Mother up and ran off, leaving the bastard with all five children and no sense."

Taking out a bar towel, the bartender began scrubbing the counter even though he'd already wiped it down twice since Khiri

293

and Kal had ordered their last pints. "Couldn't blame his girl for leaving really. All of them did, eventually, after she went. Oldest brother went searching for her not long after."

"What was her name?" Khiri asked.

"Can't remember," the bartender said with a sniff. He put some extra effort into his scrubbing as he attacked the nonexistent stain. His sneer grew as he worked. Khiri was pretty sure he was imagining a stain shaped like her own face.

Kal was pulling her toward the door when she tried one last question. "Do you recall her family name?"

"Howe? Hays?" The bartender wasn't even looking up at this point. He seemingly wanted the dirty people gone so he could clean his taproom in peace. "Something like that. Go look in the city record hall if you want to know. Someone's bound to have filed something."

TENISING'S HALL OF Records was the only all-stone building in the whole city. It towered over its neighbors; a full three stories looming over all the single story offices nearby. The city guard were stationed next door on the right, while a courthouse and two taverns shared the rest of its block. A large square with benches and statues cowered behind a wall of hedges across the cobble-paved street.

"Well, this was hardly how I imagined spending our first evening this close to an inn. But then, you're not quite there yet, are you, *laska*?" Kal sighed, but he was giving her that charming half-smile.

Khiri felt her cheeks flush in response to the implied invitation. Since the day she'd inadvertently plane shifted and ended up in Kal's arms, the lanky mage hadn't even hugged her. She did and didn't want to ask him about it. This was the first he'd broached the subject in days. Khiri had started to wonder if he'd lost interest after they'd kissed. Telgan Korsborn's name took the opportunity offered by her doubts to root itself deeper into her thoughts.

Imyn was even silent on the issue... She was often silent. If it weren't for the occasional comment or command, Khiri had a hard time remembering that the goddess was there.

"Why do you need to know who your mother was before?" Imyn chose that moment to ask, as though confirming she was present.

"I thought I knew my parents," Khiri struggled to explain. *"They were always just...my parents. Genovar and Leyani. Hunter and Trader for the Oak Wood Clan. I've learned so much about my father since I left home, I... I need to learn about my mother, too."*

"What if you are disappointed with what you learn?" Imyn inquired.

Khiri didn't have an answer for the goddess. She had been wondering the same thing after leaving the Sparkling Cider Glass, with all of the bartender's ominous, if patchy, memories. If her mother had been running away from such a family, did Khiri really want to find them?

The smooth marble floor of the records hall carried the soft tread of her footsteps and the slightly harder slap of Kal's boots into the upper reaches of the stacks. Shelves upon shelves of cubby holes filled with vellum and paper and leather bound tomes stretched from one end of the main floor to the other. Around the perimeter, the shelves lined the walls, with a large railed path at each new floor. Rolling ladders were located every few stacks. Nothing was out of reach, no matter the height of the researcher.

"At least we know to start with H," Kal said.

"Assuming that the bartender remembered that much," Khiri muttered. She hoped they'd find something before the next morning broke. Tomorrow promised to be a busy day.

ELITHANIA HAUD, Khiri rolled the name around in her head, testing it. She couldn't quite imagine her mother as an Elithania, but the elven woman described in the text didn't sound very much like a Leyani, either. Genovar Fortiva had been described much as she had always seen him—an elf of quiet dignity. Even when he was teaching his daughter to curse behind her mother's back.

The original Leyani had been a short, ruby-haired ball of trouble. She'd been arrested twice for theft, twice for initiating bar fights, and no less than eight times for disorderly conduct. It had been little wonder Genovar felt trapped by his connection to such a woman. She also seemed hampered by her Destined and his calming influence on her schemes. At least four of the former Leyani's arrests were attributed to Genovar. Things had not gone well for her after the name switch, either. In the very last file, a certificate of death for Elithania Haud had been registered.

"Last known residence: Halsh," Khiri read. "Where is Halsh?"

"It's a town on the border of Firinia. Are you wanting to visit the grave of your almost-mother?" Kal asked.

Khiri thought about it. A lonely twig of Lifewood, nowhere near the Life Trees and the Clans. Her almost-mother hadn't truly been exiled, but maybe she'd been happier away from the others. What would such a woman think about her former Destined's daughter seeking her out during her rest?

Kal's hand brushed Khiri's cheek, drawing her back into thoughts of the present. It was time to return to their other tasks.

Creeping across the city wasn't too difficult. Despite the rune lamps, the moon was hidden and the shadows were long enough to hide even Kal's lanky form. Within minutes, they were waiting in the bushes outside of the small clearing indicated on the planted note in Master Task's records. Kal cast his camouflage spell over the two of them and they began to wait. It was approaching the scheduled meeting time.

A russet haired dwarf appeared from between the trees, stumbling as the underbrush groped at his leg, as though it was unwilling to let him go. His long beard was left curly and was studded with leaves and twigs, making it look like discarded foliage was his snack of choice. His weathered cheeks were smudged with dirt and tanning oils, and something darker. Something that looked like blood. He was wringing his hands almost constantly. Whatever he was concerned about, it had him very, very worried.

Two more figures came out of the shadows. Familiar figures. Painfully familiar. Solancia and Radley. Khiri's friends from the journey to Grimson's Pass to Taman with whom she'd enjoyed many games of cards and stories over campfires. The same two that had sent her to the ambush at Master Vort's shop, she recalled. Now they were here, looking at the very unkempt dwarf that Khiri guessed was none other than Kivian Threshler.

"Where are they, Threshler?" Solancia asked. There was nothing friendly in her tone. Her eye patch, the one she had donned after losing her eye, no longer seemed cheery to Khiri despite its brilliant purple. Nightshade, always nightshade. Khiri had taken it as a joke; a pretty but deadly flower. Now she wondered if it shouldn't have been a warning.

Radley's arms were crossed, his expression no more comforting than the one his wife wore. "It's a long trip out here," he commented. "One we should never have had to make. I thought they were supposed to die in Elmesh."

"They were supposed to die with Ian Vort, but for some reason he's still ambling his way around Taman," Solancia spat. "But you do have a point. Somehow, those two keep slipping right through our nets. Tell us, Threshler, where are they now?"

"I... I don't know." Kivian Threshler looked like he was about to throw up. "I-I-I slipped the n-note right where you t-t-t-told me. Unless T-t-task found it and threw i-i-it out..."

"Enough of your stammering!" Solancia slammed a back-fist across the sputtering leather master's mouth, knocking him to the ground. "You've outlived your usefulness. The Army has no use for those that can't keep their bargains."

"No more does the Guild," Radley agreed. "He's all yours, my love. No more qualms about removing our mark of protection. If you had delivered... Maybe." The cook shrugged his large, muscled arms.

Khiri attempted to jump forward at that moment, but Kal restrained her.

"*Not yet.*" His gaze rested on the sniveling form of Kivian Threshler with a harshness that Khiri had never seen in him before. "*That 'Master' willingly bargained with both the Gray Army and the Venom Guild to have his apprentices murdered along with all of his colleagues and those in their employ, and tried to frame a long time friend. We will confront them, but not to save the likes of him.*"

"*I can't just sit here and watch him die!*" Khiri argued. "*I can't!*"

Kal searched her eyes for a moment longer, then released her with a sigh and tightened his grip on his staff.

Micah was out of his sheath and in her hand before another breath left her throat. She aimed for Solancia's hand, and released. But it was too late. The arrow punched its way through the dwarven warrior's glove only half way through the slice she jerked across the unfortunate leather master's neck. Kivian Threshler fell to his knees and toppled forward, a dark puddle forming under his head as it landed heavily on the dirt. His rump was propped in the air in a manner that would have been humorous if he wasn't bleeding out.

Solancia examined the glove almost casually, plucking the arrow out of the layered folds of leather. She gave Khiri a smile that turned the bile rising in the elf's stomach. "Shame you hadn't come out a few seconds earlier. Seems Threshler was actually pretty good at something. I could've gotten one more set of gloves out of him."

The tightness in Khiri's stomach grew. Not only had she witnessed death today, but two people she'd thought were friends were waiting to slaughter her. Unless she was willing to kill them first. Just like Fennick. She really might be sick.

Radley slowly pulled out a pair of daggers Khiri had never seen him wield before. During the trip from Grimson's Pass, he'd only engaged in one sparring match with his wife, and that had been under duress. He had fought with a borrowed sword and though he had more skill than Rigger, he hadn't seemed like much of a challenge. Khiri wondered, as the over-tall, curly blonde dwarf faced her, if that hadn't been intended to throw her off. If he could wield daggers the way he did frying pans, she was in real trouble.

Especially with Solancia closing in on Khiri's other side, her dagger ready. Solancia's short sword emerged with a flourish. Where Radley had always underplayed his skill, Solancia was very open about her abilities. Most of Captain Horis Aldash's unit had lived in fear of drawing her as a sparring partner.

Behind Khiri, Kal uttered arcane syllables under his breath. He shot his spell toward Radley. The blonde dwarf took a large boulder of ice to the chest.

"The forest is far too dry right now," Kal sent Khiri. *"I'll do my best not to set it on fire, but the moment you're in real trouble, I make no promises."*

Not trusting herself to words, Khiri gave the mage a brief nod and a flare of gratitude. She dropped Micah into the brush behind her and pulled out her father's dagger. It wasn't much, but there was no way she was going to endanger Micah again. The memory of her old bow snapping in two flashed through her mind. She'd never forget the feel of her hand around Micah's as she drove home the blow against the nearly-invincible Flayer. It was close to what she felt now. Helpless.

Tears would come later, she knew. She would cry herself to sleep the way she had when she had been in mourning for her newly-bound brother. But she *would* be the one crying. Khiri set her jaw and dug her toes into the dirt. She and Kal still had to warn Ullen.

If these two were here, Captain Horis Aldash was no longer Ullen's friend.

42

~Estan~

CATAPULT'S DISGUISE appeared as Estan and Corianne were rounding the corner. They had five or six youngsters in tow behind them.

"I can lead this lot out," Khiri's voice promised. "I can't fit past the main entry, but I can make it so they aren't seen."

Exchanging a quick nod with Corianne, Estan told the horse to do what he could. He didn't regret his phrasing until the tow-headed child's eyes lit with excitement.

"What I can?" Khiri had never sounded quite so mischievous. Estan wondered if somewhere, the elven woman's elbows were itching because of it.

Odd thing to remember, he chastised himself. Having itchy elbows when your name was used in vain was an old children's tale he'd heard while growing up. As likely as the belief everything would taste salty for a week if you stole a hat, or tales that certain areas of the forest held mushrooms that tasted like strawberries. He had yet to encounter the mushrooms, and he was pretty sure the hat was false as well. No reason Khiri would be suffering from name-related ailments.

As soon as Estan shook the children's tales from his head, he was looking at two, no three, versions of the tow-headed boy Catapult favored as his double. They were exchanging wicked grins with one another and the kids behind Estan and Corianne, which had tripled as well.

"We'll distract them while you free the others," two of the boys said.

"While I take the real ones through the other hall," the third finished. "It will be great fun!"

"Nothing dangerous," Estan chided his horse. "We want to get everyone out safely."

All three versions of the boy nodded vigorously and one of the false puppies yapped.

"*Numyri grows stronger through her connection with your horse,*" Taymahr said. "*The two are very well matched.*"

Estan tried not to grimace. They needed the High Ones to gain as much strength as they could. If Numyri grew stronger, then so would the others. Still, it was disconcerting to be told his warhorse was well matched to the High Goddess of Mischief and Mayhem. He wasn't entirely sure what he had released on the world.

Two groups of kids ran past Corianne and Estan down the hall that the knight had heard Shalora and her escort disappear into earlier, whooping and catcalling as they went. A startled cry and heavy footsteps let the adults know the diversion was working. The third group of kids made a hasty retreat following their dog-carrying boy. They were being as quiet as they could. None of them seemed as exuberant as Estan would have expected with the promise of liberation so close.

"What have they been doing to these kids?" he asked, not sure he wanted an answer.

"Nothing good," Corianne told him, her gaze echoing Estan's concern. "Don't see too many marks on 'em, but that don't mean much. Could be doping 'em with the evenin' stew, could be forcin' 'em to rat on each other... Could be lack of sun makin' the tykes shrivel like sprouts. Give 'em a few weeks, and most of the lot will even out again like it never happened."

"The others?" he asked. They approached another door and Corianne set to work popping the lock with a rune in one hand and a pick in the other. Estan leaned against the wall, trying to block the view of anyone who might come around the corner while he kept vigil.

"There's a reason rogues and thieves spring up, and those what join the grittier side," Corianne shrugged noncommittally, her tongue forming a tiny pink line against the white of her teeth as she worked the pick back and forth.

The door swung open. Footsteps came pelting down the corridor they'd been standing in only moments before. Estan didn't think, he just grabbed Corianne's arm and yanked her into the room she had just opened, which was not so much a cell as a storage closet. A few piles of blankets and a couple of mostly empty crates were stuffed into the cramped space, which now held to full-sized adults, for all that they currently looked like kids.

Corianne's breath was hot against his skin and Estan became uncomfortably aware of her proximity. He was glad it was dark, because he definitely didn't want to see her disguise at the moment. It was confusing enough to feel how hard his pulse was racing with this proximity to Corianne; not that she was unattractive by any stretch, but they were friends. They'd only ever been friends. She'd once been involved with Ullen, and that was before Estan had even met her.

"*You are surprisingly fickle for an avatar of mine,*" Taymahr commented, snapping him out of whatever had been going on.

"*It's just the situation. I'd be attracted to Resmine in these circumstances,*" Estan told his deity a bit gruffly.

Taymahr's disbelief mirrored his own. Estan shoved it to the back of his mind, telling himself he'd think about it later. He didn't have time for thoughts about Corianne, Ysinda or Khiri at the moment. They were still in the middle of deep cover in enemy territory and they had roughly twenty more kids to locate.

"Mr. Guard Man!" a child's voice rang down the corridor, followed by the sound of laughter and whooping.

"Hey, you! Get back here!" the guard pelted after the diversion, leaving Estan and Corianne to exit the cramped storage room, looking only slightly more disheveled than before.

"Bit of a heart-stopper, weren't it?" Corianne's bent over and tried to catch her breath. "Nothing quite like making it through the comb's teeth."

"Closer than I like," Estan admitted, not entirely sure if he was talking about the guard or Corianne herself. It took him a moment to realize that neither of them were disguised anymore. "Much closer."

He saw her expression change when she saw the disguises had melted. They'd done something no one would see as very child-like... But they hadn't actually *done* anything. "You... we..."

"No use worryin' about it," Corianne shrugged, though Estan could see she'd gone a little pink across the cheeks. "We've got work ahead of us, and a meet point to make."

Estan nodded. *Later.*

"LAST ONE," THE KNIGHT said, looking up and down the hall. Even with Catapult's help, Estan felt exposed. He and Corianne had wandered up and down every hall, popping the lock on any and all doors they'd come across. It was unlikely they'd get another chance to infiltrate this place, and they didn't want to leave anyone behind. Especially since they'd agreed the best way to stop its future use was to destroy it.

"I don't see a mite," Corianne said as she peeked through the bars. "But hadn't stopped us yet."

Something about this last door made Estan anxious. Maybe it was because they were nearly through and he had trouble accepting things had been relatively easy. It was a straightforward plan, with very few loopholes. But even allowing for that, it had all seemed easy. Too easy. Aside from almost running into one guard here and there, they hadn't encountered any real opposition. Not the kind of laxness he'd come to expect from the Venom Guild or the Gray Army. Neither organization had come to power by allowing their people to be lazy.

"...And done," Corianne started to smile just as a roar erupted from the interior of the room. Reacting with the instincts of a lifetime on the streets, she pulled a rune from her pouch and hurled it into the mouth aiming to chomp her head.

The creature froze. Literally. Frost crept from between its jagged teeth in trails of splintering crystals. Shards of jagged ice pointed toward the ceiling and walls like a cold explosion had centered around the creature's feet.

"What is it?" her voice was, understandably, shaky. She had avoided death by mere seconds, and whatever had attacked her was unearthly.

Estan studied the thing, though looking at it too long made him increasingly uncomfortable. Its mouth had stretched across the room leaving a trail of flesh to the bulk of its body. The creature's unfrozen flesh was an odd pinkish-gray, with great folds and wrinkles making it appear soft and flabby. Its girth was comparable to Shiv. Estan didn't doubt the creature was easily as strong as the massive thief. Instead of fingers, the beast had long, bone-like claws. Several glowing orange eyes, scattered like freckles across what passed for its face, were in the process of dulling as the thing eased into its frosty death.

"I think it's a creature of the Demon Realms," the knight said finally. "It looks like something I read about when I was a squire."

"If it be from the Realms, ain't it a demon?" Corianne asked. She was being careful not to touch it while she bobbed on her toes in an attempt to see if it was guarding anything. With a sigh, she ducked under its reaching maw and entered the room to search more thoroughly.

"I'm not sure if I would..." Estan started to warn her, but before he could react, Corianne took out another rune and smacked it on the creature's forehead. Webs of blue light crackled over the creature's skin, as though lightning had been captured beneath its hide. Blue intensified until it was practically white and then it vanished with a crack of thunder. "What did you do?"

"Exorcism," Corianne said. "Never thought I'd be needing it, but I plucked it off a wandering mage about a season ago and figured I may as well be keepin' it. Wish I hadn't lost the first. Was my favorite freezer. Only took a half-day's recharge."

Estan rubbed his chin, impressed by Corianne's display, and a bit intimidated. "As I was saying, that was not a demon, but it shares their realm. It's like their version of a gnorel. Hunts the unwary, roams the hills, that sort of thing. I think it was called a dreker. They're unable to make it through the realms without being summoned, but there hasn't been a mage willing to do it since..."

"Since Irrellian Thornne?" Corianne raised an eyebrow. "Looks like someone's bringin' home a party."

Estan shook his head. Even with the dreker's disappearance, he wasn't satisfied that he and Corianne were out of trouble. There was something he was forgetting. Something about drekers and the way they hunted.

"We've got to get out of here!" Estan shouted as the passage slammed into place in his mind. "I just remembered..."

A sound, somehow both roar and screech, echoed through the corridor, threatening to shatter Estan's eardrums. It was answered by two more cries in the opposite direction. "They hunt in packs," Estan finished with a sinking feeling deep in his chest.

Corianne didn't waste time. Grabbing Estan's arm, she yanked him out the door and down the hall. The head of a hapless guard that had been chasing Catapult's illusions disappeared into a mouth that crashed through the barred window of one of the closed rooms. The body thrashed like it still wanted to escape. Another dreker plunked its way in front of them, releasing a vicious roar. It was easy to imagine the creatures roaming through mountains as opposed to wooden halls.

"We were going to bring this place down, anyway, right?" Corianne asked.

"Yes, but we weren't supposed to be inside," Estan answered. They were still running straight for the dreker in front of them, Corianne's grip keeping Estan firmly at her side. He fumbled for his sword with his free hand, but he couldn't manage to draw it left-handed. It slid back into its sheath like a cat shifting in a warm lap.

"Never mind where we should be, this is where we are!" Corianne's eyes were wild and she had the a crazy smile playing over her full lips. "Find a way to get your horse out of here, because here's not going to be here much longer!"

She palmed a rune and chucked it. Not at the dreker that was beginning to charge toward them, closing the gap even further between its launching teeth and their fragile bodies, but at the support rafter between them. Fire flared to life. It danced its way across the beam, melting wood like it was nothing more than candle wax. The rafter fell across the creature's extended mouth and caused the dreker to come to a screeching halt as it yowled with pain. Corianne pulled Estan over the toppled creature, not even pausing when it attempted to swipe at them with its claws. A second dreker broke through the door of one of the empty cells and ambled toward its fallen brethren, chomping a big hunk out of the fallen one's flesh as the flames continued to grow.

Soon the fire was adding its own roar to the cacophony. Corianne lobbed several more flame runes and grabbed torches from the wall sconces and tossed them into empty cells. Another mouth flew toward them as she yanked a torch from its perch. She dodged and let the thing chomp down on the burning wood instead. Estan caught a manic glint in her eyes. Corianne was positively gleeful.

"There is something very wrong with you," he said, jogging with her into the night.

Catapult met them outside the door of the warehouse, his childlike disguise looking almost as excited as Corianne. He set his hand on a stack of barrels that he had found in the alley, "This may help."

Estan wasn't entirely sure why the horse had brought them flour, but Corianne let out a small excited squeal as he helped her roll them into the already burning building. They smacked against the far wall of the entry, seeming to swell. Corianne let loose one final rune and grabbed onto Estan again. If he had thought she was sprinting before, it was nothing compared to this last burst of speed.

A wave of hot air thrust forward from behind them, knocking Estan's feet out from under him. Corianne hit the cobbled street right next to him, convulsing in giggles, even as the distressed yowls faded into the roar of flames now licking up into the sky.

"Now I know why bakers invest so much in anti-fire runes," Estan gasped. His lungs felt as though he'd swallowed one of the torches as they made their final mad dash through the corridors. "You do know that you are one scary woman, right?"

Pulling herself up off the road, Corianne helped Estan to his feet, "We've got to catch up to Catapult, love. We don't want to be here when the guard shows up with their water buckets."

With a shake of his head, Estan followed her down the road, toward the group of kids that waited for them. Now, they had to make it to the meet point and find out how the others had fared.

43

~Khiri~

SOLANCIA CHARGED FORWARD, taking the offensive. Khiri, already at a disadvantage, weighed down by a sense of betrayal, barely managed to dodge the oncoming blades. How long had Solancia and Radley known it was going to come to this? Had they befriended her knowing this fight was coming?

"What's the matter, lass? Your lip's all a quiver," Solancia taunted.

The dwarven woman slashed her sword at Khiri's neck. Khiri waited until the dwarven woman was truly committed to the strike before tumbling out of the way. One shoulder hit the ground, and then Khiri was back on her feet.

"Why?" Khiri demanded. It wasn't much of a question, but it was the only one she could force past the lump in her throat.

Pivoting on her heel, Solancia was on Khiri again between one breath and the next. She blocked Khiri's knife with her dagger and aimed to plunge her sword into the elven woman's belly. Khiri dodged, gritting her teeth as the sword's edge raked along her chest plate. Grabbing Solancia's hilt with her free hand, Khiri stepped in and slammed the back of her head into the shorter woman's nose.

Solancia cursed and broke away, reassessing her opponent. Khiri had managed to surprise her. *We'll see how long I can keep it up*, Khiri thought grimly.

Across the clearing, Kal had Radley thrashing at columns of ice as they speared toward him. Khiri had been right to worry that he was better with daggers than he'd been with the sword. Despite the speed Kal was achieving with his projectiles, Radley was slicing them out of the air like it was a game.

A glimpse at the other fight was all Khiri had time for before Solancia charged again. Khiri realized her mistake in not pressing her advantage when she had the chance, but not until it was too late. Some habits were hard to break. Letting people recover was a habit that would get her killed someday.

"Why? Because Captain Aldash needs you gone. Because when Master Rhidel asks for Rad to get something done, it's best not to disappoint. Because my first loyalty is to the Gray Army, next is to my husband. Right knackered twit that you are, you told us all you were trying to gain support against the first allegiance, and then Master Rhidel comes to see us special... Says he needs you dropped, but quiet like," Solancia said. Her arms were pumping with slices and slashes in time with her confession, making her attacks a mixture of words and weapons. "First rule of being an agent for either organization: never get attached. Everyone is a potential mark. If my superiors told me to drop Radley, I'd try to make it quick."

As she parried and dodged, Khiri recalled the battlefield kiss between Radley and Solancia. It had been edged with the passion of being so close to death. At the time, Khiri had translated it into their fear for each other, but now she wondered if it hadn't been battle lust seeking a new course.

Another dumb moment of naivety, like falling for Fennick's guidance straight out of the Life Tree.

"So we were never really friends?" Khiri asked, her grip tightening on her father's knife. A wisp of hair had escaped from her tie and was dancing in a breeze over her forehead, but she didn't bother to tug it out of the way.

Solancia's only response was the cruel uplift at the corner of her mouth.

"Good," Khiri sighed, feeling something in her chest loosen. "That makes this easier."

As Solancia charged a third time, Khiri leapt into the air and caught one of the branches that hung above the clearing. If they kept fighting on Solancia's terms, it was only a matter of time before Khiri would find herself skewered. But Khiri had spent the majority of her life hunting from the treetops. There was no way Solancia could follow her up there.

It only took a few moments of stillness for Solancia to lose sight of her prey. Solancia continued trying to spot any signs of movement. After staring at one area for a few seconds, she would turn her entire body to examine another patch of leaves. Khiri watched to make sure she only moved when Solancia's eye patch was pointed in her direction. The dwarven warrior woman was on her guard, waiting for the coming attack. Surprise was the best weapon Khiri had, and Solancia was waiting for her. Scrambling up a tree limb, Khiri dropped down onto Radley.

Radley was mid-swing when her weight crashed into him, and Khiri's momentum knocked him over entirely. Rolling off of him, Khiri was nearly impaled herself as a frozen spear dropped down from overhead. It pinned the curly blonde dwarf with a sickened crunch of finality.

"Rad!" Solancia cried, skidding to her knees next to him. The cook's mouth worked, red dripping from his bottom lip. He struggled to get up even as his lungs ceased to function.

Fury burned in Solancia's remaining eye as she stood. She turned toward Khiri, both blades clutched in white-knuckled fists. "How dare you!" she hissed, swinging both arms at the elf. This was not an attack planned with the finesse of a master, but a sloppy clubbing attempt fueled by rage.

Khiri jumped back, but she tripped over the body of Kivian Threshler. She'd entirely forgotten about his body during the initial exchange with Solancia. The dwarven warrior huffed through her nose, her single eye showing white all the way around her iris, as she raised both blades over her head and plunged them toward Khiri.

Prone on the ground, Khiri reflexively curled into as small a ball as she could. She expected to feel the brutal blades pierce her vitals. Instead she heard a snarl of frustration. Hazarding a look up at Solancia, Khiri watched as the dwarven woman drew back her blades and tried again.

They bounced off a barely visible shell. One that Khiri now noticed was sending pleasant tingles through her ear tips.

Across the clearing, Kal was panting heavily, one arm extended and the runes on his staff glowing hot white. Solancia was beyond reason. She began beating against the shield with both of her weapons, hissing promises of a grim and bloody future for not only Khiri but the entire world.

"Thornne take you!" Solancia seethed. "The world will be cleansed!"

"*I think she's gone mad,*" Khiri sent, watching as the woman's hair escaped its braid and sweat dripped from the dwarf's brow. Still, Solancia hammered against the invisible dome that kept her from killing Khiri. It was as though the dwarven woman didn't even remember that Kal was present.

"*Seems it was a short journey,*" Kal agreed. "*If she weren't so dangerous, I'd leave her alone at this point. She's more like a savage beast.*"

Khiri closed her eyes. She didn't like what had to be done, but she was a hunter. Once a bear had rabies, there was only one cure. She rose to her knees, still keeping within the dome's protection. Bringing her knife into a ready position at her side she let out a deep steadying breath and sent Kal, "*When I send you the signal, drop the barrier.*"

IT WAS A LONG FOUR days back to the Eerilorian palace in Taman. Khiri had scrubbed off in every creek they had encountered, but she still felt dirty. She wanted to soak in the great tub she'd bathed in the first time at the palace, with its soft ribbons of blue and gray winding through the stone and the soft velvet of heated water enveloping her tired muscles. Too many other things had to be handled first, though.

They'd debated how to go about getting back into the palace without Captain Aldash catching wind of their return, but the palace was too well guarded. Someone somewhere had to let them in and, short of another well placed noble with questionable motives, sneaking wouldn't work. Electing for speed rather than subtlety, they went to the front gate. It took a few minutes of convincing before a runner was sent for Ullen and he confirmed they were to be allowed access.

Prince Ut'evullen met them in the halls of the main building. Khiri was slightly taken aback to see him in royal attire during the afternoon. Somehow she'd thought Ullen would stick to his travel clothes, even after a week in the palace alone.

"Khiri! Kal!" Ullen's voice was almost as soothing as the imagined bath waters, still holding all of the warmth it had on the road. She was surprised at how happy she was to see him after only a week and a half. Granted, it had been a very long week and a half. "I'm glad the two of you made it. The solstice is only a few days away, and we've already had a few delegates arrive."

"We have much to tell you," Khiri said softly. "Good and bad."

"I'm lookin' forward to the diversion," Ullen said, leading them through the ornate blue goldstone halls. "After you left, my mother came up with yet another tactic to induce me to take my brother's throne. It's been weighing on me something fierce."

Khiri caught sight of the dwarven noble woman who'd helped them out of the palace heading down an adjacent corridor. Her back was to the group and she looked to be in a hurry.

"Who is that?" Khiri asked. "And whose side is she on?"

Glancing toward the woman with the chestnut curls, Ullen turned a deep crimson and leapt back against the wall.

"Maybe she hadn't seen us yet," Ullen muttered. "Quick, duck in that ballroom. We'll try the back way." He hustled them into the door and shut it behind him softly so that it wouldn't draw attention by slamming.

"What was that about?" Kal asked. "It's not like you to get so flustered, my friend."

"That'd be my soon-to-be betrothed," Ullen sighed. "Me mum thought it'd be a fitting trap to spring on Hon'idar and me—ye see, whichever o' us wins Lady Jaspar Terilles is to gain the throne. She's already engaged to Hon'idar, but she and I had... It was a long time ago. Thing is, Lady Terilles might agree with my mum on who should rule next."

"Meaning no offense, but they might both have a point," Kal said.

Ullen shook his head and led them through the grand ballroom they'd ducked into. Its floor was a mirror of the one in the throne room, with alternating blue and brown goldstone, creating the impression that Khiri's feet were moving over pieces of the night sky and magic. "I'll be happy to leave this place behind again as soon as may be. So what did the two of you ferret out? We've heard a bit about the deaths of the leather masters, and a long letter arrived a few days out from Elmesh... Wouldn't suppose the pair of you had much to do with that?"

"That depends," Khiri sighed. "Was it from Vess or Sergeant Kari Peplar?"

Ullen stroked his beard thoughtfully. "Once we get to my tower, I'll have you start at the beginning. Given the details of that letter, I'm right sad that I didn't leave the doin' here to Hon'idar and head out with you. A bit o' trouble would do me some good."

The Odlesk mage exchanged a look with Khiri behind the dwarven prince's back. She shook her head and continued to follow Ullen through the palace. He'd know the whole of it soon enough. They'd managed to stop the flow of equipment into the hands of Flayers... Sort of. At least pieces wouldn't be coming from Kivian Threshler anymore.

Captain Horis Aldash, however, was still in a position to find a new vendor. And there was still the matter of his financial backer. Even a captain in Eerilor's army couldn't afford to equip that many Flayers out of pocket. There were still a lot of questions tumbling through Khiri's head about the whole operation, but maybe Ullen could provide some insight. He did know Eerilor far better than she did.

As they sat down in the room Ullen had briefed them in only a few weeks before, Khiri barely let Kal place a barrier before she launched into a narrative of their adventures. Ullen's grim frown told her he was taking matters seriously. Given everything that had happened lately, Khiri wondered if she should doubt Ullen's loyalties. Imyn could sense the presence of Tharothet, which told Khiri that Ullen was still the Ullen she knew. None of the gods would reside within someone loyal to the Gray Army.

"That's a real problem," Ullen sighed. "I don't want to believe ye, but I know, deep in me gut that ye'd never be fibbin' about such a thing. And it isn't just that I don't want to believe ye, lass, that makes this news a problem. A few days after you left, Hon'idar sent Horis out on an errand and he ain't been back. We thought that maybe it were he'd been abducted, but now it could be he got wind you was on his tail and he defected. He was well aware o' many o' the plans

Hon'idar and me were discussin'. He knows exactly who we're lookin' to for help."

Rubbing the back of his neck, Ullen looked like he'd aged ten years since they had sat down at the small table. "I'll have to go discuss this latest news with my brother. If I can even get him to see me."

"Why wouldn't he see you about this?" Khiri asked.

"That whole business with Lady Jaspar Terilles. He thinks I'm softening and trying to usurp him, now," Ullen said, sadness etched into the corners of his mouth. "Nevermind that I've been duckin' out o' her path and not courtin' this latest madness."

"Are you sure we can trust Prince Hon'idar?" Kal asked.

"I'm not sure, but we gotta take the chance," Ullen replied. He got up and gave Khiri a hug and clapped Kal on the shoulder. "The pair o' you are welcome to take the same rooms as before. Get cleaned up, grab a bite, and then we can all prepare for the summit. Seems this season's goin' to see one hell of a solstice."

44

~Estan~

DEWIN AND RESMINE WERE waiting for them at the designated meeting house. It was an old townhouse Corianne and Estan shared when they weren't staying at the Court's safehouse. Catapult was still outside with the kids that had been rescued. Part of the decision to use the townhouse was the courtyard across the street; it was gated, but it had high brick walls which would protect the kids from everything from prying eyes to cold winds. There was no way that a couple of hundred children would all fit in any of the safe houses or hidey-holes the Guild normally kept around the city.

"There were only about twenty in the basement where we got stuck," Resmine said. "And they'd not been kept solitary."

"Two of 'em, Bremine and Jerrin, already had a plan. Right loves, the pair of 'em. She's a right genius, and he's mechanically minded. Only twelve and already all but sprung the gate. Our whole lot was gone before an hour was out," Dewin said, leaning against an old, green velvet sofa.

Estan plopped down next to Dewin. Examining the interior of the house Corianne and her brother shared surprised him. He'd never seen either of them in anything but black; either their taste veered toward old and ornate furniture with jewel tones or they'd gotten a place already furnished. All the walls were a deep garnet hue, and most of the furnishings were very dark woods. Both a large sofa and a wingback chair had once been a bright emerald, but were now faded and worn. An ancient, threadbare tapestry hung on the wall beside the stairs, not showing a scene but a pattern of topaz, emerald and sapphire. The floors were darkly stained hardwood. A fire was blazing in the fireplace, sending warm light across the middle of the room, but making the corners seem darker. Corianne sat in a chair propped up in one of these pockets of darkness. Estan hadn't even noticed that chair until Corianne claimed it.

Everyone froze when the door swung open, not relaxing again until Tak and Shiv wandered in.

"How'd it go?" Resmine asked. When she'd come up with the plan to free the kids, she'd stepped into the role of leader for the operation. It had taken Estan by surprise at first, but the longer Resmine wore this particular hat, the better it suited her.

"Not great," Tak sighed.

"We had a confrontation with a couple of guards before we ever got there. Had to find the place by other methods. Tak used some of his contacts, through some credit out. We managed to free everyone in the building, but—" Shiv's voice cut off. The big man seemed to be fighting back tears. "By the time we got there, one of the children had been sick for a while. Couldn't take the running. Poor tyke dropped before we made it out."

The entire room fell into a moment of silence for the child they'd not been able to bring back. Granted, one out of countless others was better than Estan had expected from the night's endeavors, but that didn't make it easy to lose one of their charges.

This was the silence that greeted Risk as she entered the townhouse. It took several moments for Estan to realize that she'd arrived alone. She was alone and she looked utterly heartbroken.

"Evic is dead," she announced. "We were running, about thirty kids with us, and a team of Flayers stepped out in our path. He told me to keep going, through the main streets if I had to. He didn't pause, just ran straight for them. I told the kids to keep going. I was going back for him. And then..." Risk crossed her arms over her small chest and sank into a crouch, tears flowing down her cheeks. "I never bothered to tell him... I thought there'd be time."

The words didn't sink in for a time. Estan had never seen Risk display emotions other than cool mischief or calm superiority, but she seemed different in her heartache. More frail.

As Risk's meaning took root, Estan fell into himself a bit too. Shiv made his silent way to Risk's side and picked her up in a great bear-hug. Resmine and Tak were already moving to comfort Dewin. Her expression of disbelief struggled against the tears that were already flowing down her cheeks.

Satisfied the others were taken care of, Estan finally looked at Corianne. She'd risen to her feet and was facing the corner. Estan went to her and placed one hand on her shoulder, tugging gently. She turned and planted her face against Estan's chest, not really seeing him in her grief. He was a pair of strong arms offering comfort to a woman who had not only lost her brother, but her best friend. That's all Corianne needed Estan to be right now. Comfort. Support. A pillar in the storm.

"It's always a risk, that," she murmured. "Not coming back. Just figured we'd be crossing that gap together. The ashkeepers find us both, maybe at each other's throats during one of our rows... But I thought I'd be there."

Resting his cheek against her raven curls, Estan made soothing sounds, not knowing what he could possibly say. Memories of Khiri clutching the bow that had been her bond-brother, Micah, sprung into the knight's mind. He hadn't known what to say then, either.

Eventually Corianne pushed him away, and Dewin removed herself from Tak and Resmine's comforting. The two sisters embraced and held each other, taking solace in the fact that they still had each other. They sat on the couch, holding each other's hands as the group slowly moved back into what still had to be done. Risk watched the two of them forlornly, as though she wanted them to invite her into their familial grief.

Estan could be thick about things, but he could see Risk had loved Evic. Still loved Evic. Would probably love him for a long time to come.

It was time to get back to business, despite the dark clouds hovering over their successes.

"So we've rescued these kids. Now what?" Tak asked. "Can't exactly send them all home with notes saying, 'We took your child back from the Venom Guild. Sincerely, your friendly local thieves.'"

"No..." Estan agreed. "Anything coming directly from the Thieves' Guild would likely backfire. Ysinda couldn't issue a public statement without making herself a target for the guard and the townspeople. Their children have gone missing and for the average citizen, having something precious stolen means thieves. Guild associations, laws within the lawless, the Court... None of that would make sense to your average baker or merchant."

"You have something in mind, Estan?" Resmine asked.

"I do," he assured her. "I'm going to go straight to Orin Treag. If anything will cement his position as Lord Ilamar, it would be recovery of the city's children."

"How is that good?" Risk asked. She seemed angrier than sad now. Some people did that after the loss of a loved one. They started lashing out at anyone they could. Estan had spent enough time on the front lines to let Risk's anger roll right over him.

"He wants to keep Ysinda on her throne," Estan said. "With a battle coming between the Thieves' Guild and the Venom Guild, the city guard would be handy allies."

"I hope this works," Dewin and Resmine said together, almost in the exact same tone. Estan was feeling confident, until he realized Taymahr's voice had spoken with them.

ESTAN DIDN'T HAVE TIME to wait for Orin Treag to come to The Legend and The Knave, but Tak had access to the noble family's grounds. It was unusual, but not without precedent, for the information trader to bring his sources straight to the late Lady Ilamar. The guards didn't stop them when Tak vouched for the man standing next to him. Catapult had redone Estan's disguise, returning him to the bland, non-threatening man Ysinda had attacked at her table.

The knight wasn't sure how much longer he'd have to remain hidden from Arad Rhidel. Estan was certain that news had already reached the Venom Guild's leader about the escapes occurring all over the city. Either Arad Rhidel would decide his message to Ysinda had forced her to act, or he would suspect the message hadn't had quite the impact he'd been hoping for. Whichever way he interpreted matters, Arad Rhidel wasn't the kind of person to wait for the next move to play out. Plans would already be in motion.

Resmine had pointed out they needed some way to let Orin Treag know he was speaking to his contact. There'd been a bit of debate, but Corianne had stashed a pair of linked runes away in her room that were perfect for their present needs. She'd secured one of the runes on Catapult's halter, shaking it to make sure it wouldn't jostle itself loose. Corianne explained that once Estan said the activation word, the corresponding runestone would flash, alerting Catapult that Estan wanted his disguise removed. Then she'd turned and met Estan's eyes.

A thousand things had run through his head in that moment. From their first encounter, to her face swimming past as he died, to Risk's choked out, "I thought there'd be time..."

Estan had been on the precipice of understanding something. Something urgent, something shared. Then Corianne had pushed the rune at him and fled back up the stairs before he could say anything.

Rubbing his thumb over the runestone Corianne had shoved into his palm, Estan tried to focus on what he was going to say to Orin Treag.

"What's this about?" an older gentleman demanded. "My lord's very busy, planning for his hearing with the Council tomorrow. His sister made some very persuasive arguments during her standing today, and he shouldn't be distracted by trifles."

"Then we're just in time, Gerard," Tak smiled. His professional smile was only slightly less laid-back than his normal one. "We have information that will make his position exceedingly difficult to overcome."

With a bit more grumbling about how busy Orin was, Gerard—who was Orin's chief executive—led Tak and Estan down a cavernous hallway, decorated with a long red and gold rug, polearms, and sconced torches. It was impressive, if understated. Much like Orin Treag himself.

As Gerard opened the door to Treag's office, Estan saw a side of Orin that he'd never encountered at the pub. As a tavern regular, Ory had never appeared very noteworthy as he made his way across the sea of bar patrons. He'd only given Estan glimpses into his keen intellect, which was hardly recognizable as the regal, commanding figure standing behind the large desk. Orin was sifting through stacks of vellum, making notes on a map of the city which occupied most of the surface.

"Tak," Orin greeted the broker, barely raising his eyes as he gave a slight incline of his head. "I trust you and yours are well."

"Well as can be, your grace." Tak made a slight bow, but never quite ducked his head below his shoulder. "My companion has news that could prove very useful with your coming hearing."

"At what price?" Orin asked.

"This one..." Tak polished his fingernails against his shirt and pretended to inspect them, lending a certain amount of intrigue to the discussion. "...is free."

Orin Treag looked up from his notes and studied Tak with an intense gaze, one that Estan had been pinned by once before. The trader didn't seem to mind it in the least, but then, he dealt with people like Treag and Ysinda on a regular basis. Estan suddenly remembered Tak had been crossing Grimson's Pass alone when Estan and Dewin had first met him. It would take much more than a steely gaze from a nobleman to unsettle the man.

"Free is never truly free," Orin said. "What's the catch?"

"You continue with my contracts as your mother before you," Tak shrugged. "Deal?"

"Seems fair," Orin's suspicions were satisfied. He turned his attention to Gerard. "If you would give me a moment with these gentlemen, Gerard. I believe those contracts call for strict amnesty for all informants brought to my attention."

The older man ambled back out the door and closed it behind him, grumbling the whole way. Orin paid Gerard little attention as he gathered several of his documents and turned the pile over. It was clear he wasn't going to trust the information trader's eyes not to wander, despite whatever contracts they had just agreed on.

"So, what do you have for me?" Treag asked.

Estan spoke the word for his rune. As his disguise fell, Orin Treag, looked on with a bemused expression.

"I heard you were dead," Treag said, his voice noncommittal. He didn't seem impressed to see the knight, nor did he seem angry. What he did seem was impatient. Treag was still waiting for someone to get to the point.

"I heal fast," Estan said. "We do have news for you, though. Nearly two hundred of the city's children were recovered from the Venom Guild's warehouses during raids conducted by the Thieves' Guild."

The nobleman's eyebrows rose almost to his hairline, showing much more emotion than he had for the revelation of Estan's recovery. "That is excellent news. The best I've received in days. Where are they?"

"We have your word that you can spin this in a way that would not bring further incrimination against Ysinda and her people?" Estan asked. He knew he wasn't the official trader, but he needed the assurance.

"Don't you mean your people, Queen's Consort?" Orin Treag's mouth quirked on one side. "Yes, Ysinda and her Court will be spared further unfounded accusations. In fact, I have a thought I'd like to run by the two of you after this whole mess with the kids is sorted out. I'll arrange for a regiment to go and fetch the children immediately. I need to be a part of the group, otherwise one of my siblings will try to claim credit. If the two of you could arrange with Ysinda to meet me at the usual place, I'll explain more there."

Exchanging a look with Tak, Estan nodded, "I think that can be arranged."

"Good. I think the Thieves Guild and the guard will be unlikely bedfellows very soon." Orin's shoulders sagged, showing more weariness than he'd displayed the whole meeting. "Rothan Haud is a menace—one Jarelton can't afford to suffer much longer."

45

~Irrellian~

JARELTON'S GUARDS HAD finally stopped poking around the ashes of the warehouse, allowing Irrellian his chance to investigate the scene himself. When he'd hired Arad Rhidel to take over the city, Irrellian had been purposely vague on how he expected the task to be handled. He hadn't anticipated Rhidel would come up with a scheme to undermine the Thieves' Guild by kidnapping children.

Not that it was a bad plan. Uncontrolled crime in a city without a leader led to a great deal of chaos. Chaos was much easier to usurp than order.

"He can't be trusted," Telgan Korsborn's voice welled up from the depths. *"The leader of the Venom Guild has too much ambition."*

Ambition was exactly why Irrellian had sought out Arad Rhidel in the first place. But perhaps Irrellian's counterpart had a point. Somehow, Arad had gotten ahold of drekers. Drekers were dangerous beasts: hard to kill, harder to control.

Much like Arad Rhidel in that way.

And, once more, Irrellian had found the fingers of Seirane's Temple Hill prying into his affairs. Travin Esk had been busy, arranging for a new army of children to indoctrinate. Irrellian had watched enough of Travin's meetings to know for certain the man didn't really believe Irrellian had returned. Twenty years had worn away at

Travin's devotion and now he didn't want to give up the reins of what he regarded as his own private regime.

Soon, Irrellian would let the world know he was back. Those that crossed him would have to pay. Winter solstice seemed an excellent occasion to announce his return to the world.

He just had to decide where he would make the biggest impression.

46

~Khiri~

WALKING THROUGH THE silver mists, Khiri noticed the ground beneath her feet was paved with dark cobblestones. She reached for Micah's warm wooden grip, remembering too late he was no longer at her side. His absence made her heart ache. Instead she rested her hand on the hilt of her father's knife, even though she knew its broken blade offered no protection.

"Come to me," Irrellian Thornne's onyx skin gleamed softly, like moonlight reaching through the clouds. She didn't want to go to him, but neither did she want to fight him. She was so tired of fighting.

"Meet your Destiny."

Khiri woke with a start. The dream had come back. Sharper this time, if that was even possible. Morning sunlight pierced the flimsy curtains of the balcony in her guest room. It was only a matter of time before the Army of Three marched into her quarters to begin their assault on her hair and face. There was no time for her to seek out Kal and the comfort of his arms.

Her armor was polished and hung carefully by the door. Slipping on a fresh set of clothes, Khiri geared up as though today weren't the morning of the summit. She wanted to get out of the palace and stretch her legs.

Even as quiet as Ullen's halls usually were, the entire palace seemed oddly hushed for the morning of such a large event. It wasn't until Khiri reached the kitchens that she encountered any of the palace staff. As usual, the kitchens were bustling with cooks, undercooks, spit turns, scullery workers, and bakers, all overseen by the chef. Several of the cooks nodded to Khiri as she poked her head in. The chef, whose name Khiri had never heard, came over herself to see what Khiri was after.

"Is there something we can do for Prince Ut'evullen today?"

"I... Not that I know of," Khiri hesitated. "Why is it so quiet today, though? Today is the Solstice celebration and the Royal Summit, correct?"

"Has the messenger not made it to Prince Ut'evullen yet? Girl, turn back around and get up there at once! The prince needs to see his mother before she embraces the stone! Fetch him! Fetch him quick!"

Hustled back out the door, Khiri didn't even have a chance to clarify. When had Queen Di'eli taken ill? Surely Ullen would've mentioned it when she and Kal returned from their journey. Khiri tried to puzzle it out on her way back to Ullen's tower.

"Fortiva!"

The voice wasn't one Khiri recognized, but she looked back over her shoulder to see who was addressing her. It was the Lady Jaspar Terilles, the one Ullen said was in charge of choosing the next ruler.

"Has anyone been to see Prince Ut'evullen yet?" Lady Terilles asked.

"Not to my knowledge," Khiri said. "I'm heading there now. The chef told me his mother was in danger of embracing the stone and he needs to see her immediately."

"We must hurry! I have a very bad feeling about Hon'idar's intentions today."

Khiri rushed after the Lady Terilles, sending Kal a silent update on the situation, hoping he was awake to hear it.

"I'm afraid I'm outside the palace at the moment, laska. Someone attempted to climb in through my balcony door this morning. I've been tracking them through Taman," Kal sent back.

"Be careful," Khiri urged. Every hair on her body was on full alert. She could feel the temperature outside dropping, despite the sun's earlier greeting. There was a storm brewing this solstice.

"You as well." Kal's sending was laced with a warmth Khiri appreciated. It wasn't the same as having the mage nearby, but it was reassuring.

Lady Jaspar Terilles reached Ullen's door only a step ahead of Khiri and immediately began pounding against the heavy wood. "Ullen! Ullen, please! There's no time to waste!"

A very groggy Ullen opened his door a crack. Whatever he'd meant to say to Lady Terilles died on his lips when he saw Khiri standing behind her. "It's your mother," Khiri said. "They say she's about to embrace the stone."

"Ullen, your brother went to see her last night. The timing can't be a coincidence. We've got to see her before it's too late!" Lady Terilles said. "You can't let Hon'idar take power..."

Allowing the two women into his room, Ullen pulled a fresh set of clothes out of his wardrobe and stumbled behind a changing screen. "Why would Hon'idar hurt our mother? Her last proclamation was to pass the decision to you? What does he gain if she dies suddenly? The rumors alone would be enough to undo him..."

"I don't think he cares about the rumors," Lady Terilles said. "And unless you hurry, there's no one of sufficient rank to verify anything he decrees to have been your mother's last words."

"Didn't my mother have a will?"

"The last time she updated her will, you were still missing. Hon'idar had to be named as heir."

Khiri was barely listening to the exchange. There was something, some*one*, at the edge of her perception. She couldn't place her finger on where they were. In the room with her? Somewhere within the palace walls? Standing next to Kal, wherever in Taman he'd gone? The sensation was making her skin crawl. She reached back to make sure Micah was in his sheath at her back.

"Still here," Micah confirmed.

"Do you feel it, too?" Khiri asked.

"Afraid this one is all you," Micah said.

"Imyn?" Khiri tried.

The Goddess of Power and Change didn't choose to respond. Khiri shuddered as her sense of trepidation grew.

"What about the summit? Did he even think about the fact we're hosting foreign delegates..." Ullen muttered as he emerged from behind the screen. He didn't look either of his visitors in the eye. Instead, he kept fidgeting with the cuffs of his gloves. The dwarven prince was back in his travel garb. Khiri wondered if that had been a conscious choice or instinctive. "Eerilor won't even be able to sign treaties until a new ruler is crowned."

Lady Terilles didn't respond to Ullen's mutterings. Instead, she walked up to him and took one of his gloved hands in her own. "You don't have to do this alone, Ullen. I know the court frowns on shows of emotion, but for all her faults, Queen Di'eli is your mother."

Swallowing and giving a grim nod, Ullen allowed Lady Terilles to lead him out the door. Khiri followed in their wake, scanning every shadow in the halls as they passed through the palace. The wind could be heard through the thick walls of stone as it began to roar outside, muffling the sound of footsteps and making it impossible to detect the whisper of fabric. Still, Khiri was sure they were being watched.

"HERE HE COMES! MY MOTHER'S favorite son! And murderer!" Hon'idar sneered. He was blocking the door to the Royal Bedchamber with a handful of guards.

"Let Prince Ut'evullen pass!" Lady Terilles demanded. "It's his right as one of the royal line to see his mother before she dies!"

Hon'idar's sneer morphed into something sour and cruel. There was a smugness lurking in his eyes as he watched Ullen. "The little princling is too late. And you," he addressed Lady Terilles, "have shown where your loyalties lie. With usurpers and those who'd take power through acts of regicide! Arrest these traitors. They're all to be tried in the dome. Since the room was made ready for a summit, we may as well get some use out of it."

Ullen was strangely quiet during his brother's accusations but when Hon'idar mentioned the summit, it seemed to break Ullen out of his thoughts. "You never arranged for a summit, did you?"

Hon'idar's only answer was to chuckle as the guards swarmed past him. Khiri reached for her dagger, but Ullen signalled her to stand down. She didn't like the idea of being arrested, but Khiri trusted Ullen had his reasons.

It wasn't until they moved out from behind Prince Hon'idar that Khiri recognized the guards as Captain Horis Aldash and his most trusted lieutenants. Ullen and Khiri would find no sympathizers in this crowd. But it did solve one mystery for her.

"I think I figured out who was funding the armored Flayers," she sent Kal, along with a mental playback of the last few minutes. *"He's having us arrested for the death of the queen."*

"Shit! I'll come right back—"

"No!" Khiri interrupted. It was hard to focus on the internal conversation and her footing while two guards grabbed her by the arms. She was being dragged more than she managed to walk as the guards followed the rest of their unit. The tubular hallway between the queen's tower and the main body of the temple was already coated

with snow, making the journey darker. *"If you come back now, they'll grab you, too!"*

"Laska, if he's framing Ullen for regicide, he's going to kill anyone that can bring evidence against him. Aldash already knows what we were out there investigating. The longer they keep you alive, the harder it will be to keep you quiet. They will kill you."

"Don't come!" Khiri insisted. *"Ullen's smart and Lady Terilles is with us. The three of us can figure something out."*

Kal was right, though. It didn't make sense. Killing Ullen would ensure there was no one else to take the throne, and Khiri knew dangerous secrets about Prince Hon'idar. Given how willing Lady Terilles had been to switch sides, she likely had her hands on plenty of dangerous secrets, too. If Hon'idar was going to kill them, why hadn't he done it already? Why was he taking them to the central dome?

"He wants a spectacle," Imyn said. *"There are many who won't accept Hon'idar's rule without a trial. Especially given how much the late queen lauded Ullen and her preference for his succeeding her."*

"Imyn! Please, can you tell me—"

"I've said more than I should. This is a nexus of paths. We are not allowed to affect the outcome."

Khiri cursed under her breath. The guard on her left jerked her arm as a warning to be quiet.

During the trip from Queen Di'eli's tower to the main dome, Khiri's sense that someone was watching her only increased. Someone was here. Someone that didn't want to be seen. Someone powerful enough to hide from Micah's unique perception. There was only one person in all of Arra that Khiri knew to be that powerful.

TELGAN KORSBORN, the name inside of Khiri, agreed. It smoldered under her skin like a brand the moment the guards towed her across the threshold of their destination.

Khiri'd thought the summit–had one been held–would've been arranged in the throne room, under its frozen galaxy of a ceiling.

She hadn't realized how much grander the palace of Eerilor could get. In this, the top room of the palace's main dome, huge sections of wall were transparent, with large verandahs arranged on all sides. Vast gossamer curtains were pulled back from the gigantic windows and gathered with jeweled chains against four massive goldstone pillars, allowing a magnificent view of Eerilor's mountains and Taman most days. Right now, the only thing visibly surrounding the grand room was a blizzard. The stairs had belched Hon'idar and his retinue into the room through an arch to the north of the central chamber. Several rows of ornately carved benches encircled the roofed space in the center of the floor. Nobles and courtiers were huddled on the benches, clearly waiting for something to begin.

When Prince Hon'idar entered the room, the courtiers stood. The moment the guards entered with their prisoners, the nobles melted from respectfully hushed to pure bedlam. Several were trying to shout over each other, demanding recognition.

"What's this about Queen Di'eli's embracing the stone last night?" one of them demanded. "She was the picture of health when I spoke to her yesterday!"

"You'd have to ask my brother, Earl Terilles... Or perhaps your daughter," Hon'idar said. "I caught them leaving my mother's chamber with their elven assassin."

"Assassin?!" someone else exclaimed. "We were told she's the daughter of Fortiva! How could a Fortiva be an assassin?"

"Ask her yourselves," Captain Aldash spoke. "She'll tell you she's personally responsible for the deaths of two of my best."

The hands gripping Khiri tightened sharply at that. She winced, both from the reminder that she'd taken more lives and the rough treatment. "I've got quite the story if they'd like to listen," Khiri growled. "And proof. Do you have proof, Aldash?"

Captain Horis Aldash's response was to punch Khiri in the stomach. The pain doubled her over and blurred her vision. One didn't get to be the captain of a regiment without being able to deal a solid blow.

Because of her preoccupation with the blow she'd been dealt, Khiri thought the gasps of horror were for the way Captain Aldash dealt with a prisoner. It wasn't until her vision cleared that she was aware of Irrellian Thornne standing between her and the burnt out shell that had been Captain Aldash.

"I think that's enough of the melodrama, Hon'idar. You agreed to my terms. I specified this one was not to be harmed." The Flayer Mage's voice was as calm and deep as it had been in Khiri's nightmares. "She belongs to me."

"No!" Khiri tried to scream it, but the word practically dried up in her throat.

The two guards that had been holding her up dropped her and backed as far from Irrellian Thornne's notice as they were able. Khiri, suddenly free, scrambled to get away from the villain and the pile of ashen bones that used to work for him.

Irrellian turned toward her. He said nothing, but Khiri's body stopped moving. It reminded her of the sensation she'd had when holding the control rune Fennick had given her only months before. No matter how she pulled and tugged, her body wouldn't respond. She found herself standing next to the Flayer Mage despite her wishes to run screaming in the opposite direction. His shimmering face twisted into a grin as though he was at her inner struggles.

"Now, you've more than enough nobles here to cement your title as king. Those that pledge fealty, live. Those opposed, die. And then Eerilor becomes the foundation for my new army. Hurry this along. The Solstice is a busy day for me," Irrellian said.

There was rustling among the courtiers. Some surged forward, more afraid of death than pledging away their honor or freedom. Others tried to move back, hoping for some sort of barrier between them and the returned Flayer Mage. Khiri only spotted a few nobles in the crowd that didn't move in either direction. They stood like trees, rooted in place, glowering at Irrellian and Hon'idar with undisguised hatred. Khiri found herself on the receiving end of a few of those glares.

They can't tell I'm being controlled, she thought. Tears sprang to her eyes, despite her inability to break free.

"Hon'idar, why? Why betray your country? Why kill our mother? Why would you do any of this? I would've willingly given you all of it!" Ullen's voice echoed despite the howling winds outside. Khiri's friend seemed utterly defeated. He wasn't even fighting the two guards holding him in place. His hair hung around his face like a curtain, closing his expression off from Khiri's view.

"Why, my brother? Why did mother choose to ignore my claims not only to the throne, but my claims to her affection as a son? You left thirty years before there even was a Gray Army, and yet daily, she spoke of the day you would return; her son, her only *true* son," Hon'idar spat. "And then you returned, and it didn't matter you'd neglected your duties for more than fifty years. Her true son had returned! I meant nothing to her. Less than nothing! And that has been my reality ever since our father died. Irrellian promised me a better world, and damned if that doesn't sound like a fine idea—I think the best improvement Arra could have is to move on without you!"

Hon'idar's sword slid from his sheath and rose above his brother's head. Khiri couldn't close her own eyes any more than she could look away as the sword made its descent. No one in the room had time to intervene. Helpless tears were blurring Khiri's vision. She struggled even harder against the mental bonds, hoping to throw herself between Ullen and Hon'idar. The most she managed was the twitch of a finger. Just when the last of Khiri's hope evaporated, Hon'idar's sword bounced off a transparent blue shell.

Kal stood on the windowsill, a halo of snow blowing in around him. Khiri's father was next to him, aiming an arrow at the Flayer mage's heart. Even though Khiri found the idea of a single arrow actually posing a danger to Irrellian Thornne unlikely, the Flayer Mage spread his hands in a show of momentary surrender. Genovar had been the one to trap Irrellian in the past, so perhaps there was more to this encounter than Khiri was seeing. She was so excited to see her father, she barely cared if the situation made sense.

"How on Arra did you find my father?" Khiri asked.

"He was the person I tracked across town. Apparently, he's been in Taman for a bit. Got a letter from Ullen shortly after we arrived. He's been waiting for the summit to begin. Worried when no delegates showed."

"Those who stand against the Gray Army, to me!" Genovar called.

The force imposed on Khiri's body suddenly broke as a shield popped up around her. Lady Terilles and the captive nobles were enveloped by blue shields bubbling into existence all over the room. They were free! Lady Terilles grabbed hold of Ullen and yanked him toward the exit as fast as she could run. Khiri fell in behind them, eager to leave the Flayer Mage in her wake.

Irrellian grabbed Khiri's arm as she passed, as though Kal's shield didn't exist. A cold that had nothing to do with the storm outside shot through Khiri's system. Irrellian was letting her go. Letting them all go. Again. "You will come to me, one day," he promised. Then he released her, leaving her to flee into the storm.

Sliding down the side of the dome into a pile of snow, Kal latched onto Khiri's hand and dragged her along in the wake of the rescued courtiers. Genovar was bringing up the rear of the party. Armed men and women shoved the civilians of Taman out of the way. No one slowed down until the palace of Eerilor was no longer visible.

"My friends, remember this day," Genovar said. "This solstice marks the dawn of a new war. Our foe, my foe, awakened by my own blood." As he said, this Genovar spat, giving Khiri a heart-wrenching sneer. He hated her. Her own father. "He has made an error, allowing us to know who our enemies are! Gather your armies, for on this day, Eerilor has fallen. She will be avenged!"

"Father..." Khiri began, "I didn't..."

"From this day forth," Genovar said, "I disavow you as a member of my house. You and those with you have until sundown to make your way out of my sight, or you will be shot down as traitors."

The coldness in his voice wounded her as nothing else could have. Ullen, as defeated and grieving as he was, stood up to his old ally and said, "Surely that's a bit harsh, Genovar. You know as well as I—"

"Don't try me, Ullen. Go with her and leave my sight, or take your throne and serve." Genovar turned his back on the dwarf. "I've got a war to organize."

With a sigh, Ullen pulled Khiri in for a hug. "I'm sorry, lass. I've never wanted to rule less. But Eerilor needs me. I canna keep runnin'. I hope we see each other again, when this is all done." When he released her, he went to stand with Lady Terilles and the other nobles.

Khiri felt numb. First rejected by her father, and now abandoned by her friend. She understood Ullen's reasons, but her head was still swimming from Genovar's denouncement. He couldn't really mean to have her shot, could he?

Kal took Khiri's arm, tugging her away from the elf that had been her father. Was her father. Would always be her father. She was too stunned to make sense of the solitary trail of moisture running down Genovar's cheek.

47

~Estan~

THE STREETS OF JARELTON were packed with people waving pennants and screaming with wild abandon. It was Coronation Day for the new Lord Ilamar, and Orin Treag had been received by his people as the city's savior. He'd returned many of the lost children to their homes, and made promises to continue the investigation. Crime had lessened throughout the streets, and the people felt this was a sign that criminals were intimidated by the man that had been named Guardian of Jarelton.

Estan was less convinced the quiet of the last two days was caused by the Venom Guild's full retreat. He'd seen lulls in battle. Friendly banter between opposing sides could result in even fiercer fighting the next day.

Resmine and Dewin shared his anxiety. The High Ones were restless. Even Catapult could feel it, though he hadn't used his illusions to speak since the news of Evic's death. The knight hadn't realized how fond his horse had been of Dewin's brother, but then, Catapult was always full of surprises.

Edging his way into the crowd in Dothernam Square, Estan held his cloak tight over his shoulders. The solstice promised a hard winter, nipping at Jarelton with a frosty bitterness despite the warmth of many bodies pressing against each other in the crowded streets. Beer and other alcohols tainted the air with an acrid musk. Tak shoved his way in next to Estan. The treaties keeping thieves out of the square had been rescinded, but Corianne and Ysinda were nowhere to be seen. Risk was perched on the awning of one of the many food carts that had been maneuvered into the square in the early morning hours. Shiv towered over several nervous looking vendors on the opposite side of the square.

"What exactly are we watching for?" Tak asked.

"I don't know," Estan sighed. "Maybe I should've stayed at the Court like Ysinda wanted. I just... I have to be here."

The information trader gave a shrug and a lop-sided grin, "That's pretty much what Dewin said."

A space opened next to Estan, and the hybrid version of Tak and Evic that Catapult had worn almost a week before ambled into it. The disguised horse blinked innocently at his rider, as though inviting reproach.

"Took you long enough," Estan muttered.

Catapult whinnied his approval and stamped his feet impatiently.

"The door's opening!" someone at the front of the crowd cried. The crowd surged around them, straining the guards' abilities to keep the civilians away from the dais. Treag walked down the steps of the stage next to the wall and made his way toward the dais in the center of the square. It was his desire to have as many eyes on him as possible, but Estan felt a spike of fear course through him.

"Treag's in danger!" he shouted at Tak.

Tak eyed the crowd and along the upper edge of the wall, "I don't see anything. Are you certain!"

"We've got to get up there." Estan attempted to push his way through the packed bodies, but it was impossible to find enough space in the crowd. Even Catapult's massive form was having trouble moving in the sea of faces. There wasn't any sign of danger. But even with Taymahr being silent on the matter, Estan knew deep in his gut that something was wrong.

"People of Jarelton," Treag said, the crowd stilling as though the noble's words held a spell to quiet them. "I am greatly honored by your warm reception. I will do my best to fill the void left by my mother's passing, but she was a great woman and a greater leader. She saw this city through the War of the Burning Valley and made us strong in a time of hardship. Therefore, it is with a heavy heart, I solemnly..."

A scream erupted from someone in the front row as a long blade burst through Treag's chest. Arad Rhidel, appearing from seemingly nowhere, stepped out from behind the new Lord Ilamar's body. Treag's mind hadn't ceased to function yet, and his eyes widened at the sight of the sword puncturing his heart. Rhidel planted his foot on the man's back and shoved the dying Treag forward into the crowd.

"Ladies and gentlemen, I regret to inform you that the Lord Ilamar has passed on!" Rhidel announced. "I claim this city in the name of the Venom Guild and all who do not wish to die now, had better run!"

Flayers appeared at every door, swiping bloody trails through the panicking crowd. People who'd seen Treag die were running into the wave of those surging away from the Flayers. Estan jumped onto Catapult's back, the warhorse suddenly visible as the crowd parted around the horse's solid form. Resmine and Dewin were already on the dais, weapons in hand.

"It looks as though my old friends came to play on the day of my triumph," Rhidel laughed. "Too late to save the city, I'm afraid!"

Resmine raised her whip, but Dewin held up one hatchet and shook her head at her lover. "*Bless this offering, with which I seal our covenant,*" the former thief's voice was barely a whisper, but it echoed off of the walls of the square, rumbling through the stones paving the yard and shaking the earth itself.

The lines that Estan and Tak had spent hours chiseling through the night, so long ago it seemed, broke forth with radiant white light, incinerating the Flayers that got too close. Rhidel was thrown from the circle, crashing into a fruit stand. Estan watched helplessly as the leader of the Venom Guild escaped through the door Treag had come through only moments before. He, Resmine, Dewin and Catapult were glowing every bit as brightly as the lines of the consecrated temple below them.

"I am sorry, my child, but we must leave you now. The portal is open," Taymahr said. Estan felt a kiss he couldn't see touch his forehead. *"We have our own battle awaiting us, but what you do here will affect us there. One's strength is shared, and We will listen."*

"My Goddess," Estan felt tears running down his face. *"What about...?"*

"Your abilities will one day fade, though it may take one season—or it may take one hundred. One of us will stay to guard, to watch, and to guide, but I cannot say which. Good luck, dear one." Taymahr's presence began to fade, leaving the knight feeling empty within his own skin. *"The War has started."*

THE NEWLY CONSECRATED temple had emptied of nearly everyone but the former avatars and what was left of the Thieves' Guild. Treag's body, used as a stolen sacrifice for Adari, Goddess of Greed and Guile, had vanished into the carved circle. Estan wanted to feel guilt for dragging the reluctant noble into this mess, but it was too much. There were other bodies. More important bodies.

Ysinda had been cut down during the initial wave of Flayers. No one had seen it happen. Shiv had retrieved her body from the side and brought her to the center of the courtyard.

"We got separated during the initial surge. She had a child under her. May have been trying to play the hero, or she might've just been another unfortunate thrown on a pile. I'd prefer to believe the first one. Ysinda always had more good in her than she cared to admit," Shiv said.

In death, Ysinda wore an expression of peace. Estan pulled off his cloak and draped it over his lover. He hadn't expected their relationship to be cut short like this. Death was always a possibility for people like Estan and Ysinda, but she'd always seemed so careful, so confident...so dangerous. If Estan could give someone his healing ability, he'd have done so gladly to give the city back one of its rulers. Ysinda had cried for Estan when he'd died. It was time for him to repay those tears. He didn't bother to hide his face.

"I can't do this anymore. First Evic, now Ysinda. I can't do this anymore!" Risk dropped to her knees next to Ysinda's draped form and pounded a fist against the cobbles. Before Shiv could reach out to touch the exiled elf's shoulder, she was back on her feet. She sprinted out of the courtyard and kept running.

"She's not coming back," Shiv sighed. "More's the pity. With Ysinda gone, Risk was one of the best candidates to replace her."

Estan's gaze flicked from the big man to Corianne's back. He wanted to go to her, to put his arms around her the way he'd done when they'd lost Evic. But it felt inappropriate with Ysinda laying on the ground between them. Corianne had turned away the moment she'd seen what Shiv carried, and her shoulders trembled with muffled sobs. Using the cleanest edge of her cloak to wipe her face, Ysinda's most faithful lieutenant turned back to those remaining mourners. "Can't say I'm not right tempted to run off myself, but someone's got to be a love and see things settled right. Ain't no new leader what's declared by combat. Flayer damned took our throne and got itself splice by a god. I'm all for following Adari, but can't exactly have her down in the Pit handin' out orders."

"What about Dewin?" Resmine asked. "She's technically the priestess of this temple."

"Nothing doin', love," Dewin said. "I was given a pardon by Ysinda, but none of the rest of the Guild would take me serious. I wasn't ever any good at the minor jobs."

Resmine wrapped an arm around Dewin and bumped heads gently with the former thief. The body language seemed to say that Resmine couldn't imagine Dewin being bad at anything, but accepted her decision. Even though the two lovers seemed to be having their own conversation, Resmine asked, "Corianne? Why not you?"

"No, no, love. I'm a true lieutenant, but ain't never one to court power outright. That's a heavy crown and I ain't the one to bear it. Soon as the new one is settled, I'm off, too. Risk ain't the only love what feels the need to move on."

"How about Resmine?" Shiv said.

The entire group shifted to look at the large man.

"Me?" Resmine rocked back on her heels. As strange as the proposition was, Estan was shocked to see his childhood friend was actually considering it. "I'm not even technically a Friend of the Guild. Why me?"

"You beat me at Knives and Nobles. You managed to wheedle your way into our taverns twice without invitation. Saw you fight during the tavern riots, and I'd say you do at least as well as Corianne. Led us through the last operation like you were born to it," Shiv shrugged. "Guild could do a lot worse."

Estan held his protests. If this had been discussed in front of him the last time he'd been in Jarelton, he would've intervened. He would've grabbed Catapult's reins and stormed out, expecting Resmine to fall in behind him as they left the lawless in their wake. A lot had changed during that time. Estan had changed. He'd been Consort to the former Queen of Thieves. He could find it in himself to be brother to the next queen.

"I've no qualms," Corianne said. "Rulers for our sort come from all walks, yeah? If this be serious, you're to be put through the trials, though. Can't take the crown without a test."

With a nod, Resmine said, "Let's do this."

Estan left them to plan as he and Tak went to fetch an ashkeeper. Ysinda deserved a proper send off.

48

~Irrellian~

"HOW COULD YOU LET THEM get away?!" Prince Hon'idar demanded. His blonde mane was partially undone and the sword he'd been holding over his brother lay forgotten on the ground. Madness gleamed in his wide eyes. If he could've reached Irrellian's throat, it seemed likely he was far enough gone to attempt throttling the Flayer Mage. "We had a deal! Do you have any idea what you've done?!"

Irrellian contemplated the seething prince. Perhaps it had been a mistake to dispatch Captain Aldash so thoroughly. Even if the captain had overstepped, he'd at least proven a competent lackey. "I let a gaggle of courtiers run off to collect masses of soldiers to combat me."

"They didn't confirm me! My brother is not only alive, but unconvicted! I can't conscript their armies! You gained nothing from this!"

"*I* gained everything from this," Irrellian corrected. "Those nobles will return to their homes and tell everyone about their brush with death against the returned Irrellian Thornne. They will build forces, forces with one purpose. To fight against the Flayer Mage. Neighboring countries, the ones alerted to the filtering of armed clutches of demon-bound across their borders, will begin to look into Eerilor's building armies against me. The nobles I just released will

346

point to you, my seeming ally. They might even find the evidence Khiriellen Fortiva spoke of, that links you directly to the Flayer scheme. Eerilor, the nation that supplied the largest army against me in the former war, will either be lost in a civil conflict or destroyed in an effort to root me out of my seeming base. It doesn't matter. The important thing is that each and every soul out there, for me or against will be sending me power through their belief. With enough belief, even a mortal can rival the gods."

Hon'idar collapsed to his knees as understanding sank in. "You were the one that gave Aldash the Flayer scheme... He said, we were going to look like saviors to the other nations and no one would ever link it back to us, but you... you wanted the nobles to know, and you wanted them to run away. You were counting on Genovar Fortiva to come and save them... You used me."

Irrellian didn't bother to continue talking with the broken prince. He had used Hon'idar, but the prince hadn't even bothered to hide his attempts to use Irrellian. Perhaps Hon'idar had assumed Irrellian wouldn't notice. More likely the prince had believed himself more clever than the Flayer Mage.

Hon'idar could threaten not to continue his war against Prince Ut'evullen, but it would be a pointless gesture. He wanted the throne too badly to give it up in an effort to thwart Irrellian, and they both knew it.

It was then that Irrellian felt something change. Like hearing a bubble pop from a mile away, it shouldn't have been possible. The portal to the heavens had opened. Somewhere along the way, one of his plans had gone terribly wrong.

~Acknowledgements~

This one was dedicated to my cousin Michelle because without Michelle, there wouldn't be *this one*. I'd finished my first draft of Waking the Burning Valley, but I wasn't convinced it was a project worth pursuing. I'd begun the first draft a few years before I dug it out and wrote the end, but I was hitting a mental wall. I didn't think anyone would like it. She convinced me to let her read it, and then basically knocked me over the head with my own book and told me to get off my butt and write the next one. So I did. I spat out the first draft of Dropping the Keystone in less than ten weeks. Thank you, cuz, for being both an ego boost and ass kicker all-in-one. Love you.

Thank you to Mom, Stephen, Dad, Sean, Michelle (yes, a different one), and the whole rest of the family for their continued support. When the house is falling down around us because I'm too focused on my work to notice, I know help is only a phone call away. Much love to you all.

A huge thank you to my beta team. As usual, you guys helped make this book so much better than I could've done on my own. Wendy and Katja: as usual, you two really went above and beyond for me. I've barely got the words to express my gratitude.

Thank you to the Writers' Room for the late night fixes, soundboarding sessions, and countless other ways you guys have been there for me. Much love and luck on all of your personal projects. If any of you need help, I'll endeavor to lend a hand.

I'd also love to thank brosedesignz for another amazing cover. People do judge by covers, and you always make my books shine.

As always, thank you to Terence. You beautiful, beautiful weirdo. Thank you for everything you do and everything you are. There's no one in the world I'd rather spend my days with. I love you.

About the Author

When she was younger, Christina lived in Michigan, where she earned a black belt and took archery classes. She loved running through the forest, climbing through sand dunes, and swimming in Lake Michigan. She started writing in the fourth grade, with a story about her big, orange tabby cat wanting to be a rock star.

Now that she's older, Christina lives in Texas with her husband and their three cats: Scythe, Amulet, and Mad Cat.

She's worked all kinds of jobs--from retail to waiting tables to warehouse to massage therapy to management. She has earned her Associate Degree with focuses on Creative Writing and History. Through all of it, her dream was to see her work in print on someone's shelf.

Christina's hobbies include playing board games, role-play games, video games... basically games... reading, and traveling. She's always up for a ren faire, exploring an ancient ruin, or taking a cruise.

Read more at https://christinadickinsonwrites.com.